fair game

Books by Elizabeth White

Fireworks

Prairie Christmas

Sweet Delights

The Texas Gatekeepers

Under Cover of Darkness

Sounds of Silence

On Wings of Deliverance

fair game

elizabeth white

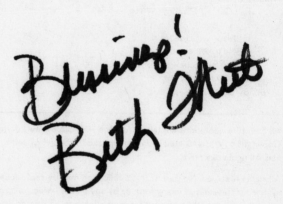

 ZONDERVAN®

ZONDERVAN.com/
AUTHORTRACKER
follow your favorite authors

ZONDERVAN®

Fair Game
Copyright © 2007 by Elizabeth White

Requests for information should be addressed to:
Zondervan, *Grand Rapids, Michigan 49530*

Library of Congress Cataloging-in-Publication Data

White, Elizabeth.
    Fair Game / Elizabeth White.
      p. cm.
    ISBN-10: 0-310-26225-9
    ISBN-13: 978-0-310-26225-1
    1. Wildlife rescue—Fiction. I. Title.
PS3623.H574F35 2007
813'.6—dc22

                                           2006025513

Published in association with the literary agency of Alive Communications, Inc., 7680 Goddard Street, Suite 200, Colorado Springs, CO 80920.

Make-up and hair for cover model by Kim Recketts

Interior design by Beth Shagene

Printed in the United States of America

---

06 07 08 09 10 11 12 • 22 21 20 19 18 17 16 15 14 13 12 11 10 9 8 7 6 5 4 3 2 1

ACKNOWLEDGMENTS

Gratitude goes to my wonderful agent, Beth Jusino at Alive Communications. And to Karen Ball for seeing me through the acquisitions process. It's a joy working with you both.

I am indebted to those who helped me with critiquing and editing *Fair Game*—not least, of course, my stellar editor at Zondervan, Diane Noble. Also, my husband Scott, Tammy Thompson, Sheri Cobb South, and Anne Goldsmith read various drafts of the manuscript and contributed invaluable experience and wisdom, not to mention the laser eye of logic.

For story development, I thank my cousin, Dina Kennedy Hawkins, and my friend, Scott Vernon. Dina supplied her expertise in wildlife rescue and rehabilitation techniques, and Scott allowed me to pick his brain about bow hunting. Dr. Andrew Duke (who for the last ten years has taken excellent care of my Boston terrier, Angel) allowed me to consult with him and his assistant Melissa on veterinary questions—thanks, Andy, for serving as a great model vet.

Four years ago I spent a lovely fall day with Steve and Betty McKenna and their son Mark on their ranch in Pachuta,

Mississippi. The McKennas allowed me to ask questions, take pictures, and tramp around their property learning how a hunting camp works. They were gracious hosts, even though they probably thought they'd never really see a book out of the crazy lady with the notebook.

I would like to extend my gratitude to Mrs. Maxine Cumbest and, posthumously, her late husband, Orris—the inspiration for my game warden, CJ Stokes. Maxine served me coffee at her kitchen table while Orris told story after story of Jackson County, Mississippi, wildlife management adventures. I'll never forget the experience, and it lent richness of story detail I couldn't have found anywhere else. Appreciation also goes to game warden Keith Carter, who answered questions over the phone when Mr. Orris wasn't available. Oh, and thanks, Aunt Nell and Uncle Bob, for arranging these contacts.

I owe Chris and Kristy Skinner a big thanks for letting me experience an afternoon on their houseboat. What a cool way to live!

The businesses in this story are all products of my imagination, except for Cole's Drive-Inn, which is a Vancleave, Mississippi, landmark. The owners and operators of Cole's graciously let me "feed" my people there. The folks at the Hurley Farm and Feed allowed me to come in and look around, giving me the basis for Alvin's store. I appreciate their hospitality.

Last, but not least, I'm blowing a kiss to my niece Susannah, who can do anything if she just has the dress.

A NOTE FROM
THE AUTHOR

Most readers seem to be interested in "where the story comes from." Several years ago my family formed one of those chatty email loops—my mom and four aunties, my three sisters, and four girl cousins, with a husband and boy cousin or two allowed to participate on occasion. The kind of loop where the funny, tragic, or just plain weird events of life are logged daily, almost like a diary. It didn't take this writer long to realize I was being sent story fodder in abundance, and often my response to an email was "Can I borrow that?"

My cousin Dina, who volunteers at the Wildlife Center of Silicon Valley in San Jose, California, often sent poignant or funny stories and pictures about her animal adventures. Eventually it occurred to me to wonder what would happen if a woman with that kind of love for animals fell in love with a guy whose main joy in life was the sport of hunting—and believe me, there's plenty of inspiration for that kind of hero right here in south Alabama! Interviewing my friend Scott and learning to shoot a bow myself were two of my favorite parts of the development of this story.

I found the philosophical debate of animal rights/animal protection versus hunters' rights/wildlife management a fascinating subject for research, especially as a biblical topic. I hope I've dealt with it realistically, without enraging either side too much. I'm always more interested in interpersonal issues, anyway. How do Christians respond to those who offend? Is it possible to mend a relationship when one or both parties have intruded on a deeply felt belief? The Bible commands us to do so. Conviction fell on me as I wrote. I pray that in all "disputable matters" I can be full of grace toward my brothers and sisters in Christ.

May the Lord grant you peace, dear reader.

chapter 1

Jana Cutrere had just run over a Black Angus cow in broad
daylight.

Maybe it wasn't the worst thing that could have happened on
her first trip home in ten years. And technically speaking, she
hadn't run *over* it. After all, she'd been going less than twenty
miles per hour in a geriatric Subaru, not a Sherman tank.

The ink barely dry on her vet school diploma and already she'd
committed bovine homicide.

Her eight-year-old son, Ty, was staring wide-eyed at the steam
oozing out from under the crumpled hood of the car. "Look out,
Mom, she's gonna blow."

Presumably he meant the radiator and not Mrs. Angus, who
rolled over with a grunt, lurched to her feet, and lumbered off
down the highway. Jana's relief was short-lived. Four-year-old
LeeLee, buckled into her booster seat in back, chose that moment
to start screaming her head off.

Jana scrambled out of the car, yanked open the rear door,
and scooped her daughter into her arms. "It's okay, sweetie." She
hugged LeeLee until the screams subsided into muffled hiccups.
"You're not hurt, are you?"

LeeLee clamped her arms and legs around Jana. "I'm all shook up."

Jana laughed shakily. "You're a trooper, kiddo." She squeezed her preschool Elvis freak and looked to the cloudless blue sky. "Thank you, Lord, we're all okay."

The front passenger door opened, and Ty poked his head out. "It's hot in here, Mom. Can I get out?"

It was hot outside too. Sweat beaded under Jana's bangs and ran down her back. Barely into summer and the temperature was already over ninety degrees.

Welcome back to the Gulf Coast.

"Okay, but stay close. I don't need you to get run over too."

"I'm smarter than some old dumb cow." Ty tumbled out of the car and wandered over to inspect the roadside ditch, filled with water from a recent rain shower. No telling what wildlife she'd find in his pockets later.

With a final hiss the car fell silent. Maybe the cow had survived, but it sure had done a number on Jana's transportation. Now what was she going to do? Even if she'd wanted to hitchhike, not a single car had passed in several minutes.

When LeeLee began to wriggle, Jana set her down and looked around to assess the situation. Dense woods stretched off to the right, and across the highway ran a rolling pasture that hosted the cow congregation. She should have been paying attention instead of rubbernecking with the children. Pointing out the cypress knees poking out of the swamps, she'd forgotten that something might appear around one of these dogleg bends.

"Mommy, this car is a mess!" LeeLee planted her fists on her hips, a ferocious gesture mitigated by the sticky blue ring around her mouth.

Jana sighed. "I know. We'll either have to walk or call Grandpa to come get us." Rats. This old car would be the first thing she replaced when she got her practice going.

She reached through the open window for her cell phone. At least Grandpa wouldn't have far to go. The Farm and Feed was three miles down the highway in Vancleave. Grabbing LeeLee's hand to keep her from running out into the road, she began a one-thumb search of the phone menu.

"Mommy ..." LeeLee tugged on her hand. "I'm not tattling, but where's Ty going?"

Frowning, Jana looked around. LeeLee had figured out that what Mommy noticed for herself couldn't be called tattling. Ty had vanished.

She clutched LeeLee's hand. "Where did he go, baby?"

"He ran into the woods."

"The woods!" Jana jammed the phone into her pocket. "Which direction? Show me."

LeeLee pointed.

Jana swung her daughter across the ditch, then jumped over herself. When LeeLee couldn't keep up, Jana picked her up and walked faster. Tall switches of Bahia grass stung her bare legs and left black seeds clinging to her socks. All three of them were going to be sweaty, itchy, and miserable by the time they got to Grandpa's.

"Ty, where are you? Ty!"

Jana stepped into the woods—Grandpa's woods, known locally as Twin Creek Refuge—a typical Mississippi forest of oak, sweet gum, and pine, overgrown with scrubby underbrush and briars. Pine needles and rotting leaves created a slippery foundation beneath her tennis shoes, and a sharp, whining drone buzzed in her ears and nose. Ty shouldn't be in any real danger, but the mosquitoes would eat him alive. It wasn't like him to run off.

LeeLee leaned back and patted Jana's cheeks. "If Ty's lost, he's supposed to go to customer service, right?"

Jana blew her bangs out of her eyes. "This isn't Wal-Mart, baby. But we'll find him." *I hope. Please, Lord.* "Ty!"

She hadn't walked much farther before she realized they were following a path. Orange plastic ties marked a few skinny white oaks, and reflective tacks were stuck here and there at eye level. She stopped. "I thought we were on Grandpa's property, but it looks like somebody's been hunting it."

"Hunting's bad, Mommy."

"That's right." Deer season didn't open until October, so they should be safe. A thought came to her. "Poachers."

"Could I have a poacher egg? I'm hungry."

"Honey, poachers are bad people who kill animals. We'll eat as soon as we get to Grandpa's, but first we have to find your brother. Ty! If I find you hiding, that Game Boy is mine!" She waited, shushing LeeLee with a finger on her lips. Nothing.

A gunshot ricocheted through the woods.

"Ty!" Jana tore through the trees, unable to hear anything except the thudding of her heartbeat and her own gasping for breath.

A moment later a faint but clear boy soprano drifted through the woods. "Mo-o-om!"

Relief weakened her knees as she followed the direction of his voice. "Where are you? Are you okay?"

"Mom! C'mere!" Ty's voice came from the right, a few yards ahead. "Come see what I found!"

With LeeLee still clinging monkeylike to her neck and waist, Jana pushed through a brushy growth of oak and magnolia seedlings. She almost stepped on Ty, who sat cross-legged in a nest of pine needles with a tiny spotted fawn cradled in his lap.

"Ooh, look, Mommy." LeeLee leaned down. "It's Bambi."

Ty looked up, cheeks poppy red, sweaty blond cowlick standing at attention. A cut on the back of one hand bled freely, but otherwise he seemed healthy and whole. Jana closed her eyes in relief.

"I think his leg's broke, Mom. Can you fix him?"

"I don't know." Jana set LeeLee down and sank to the ground beside Ty. "He's so little. How in the world did you find him?"

Keeping an eye on the knifelike hooves, she examined the quivering animal as best she could. Its liquid brown eyes were wild with fear.

Ty looked up at Jana, absolute faith in her healing abilities shining in his dark blue eyes. "I saw him at the edge of the woods. I could tell there was something wrong with him, so I ran after him to see if I could help." He shrugged. "I didn't have time to call you 'cause he was running so fast. Then he sorta fell down, so I waited 'til you came."

The tenderness of her son's sturdy, sun-browned hand stroking the deer's back stayed the lecture poised on Jana's lips. "Sweetie, his mama will come after him. I'm sure she just went looking for food. If we take him out of the woods, she'll worry—just like I did when you ran off."

"But, Mom!" Ty blinked back tears. "If we leave him here, he'll die."

"Not necessarily—"

"Mommy!" LeeLee tapped Jana's shoulder. "There's GI Joe!"

Jana looked around to see what LeeLee's spectacular imagination had conjured up this time. A young man, perhaps in his early thirties, dressed in faded jeans and a maroon cap worn backward on his head, stepped through the woods behind her. A camouflage T-shirt stretched across shoulders as wide as any action figure's, and he carried a bow-shaped contraption that looked like some kind of military weapon. He had a quiver full of neon-fletched arrows strapped on a belt at his waist.

"Did you folks know you're trespassing on private property?" His slow, pleasant baritone belied the threat of the weapon. He propped his arm against a tree. "If you're lost, I'll be glad to show you the way out."

Jana was incapable of answering. The moment she'd jerked her gaze up from those shoulders to look at his face, a crazy mixture of humiliating memories nearly shut down her brain. Grant Gonzales had changed: the facial bones had sharpened and hardened with manhood, and his curly dark blond hair was hidden under the cap. But those brown eyes—the only remnant of fourth-generation Hispanic descent—still had a lazy, deep-lidded droop that told you he knew more than he was letting on. More than you wanted him to know.

Of all people to run into when she wasn't prepared for confrontation. And here of all places.

She struggled to speak in an even tone. "I'm not trespassing. This land belongs to Alvin Goff."

"Not for long. I'm in the process of buying it from—wait a minute!" His gaze raked her, eyes alight with an appreciative gleam. "Jana Baldwin. I thought you looked familiar."

Jana's heart pounded in her throat. *He* was the one buying Grandpa's property? She'd come home not a moment too soon. The nebulous "really good offer" had turned into the person of her first high school crush.

"It's Jana Cutrere. Richie and I got married." She rose, silencing the children with a look at Ty and a hand on LeeLee's shoulder. "And we're not lost. After all, I grew up here." When Grant frowned, she felt compelled to explain their presence further. "Ty saw the fawn and followed him to make sure he was okay."

Grant's gaze homed in on Ty. The small space seemed to shrink as he stepped into the glade with them. Kneeling with a graceful fold of his body, he gave Ty a sharp look. "Did you see his mama?"

"No, sir."

Grant glanced at Jana, his expression awkward.

Ty's eyes widened. "You killed her, didn't you?"

"This time of year? Of course not!" Grant looked shocked. "I was out here marking trails for an archery shoot. Didn't you hear that gunshot? I'd just found the doe when I heard y'all hollering. I didn't want to move her until the game warden—" Apparently realizing he was still under accusation, he appealed to Jana. "I didn't know she had a fawn. Listen, the poacher may still be out here. You all better go back to your car."

Jana shook her head. "We can't leave the fawn—its leg's broken. It'll die without its mother."

"I'll tell the warden where it is." Grant stood and extended a hand to Ty. "Come on, I'll walk you out."

Jana wasn't about to leave an injured deer in the care of this man and his weapon. "Go on back to your scouting, Hawkeye. We'll take the fawn with us." She took the animal from Ty and stood up. It squealed and struggled, but she managed to calm it in spite of her own agitation. "Ty, hold your sister's hand." She headed for the road.

Ty jumped to his feet. "But, Mom—"

Jana resisted the urge to look over her shoulder to see if Grant followed. "My supplies are all packed up, but we'll take the fawn to the vet."

She might have known Grant wouldn't be gotten rid of so easily. He caught up in two strides. "At least let me carry him for you." He stalked beside her, pushing tree limbs out of the way before they could slap her in the face.

"I've got him. We don't want to upset him any more than he already is." She gave Grant points for chivalry, though she wished he would go away.

Such wishful thinking came to an abrupt end when Jana emerged from the woods. Her disabled car still hunkered like roadkill in the middle of the highway. She had no way to get to a veterinary clinic—or anywhere else for that matter. "Oh, man."

"What happened to your car?" Grant's voice vibrated with amusement.

Seeing the pathetic, overloaded little wagon through his eyes, Jana could have died of mortification. "We had a minor confrontation with a cow."

"Looks like the cow won," he drawled. "The vet clinic's five miles away. You planning to walk?"

Jana gave him a pained look. "I was just about to call my grandpa." Balancing the fawn in one arm, she dug the phone out of her pocket. "If you'll excuse me ..."

"No, wait." Grant blew out an exasperated breath. "It's right at a hundred degrees out here, and Little Bit's liable to melt if you have to wait on Alvin." He grinned at LeeLee, who was all but turning herself wrong-side-out trying to reach a mosquito bite between her shoulder blades. "I'll take you wherever you need to go. And I'll call my brother-in-law to come tow your car. You remember Tommy Lucas?"

"Of course I do. We grew up in the same trailer park." Jana paused with Grandpa's number half-dialed, considering her options. "I guess it *would* be faster if you took us to the vet so Grandpa wouldn't have to leave the store. Where's your vehicle?"

"Not far. Just around the next bend."

While Jana locked the Subaru—not that there was much in it worth stealing—Grant checked the padlock on the U-Haul and handed his bow to Ty.

"Take care of that for me, would you, bud?" Without asking Jana's permission, he reached down to hoist LeeLee onto his shoulders. "Come on, Sally, let's go for a ride." He set off down the side of the road.

"My name's not Sally!" LeeLee squealed, clutching his forehead.

"It's not?" Grant turned to walk backward and winked at Jana. "Then it must be Snigglefritz."

"No!"

"Pudd'n'tain?"

"No! It's LeeLee Annabelle Cutrere."

"Hey, I was close, wasn't I?"

"Yessir. Mommy, look at me, I'm tall!"

Jana swallowed. "I see you, honey." Grant was well over six feet. Even walking backward through clumps of weeds reaching to his knees, he moved with an athletic grace that attested to a life spent outdoors. Why didn't he turn around and quit looking at her? Did he remember the last time he'd driven her home—and what he'd said?

Jana hadn't forgotten. "You better watch where you're going, she warned."

"Oh, backseat driver, huh?" He turned around with a sudden dip of the knees that made LeeLee giggle.

Another few steps and they rounded the bend in the road. An enormous dark green pickup was parked on a red dirt track extending off the highway. A steel toolbox took up a third of the truck bed, and through the back window she could see the inevitable gun rack. The undercarriage and wheels were coated with fresh mud, but the top half of the vehicle gleamed with a recent waxing.

Here was a man who cared for his possessions.

The thought gave Jana a funny pang, but before she had time to question it, Ty raced past her and clambered over the tailgate.

"Mom! Can I ride in the back?"

"No!" she exclaimed at the same moment Grant said, "Sure."

He held both of LeeLee's small sandals in one hand while he dug a set of keys out of the front pocket of his jeans. "It's okay. He can't hurt anything back there."

She gave him an annoyed look. "It's illegal to ride in the back of a truck."

Grant's wide mouth quirked. "Don't worry. My uncle Dewey's still the sheriff." He laughed as Jana opened her mouth to protest. "Haven't you ever let this boy ride in the back of a truck? That's a crime in itself."

She tried to think of an answer that wouldn't make her sound like an overprotective mother. "Who do you think you—"

"Look, we're way out in the country. He can sit close to the cab, and I'll go slow as my grandma." He shook his head. "On second thought, Granny's not such a great role model. Make that slow as your grandpa."

She could stand here arguing all afternoon, then wind up having to call her grandfather after all. The stubborn glint in Grant's brown eyes was all too familiar. He'd made her get in his truck once before, then proceeded to humiliate her. But that was a long time ago. She was an adult now, and she'd had a lot of experience taking care of herself.

Some battles weren't worth fighting. "All right. Sit down, Ty, and I'll let you hold the fawn—but only if you promise to be still! No arms or legs or any other part of your body hanging over the sides." She turned to Grant. "And remember you promised to drive slow. *Real* slow."

"Yes, ma'am." He stowed LeeLee in the backseat of the cab. "I hear and obey."

Grant had been hunting the woods of Jackson County since he was eight years old, but hauling out a beautiful woman, two kids, and a live deer was a first.

He glanced at Jana. Good night, it had to have been at least ten years since he'd last seen her. No wonder it'd taken him a minute to recognize her. Back then she was a tall, leggy wild child with a long gypsy mane and too much makeup. Eye-catching, for sure. But look at her now—dark hair floating around her face in short, glossy waves, dark blue eyes brilliant as gemstones, mouth full and curling at the corners.

There was something different in her expression too, something he couldn't quite put his finger on. She sat crowding the door, hands clasped in her lap and narrow feet straddling the hatchet and industrial-sized flashlight he'd left on the floorboard. He couldn't help wondering at the tension that all but vibrated from her slim shoulders. Surely she didn't still hold it against him that he'd bloodied her boyfriend's nose at the prom.

He could hardly believe she'd married that yahoo.

Curiosity sneaked under his guard. "So what's old Richie up to these days?"

"Daddy's in heaven, playing guitar with Jesus," LeeLee lisped, right into his ear.

Grant nearly ran the truck off the road.

"LeeLee! Sit down and put your seat belt on!" Jana glanced through the back window, then frowned at Grant. "You promised you'd go slow."

"Sorry." He gave her a cautious glance. "So Richie's, uh …"

"Yes." Her voice was tight. "Three years ago."

Grant glanced at the dark-haired little widget in the rear-view mirror. She was singing what sounded like a list of Eastern European countries. He shook his head. She couldn't be more than four or five.

Jana cut a glance at him. "LeeLee never knew her daddy, but I told her he's in heaven."

Lifelong acquaintance with the Cutrere clan made Grant doubt that, but he kept his reservations to himself. Already he'd betrayed his number one motto: *Never ask a woman questions; you'll get way more information than you need.* He wasn't about to break rule number two: *Never let on how much you know, or you'll wind up with an extra job.*

"Hmph." He returned his attention to the zigs and zags of the winding county road. There was a moment's quiet, except for the little voice warbling in the backseat.

He was trying to think of a safe topic of conversation when Jana cleared her throat. "So which one of your sisters married Tommy?" She still didn't look friendly, but at least she seemed to have reined in her overt hostility.

"He hooked up with Carrie."

"Tommy's my age! Carrie's older than you, isn't she?"

Grant glanced at her, amused. "There's only about five years' difference between them."

"But Tommy was even wilder than—"

He knew what she'd been about to say. Tommy Lucas and Jana Baldwin had both been known as "hoods." At first Grant hadn't been thrilled with his sister's choice of husband, but Tommy had turned out to be as grounded as a Mississippi live oak. The guy worshiped the ground Carrie walked on.

"He became a Christian." Grant glanced at Jana to gauge her reaction.

A radiant smile bloomed on her face. "Did he really? So did I!"

Well, that was interesting. No wonder she seemed different.

He hesitated. "I noticed the U-Haul. Are you moving back here after all this time? I assume you're gonna stay with your grandpa for a while."

She didn't answer for a long moment. Then, "Grandpa's getting older, and I felt like he needed me."

"I know he'll be mighty glad to see y'all." He slowed to turn into the driveway of the veterinary clinic. He'd promised to go by Carrie and Tommy's this afternoon and stay for supper, but he couldn't just dump off Jana and her kids and leave. Well, he could, but he had a thing about making sure his responsibilities were settled.

He preferred not to think too closely about why he felt responsible for Jana.

chapter 2

Redmond Animal Clinic, a two-story barnlike building sided in weathered gray cedar and roofed with green Italian tile, sat on a grassy hill just south of the Vancleave city limits. Grant parked in the side lot near the small animal entrance, setting the brake so the truck wouldn't roll backward into the goldfish pond at the edge of the property. Which had happened a few weeks ago, and Heath had yet to let him forget it. A part of him even suspected the pond was there for the express purpose of humiliating Grant Gonzales.

Heath Redmond had studied pre-veterinary medicine at Mississippi State while Grant was there majoring in sorority girls and minoring in mechanical engineering. The two had grown up together, played baseball on the same team, marched in the Vancleave High School band, and competed as seniors for valedictorian. The fact that Grant had missed it by two-hundredths of a point remained a sore subject.

Still, on behalf of his pure-bred bluetick coonhounds, Grant was glad his old rival had set up practice in their hometown. Redmond might be a wise-cracking oddball, but he was a stellar veterinarian.

Inside the reception area, Dora King hung up the phone, her eyes lighting when she saw the fawn. "Oh, look at the baby!"

Jana walked up to Dora's window. "Could we see the vet? It's an emergency."

Emergency? "It's just a deer," Grant muttered, earning a dirty look from Jana.

"We were just about to close up for the day, but I'll see if Dr. Heath is still here." Dora bounced to her feet and returned in a moment, beaming. "Bring him on back, right through that door."

Since Grant had no desire to sit there listening to the Bill Gaither CD blaring through the waiting room, he followed the Cutreres. He could always entertain himself by giving Redmond a hard time.

Except for the obnoxious tile roof, the clinic was nothing fancy. Everything was clean, orderly, and built on sturdy lines—even Dora. She met them in a hallway lined with shelves of animal food and supplies. "Y'all wait here." She opened the door of an exam room and gave the deer a goo-goo-eyed air kiss before disappearing.

"Y'all sit down and be quiet." Jana cradled the fawn close, supporting its broken leg in one hand.

Grant hoped she wasn't talking to him.

Ty plopped down in a plastic chair against the wall, pulling his little sister onto his lap. Eyes as big as china-blue saucers, LeeLee took in the jars of animal organs displayed on an overhead shelf.

She pointed at a jar. "Those are heartworms and tapeworms." She squinted up at Grant. "Have you ever had one?"

"Uh, no." Grant grinned a little. "At least not that I know of. Have you?"

She grinned back at him, eyes sparkling. "No, sir, but Ty got ringworms on the bottom of his feet last summer."

"LeeLee, hush." Jana met Grant's eyes, cheeks pink.

Fingers tucked into the back pockets of his jeans, Grant stood in the doorway watching Jana stroke the fawn's white-spotted coat. She was a beautiful woman, but it was best to keep his mind on the fawn. Maybe if Redmond fixed it, it'd grow into a handsome spike by this time next year. He couldn't wait for deer season to open. The investors in Mobile were champing at the bit, and he had less than four months to get the camp running. Alvin had better turn loose of that property quick.

"I'm sure Forrest is gonna be okay." Jana gave LeeLee a smile. The little girl had insisted on giving the fawn a name, and Jana suggested Forrest Gump. It fit, down to the gimpy leg.

Somebody shoved at his shoulder from behind. "Move it, Gonzales. Lemme see what's got Dora in such a twitter." Heath Redmond's tall, rangy frame overwhelmed the tiny exam room as Grant stepped aside. Dressed in a red-and-white Hawaiian-print shirt and green scrub pants, Redmond was evidently in a *Magnum, PI*, mood today. "Well, look at this." He stooped to peer at the fawn. "I can see why you're the center of attention."

"You shouldn't look him in the eyes." Jana backed up a step. "Wild animals find that threatening."

Heath blinked. "I knew that." He turned his raffish smile on Jana. "I'm Heath Redmond."

"I remember you. I'm Jana Cutrere—used to be Baldwin."

Redmond's heavy brows rose for a second before his grin turned wolfish. "Oh yeah ..."

Jana reddened.

Grant was startled by the protective instincts that knotted his fists. He had no reason to care what Heath Redmond thought about Jana; still, she had only these two kids and old man Goff to look out for her. He cleared his throat. "Hey, Dr. Dolittle, what about the deer?"

With a speculative look at Grant, Redmond gestured for Jana to lay the fawn on the stainless steel examination table. "What are you doing here, Gonzo? I wouldn't think you'd be interested in rescuing venison. Hold him still for me, would you, Jana? I don't want him any more agitated than we can help."

"He's so scared." She leaned close as the doctor ran experienced hands over the animal's quivering little body. "I'm pretty sure his leg's broken. See?"

"Hmm. Looks that way. We'll need X-rays, though." He tugged one side of his mustache. "My assistant's gone for the day."

"I just graduated from vet school at UT Knoxville. I don't have my Mississippi license yet, but—"

"No kiddin'! Congratulations, Dr. Cutrere. You looking for a job?"

She blushed. "My plans aren't firm yet."

Redmond's appreciative smile set Grant's teeth on edge. He stepped into the room. "I'll just take the kids and entertain them outside."

"No, they can watch." Jana didn't even look at him.

So Grant was forced to loiter by the door like a redheaded stepchild while Jana and Redmond anesthetized the little animal. They weighed it in at a whopping 5.9 pounds, then took X-rays and conferred in the manner of lifelong partners. Within another hour or so, the deer was lying asleep on the table with a soft plaster cast stabilizing the broken leg. Somehow it looked even tinier and more fragile than before.

"What's going to happen to it now?" Grant blurted. Not that he cared.

As Redmond washed his hands at a sink in the corner, he looked over his shoulder. "That's a bit of a problem. We're not equipped to keep it here. The wildlife conservation people get nutso about permits, and he's going to need round-the-clock care for a while. At least until he's weaned."

"Weaned? You mean he'll have to be bottle-fed?"

"Well, what did you think?" Jana touched the deer's lax body. "His mother's dead."

Ty bounced a little. "We can take him home. I'll feed him!"

"Baby, we can't show up at Grandpa's with a deer."

"Why not?"

"We're just getting here. It would be bad manners."

There was no reason Grant should feel responsible for the unconscious animal on the table. It wasn't *his* fault the poor little guy had a cast on his leg. So what if Ty looked like somebody had run over the family dog? The kid would just have to get over it.

Then he saw LeeLee's bottom lip tremble and tears swimming in her enormous blue eyes.

"I'll take him," Grant said, to his utter horror.

Everyone in the room looked at him as if he'd just shot a gun at the ceiling.

Redmond burst into guffaws. *"You?"*

"Why not?" Grant shrugged as Jana stared at him with that sweet Meg Ryan mouth ajar. "I'm good with animals too."

"Gonzales, you have two hunting dogs. Don't you see a small conflict of interest there?"

"They're coon dogs, not deer hounds." Heath Redmond was not going to tell him what he could and could not do. "Besides, my place is in the woods. I'll build a pen and feed it what and however often you say." And maybe, a sneaking little voice in his head whispered, Jana would volunteer to keep an eye on him. Maybe this wouldn't be such a bad thing after all.

Redmond, still snickering, dried his hands on a paper towel. "The game warden would have a stroke."

Jana glanced at both men. "I can get permission. The fawn needs to be in the woods, Dr. Redmond. Why not let Grant keep him, and I'll check on him every so often." Her dark blue eyes glinted with mischief as she looked at Grant.

Grant swallowed. He'd just been had.

Jana's heart raced with a mixture of excitement and apprehension as Grant stopped the truck in front of the Farm and Feed. She'd missed this place—from the organized clutter of the store to the acrid odor of fertilizer and sticky-sweet smell of molasses in the feed warehouse. During the chaotic violence of her growing-up years, Grandpa's store had been an asylum of safety.

This first meeting with her grandfather came loaded with snares. One reason she'd held off asking him for the land had to do with her own pride and stupidity. The night after high school graduation, Grandpa had told her he'd give her enough land for her own trailer if she'd let Richie go and come to work for him in the store. But at eighteen she'd been impatient to escape—impatient to *live*. And she'd refused the gift with barely a word of thanks.

Now, ten years later, the prodigal somehow had to find the nerve to ask for more than just a postage stamp big enough for a trailer. She needed the whole doggone Twin Creek property. Judging by the state of Grandpa's store, fatted calves and signet rings weren't likely to be in her immediate future.

There was the same American flag drooping from a metal pole fastened to the porch rail. John Deere and Nexus feed advertisements hung in the windows, and riding tack filled the back wall. The maroon awning over the entrance looked fairly new; it was a bit faded in places, but not yet rotted by the sun.

"It hasn't changed at all." She glanced at Grant, who was observing her with one wrist propped on the steering wheel.

"Not unless you count the price of the drinks in the Coke machine."

Jana smiled, his dry humor settling her nerves. "Looks like Grandpa still rolls up the sidewalks at seven too." The parking lot was empty except for her grandfather's dark blue El Camino and a dusty red Chevy pickup she vaguely recognized. She reached for the door handle. "Thanks for the ride over here, Grant. Tell Tommy I'll get my luggage out of the car tonight when Grandpa's free to bring me."

"I'm going over there for supper. I'll bring it to you so y'all won't have to get out again."

"That's very nice of you." She wasn't sure she wanted to be in his debt any further. "You'll take good care of the fawn, won't you?" Why had she agreed to the arrangement? Was she crazy?

"Jana." He released an exaggerated sigh. "You think I'm going to execute little Forrest the minute you turn your back? Look, I've got a significant investment in that animal already, what with X-rays, anesthesia, and antibiotics."

"I guess you do. Thank you for that too." She would have offered to pay Dr. Redmond herself, but she barely had enough in her checking account to buy another tank of gas. "He should stay unconscious until you get him home. Just don't forget to give him his antibiotics twice a day." She stopped when the corner of his mouth curled.

He gave her a little salute.

"Sorry, motherhood is ingrained. Come on, LeeLee, let's go see Grandpa."

But her daughter had already hopped out of the truck and made a beeline for the store. She stood on the porch, yanking on the wooden-spool knob on the screen door.

"LeeLee, wait on me!" Jana lingered to make sure Ty got away from the truck before Grant backed out and turned onto the highway. "Come on, Ty, we'll go visit Forrest soon."

"Hurry up, Mommy, I gotta go!" LeeLee hopped from one foot to the other.

Jana hastened to help her daughter with the warped old door. "You were fine just a minute ago!" The door spring screeched as Jana stuck her head inside. "Grandpa, we're here! I'm sorry we're so late, but we need to use your—"

She stopped. An elderly fellow in camouflage coveralls and a pair of impressive white sideburns leaned against the counter, chewing on a pipe and looking at her with open amusement. CJ Stokes, the owner of the red truck, lived half a mile from her grandfather's house, right about where she'd hit that cow. As children, Jana and her brother had snitched many a watermelon out of his patch.

He removed the pipe from his mouth and smiled. "Hey there, young lady." His gravelly drawl hadn't changed one iota.

Flustered, Jana looked around for her grandfather and found him seated behind the counter, engaged in counting a pile of bolts. He raised heavy gray eyebrows. "We been looking for you, girl."

Jana felt a tug on the back of her shorts. "Mommy!"

"Grandpa, is the restroom in the same place?"

He pointed. "Back corner of the storeroom."

"Thanks. Be right back." Jana hustled LeeLee toward the storeroom.

When she returned, Ty was sitting on the counter, swinging his feet and regaling the grown-ups with his cow-hunter-deer-veterinarian adventures. Grandpa leaned back in his chair, arms folded, rubbing his beaky nose to hide a smile.

"And you should see Mr. Gonzales's truck!" Ty took a gulp from a can of grape soda, brandishing it with dramatic flair. "It's a Ford F-250 King Cab, with dual exhaust and four-wheel drive. And he let me ride in the back!"

"Sounds like you kids had you a real time." CJ grinned around his pipe. "Good thing you run up on young Gonzales when you did, though, 'cause you could've got hurt bad. Alvin, I told you there's been poachers runnin' all over them woods. I'll stop by there before I go home for supper. See what I can pick up from lookin' at that doe."

"I'd appreciate it." Grandpa slid off the stool and limped around the counter toward Jana. "How's my girl?"

"Glad to see you," Jana said, throat thick with emotion. "Oh, Grandpa, I missed you so much—"

He grabbed her in a vertebrae-cracking hug, the scent of peppermint and Old Spice watering her eyes as she buried her face in his neck. He was still tall and straight, his white hair thick as ever, but his body felt thinner and frailer than she remembered.

"Me too," he whispered, chin against her temple. "Glad you're home."

Guilt hit hard. It had been four years since he'd flown to Knoxville for a brief visit after Grandma's death. Jana had needed help then, and he'd come through.

"I'd never have made it through vet school if you hadn't been my rock."

"Aw, now, that's what family's for." Stepping back, he took off his black-rimmed glasses and polished them on a clean white handkerchief. "CJ, you remember Jana, don't you?"

CJ doffed his hunting cap, giving Jana a courtly little bob of his grizzled head. "Sure do. Always walking around with a stray animal under her arm. Mice, birds, even a skunk one time, if I remember right."

"That was me. Are you still the game warden?"

"Yes, ma'am, one of 'em at least. The community's grown so much we got a whole unit now, and a station up at Parker Lake. Don't have to work out of my house no more."

"That's good." Jana wrapped her arm around Grandpa's waist. "That fawn is going to need a lot of care, so I let Grant Gonzales take it home. Is that okay with you? I'll make sure it gets released back to the wild by the end of the summer."

CJ tipped his head. "Sounds like a plan. One less thing for me to worry about."

"Good!" Jana smiled at him.

"CJ, this is my favorite number one great-granddaughter." Grandpa pinched LeeLee's nose. "How about a soda pop, Shorty?"

"Okay," LeeLee sighed, "but my name isn't Shorty. Can't anybody remember that?"

"Don't be rude, LeeLee." Jana shook her head. "Why don't you give Grandpa a Yankee dime?"

Eyes twinkling, Grandpa squatted to LeeLee's level. "I'd rather have a kiss. No place to spend a Yankee dime around here."

LeeLee rolled her eyes at this grown-up stupidity. "A Yankee dime *is* a kiss!" She leaned over and gave Grandpa's leathery, red-veined cheek a loud smack.

Grandpa patted her head and rose, looking pleased, then went behind the counter to fill a plastic sack with the bolts he'd been counting. "Here ya go, CJ. You better get home and mend that fence before Jana runs over the rest of your herd."

"Oh my goodness! Was that cow yours?"

"'Fraid so." CJ chewed on his pipe, lips twitching.

Jana put a hand to her forehead. "I meant to give her a closer examination, but I got sidetracked by the deer. I'll run over to your place tomorrow morning and check her over."

"That'd be just fine." CJ took his sack of bolts and headed for the door. "Alvin, I'll be back to stomp you in a game of checkers over lunch tomorrow. Nice to see you again, Miss Jana. Don't worry about the cow, you hear?"

"Beat me at checkers—like that's gonna happen." Shaking his head, Grandpa handed Ty a canvas bag full of coins along with a stack of paper wrappers in a rubber band. "Let's see if you can deal with this for me."

"Yes, sir!" Ty grinned and dumped the coins on the counter.

Grandpa limped over to flip the hand-lettered "Open" sign to read "Come back tomorrow." Pulling a big wad of keys from his belt, he locked the door. "Let me finish my cash drawer, then we'll go to the house and throw together some greens and corn bread."

"Mommy, I don't like green corn bread," LeeLee whispered loudly. She'd discovered a martin house made out of a gourd and was trying to peer inside its tiny door.

Ty rolled his eyes. "Green corn bread—"

Jana shushed him with a look. "That'll be fine, Grandpa." She located the big push broom and set to work sweeping the aisles. She knew the closing drill.

"Good kids you got here, Jana." Grandpa crammed money into a nylon zippered bank bag.

"I think so." Sweeping her way past the seed bins, Jana watched to make sure LeeLee didn't move the gourds. She was a curious little thing, and Grandpa didn't like his merchandise out of place. "They sure wanted to bring that fawn home with us."

"Well, I don't like the idea of mixing wildlife with my livestock, so it's a good thing you didn't."

Jana sucked in a breath. Oh dear. Didn't bode well for the wildlife refuge center idea.

Grandpa looked up from the cash drawer, his light gray eyes piercing under those thundercloud brows. "I guess the kids take after you in the animal-lover department."

"They were practically raised in the clinics at the vet school, and they helped me with the Andrewses' horses." Jana had worked on a horse-breeding farm to pay some of their expenses. She and the children had lived rent-free in a small trailer close to the barns.

"And you got it from your grandma, you know." Grandpa moved aside to let Jana empty her dustpan into the trash can. "She was an animal lover too. It was *people* she didn't handle so good sometimes."

Jana looked up, ready to deny any resemblance to the irascible Imogene Goff, but she had to smile at Grandpa's wistful expression. "You miss her a lot, don't you?"

"Well, after 'while, a man develops a taste for chili peppers, if he eats 'em every day of his life."

Jana laughed. "Mama never got used to Grandma's bite. I got a whipping every time I snuck over to y'all's house."

"That was the thing about those two. So much alike they couldn't stand one another as adults. And your daddy—" Grandpa whistled, shaking his head. "Thought Imogene was gonna bust an artery when Paulette run off to marry Aaron Baldwin."

It had taken a long time, but Jana now found it possible to think about her mother and father without flinching. "Mama should've listened to Grandma on that one."

Her grandfather's tone was tender. "Well, now, if she had, you wouldn't be here. And I'd be mighty sorry about that." Grandpa closed the cash drawer with a bang. "Hey, buddy-roe." He crooked a finger at Ty. "Why don't you get your sister and let's blow this joint. You can finish wrapping them coins at home."

"Okay." Ty scooped the loose change back into the canvas sack, along with the rolls he'd already finished. He headed for the back of the store, where LeeLee could be heard singing "Little Blue Man."

Smiling at the sweet sound, Grandpa followed Ty with his eyes. "Who does the boy favor? Don't look like none of our people."

"He's Richie all over again. Cowlick and all." She sighed. Maybe she could talk about her parents, but she didn't want to discuss her late husband. When all was said and done, her choice hadn't been any better than her mother's. Maybe worse. "But Ty's a steady kid for his age. He's smart, and I think he'll make a good vet one of these days."

"You planning his future for him already?"

Jana winced at the irony in her grandfather's voice. "I know. It used to drive me insane when Grandma would do that to me. But Ty does have a knack for dealing with animals. You should have seen him with that little fawn this afternoon. I never would have noticed him, but Ty tracked him all the way to his hiding place."

"Pretty smart, I'll have to agree. You too." He shook his head. "I still can't believe you conned Grant Gonzales into taking on an orphan deer."

Jana grinned. "Yeah, I'll have to keep an eye on him." Grandpa stared at her until she felt a blush creep up from the neck of her T-shirt. "The fawn, I mean."

"Uh-huh." Grandpa snorted. "I appreciate young Gonzales helping you get your car situated, but you'd best not take him too seriously. Bet he thinks he's working another angle to get ahold of my Twin Creek property." Grandpa's hatchet-thin features took on a cagey expression. "The boy's got a reputation for turning a sharp deal, but he's met his match in old Alvin Goff."

Jana sent him a casual glance. "Are you really thinking about selling it outside the family?"

"Yep." Grandpa reached under the counter to retrieve his walking stick.

Worry knifed through Jana's stomach. Had her vet school bills left her grandfather needing money badly enough to give up fifteen hundred acres of priceless woods, water, and fertile soil that had been in her family for generations? Knowing that he'd once offered it to her and she'd given it up for Richie Cutrere strengthened her remorse.

Oh, Lord, I was so stupid. Can you please redeem my mistakes?

Grandpa, leaning on the hand-carved top of his cane, looked every bit of his seventy-five years. If she asked him for the land she needed for the wildlife refuge, would he think that she too was "working an angle"?

"Did you tell Grant you'd sell it to him?"

Grandpa shrugged. "I'm entertaining his offer. Mind you, I ain't signed on the dotted line yet, whatever he says." He looked around. "Now, where you suppose those two younguns of yours got off to? Reckon they're playing in the mop bucket like you used to do?"

Pondering her dilemma, Jana rounded up Ty and LeeLee and herded them out into the stifling heat. As Grandpa locked the door and crossed the gravel parking lot toward the El Camino, teasing the children all the way, Jana noticed how heavily he leaned on the cane.

Please, Lord, let me and the children be a blessing to Grandpa, not another worry.

She'd better wait and see if he would offer her the land. Then she would know the Lord was with her in this venture.

chapter 3

Okay, dude, it's just you and me tonight." Grant squatted in the doorway of the tiny laundry room of his houseboat, observing his unwanted houseguest. "Hope you don't snore."

The sleeping fawn twitched. Nestled on a couple of old towels between the wall and the dryer, the broken leg poking out to one side, he otherwise looked like the Grand Poobah.

The dogs, even when they were puppies, had never been this much trouble. Baby bottles, formula, medicine. There were cuts all up and down Grant's forearms from those lethal hooves. He even had a gash in his chin, which had bled all over his favorite T-shirt before he'd managed to get the antibiotics down the fawn.

"And Dolittle says I'm stuck with you for three months."

Heath had called to tell Grant not to leave the deer out in the open until the cast came off. The vet had then proceeded to give instructions for building a shelter, as if Grant didn't know how to nail a few pieces of plywood together.

"But I don't have time to build it tonight," Grant had insisted.

"Just shut him in a room on the boat. He'll be fine."

Then Grant discovered what one had to do to make an infant deer relieve himself. "You have got to be kidding!" he'd shouted, while Heath just about hurt himself laughing.

He ought to dump the responsibility back on Jana Cutrere, since *she* knew so much about wild animals. The only thing that kept him from doing so was his pride. And the fact that he didn't want to disappoint her.

"We can do this," he told the fawn, even though the little guy had started snoring like a chain saw.

Looking at his watch, he pushed to his feet. It was nearly nine o'clock and he still had to go by Tommy's garage to pick up Jana's luggage.

I'd about decided you weren't going to come over after all." Jana opened the screen door, and her smile almost made Grant forget how tired and aggravated he was. He'd missed supper. Carrie had reamed him out for not calling to cancel, and it had taken him half an hour to unhitch the U-Haul from the Subaru in the dark and move it to his truck.

"I said I would, didn't I?"

"Yeah, you did." Jana wrinkled her nose. "Sorry about the way I look. I've been helping LeeLee get a bath. Come in."

He didn't see any problem with the way she looked. Her hair curled around her face, loose and a little wild, reminding him of the way she'd looked as a teenager. Something in him that had long been asleep woke up, making him feel a bit like he did on the first day of hunting season. Eager, expectant, fully alive.

He stepped inside, trying not to stare at her dainty bare feet and the damp splotches on her shirt. "If you'll give me the key to the trailer, I'll start unloading."

Jana blinked. "It can wait 'til morning."

"Don't you need your clothes? Come on, it won't take long if we work together."

She gave him a long, indecipherable look. "Okay. Let me find my shoes."

While he waited, he looked around Alvin's small living room. He could hear the shower running in the old man's room, but there was no sign of the kids.

Jana came back carrying her sneakers and sat down in the brown Naugahyde recliner to put them on. Boy, she had little feet. She caught him staring and tucked her hair behind her ear.

"Kids asleep?" He swerved his attention to a photograph of Mrs. Imogene that sat on the television. That disapproving stare would curdle milk.

"Yep, they were worn out." Jana snagged her keys off the mantel. "Too much excitement for one day." She led the way outside, pausing to flip on the porch light. "Did you get Forrest settled for the night?"

"Who?"

She huffed. "The fawn."

"Oh yeah, *Forrest*." Grant snorted in disgust. "Why couldn't you give him a *guy* name like Spike? He's taking his bottle like a man." He shot her an accusing look. "You didn't tell me he couldn't even go to the bathroom by himself."

"You didn't know that? The big game hunter?"

Grant let her unlock the trailer, then nudged her aside so he could let down the ramp. "I also didn't know he was going to be my roommate tonight." His mouth fell open when he saw how much junk was crammed in the tiny U-Haul. "Hey, if the vet thing doesn't work out, you've got a career in professional packing."

Jana made a face. "Another thing that comes with motherhood." She hauled out a gym bag and an Easy-Bake oven. "I'll come check on Forrest as soon as I get my car back. Where do you live?"

"Out at Ketchum's Landing on Twin Creek."

"That's right next to my grandpa's property. Mr. Ketchum used to let Quinn and me swim off his houseboat."

"Yeah, I bought it when they moved Mr. Ketchum to the nursing home."

"Oh." By the light of the porch, Grant could see the distress on Jana's face. "I didn't know he'd gotten that sick."

"Not sick. Just old. Jana, he's nearly ninety." He set down his armload of boxes and opened the door. "You want to just leave this stuff in the living room for now?"

"I guess so." Jana led the way inside and dumped her load in the middle of the braided rug. "Just a minute."

He paused with a hand on the door. "What's the matter?"

She bit her lip. "Grandpa said you wanted to buy his property out there."

"Yeah, I told you that this afternoon."

"I guess I didn't take you seriously. I know this is going to sound nosy, but—he hasn't signed a contract, has he?"

"No, but I made an offer and we have a verbal agreement. Why?"

"Grant . . ." Jana's big-eyed gaze dropped, then flashed up to his face. His stomach clenched. *Sympathy?* "Something Grandpa said to me tonight made me think he may be reconsidering selling."

"He can't reconsider. That property lies between me and the road. I have to have it in time for hunting season." Actually, he needed it *now*, but if Alvin thought he was desperate, the old man was likely to hike the price. And Grant couldn't afford to pay more.

But he didn't have to tell Jana that. Her loyalty would be to her grandfather, and maybe he'd already said too much. He took a deep breath and pushed the screen door open. "Look, I'm a big boy, and I can deal with your grandpa. Don't worry about it. Come on. Let's get the rest of your stuff in."

Jana looked at him, her expression troubled. He waited for her to say something else, but after a moment she sighed and trudged down the porch steps.

He followed, wishing he could take some of the responsibility from those slim shoulders. It couldn't be easy, moving with two kids all the way from Tennessee, dealing with a wrecked car and a wacky old grandfather all by herself.

He carted box after box of childish and feminine junk from the trailer into the house and twenty minutes later faced Jana on opposite sides of the screen door. "I have an errand in Mobile tomorrow, so I'd be glad to take the U-Haul back for you."

"You don't have to do that—"

"No big deal. Your car's out of commission, and besides, I know you've got unpacking to do around here. Just take it easy, sleep in tomorrow." He noted the dark shadows under her eyes. "And don't forget my granny's right across the road, so you can call her for anything. She loves to interfere."

Jana smiled. "Grant, thanks. You've been a real godsend today."

He backed away from the door. "Well, I don't know about that."

He'd only lent her a hand, just as he would have for any lovely woman who'd once been—well, maybe not a friend, but someone who'd flashed across his life and left him changed. He was likely to make her life uncomfortable in a major way if things got nasty between him and Alvin.

Early the next morning while the children still slept, Jana sat on the front porch with Grandpa, watching a pair of jewel-bright hummingbirds come to blows over a plastic feeder hanging from the eaves. The dew sparkled on the grass, and a fine haze filtered weak sunlight into splotches of shadow around the fruit trees in the yard. Grandpa's ancient shepherd dog sprawled at his feet, emitting an occasional geriatric snore that made Jana want to laugh. Perfect morning. *Thank you, Lord.*

She took a sip of Grandpa's axle-grease coffee and winced. Well, nearly perfect.

"Wish I could stay home and entertain you." Grandpa slurped his coffee. "Don't seem right for me to go off to the store and leave you stranded when you just got here. When will your car be ready?"

"Grant said a couple of days." She hadn't mentioned last night's conversation to her grandfather yet.

"I'm a big boy, and I can deal with your grandpa." What did that mean? Was he going to break Grandpa's legs if he didn't follow through on their "verbal agreement"? That was ridiculous, right? Grant's behavior toward her had been generous.

Then again, that could be explained by the fact that he seemed to like the way she looked. She'd lain awake last night thinking about it. She shouldn't feel guilty for wanting that property. It was hers. Grant had always gotten everything he wanted, and she didn't have to hand him one more thing on a silver platter.

"It's okay, Grandpa. Being without wheels for a couple of days will give me a chance to get organized around here. Then I'll see what I can do to help you at the store."

Grandpa frowned. "I don't need any help. Besides, you got no business running a cash register."

"What do you mean? I haven't forgotten how to—"

"Of course you haven't." He waved his hand. "But you're a doctor now. You got more important things to do. You never said where you were gonna put your clinic. Or were you planning to go into practice with the Redmond boy?"

That had never crossed her mind until yesterday when Heath mentioned it. She had no interest in a partnership. "I didn't even know Heath was here. But I *have* been thinking about my practice." She paused. "You know the wildlife research I did in Knoxville?"

"You mean all that fooling around with squirrels and deer and all them other rodents?"

"Deer aren't rodents!" She smiled. "But yes, sir, that's the kind of practice I want. Not just ordinary domestic animals."

"You're joking me, right?" Grandpa set his mug down on the arm of his rocker, hard enough to slosh his coffee. "You can't make no money doctoring wild animals!"

"I wouldn't refuse to treat pets and farm animals. But there's been so little research on wildlife, and new diseases are cropping up all the time. Eventually they're going to affect humans—"

"Are you talking about that evolution baloney?" He scowled. "I happen to believe God created separate species from the very beginning, and I'm not catching no monkey pox!"

"Okay, listen, Grandpa." She put her hand to her forehead. Maybe she'd jumped the gun, but she'd worked too hard for too many years to kill her dream before she'd even had a chance to pursue it. "I don't believe in evolution any more than you do. All I'm saying is, God put us humans in charge of his creation, and it's our responsibility to take care of it. He's given me a gift—and a special concern—for treating wildlife."

Grandpa's expression softened. "Maybe so, but I happen to know how much you got invested in school loans. Baby doll, you gotta start earning a living sometime!"

"I know." She was going to have to explain this carefully. "And I will, eventually, because I plan to write a textbook based on my research. I've got a federal grant to establish a wildlife refuge, but it's on the condition that I provide land to build it. The grant runs out the first of next year if I don't use it."

Grandpa's brows beetled. Maybe he'd only made it through the eighth grade, but he was no dummy. "Where you gonna get the land?"

Jana swallowed. "Well, I need at least a thousand acres."

His eyes widened. "A thousand—What for?"

"I need that much room to release the animals after I treat them." She waited.

Grandpa's watery gray eyes shifted and narrowed. "Would you look at that?"

Following his gaze, Jana caught her breath. A beautiful full-grown doe stepped daintily across the yard, approaching Grandpa's prized peach trees that grew alongside the toolshed. It was a rare sight.

Grandpa put a finger to his lips and slid to his feet. "Don't move," he whispered. "I'll be right back." He noiselessly opened the screen door and disappeared.

Assuming he'd gone to get a camera, Jana sat still and watched the doe, enthralled. Maybe she'd adopt Forrest when he was well and strong enough. What had she been thinking to let Grant take him? He was the Hunter—capital *H*, like Felix Salten's villain in *Bambi*. She'd read that book over and over as a child, seated on her favorite vine swing in the woods.

The only explanation was that Grant had lulled her with his reluctant chivalry and that lazy, lopsided grin. She couldn't help remembering the night of the prom—an event stuck in the back of her mind, a conundrum to be brought out over the years, held up to light, and pondered.

She was going to be more careful this time. *Shrewd as a serpent, innocent as a dove.* She watched the doe lift her head. The large, delicate ears twitched.

The screen door opened behind Jana, and Grandpa stepped out carrying his shotgun. To her horror, he lifted it and aimed at the deer.

"Grandpa!" She jumped to her feet as the deer bolted for the woods. "What are you doing?"

He lowered the gun and gave her an irritated look. "Dadgum deer always get in my peaches before they get ripe enough to eat."

Jana spluttered, unable to articulate the depth of her outrage. "You can't shoot a deer this time of year, especially aiming toward the road! What if you hit somebody!"

"I know that. What do you think I am, crazy?"

Jana just gaped at him. She did wonder if all her grandfather's synapses were firing.

"I wasn't aiming *at* the deer, anyway. I was just gonna shoot over its head and scare it away."

"But, Grandpa, why didn't you just yell at her, like I did? She ran right off."

He propped the gun against the porch rail and dropped into his rocker. "I yell myself blue in the face and they just keep coming right back. I figured a little more noise would do the trick."

Jana took a deep, cleansing breath and sat down, eyeing the gun. "Okay, I'll work on the problem. But we've got to talk about this gun being in the house. I've got two curious kids, and it scares me to death that one of them might get hold of it."

Grandpa folded his arms. "My daddy taught me how to use this gun when I was just a little fella. I'll teach your boy to use it too. This is south Mississippi, girl, and hunting's our way of life. You knew that when you moved back here."

Tears stung the back of Jana's nose. She'd never anticipated this sort of contention with her beloved grandfather. Maybe she should start looking for another place to live. She couldn't stand the thought of Ty picking up a gun at all, much less to aim it at an animal.

But how would she pay the rent? Vet school had wiped out all her funds, she owed Grandpa thousands already, and now she needed him to give her that property.

She doubted he was going to be in any mood to give her anything in the near future. Her whole body shook.

Oh, Lord, what a mess. What am I going to do?

Grant pulled an arrow from his quiver, nocked it, and sighted the latest fully rigged Mathews bow at the center target at the end of the room. His friend Bo Eubanks had added on a practice range to his pro shop, turning it into such a first-class operation that Grant wondered how Bo could spare the capital. Grant would be there every day if he could, but the shop was a full hour's drive from home. He had to settle for a once-a-month fix.

The arrow flew straight into the center of the target.

"I'd buy it if I were you, Doug. It's hard to miss with this thing." He'd just bought a new bow himself after Christmas. Already improvements were coming on the market.

"Yeah, if you're Robin Hood in blue jeans." Mobile attorney Doug Briscoe gave Grant an envious look. He took the bow and shot quickly with more enthusiasm than skill, sending the arrow wide of the target. He'd been gun hunting all his life but had recently taken up the more challenging sport of bow hunting. Doug nocked another arrow. "I can't wait to get out in the woods and go after the real thing. You said you're putting together a tournament for this summer?"

"Yeah, in July, before the national championship in August. Keep practicing and you'll be ready."

Grant watched Doug let fly several more shots, giving him brief tips to correct his aim. Eventually Doug lowered the bow and gave Grant his no-nonsense in-the-courtroom look. "Okay, sport, you've been buttering me up for the last fifteen minutes. Now, what legal advice are you after?"

Grant grinned sheepishly. "I thought I was being subtle. No wonder you're the terror of the Mobile County legal system."

"Look, I told you you're well out of that mess with the guy in Atlanta." Doug walked down to the end of the room and started plucking arrows out of the target. "He can't touch you, no matter what the bank says, so just ignore their nervousness."

Then why was he having so many sleepless nights? Grant folded his arms and leaned against the wall to avoid towering over Doug, who had height issues. "That's not the main thing on my mind right now. But I do have a potential problem." He hesitated. The man tended toward volatility in more than his shooting.

"Oh yeah?"

Grant nodded. "You know that easement property—the thousand acres that fronts the highway?"

"The deal you said was sewn up, just a matter of crossing t's and dotting i's?" Doug walked toward him, his bantam-rooster strut pronounced. "What about it?"

"It may not be as clear-cut as I thought. I have a verbal agreement, but old Mr. Goff's decided to play hard-to-get. Do I have any way to legally force him to act?"

"Depends. Do you have ingress and egress otherwise?"

"No. He's been letting me cross his property, but if he decides to close the road off to me, the only way I can get to my land is by boat. I'm boxed in on the other two sides by federal land."

"Then he has to sell." A frown gathered on Doug's round face. "But if you have to sue him, you won't get the whole acreage, just enough for a road. And you could be tied up in court for up to two years if he decides to fight it."

"No way!"

"Afraid so." Doug took off his glasses, his blue eyes suddenly hard. "And I have to tell you, I'm not going to wait that long to get in on a hunting club. I want to hunt this fall, and so do the other guys."

"Doug, if you three pull out on me, I'm dead in the water!" He couldn't develop the camp without his investors. He would lose a huge chunk of change, and his reputation along with it. The pit of his stomach tightened into a burning knot.

"Then you'd better start sweet-talking that old man and get him to sign the contract." Doug sighted and let an arrow fly, sending it into the ceiling. He snarled out a crude word and tossed the twelve-hundred-dollar bow onto the concrete floor. "Maybe I should take up bowling."

Friday morning the phone rang as Jana was finishing up the breakfast dishes. Grandpa had already left for the store, and the kids were outside playing in the pump house, so she picked it up on the second ring. "Hello?"

"Hey, Jana."

Her stomach flipped at the sound of that slow voice. "Is Forrest okay? I'm going to come see him as soon as I get my car back—"

"He's fine. In fact, I called to tell you your car's ready."

"That's good." Tucking the phone between her shoulder and ear, she dried the frying pan to occupy her hands. She'd been in touch with Tommy, and he'd said the repairs could be finished any day now. But what did Grant have to do with it?

"Yeah." He hesitated. "I was headed over to the garage this afternoon — Tommy and I are meeting for Bible study — so I thought I'd see if you wanted a ride."

"That's very nice of you." She'd assumed she'd mistaken his interest in her when he hadn't made contact in three days.

"It was Tommy's idea."

Of course. No reason to be disappointed. "I'll have to bring the kids with me."

"Okay." He almost sounded relieved. "And Carrie wanted me to tell you to stop in and say hello while you're there. Her shop's right next door."

"I guess I could do that." Grant was likely to bring up the subject of her grandfather's property, and she wasn't ready for a confrontation. Not until she'd at least convinced Grandpa that a wildlife refuge was a worthy enterprise. On the other hand, she could use a friend, even Grant's sister. "When should I be ready?"

"Around one, I guess. No big rush. Well, I mean, except for you wanting your car." He sighed. "I'm sorry, are you in a hurry to get there?"

"Not really." He sounded so flustered she wanted to laugh. "I'll be ready." She hung up the phone, feeling giddy. It had been a lonely few days, dodging boxes all over the living room, Grandpa looking sour, and the kids stuck in the house because of rain.

She skated across the linoleum on her sock feet. She had to figure out what to wear — to meet Carrie, of course. Adult conversation would be nice. She just had to remember to keep her mouth shut about real estate.

chapter 4

Be cool, Grant told himself as Jana scrambled out of the truck to open the door for the kids. Ty and LeeLee had jabbered in his ear all the way over to Tommy's garage, asking questions about the deer and telling him about the horses they used to ride in Tennessee. Jana had hardly said two words to him. She'd seemed to want to join the conversation, but then she'd look at him and get this stricken expression and clam up again. *Now* what had he done?

"Yo, Tommy!" He got out of the truck and pocketed his keys.

His brother-in-law waved a greasy hand. He had his head under the hood of a Bronco parked inside one of the bays recently added on to Lucas Import Service. Two years ago the place had been a dump, but Tommy was taking better care of his surroundings now that he had Carrie in tow.

Jana sent the kids to climb a pecan tree in the stretch of lawn between the garage and the candy shop. He wondered if she got as bent out of shape over junk as his sister did. She probably wouldn't appreciate living on a houseboat. He kept his place neat, but it was pretty tight quarters.

The implication of that thought shocked him into a lope across the parking lot.

"Hey!" Tommy lowered the hood of the truck, then pulled a rag out of his back pocket to wipe his hands. He hooked a boisterous arm around Grant's neck. "Dude, where's your Bible? And where's Jana?"

Grant shook hands and whacked his friend on the shoulder. Tommy was the closest thing he had to a brother here in Vancleave. "Bible's in the truck. Jana's—here she is."

She approached, looking oddly vulnerable with her arms folded across her stomach. It was hard to imagine anybody being intimidated by Tommy. "How are you, Tommy?" She extended her hand, smiling, but Tommy ignored it and pulled her into a hug.

"I'm great!" he shouted. "God is good!"

Laughing, Jana returned the hug. "Yes, he is. All the time." She stepped away. "It's so good to see you again."

"You too. We've got a lot to talk about, but first let me show you your car. I got it running like a little orange sewing machine."

"I'm so relieved. It didn't take as long as I was afraid it would." Jana's gaze flickered toward Grant as they walked toward the Subaru. "Can we, um, work out a payment plan of some kind?"

Tommy smiled. "It's taken care of."

Jana's eyes widened. "Oh, but you can't—"

"I didn't—" Tommy stopped when Grant shot him a warning look. "I mean ... the first service is covered under my, uh, new residents' plan. We want your repeat business."

"I'm not planning on running into any more cows."

Grant couldn't resist. "You sure taught *that* one not to jaywalk."

Wrinkling her nose at his teasing, Jana got into the car and cranked it. "It hasn't sounded this, um, normal in ages." She removed the key from the ignition and got out, smiling up at

Tommy. "Thank you *so* much. I've got to at least pay you for the parts, though. Do you have any pets? Maybe you could bring them to me for a checkup, soon as I get my clinic set up."

Grant was tired of being ignored. "I don't know if you'd call Skywalker a pet. He's more like a sociopathic mooch."

"Hey..." Tommy feigned offense.

"Come on, let's head next door." Grant popped the hood of Jana's car with his hand. "Carrie said she'd make me some oat-meal cookies."

Tommy shook his shaggy dark head. "The man is a total slave to his stomach."

"Says the guy who married a professional caterer." Grant winked at Jana.

He felt better when she smiled at him. *Finally*.

I'm so glad you had time to come by." Carrie Lucas served Jana a glass of raspberry iced tea along with a warm smile. Stepping over Grant's big, booted feet, she placed the tray on the coffee table, then sat down beside her husband.

"So am I." Jana smiled her thanks. Grant's older sister was brown-eyed like him, but blonde and slender in a soft yellow summer dress. "Looks like you needed a little break."

Settling under Tommy's arm, Carrie sipped her tea. "I'm tired." She slipped off her sandals. "The store's been busy today."

"It's beautiful. I can see why people like to come in here."

The four of them sat in the lattice-screened alcove where Carrie held her catering consultations. Greenery warmed every corner of the store, with attractive gift baskets displayed on white-painted shelves and gauzy curtains at the windows. Jana covertly watched Grant, who looked wildly out of place in this feminine niche. He sprawled in a floral-upholstered wing chair under the window, where the afternoon sun painted gold streaks in his hair.

"Trust me." He helped himself to an oatmeal cookie. "It's the food, not the decorations." He bit off half the cookie, closing his eyes in ecstasy.

Feeling suddenly hot and fidgety, Jana bent to check on LeeLee, who had crawled under the table to play with a smoke-colored kitten. Ty was outside playing Tarzan in the tree.

"It takes so little to make them happy." Carrie exchanged an amused look with Jana. "Your grandpa's been so excited about you and the children moving back."

Tommy winked. "Yeah, every time we see him in church, he'll say, 'Did I tell you my little Jana's moving home this month? I ask you, what am I gonna do with her and two younguns in that little bitty old house of mine?'"

Jana laughed at the dead-on imitation of her grandfather's grumpy drawl. "I should have come home a long time ago. He's getting frail, especially since my grandmother died."

"Well, it's never too late," said Tommy. "You and the kids will perk him up, just being in the same house. He's about to bust his buttons because you made it all the way through college and vet school."

Jana smiled at her old friend. "You've made something of yourself too."

"Thanks to the Lord Jesus." Tommy squeezed his wife's shoulders. "Where I'd be if I hadn't met him — man, I don't even want to think about it." He gave Jana a rueful grimace. "We used to think we were so cool, didn't we? Don't you wish you could go back and undo things?"

"Sure. But maybe those of us who've come out of the pits understand God's grace better than anybody." Jana's gaze flickered to Grant. His watchful eyes narrowed as if he wondered how deep a pit she'd occupied. She looked down at her hands. *Try the Grand Canyon.* "I could've come home sooner, but I kept putting it off. There were so many things I didn't want to revisit. People ask so many questions ..."

"I know." Carrie gave Jana a sympathetic look. "My family nearly drove me crazy when I first moved home. Interfered in everything. But then I realized they just cared—because they love me."

"Huh. You should have seen the wall of relatives I had to climb over to get to her." Tommy winked. "But my charm and automotive skills won them all over. Even Gonzo the Great here."

Grant pointed a lazy finger. "Hey, the jury's still out. You still haven't replaced my rod and reel you left in the bayou."

"*You* were the one who said there was plenty of room to cast under that cedar limb."

"There *would* have been if your dumb dog hadn't decided to jump out of the boat right then. Was I supposed to let him drown?"

"Skywalker's not dumb, and he swims better than you do."

"Boys, boys." Carrie exchanged a look with Jana.

She found herself grinning. "Oh, don't mind me. Makes me feel right at home."

Carrie rescued the cookie jar from Grant. "Give me that, you big hog. I want to send some cookies home with the children."

"You mean this is all there is?" Grant peered into the jar.

Tommy snorted. "She rations those things like gold."

"I'll say. Granny always—yeow!" Grant leaned over to pluck the gray kitten's needlelike claws out of the leg of his jeans. He handed it to LeeLee when she poked her head out from under the table. "Hey, Sally, would you like to take this pest home with you?"

"Yes, sir, I sure would." LeeLee enfolded the kitten in an exuberant hug. "But I *told* you, my name's not Sally."

Jana held up a hand. "Grant! You can't give away Carrie's cat."

"Yes, he can." Tommy nudged his wife. "Skywalker'll have to go into therapy if he keeps finding kitty litter in his water bowl."

"Look, Mommy, she loves me." LeeLee rubbed noses with the purring kitten. "Can I please keep her?"

"No, darlin', that's Miss Carrie's cat."

"Actually, I'm not that attached." Carrie looked apologetic. "But I understand if you don't want the extra trouble."

"Her name's Glitter." LeeLee giggled as a rough pink tongue bathed her chin.

Jana looked from Carrie to Tommy, then found her gaze drawn to Grant.

A dimple creased his cheek, making him look both smug and wretchedly attractive. "Come on now, if I could take on old Spike, I know you can handle one measly little kitten."

Trying not to grin, Jana met Grant's smiling brown eyes. "Okay, but if she terrorizes Grandpa's dog, you'll find yourself adopting a cat as well as a fawn."

"Just what every skipper needs on his houseboat—an attack cat."

Carrie wrinkled her nose at her brother. "If you knew what you needed, you'd be married." She ruffled LeeLee's hair. "I think Glitter's a beautiful name."

"Yeah, right up there with Forrest." Grant stood up, stretching. "Come on, Tom, I came over here for Bible study, not a tea party. Jana, tell your grandpa I'll stop by to see him on my way home."

"All right." She hid her dismay. What if Grant talked her grandfather into signing a contract before she'd had a chance to change his mind? "Tommy, thanks again for fixing my car."

"No problem."

The two men left, arguing amicably over dogs and fishing poles, leaving Jana to help Carrie clear away the tea things. Terrifying that Grant Gonzales could reel her in for the second time in her life. He was even more attractive than he'd been as a teenager, and still funny in that teasing way that slid under her guard and made her stomach fizz.

Worst of all, she knew who'd paid for her car to be fixed. She hadn't missed the look exchanged between Grant and Tommy when she'd mentioned the bill. She was such a sucker for secret kindness. Why did it have to be his property that she needed?

Grant shoved open the screen door of the Farm and Feed, disappointed that Jana's little Subaru wasn't in the parking lot. Good thing she wouldn't be around to distract him. That sweet, curling mouth invited kissing, especially when it hung open after he'd teased her. You couldn't go around kissing a woman you'd only talked to twice in ten years.

He'd have to learn to hide his attraction, though. Tommy had spent the first fifteen minutes of their Bible study giving him a hard time about Jana and the deer. Their prayer time had been productive, although Tommy tended to probe into emotions Grant would just as soon ignore. An engineer through and through, he liked things cut and dried. Just the facts, ma'am, like Sergeant Friday.

Listening to Tommy pray for his wife was a revelation. She wanted a baby more than anything, and Tommy was feeling the pressure. How goofy was that? As if it were his fault.

They'd prayed for Grant's former business partner too, despite his firm conviction that the guy was beyond redemption. As costly as the split had been, he was well out of that affiliation, and he was determined to be more careful about future partnerships.

"Hey, Alvin?" He stood in the front of the store looking around. The old man wasn't behind the counter, but a lot of times he hung out in the rear of the store with his buddy CJ or his twin brother, Elvin.

Sure enough, he heard "Back here" coming from somewhere near the warehouse entrance.

If *he* ran this place, he'd have somebody at the front to make sure people didn't walk out with the merchandise. No telling how many customers Alvin lost while he was occupied playing checkers.

Grant found Alvin and CJ perched like Hekyll and Jekyll on each side of a burlap checkerboard. Old metal soft-drink tops served as game pieces. Grant dropped down on a sawed-off stool and tipped it back on two legs. Hard to gauge Alvin's mood. The old man looked sanguine for a change. Maybe he was eating better now that Jana was cooking for him.

Alvin moved a Nehi Grape cap and peered over his glasses at Grant. "You need some help with something, boy, or are you just in here to pester me about that Twin Creek property again?"

So much for an oblique attack. "You told me you were ready to sell, so I had an agent draw us up a contract. I've been carrying it around in my car for weeks. I can't develop my camp property until I can put a road in there."

Alvin's sharp old eyes narrowed. "Been meaning to talk to you about that."

An old ulcer in Grant's stomach started to ache.

"You may have to find another piece of property." Alvin studied the checkerboard. "I'm thinkin' about hanging on to that one."

Grant had known he might have to wait. But he'd never imagined the old man might completely back out. "Mr. Alvin, there's not another piece of property for miles that isn't owned by either the state or the feds. You promised—"

"Now, look. You and I both know it ain't a done deal until both of us sign on the dotted line. Don't get all bent out of shape. I just said I'm reconsidering my options."

"But I don't have any other options!" Grant had been taught all his life to honor and respect his elders, a philosophy that had, for the most part, served him well. He had to slam his teeth together and mentally recite the preamble to the Constitution to keep from forgetting he was a Christian and a gentleman.

There was something under that veneer of calm, something watchful and conniving. Was the old man out for more money? Grant's offer was above fair market value—more than he could afford. He corralled his temper and his tongue. His mother would have been proud of him. Besides, he didn't have any choice. Doug Briscoe had told him the legal options were more complicated than he had time for. The truth was, he'd acted on presumption.

He was not going to go through this again.

He took a deep breath. "Okay, Mr. Alvin. You reconsider your options. But I sure hope you're gonna be reasonable."

"I'm the most reasonable person in this county." Alvin wagged a knobby finger. "You can take that to the bank."

"Alvin, it's your turn." CJ frowned, gesturing with his pipe.

Grant had forgotten all about him. He grabbed for the lesson he and Tommy had just worked through from the book of Jeremiah. Broken cisterns a person dug for himself wouldn't hold water. The more he pushed, the more obstinate Alvin was going to get. And he was out of time. *Lord, I was sure you wanted me to open this camp. What do I do?*

Jana's pretty face swam across his mind's eye. What if he could get her to intervene with her grandfather? He was already baby-sitting her fawn. Maybe he could invite the kids to swim off his houseboat. Ty was a nice kid, after all, and LeeLee was cute as a button. He could even help Jana find a place to build her veterinary clinic.

He surged to his feet. "I'll leave you alone for now, Mr. Alvin, but don't forget about me, okay?" He picked up an Orange Crush checker and took a jump CJ had missed. "Crown him." He headed for the door.

After a storm that crackled and boomed and poured all weekend, Monday dawned with a hot sun that sent blinding sparkles dancing along the river. Grant decided to spend the morning sanding the deck of the houseboat and tweaking his battle plan.

The main strategy was patience. He was good at being patient. His mother translated that as "bullheaded," but whatever. One of his favorite Scripture passages was the one about the lady who kept harassing the judge until he gave her justice.

He scrubbed his wire brush across the deck. *Come on, Lord, I need that property.*

A distant whistle shrilled over the jam box blasting Audio Adrenaline through the open window of his sleeping berth. He looked around, but all he saw were a couple of seagulls squabbling over a fish out in the water. The whistle sounded again, louder this time, from beyond the tree line at the top of the bank.

Checking his watch, he got to his feet. Just past nine o'clock. The only drawback to not having office hours was that people assumed you weren't busy and dropped in without notice. Grabbing a T-shirt off the rail, he jumped to the pier and took the cedar steps up the steep bank three at a time.

"Down here!" He wiped paint flecks and sawdust off his hands as he went. "Who's there?"

As the boom of the bass from the CD player faded, he heard someone—from the amount of noise, probably two someones—shoving through the trees. A few months ago he'd built a long pier, starting from the end of Alvin's road and winding through a tangle of trees and underbrush, out to the river where he'd anchored the *Minnow*. So far, Alvin had let Grant cross his property without interference, but he was going to need true ingress and egress for construction crews to come in.

There were two rough cabins already on the property, but he had to have better facilities if he expected to make the business grow. Mainly he needed a lodge with a kitchen. The best place for that would be Alvin's property, which was on high ground fronting the highway.

He stopped and shaded his eyes against the sun with one hand. Willis and Crowbar Dyer tottered at the top of the bank like a couple of denim-and-plaid babushka dolls.

"Hey, boys. What's up?"

For a couple of weeks now, the Dyer brothers had been parking their camper on his property, essentially trespassing. Knowing they'd both been laid off from the shipyard and evicted from their trailer park, he let them stay. They'd move on when work picked up again.

"Hey, yourself." Crowbar's ferretlike features were framed by a bleached blond mullet haircut and a drooping, straw-colored mustache. "How's it going down there?"

"Well, maybe I won't have to bail next time it rains." Were they looking for food?

Willis grinned, looming close to seven feet tall with sweat pouring down a face as red as his nylon-mesh cap.

Jerking a thumb in the direction of the *Minnow*, Crowbar produced an ingratiating smile. "Got her looking good."

"Thanks." Grant turned to survey his project. From this distance and elevation, the houseboat listed a bit to port. With half her paint sanded off, she looked as if she had a bad case of mange. "But I'm sorta busy. What can I do for y'all this morning?"

Crowbar stuck his thumbs in his belt. "Thought you might want to know old man Goff's granddaughter and them two kids are up there fooling around with your deer."

"It's not my deer." Still, his heartbeat accelerated as he headed toward the clearing where he'd set up the deer pen.

The Dyers tromped along behind him. They seemed to have a mighty proprietary attitude toward what didn't belong to them. He turned to find the brothers looking around, Crowbar muttering to himself and Willis happy just to have someone to follow.

"Guys, I have an idea. Why don't you go see if Mr. Alvin needs some help down at the feed store? He was in there all by himself the other day."

Crowbar shook his head. "Already asked him. Says he don't need no help."

Grant winced when Willis's stomach gave a mighty growl. "Well, if you don't have anything else to do, you can go back down to my boat and finish sanding it for me. I'll buy you lunch."

Willis's expression lightened, but Crowbar scratched his chin. "Lunch and fifty dollars if we paint too?"

Grant sighed. "Oh, all right."

The brothers high-fived one another and disappeared.

As he walked into the clearing, he saw both of his dogs lolling against Ty Cutrere, who had knelt to scratch their bellies. LeeLee sat on a fallen tree nearby, singing to her kitten. It had on a—he looked again. It had on a *dress*.

And there was Jana, kneeling inside the pen, feeding the fawn from a plastic baby bottle. He hadn't seen her since Friday. Coming upon her on his turf was an unexpected gift. He'd been trying to figure out how he was going to approach her. Laughing at the deer's greedy sucking, she looked like a wood sprite dressed in dark green shorts and a knit top. A really hot wood sprite.

"Y'all are up mighty early this morning." He skinned his hand across Ty's head. "Boy, watch out, that dog'll take your arm off."

"Yes, sir." Ty grinned as Josh swiped a tongue across his hand.

Jana looked around, her smile open and warm. "You've done a good job taking care of Forrest. You'll have to build a taller fence, though, or he'll be jumping out of here as soon as his cast comes off."

Elated at her praise, Grant opened the makeshift gate in the enclosure he'd fashioned from two-by-fours and a roll of chicken wire. "How long will that be?"

"About five more weeks. He's young, so the bone will knit fast. Heath did a good job setting it." The deer's ears twitched as he followed the movement of the bottle in Jana's hand.

She complimented everybody, even Redmond. Realizing she was craning her neck to talk to him, Grant crouched beside her. The fawn jumped away. "Hey, buster, who's been manning the chuck wagon around here for two days? Let's have a little gratitude." When Jana laughed, he met her sparkling sapphire eyes. "He seems to like your bottle better than the one I've been giving him."

"This is goat's milk. A lot closer to what his mommy would have fed him, since the white-tail deer formula I ordered hasn't come in yet."

"Now how come Redmond didn't tell me that?"

"He probably didn't know. I volunteered at a wildlife center while I was in vet school."

Her gaze skittered away from his, a bit like the fawn avoiding his touch. He remembered kids in high school calling her "Wild Child" behind her back. And it hadn't been a compliment.

Grant studied the irresistible sprinkle of freckles across her nose and cheeks. His gaze dropped to her long fingers, strong and gentle and comfortable handling the little animal. A fleeting male curiosity about the texture of those fingers breezed across his brain. "Did you always want to be a vet?"

"Pretty much. I never would have done it, though, if the Lord hadn't intervened." She gave him a shy glance as she pulled the nipple out of the fawn's mouth with a soft pop. The deer let out a burp as he lurched for the empty bottle again.

Grant laughed with Jana. "Where are your manners, boy?" He took the bottle from her and examined it. "Goat's milk, huh? Guess I'll have to drive into Mobile for that. Don't think they carry it at the Quick-Stop."

"Grandpa has a nanny goat. I'd be glad to send Ty over here a couple times a week with some milk."

Resting his forearms on his knees, he gave her an exasperated look. "You could've taken this thing home with you that first day! How come you dumped him off on me?"

She blushed. "Well ... Grandpa's not crazy about wild animals. They get into his garden and eat his peaches. Besides, I thought it would be good for you to take care of a sweet baby like Forrest."

"You thought it would be *good* for me, huh? What is this, ruminant therapy?"

She grinned a little. "Did it work?"

"No, ma'am, it did not. This deer gets big enough to fend for himself, and he's out on his little white tail. Which reminds me ..." He looked at her sideways, tugging the bill of his cap down. "I need a favor."

"A favor?" Her expression turned wary. "What is it?"

"I'm not asking for your firstborn child. I just need you to help me out with your grandpa. You were right about him balking on selling me his property. I have to tell you I'm getting just a little desperate."

She swallowed hard. "Do you mind telling me what you want it for?"

"I can't believe you've been in Vancleave a whole week and nobody's told you I'm setting up a hunting camp."

c h a p t e r   5

Jana felt as though she'd been punched in the stomach. "A *hunting* camp?"

"Well, yeah. In my old job I brought clients who did a certain amount of business down here, and I'd give them a free hunt. I decided that was more fun than selling surveying equipment." Grant pulled that faded maroon cap down over his eyes again.

She was too upset to be interested in his old job. The current one was bad enough. "Why do you need my grandpa's property? Don't you have enough?"

"Jana, do you know how much land it takes to run a hunting camp?" He looked at her as if she were nuts. "Besides, Alvin's location is critical. He's got me landlocked, and if he decided to, he could keep me from getting to my property except by boat."

She scrambled for a way to refuse his request without telling him why. "I ... I just can't stand the thought of Grandpa aiding and abetting animal slaughter."

His eyes widened. "Are you one of those animal rights wackos?" Clearly he classified them right up there with serial killers. "I'm not interested in *slaughtering* anything. Serious hunters follow the laws, and it's the most humane—"

Suddenly one of Grant's dogs snarled, and the other sent up an ear-splitting bark. As Jana looked around to see what had set them off, the kitten let out a piercing yowl and took off up the nearest pine tree.

"Mommy!" LeeLee screamed.

Ty jumped to his feet. "Whoa, look at that cat go!"

The terrified fawn skittered under his shelter. Jana left the pen through the gate, while Grant vaulted the fence, yelling at his hounds. The male came to heel, growling as Grant clipped a leash on him. The female, however, circled the base of the tree, hackles raised and baying, until Grant dragged her away and shut both dogs in the cab of his truck.

The noise level dropped dramatically, except for LeeLee's sobs of rage. Picking her up, Jana squinted upward. The kitten, still in its doll dress, trembled at the end of a skinny branch about fifteen feet straight up. "What happened?"

Ty shrugged. "I don't know. The dogs just went crazy."

"I wanted Glitter to make friends." LeeLee sniffed. "But they wouldn't play nice."

Jana squeezed her daughter. "My budding Secretary of State."

"Come on, Sally, knock it off." Grant tweaked one of LeeLee's curls. "Did you ever see a cat carcass in a tree?"

Wiping her chubby cheeks, LeeLee blinked, wide-eyed. "What's a car cuss?"

"Never mind, sweetie." Jana frowned at Grant. "What did you mean by that staggeringly insensitive remark?"

Grant shrugged. "Cat gets hungry enough, it'll come down."

"But she's *skeered*!" wailed LeeLee.

"She's going to fall off that limb if you don't do something, Grant Gonzales." First the "wacko" remark, and now this.

"Do I look like the fire department?"

"It was your dog that sent her up there!"

Grant looked harassed. "I have an idea. Be right back." He strode off in the direction of the river.

Ty jumped up and down. "Mom, can I go too?"

"I suppose." With a sigh, Jana sat down on a tree trunk as Ty sprinted after Grant. She and LeeLee peered up at the kitten. Refusing to make eye contact, Glitter mewed in piteous accents.

"She fell up, and she can't get down." LeeLee placed her palms together. "Let's call Jesus."

Jana smoothed her daughter's sweaty curls. "Good idea. You start."

"Jesus, please help Glitter get down before she turns into a car cuss."

As LeeLee continued her usual rambling prayer, Jana contemplated her disappointment in Grant. She'd known he was a hunter, but she'd hoped they could be friends in spite of that. And now to find out he wanted to turn the land into a hunting camp!

Jesus, please help me stop him before he murders all these animals.

A few minutes later Grant strolled, whistling, into the clearing. He carried a two-gallon plastic bucket, and a coil of rope was slung over his shoulder.

Ty kept up as best he could while copying Grant's lazy stride. "Hey, Mom! You should see Mr. Grant's boat!"

"What are you going to do with that?" Jana didn't even try to hide her skepticism.

"Watch and see." He dropped the bucket and smiled straight into her eyes. She almost smiled back.

"Pee-yew!" LeeLee pinched her nose. "That stinks!"

"Hopefully your kitty will think it smells like dinner." Grant knelt to tie the end of the rope to the bucket's handle.

Jana peered into it. "Fish heads?"

Grant made an efficient knot, winked at LeeLee, and stood up. "I saw an episode of *Emergency Vets* where they got a ferret down off a telephone pole." He hefted the rope like an Old West cowboy aiming to lasso a steer. "Y'all back up and give me some room."

Jana found herself watching Grant rather than the cat. He had little room to get a good toss at the limb because of the surrounding trees. His paint-stained T-shirt, ripped at the neck and hacked off at the bottom, left ridges of flat belly showing when he swung the rope. Jana lifted her gaze to the dense muscles bunching and flexing across his shoulders.

That was no better, so she concentrated on the cat, squeezing LeeLee's hand until her daughter squealed. "Sorry." Jana relaxed her grip.

The kitten flinched when the rope came hurtling past her nose, but managed to keep her balance. Grant caught the end of the rope as it came down, then tugged until the bucket slid upward. When it bumped the bottom of the limb, Jana held her breath.

Glitter minced over to investigate.

"Come on, you little sissy," Grant crooned in a singsong falsetto. "Gourmet feast right there under your nose—all you gotta do is step in."

Ty laughed when the kitten leaned as far over the limb as possible without falling in. She gave her audience a disdainful look before plunging into the bucket.

They all cheered as Grant lowered it to the ground. "Gonzales Elevator Service to the rescue." He plucked the kitten out of the bucket and handed her to LeeLee.

"Glitter, you need a Tic-Tac." LeeLee looked up at Grant. "*Thank* you, Mr.... Mr.... I forgot your name."

"Grant." He untied the rope from the bucket and coiled it around his arm. "Can't anybody remember that?"

LeeLee turned to her brother. "Let's go pet Forrest."

Grant picked up the reeking bucket. "Good thing I decided to go ahead and fillet this morning's catch."

"Good thing you watch *Emergency Vets* too. I'm not even going to ask why. Could I have the rest of those fish heads?"

Grant tipped his head. "I wouldn't have taken you for a sushi fan."

She rolled her eyes. "I want to fertilize Grandpa's peach trees."

"What'll you give me for 'em?" The lazy grin was back.

Jana tried to drum up indignation. Those brown eyes … Oh, she could get drawn in again so easily. She turned her back. "Never mind, Gonzales. Keep your fish heads."

She felt his hand on her shoulder. "Come on. I'll walk you and the kids home. I'll even help you with your fertilizer." She turned around in surprise and found his eyes twinkling. "I'll collect later."

Ha. Not likely.

Grant led his small parade through the woods toward Alvin Goff's place. Jana followed him, holding LeeLee's hand, and Ty brought up the rear, the bucket banging against his bare legs.

At the edge of a broad, grassy field crossed by a string of power lines, Ty took off at a run. "Come on, LeeLee! I'll beat you back to Grandpa's!"

"No, you won't! Mommy, would you please hold Glitter?" LeeLee passed over the kitten and tore off after her brother.

"Be careful!" Cuddling the kitten under her chin, Jana looked up at Grant. "They know the way from here. We came out in this field yesterday to pick wildflowers."

He looked around the familiar place, trying to see it through the children's eyes. The power line poles rose like gigantic saguaros, turning the pastoral setting into an alien landscape. Tall grass sprinkled with yellow and white wildflowers stretched over nearly an acre, bracketed by the woods.

"This is where my property ends." He paused. "At least until Alvin sells the rest to me."

"For the hunting camp."

"That's right." He tried to sound nonthreatening. "You said being a vet is all you ever wanted to do. You gotta understand, owning a hunting camp is something I've wanted since I was eight years old."

"Oh, please—"

"It is! I got a Red Ryder BB gun for Christmas that year."

"I bet your mom warned you not to shoot your eye out."

He couldn't help grinning. "How did you know?"

She sighed. "I'm the mother of an eight-year-old boy."

"Who needs to learn how to handle a gun too." At her disapproving look, he backpedaled. "Anyway, when I was thirteen, my grandfather gave me his Winchester .22 rifle, and I Became a Man." He hammed it up to make her laugh.

She grimaced. "I don't want to hear about your first kill, Grant."

His humor faded. "No, I guess you wouldn't understand."

Her luminous eyes were troubled. "Grant, you have every advantage—you're smart and have a college education, you have a strong family base and plenty of money. You could do anything you want to with your life. Why waste it tromping around in the backwoods of Jackson County, Mississippi?"

His family had all been wondering the same thing. He'd gotten the questions many times since he'd dissolved his business partnership and come home. Blunt questions, nosy questions, teasing questions, all of which he'd avoided on the grounds that his finances were his own business.

But he wanted Jana to understand him and almost told her about losing his business to his partner. He stared at her for a few seconds before shame stopped him.

Breaking eye contact, he shrugged. "It's just fun to me." He waved his hand to indicate the whole stretch of grassy field. "This will be the salad bar."

"Salad bar?" She wrinkled her nose. "You're opening a restaurant?"

"A food plot, which is a little like a restaurant for the deer. During the winter when there's not much for them to eat, they'll come here to feed. In September I'll plant rye, wheat, barley, oats, clover, and purple-top turnips—man, the deer love those things. Lots of protein in 'em for building antlers."

"You're feeding them so you can kill them later." There was an edge to her soft voice.

"Jana ..." Exasperated, he kicked at a spray of Queen Anne's lace. "Feeding the deer, enjoying their beauty, hunting them for food is the natural cycle of things."

"But—"

"Listen, if you don't feed them in the winter, some will die of starvation. And if you don't harvest some, they overpopulate because there aren't any natural predators anymore, and they become road hazards."

"*Harvest?*" Jana folded her arms and looked at him with stormy blue eyes. "What a cold-blooded term!"

Grant tugged at the bill of his cap in frustration. "It's the best I can do at the moment."

For an intelligent woman, Jana had a mental block on this subject that no amount of explanation was going to break through. In her vocabulary there were no acceptable terms for hunting. Still, he admired her tenderness toward living things, and he'd seen none of the belligerence common to the animal-rights activists with whom he butted heads. Despite what he'd said earlier, she wasn't what he'd call a serious wacko.

She must have read his mind. As they entered the strip of woods bordering Alvin's house, Jana bent to snatch up a spray of goldenrod and cut those jewel-like eyes at Grant. "I'm not an activist. I just resent my family property being sold for something that opposes my whole way of life."

"You know, in a real backward, inside-out kind of way, I sort of respect that." He caught the other end of the goldenrod stalk and tugged her closer. She took a reluctant step, and he smiled down at her. "Is there any way we can agree to disagree until we get reacquainted?"

She looked down at their two hands clasped around the flower—his enormous, rough, and scarred; hers slender and smooth. He was pleased when she didn't pull away. A long moment went by. "That sounds like a good idea."

"Okay, then I have a question." No time like the present. "How'd you manage to get your undergrad degree with two kids and Richie—" he stopped when Jana flinched, dropping her end of the goldenrod stalk. "I'm sorry, maybe that's something else we shouldn't talk about."

Jana's laugh was awkward, but she gave him a frank look. "No, it's okay. After Richie left us—"

"You mean when he died?"

"No. He disappeared the day LeeLee was born."

"He *left* you? With those two kids?" Grant didn't know what to do with the sudden irrational urge to punch a man who was already six feet under. He turned toward Alvin's house, and Jana fell into step with him.

"It was better after he left. I hit bottom and had to scream for help. The Lord rescued us, just like he promised he would."

He expected her to continue, but when she was silent for several paces, Grant tickled her cheek with the flower petals until she looked at him, smiling. "What?"

"I like the way you said that. Sounds like something Tommy would say."

"It's just the truth. There's a verse in Proverbs about the Lord caring for orphans and widows, and I never get tired of telling how he did that for me."

"What did that jerk do to you?" He was horrified at how much he cared.

She gave him that serene look that sat so oddly on her young face. "I don't do the poor-me act, Grant. It doesn't matter anymore. Richie's gone and can't hurt us now." She hesitated. "Let me tell you one of *my* memories of Twin Creek. When I was about LeeLee's age, I found my first bunny nest there. I've always wanted to be a veterinarian, and I'm not going to let anything stop me now. The Lord's already providing. Heath Redmond has promised to help me—"

"Has Redmond been calling you?"

"Not exactly. I saw him at church yesterday."

Grant had missed yesterday's services for the first time in months. The *Minnow* had sprung a leak, and it was either stay home and fix it or find his bunk in the bottom of the creek. "Redmond hasn't been to church since Easter. It figures the first time a pretty woman shows up he'd—" he broke off at Jana's puff of laughter. "What?"

"He said he came to hear you play your trombone in the orchestra. Only you weren't there, and he looked sort of lost, so I asked him to sit by me and the kids."

Grant gaped at her. "He came to hear me play my trombone? And you believed that?"

"Don't you play the trombone?"

"Well, yeah, but—good night, what an Eddie Haskell." He pushed through the woods, hardly aware of Jana trotting behind him, trying to keep up with his long strides. He was going to plant those fish heads and then go over to Redmond's clinic to tear a strip off that con man's beanpole hide.

"Grant!" Panting, she grabbed the back of his shirt. "Aren't you glad Heath came to church yesterday?"

He slowed to let her catch up with him. "Of course I'm glad." He hoped she couldn't see the reluctance of that concession, because he couldn't have explained why he was so disturbed at the idea of Heath Redmond sitting with Jana and her children in church.

He wasn't sure he understood it himself.

Grandpa, I don't understand what you've done here with these invoices." Rubbing the back of her neck, Jana looked up from the computer. She'd spent her first week home getting her belongings in place and giving Grandpa's house a serious scrubbing. This week she'd been at the store every day, helping him catch up on a mountain of billing.

Ty was working in the warehouse with a couple of teenagers hired for the summer, and LeeLee had taken the kitten into the storeroom for a saucer of milk. Jana was free to obsess over numbers to her heart's content.

Grandpa poked his head around the end of the fertilizer aisle. "If it's too complicated, just leave it for me. I'll get to it after lunch."

"Grandpa, I have a doctoral degree and a medical license. A seed invoice is not too complicated. What I don't understand is how old these things are. How long's it been since you purged your files?"

"Maybe I'd better do that and let you price these bags." Grandpa hobbled toward her. "I hear Little Bit putting on a Broadway show back there. Where'd she get that pretty voice from?"

"I don't know—Richie, I guess." Jana refused to be distracted. "This one says you owe Litton Manufacturing thirty thousand dollars for a Bush Hog. It's dated over a year ago."

"They got a top-notch kids' choir program down at the church. You ought to sign her up." Grandpa leaned around Jana to close the computer screen.

"I'll look into it." She flicked the window back open. "Grandpa, I don't see where this has been paid."

Grandpa was rubbing a hole in the lens of his glasses with a white handkerchief. "I'll look into it," he said, echoing her words, adding in an undertone, "even though it ain't none of your business."

Jana stared at him. "I'm just trying to help."

"I appreciate it, but ain't it about time you got busy on your real job? Let me get on with mine?"

"I'd love to, but I don't have a place to put the wildlife center yet. I just thought I'd give you a hand while I'm waiting, instead of sitting on my blessed assurance at home." How did the conversation get so deftly turned from Grandpa's bills to herself? "Besides, I *like* to work."

Grandpa pushed his glasses back onto his face. "Then why don't you go work for the Redmond boy—pester *him* for a while? I hear he's got more than he can handle."

Jana sighed. Heath was attractive in a lanky, off-the-beaten-path sort of way, and he had a thriving practice. But the way he'd looked at her Sunday had made her uncomfortable. Her instincts told her to be careful, and it was safer to work in Grandpa's store. Besides, he *needed* her here, if this invoice situation was any indication.

Before she could pursue the matter, the cowbell on the door jangled.

"Hey, Mr. Alvin." Carrie Lucas walked in, offering her bright smile and a Styrofoam plate covered in plastic wrap and tied with a jaunty blue polka-dot ribbon. "I brought you some raisin bran muffins."

"Well, ain't you sweet?" Grandpa took the plate, raising it to his nose to take a deep sniff. "How'd you know they was my favorite?"

"I saw you stick a couple in your pocket at the last church potluck." Carrie winked at Jana. "Sneaky, sneaky."

"Grandpa, you're busted. You'd better give Carrie a good deal on whatever she came in here for."

"I don't need anything. I just saw Jana's car and came in to visit for a minute."

"I'm glad you did." Warmed, Jana smiled at Carrie. Maybe this connection would turn into friendship.

"Do you think you could get away for lunch? We could walk down to Cole's Drive-Inn and be back within an hour."

"I don't know …" Jana glanced at her grandfather. "I have the kids with me, and they haven't had lunch yet."

"Aw, I'll feed 'em a peanut-butter-jelly and keep 'em out of trouble for a while." Grandpa came around the counter to commandeer the computer mouse. "You go on and enjoy yourself."

No telling what he would do to those computer files while she was gone. But she needed some adult conversation. It took her about a nanosecond to make up her mind. "Okay, Grandpa, thanks. We'll talk about Litton Manufacturing when I get back."

She ignored his truculent look. "LeeLee! Come here, sweetie, I need to talk to you for a minute."

LeeLee skipped from the back of the store with the long-suffering kitten draped over one arm and a black plastic purse on the other. She had dressed herself this morning in a pair of flowered pink shorts and a green fish-print top. "Good morning, ma'am!" she chirped when she saw Carrie. "What can I do for you today? We have some lovely birdbaths outside in our garden shop."

Jana tugged one of the four short ponytails sprouting from the top of her daughter's head. "Meet Grandpa's top sales associate."

Carrie bent to LeeLee's level. "I might look at a birdbath later, but can I take your mommy to lunch first?"

LeeLee stooped, copying Carrie's posture. "I guess so, if you'll be very careful with her."

"I promise." Carrie crossed her heart.

"Mind Grandpa," Jana said, "and don't let the kitten wander around loose."

"Okay." LeeLee reached into her purse and pulled out a penny, which she handed to Jana. "Here. Don't forget to leave a tip."

chapter 6

Jana put a quarter in the jukebox and punched a button to make her selection, sending the mellow voice of Patsy Cline flowing through the open-air dining room of Cole's. "Crazy" suited her emotions to a T.

"I can't tell you how glad I am that you came by." Jana sat down across from Carrie at a picnic table near the jukebox. "I'm feeling a bit overwhelmed at the moment."

Carrie squirted ketchup on her French fries. "I can't imagine how difficult single motherhood must be." She hesitated. "Grant said you've been alone since LeeLee was born."

Grant had been talking about her to his sister? Jana nodded, braced for censure. "I don't recommend it."

But Carrie's smile was sympathetic. "I know what you mean. I imagine our circumstances were similar."

"Really?" Maybe this explained the instant bond she'd felt with Carrie.

Carrie bit her lip. "I won't go into the gory details, but my first marriage wasn't happy." Jana took an involuntary breath. She hadn't known Carrie had been married before. "When my husband died, I was feeling this huge load of guilt. I came home to heal and found Tommy—right next door to me!"

The implication being that all you had to do was wait for romance and happily-ever-after to pop up like a wildflower on the side of the road. Jana studied the sweet sincerity on Carrie's face. "That's wonderful, Carrie, but if you're hinting at what I think you are—" she toyed with her Styrofoam cup, choosing her words. "I got over Richie a long time ago, and I'm happy with my life as it is. I'm not interested in taking any more chances."

"Believe me, I understand that. I felt the same way. But I hope you'll be open to letting friendships develop." Carrie tilted her head. "Are you considering going to work with Heath Redmond?"

"Did Grant tell you that too?"

"No, but when Heath came to church Sunday and sat with you, I wondered."

Jana never would have believed so many people would be interested in pew arrangements. "Heath hasn't officially asked me. I'm sure he'd be very careful about a business arrangement like that. For that matter, so will I. What do you know about him?"

Carrie shrugged. "Almost nothing as an adult. He hardly ever comes to church, so we don't cross paths that often. Which … worries me a little."

"He seems like a lot of fun. And he's a good vet, which is the most important thing."

"So you're seriously thinking about it?"

"Let's just say I'm *praying* for God's will." Jana almost told Carrie about her plans for the wildlife center. But Carrie was close to her brother. What if she told Grant? The longer she could keep him from knowing details, the better chance she had of swaying Grandpa to her side. She held her tongue.

"That's good. That you're praying, I mean, and I promise I'll pray with you about it." Carrie hesitated. "I hope you'll give yourself a little time to get grounded around here before you jump into something that important."

Solid counsel. How many times in the past had she made a stupid emotional decision, then regretted it?

"Oh! That reminds me!" Carrie's eyes lit up. "I nearly forgot the main thing I came over here for. There's a ladies' Bible study at the church on Wednesday nights, and I wanted to make sure to invite you. There are about ten of us, a mixture of ages."

"Count me in. But what about the kids?"

"Children's choir is going on then." Carrie laughed. "Your LeeLee seems to be quite the drama queen—in an adorable way, I mean," she added when Jana opened her mouth to express her alarm. "You can just see that little brain working overtime."

Jana smiled. "She's about more than I can deal with. I'm starting her in kindergarten this year, even though she won't be five when school starts."

"Parenting has got to be the hardest job in the world." Carrie's expression was wistful.

"Are you and Tommy planning to have kids? You'd make great parents."

"We'd like to." Carrie looked away. "We've been trying for over a year."

Jana could have bitten her tongue. Why hadn't she thought before asking such a personal question of someone she didn't know well? "I'm so sorry—"

"Goodness, it's not your fault." Carrie's smile was quick and reassuring before she ducked her head. "It's not mine or Tommy's either, for that matter, although he's such a fixer he almost wishes it was."

More than once Jana had wondered why God allowed children to be born to unqualified parents like herself and Richie, when couples like Tommy and Carrie went childless. Mute, she stared at the top of Carrie's blonde head. *Father, what do I say?* "I'll pray," she blurted, then realized that it was the only and best thing to say. "I want to pray for you, if you'll let me."

Carrie looked up, tears shimmering in her eyes. "I'd like that, though I can't share all the details right now. I'm in a place now where I have to give my desires to the Lord, over and over. It's ... harder than it ought to be."

Jana shook her head. "I haven't been a Christian as long as you, but I think you expect too much out of yourself."

"Maybe. I just know I have so much to thank God for. I have a close family, a job I love, and I'm so happy with Tommy." Carrie smiled. "You know, you're very easy to talk to, Jana. It makes me wonder if Grant has told you what's bothering him. Our family's pretty worried about him."

Blindsided by this sudden shift in the conversation, Jana searched Carrie's face for any hint of teasing. She seemed to be dead serious. "What do you mean?"

"Well..." Carrie pursed her mouth. "Grant's always been a very focused person. He went after that engineering degree and sailed right to the top. He invented this ... this surveying thingie, don't ask me what it's called, and was making buckets of money jetting all over the world selling it. All of a sudden, one day he calls Dad and says he's selling the patent rights, dissolving the partnership, and moving home." She frowned. "Now it's like he's obsessed with this hunting camp—I *know* he's talked to you about that?" Jana nodded, and Carrie shrugged. "That's just it. He's such a planner, and he gets all bent out of shape if things don't go to suit him. He is definitely bent right now."

"Hmm." Jana stalled. What did all this have to do with her? "Grant and I are just acquaintances, really, not—not friends." She wasn't about to tell Carrie that she'd had a crush on her brother fair game

since she was fourteen years old. "What makes you think he would tell *me* something he wouldn't even tell his own family?"

"He's said more about you in the last two weeks than any other woman in the last five years. Besides, I saw the way he looked at you when you were together at my store the other day."

How he looked at me? Elation clanged against alarm. "I think you're mistaken. We've only had four conversations since I've been here."

Carrie's mouth curled. "That's so cute—you counted!"

"No, I did not." Jana waved her hand. "Well, I guess I did, but it's just that he's so ... so ... I mean, he was sweet to LeeLee when her cat got stuck in the—and he helped me out when I crashed into—but that doesn't mean I—" Jana gave up and stared at Carrie's laughing face. "All right, I was looking at him too. He's pretty hard to miss." She clamped her lips together to keep from blurting out anything else, then couldn't resist. "What do you think is the matter with him?"

Carrie grinned. "I have no idea, but you'll tell me if you find out, won't you?"

Sorry about the mess, y'all." Tommy moved a stack of library books off the extra chair in his office. "We'd have more room if we met over at Carrie's. She wouldn't mind."

"She wouldn't let CJ smoke his pipe." Grant sat down and tipped the chair against the wall. "And every woman in there would give us a dirty look just for breathing in her space."

"I guess you're right." Tommy swiveled his padded office chair around for CJ and shoved a pile of files to the back of the desk before taking a seat on it. As usual on a late Friday afternoon, he was dressed in disreputable jeans and a Jars of Clay T-shirt streaked with motor oil. An Ole Miss baseball cap covered his dark hair. "But I'd brave the gauntlet for a praline right now."

"Pearl's been making me smoke outside for years." CJ reached into the pocket of his uniform pants for his pipe and looked around for a trash can in which to empty the bowl. "Gonna quit next week, though."

Grant snorted. "CJ, you've been saying that ever since I've known you." The game warden had taught his first gun safety class and had been his Boy Scout troop leader, a mentor as well as a friend. "I'm glad you could stop by for a few minutes." They'd met to discuss the archery tournament in July to be sponsored by their church as an evangelistic outreach. It was Grant's brainchild, but he'd pulled in Tommy and CJ for creative input.

"Appreciate the chance to put my feet up for a minute," CJ sighed. "Got up at the crack of dawn to get a bunch of baby gators off the Cumbests' back porch. All this rain and they get stranded." He pulled a packet of tobacco out of the pocket of his shirt and used his thumb to tamp a pinch into the pipe. "I'm getting too old for this nonsense."

Tommy snorted. "You'll still be ticketing headlighters when the rest of us are in the nursing home."

CJ grinned, not bothering to deny it. Hunting deer at night with lights was not only illegal; it was the worst sort of unsportsmanlike conduct—and CJ was passionate about eradicating the practice on his turf. Grant hoped his old friend, the closest thing he had to a grandfather now, would be around for a long time to come.

"How's the investigation of that poacher situation coming along?" Grant folded his arms. "You got the bullet out of the deer, right?"

"Yeah, but it turned out to be a common size and gauge, so it wasn't much help."

Grant shook his head. "That was way too close to home for my comfort. Puts me in a cold sweat to think of a stray bullet hitting anybody." Particularly Jana and her kids.

Tommy whacked the bottom of Grant's foot propped against the desk. "So how're things out at Walden Pond?"

"Pretty good, I guess. I'm getting more hits on the website every day. Hired Crowbar and Willis Dyer to build me a couple of shooting houses."

"Then what's the matter?" Tommy gave him one of his perceptive stares.

Grant would just as soon not admit there was anything he couldn't handle, but Tommy wouldn't leave him alone until he'd confessed. "Well, I've run into a snag with Alvin Goff's property. CJ, you heard him the other day. You got any idea why all of a sudden he's backing out on me?"

"Not really." CJ struck a match on the bottom of his boot, filling the room with the odor of cherry tobacco. "Alvin's daddy gave him that land when he got back from Korea, but he never built on it. Said he wanted to put the feed store closer to town." He drew on his pipe. "I'm surprised he's held on to it for this long."

Grant tugged the bill of his cap to mask his frustration. "Three weeks ago he was ready to sell it to me. I just don't understand it. I've tried everything but threatening to sue. Even tried to talk Jana into running interference."

He realized his mistake when Tommy grinned. "I told Carrie she was crazy, but it looks like she was right."

"What do you mean?" Grant glanced at CJ, who raised his brows.

"She said there was something going on when you brought Jana to the shop to pick up her car." Tommy pulled his cell phone out of his pocket and started dialing.

"What are you doing?"

"Calling my wife. I owe her dinner and a movie."

"Give me that." Grant grabbed the phone and canceled the call, ignoring CJ's chuckle. "There's nothing going on. And you two quit discussing me behind my back."

"Okay, I'll discuss it to your face." Tommy grinned. "I think you're just as interested in Alvin's granddaughter as you are his thousand acres."

While Grant searched for a way to deny the obvious, CJ nodded. "Jana's always been a cute little thing, even if she *was* wild as a hare as a kid."

Grant looked at the old man, arrested. "Did you know her when she was growing up?"

"Me and Pearl used to talk about getting her and her brother out of that hellhole." CJ shook his head, mouth grim. "Too many complicated family dynamics, though. Alvin should've been the one to intervene."

"Why didn't he?"

"Imogene wouldn't let him, I imagine. She'd thrown her daughter out and told her not to come back."

Good night, what pride. Poor Jana.

"I was there, hanging out with Quinn, the night Jana's dad killed her mother," said Tommy quietly. "Man, that was awful. Thank God Jana was gone."

The Baldwin family's murder episode had been a regional news sensation right after Jana left town with Richie. "Old man Baldwin's still locked up, right?"

Tommy nodded. "Life with no chance of parole."

Grant winced. It was a sobering thought. Was Jana even capable of a healthy relationship — supposing he decided to pursue her? He had to admit that he'd been thinking about it. But there were way too many red flags attached to Jana Cutrere for him to admit it to anybody else.

"You take Carrie out for dinner if you want to, but don't blame it on me. Now let's get to work on this tournament." He reached for the manila folder he'd placed on the file cabinet when he came in. "I put flyers in the pro shop and on my website, and every place in town I can think of. Got several sponsors already."

Tommy gave him a long, indecipherable look, then nodded as if accepting the change of subject. "Don't forget I'll donate a free lube and oil change as a door prize. You're gonna have junior and ladies' divisions too, right?"

"Sure. ASA competition rules right down the line." He'd belonged to the Archery Shooters Association for years. "Is Carrie planning to enter?"

"Yeah." Tommy smiled. "She thinks she's gonna beat my score."

"It could happen. After all, I taught her." Grant jumped when his cell phone rang. "Hello?"

"Are you busy?" growled a deep, aged voice without preamble.

Alvin Goff. Maybe he'd changed his mind about selling the property. "No, sir. I was just about to go get some lunch. What can I do for you?"

"I need you to run over to my place and give Jana a hand. She just called and said my nanny goat's fixin' to kid, and the mules are giving her a hard time."

"What does a mule have to do with a goat giving birth?" And why would Alvin expect him to do anything about it? Jana was a licensed veterinarian. He grimaced at Tommy, who, apparently having overheard Alvin's stentorian command, was grinning broadly.

"I don't know, and I didn't have time to ask her before her phone went dead. Anyways, I can't leave the store, and I'm worried about that goat."

"Okay, but why me?" Grant didn't mind helping, but this was too bizarre. "I'm sure Heath Redmond would—"

"I called him, but he's out at the emu farm up at Cumbest Bluff. Look, boy, this is an emergency. You've helped your coon dog deliver puppies before, ain't you? It's only Daisy's second kidding, and I'm afraid it's twins." By now Alvin was shouting so loudly that Grant had to hold the phone away from his ear. He gave Tommy a pleading look.

Tommy flapped an imaginary apron. "Miss Scarlett! I don't know nothin' about birthin' no babies!"

CJ poked Grant with the stem of his pipe. "This is a job for Superman."

Grant closed his eyes in defeat. "Okay, Alvin. I'll go play mule psychologist or goat obstetrician—or whatever Jana needs."

Jana was quite literally at the end of her rope when she heard a truck drive up fifteen minutes after her SOS to Grandpa.

"Thank you, Lord." With the back of her wrist she wiped away the sweat pouring into her eyes. "The cavalry has arrived!"

"There my button soul foun' liver tea, at Ca-val-reeeee!" LeeLee was perched on a bale of hay in the corner of the barn. Her kitten, stretched out in her lap like the Queen of Sheba on a Persian rug, was enjoying a stomach rub.

Smiling at her daughter, Jana continued her desperate effort to tie up the two mules. Poor pregnant Daisy bleated piteously in the end stall. When Jana came out to feed the animals this morning, she realized the goat was going to need one of the two bigger stalls for a delivery room. The mules would have to double up in the other. But like children with a nasty case of sibling rivalry, the female refused to share a stall with the male and kicked the gate off its hinges. While trying to catch them, Jana had narrowly avoided getting her shins bashed by flailing hooves.

"Come on, Grandpa." She wrapped the john's lead more securely around her hand. "Daisy's about to explode." The mule butted her shoulder hard, and the molly let out a wheezing bray as she skittered out of reach.

Suddenly a masculine voice outside roared Jana's name. The mule, startled into sudden capitulation, sent her sprawling backward into the mud and hay.

LeeLee peered out the door. "The cava'ry sounds mad, Mommy."

Busy trying to catch her breath, Jana couldn't answer for a moment. The john lipped her shoulder as if to apologize for his fit of temper, and she shoved his whiskery muzzle away. Grandpa had apparently met with some mortal injury out in the yard. She was going to have to check on him.

She struggled to sit up. Then almost lay down again.

Grant Gonzales stood in the doorway looking like an irate Poseidon in camo. Water dripped from the bill of his cap, his T-shirt stuck to those big shoulders and chest, and his jeans streamed water into a puddle of mud around his sneakers.

"Oh no!" She forgot about her bruised rear. "What were you doing near the peach trees?"

"I wanted a peach." He wiped his face with one wet hand. "Are you all right?"

She nodded. "I didn't know you were coming, or I would have warned you—I mean, Grandpa knew about the water scarecrow."

"Water *scarecrow*?" Grant extended a hand to help Jana up. She looked at the strong, tanned fingers for a moment, then let him pull her to her feet. "Is this Alvin's idea of a security system?"

Jana stepped away, snatching her hand behind her back. "It's a motion-sensor sprinkler. Supposed to keep the deer away from the peach trees so Grandpa won't shoot them." She grabbed the john's halter.

He took a squishing step toward her. "I might have known this was your doing."

She backed against the stall door. "What are you doing here?"

"Your grandpa sent me." Frowning, he wrung out the hem of his T-shirt. "He didn't tell you I was coming?"

"No, I—"

"Hey, Mr. Grant!" LeeLee, whom Jana had for the moment forgotten all about, pushed between them and wrinkled her little nose. "Are you the cava'ry?"

He shook the water off his cap and plopped it on LeeLee's head. "Guess I am. How you doing, Sally?"

"Fine, but my name's not Sally." The kitten jumped down and tried to wind herself around Grant's legs. Finding them wet, she stalked outside with offended dignity.

"Guess you're gonna have to wear a name badge." Grant squatted to LeeLee's level and opened his arms. "Want a hug?"

"No! You're wet!" Giggling, she ran after the kitten.

Grant looked up at Jana. "So where's the maternity ward?"

Jana smiled in spite of her distress. "Daisy's down in the other stall. Molly here wouldn't let her sweetie in and kicked the gate down. If you'll grab her, we'll get them fed and tend to Daisy."

By some fluke of nature, the molly thought Grant was Master of the Universe, and the john followed where she led. Jana sent LeeLee to the house to feed the kitten while Grant jerry-rigged the broken gate with a length of telephone wire. Ten minutes later both mules were chowing down oats in the middle stall.

"Poor little lady." Jana knelt in the straw beside the goat's heaving, swollen body. "You ready to have these babies?"

Grant crouched beside her, stroking the goat's neck. "How long's she been in labor?"

"About an hour. I tried to call Heath, but he's—"

"Vaccinating emus. Alvin told me. Have you delivered a goat before?"

"Well, not personally. Just Ty and LeeLee." He blushed, and she poked him in the ribs with her elbow. "Just *kidding*."

He groaned at the pun.

She laughed. "I've helped deliver just about everything else. Puppies, kittens, foals, calves ... Daisy will do most of the work, but she's young, and she might need some help."

"What can I do?"

J ana watched as the two tiny kids bumped their mother's bag looking for milk. Finally, the black-spotted female latched on and began to gulp her lunch. The white male was slower, but after some rooting around, he got the idea. With her little ones nursing, Daisy, like any smart new mother, promptly went to sleep.

Jana looked around for Grant and found him sitting against the outside wall of the stall with LeeLee in his lap. He was watching Jana, his eyes thoughtful.

"LeeLee, what are you doing back in here?" Jana resigned herself to answering unanswerable questions for the rest of the day.

"I watched the baby goats be borned. Yuck." Her daughter grinned up at Grant.

He grinned back. "Double yuck. But kinda cool, huh?"

"I didn't mean for her to see this." Jana sighed. The stall was a mess.

"I knocked on the door, Mommy, and Mr. Grant said I could come in if I was quiet. Wasn't I quiet?"

"As a mouse." He flicked the bill of the oversized cap down to cover her face. LeeLee squealed, but his gaze remained on Jana. "You did a great job."

She looked away. "I couldn't have done it without you. Daisy thanks you."

"I'm always on call." The corner of his mouth tipped as he watched the nanny, snoozing away while her babies nursed. "I'll send Willis over to do a better job on that gate, though. Turns out he's a pretty good handyman."

"Okay, that would be good." Jana moved to sit beside him, and his damp sleeve brushed her shoulder. Yesterday's conversation with Carrie echoed in her mind. Yes, Grant was often focused to the point of obsession, and he had not been happy about getting soaked by the sprinkler. But right now he was the epitome of laid-back charm.

A moment of sweet quiet fell as the three of them watched the goat family. LeeLee leaned back against Grant's chest. He curled his arm around her pudgy middle and rested his chin atop her head. A surge of a dangerous, soft emotion washed through Jana's chest.

Oh, Lord, this is so scary. I can't help liking this guy when he's so sweet to my little girl. Please help me keep my feelings under control.

Grant rolled his head slightly. "Hey, do we *have* to warn Willis about the water scarecrow?"

"You are so bad." She poked him. "You do a good deed, giving those two a job, then go and ruin it."

His cheeks reddened. "How'd you know I gave them a job?"

"I had lunch with your sister yesterday."

"Uh-oh. It's not true, any of it."

"What's not true?"

"Anything she said about me." His eyes twinkled. "Unless it was good."

"Your sister loves you a lot. I like her. I'd like to meet Miranda again too." Their younger sister, according to Carrie, had married and moved to New Orleans.

"She always comes home for Christmas. She has a boy and a girl." Grant shifted LeeLee, who had fallen asleep in the crook of his arm, and looked down at her with an awed expression that stung Jana's heart. "I've never been around little kids much. I didn't know they could be so much fun."

"She's a mess." Jana smiled. "I'll take her if she's getting heavy."

"No, she's fine. Where's Ty?"

"He's been helping Grandpa in the warehouse, earning a little pocket money. I don't know what he's saving for." She shook her head. "Probably something inappropriate or dangerous."

"Lady, your life would be a lot easier if you relaxed. Listen, why don't you bring the kids out to the creek one day next week. They can swim off the houseboat and I'll grill some hot dogs—" He stopped at Jana's look. "What?"

She sighed. "I'm a vegetarian."

He rolled his eyes. "I should have known. Okay, nix the hot dogs. Do you have any objection to offing peanut butter?"

chapter 7

Sunday morning Jana applied a coat of dark coral lipstick in front of the full-length mirror hanging on the bathroom door. She was clad in her one dressy outfit, a turquoise chiffon-over-silk skirt with a gauzy floral blouse, which she rarely wore. Folks in her church in Knoxville tended to dress casually—and she couldn't remember the last time she'd dressed up for a date.

Maybe never.

But "Sunday best" was de rigueur at Vancleave Church. She wouldn't for the world offend anyone. Ignoring his protest—"Mom, are we going to a funeral?"—she made sure Ty had on his only pair of khakis and a blue-and-red-striped polo shirt. All morning LeeLee had been pirouetting like a ballerina in a smocked dress that Jana had bought at a consignment shop.

She could be proud of her little family.

Though really, there was nobody in particular she wanted to impress.

Right, Jana. Last Sunday she had caught herself looking for Grant in church and squelched disappointment when he didn't show up. Surely he would be there today.

Impatient with the direction of her thoughts, she jerked the bathroom door open. "Grandpa! We're going to be late if we don't hurry."

The organ prelude had just begun—making Jana rethink her laughing answer to Ty's question about going to a funeral—when she spotted Grant. Seated on the platform with the rest of the orchestra, he was oiling his trombone slide while making some laughing remark to the trumpet player next to him. So he did play in the church orchestra. She hadn't quite been able to picture it.

"We got one of them 'blended' services now." Grandpa's loud whisper jerked Jana out of her thoughts. "I like this part, but when they crank up the drums and guitars, I just turn my hearing aid off."

Smiling at Grandpa, she snagged Grant's frowning gaze. Did she have her blouse on backward?

Then she realized he was looking past her. Heath Redmond stood at the end of the pew.

"'Scuse me, pardon me." Heath stepped over people until he reached the space she'd made for him by pulling LeeLee into her lap. He sat down, smelling like aftershave, and flung his arm across the back of the pew behind Jana. She inched closer to Grandpa. There wasn't much wiggle room.

By the time she snatched another glance at Grant, the music director was asking the congregation to stand, and the orchestra members had raised their instruments. She tried to forget everything except worship. This place in particular intensified her gratitude to God. Even when she'd been a little girl dressed in clothes bought at Goodwill—seated on the front row with the other "bus ministry" kids—the Lord had said, "That one's mine."

She could remember one morning when she was about seven that her father had sent her to the 7-Eleven for a six-pack of beer. While paying for it, she overheard a woman who'd stopped for a quart of milk. Dressed in Sunday finery, the lady elbowed her daughter. "What a shame that little thing has to buy that stuff. You think we should call the police, honey?"

Call the police! Jana had thought in terror. *I don't want to go to jail!*

Now, of course, she realized the lady had been considering calling the law on the store owner for selling alcohol to a minor. For a long time, though, she'd lived in dread of an officer knocking on the door and hauling her off to prison. One Saturday about a year later, she'd opened the door of her parents' trailer to see the woman from the 7-Eleven standing in the weedy little yard.

"Morning, honey," the lady had said and introduced herself. "Would you like for us to come pick you up for Sunday school tomorrow morning?"

Jana had never been to Sunday school before. Her grandparents, then members of a little independent church way out in the sticks, wanted nothing to do with their prodigal daughter's family. Jana's mama was too ashamed to go to church, and Daddy got mad if anyone even mentioned it.

She was thrilled to walk into the white-painted children's rooms of this friendly old church. An assortment of faded, old-fashioned prints decorated every wall—pictures of the Creation, with Adam and Eve hiding behind the bushes. Beautiful Queen Esther, Ruth and Boaz, and Mary and Joseph with their sweet baby. Best of all were the paintings of Noah and all those amazing animals. Jana could have looked at them all day.

Those pictures had drawn Jana back there Sunday after Sunday, even when the "regular" children whined about sharing cookies and Kool-Aid with the "bus kids." "Ooh, she's got cooties," she heard more than once, and she was always terrified that her dress might flip up and show the holes in her panties.

Blinking back tears, she looked down at her own sweet baby, who stood on the pew, singing along at the top of her lungs with a chorus they'd learned at their Knoxville church. Even Ty, who was reticent about singing, seemed to enjoy the rhythm and joy of the music.

Thank you, Lord, for bringing us here.

And like an extra blessing, there was Grant Gonzales, playing his instrument with enthusiasm and a surprising amount of skill. It would be very easy to fall for him. The problem was, he was going to be very angry if he couldn't have her grandfather's land.

He'd never forgive her. And the kids were already looking forward to going swimming off his houseboat. They would be so disappointed if that didn't work out.

Her glance caught Heath's, and he winked. She blushed as if he could read her thoughts. Better quit worrying and pay attention to the service.

Hey, bud, you okay?" Tommy stood up to let Grant slip past him into the pew with the rest of the family.

Grant smoothed the frown from between his brows. He wasn't going to let Heath Redmond ruin his day. He nodded. "I missed being here last week."

Tommy sat down and grabbed Carrie's hand as she handed him his Bible. Farther down the pew were Grant's parents. He slid in beside his grandmother and, hiding a smile at the plastic canary nesting in the brim of her black hat, gently squeezed her shoulders. Granny was always good for a fashion statement. He glanced to his left, where Jana and her kids sat with Alvin and Dr.

Dolittle. Hah. There was a lot to be said for the safety of having your arm around your grandmother.

He'd seen Heath come in and trample a row full of people to get to Jana. Well, it was no wonder, because she looked like a model in that flowery outfit. He liked the way her hair curved around her ear and tangled in the turquoise drops dangling there. What he didn't like was the way Redmond's arm brushed her shoulder.

At the end of the service, Grant stood up so fast he jostled his grandmother's hat. "Granny, can I bring somebody with me to lunch? Four somebodies?"

"Of course you can." She gave him a quizzical look. "Who—"

"Later." He bolted around to the center aisle.

He arrived as Jana exited the pew. Holding LeeLee's hand, she was answering Ty's excited questions, handing her grandfather his walking stick, and smiling at Heath all at once. The smile unraveled all Grant's good intentions.

"Hey, Redmond." He offered his hand. "If I'd known you were going to be here, I would've worn my hard hat."

Jana looked at him, her eyes scrunching.

"In case the roof fell in," Grant added.

"Very funny." Heath's grip was crushing, and Grant resisted the urge to wince. Any minute now the guy was going to pull out a peashooter. The big jerk smiled down at Jana. "I'd have been in church a long time ago if I'd known how nice the decorations were."

"You always did have such pure motives."

Heath just grinned. He jerked a thumb in the direction of the orchestra section, where Grant had left his trombone case. "I heard you were still playing the old ax, but I had to see it for myself. Not too shabby, boy."

"The music was beautiful, Grant."

His attention swung to Jana, whose expression was warm — but definitely amused. "Uh, thanks."

"Mr. Grant, I watched you blow that slide thing!" LeeLee reached up to tug on Grant's tie. "Boy, your face sure got red. Can I play it?"

"Sure, sometime. Jana, I came over here to see if—"

"I pulled out my saxophone the other day," Heath interrupted, "and didn't sound half bad. Would y'all mind if I sat in on your next rehearsal, knock some of the rust off?"

Now what was the guy up to? "Sure, I mean — no, we wouldn't mind." He glanced at Jana. "We rehearse on Wednesday nights, upstairs in the educational building."

Redmond nodded. "Good. I'll be there."

"Okay, whatever." That was the most enthusiasm he could muster at the moment. He smiled at Jana. "Granny sent me to invite you to lunch. We do this family thing every Sunday, and—"

"I'm sorry, but Heath's taking us to the Tiki for lunch."

Was it his imagination, or did Jana seem disappointed? Out of the corner of his eye, he could see his grandmother giving him a "What are you up to?" look. Then she grinned and gave him a thumbs-up. He took a deep breath. *Well, here goes nothing.*

"Why don't you *all* come? Granny and Mom and Carrie always cook enough to feed a small third-world nation."

Jana looked alarmed. "Grant, we can't invade your family at the last minute like this!"

"Why not?" Alvin demanded. "That Tiki place gives me heartburn, and Roxanne makes the best pot roast and gravy in Jackson County."

When Jana gave Heath a questioning look, Grant wanted to clash antlers. He put on an affable smile, however, and pulled out the big guns. "Ty, how'd you like to learn to drive a four-wheeler this afternoon?"

The boy lit up like a Roman candle. "Yes, sir! Mom, can I change clothes first?"

Heath wasn't going to let himself be outmaneuvered. "Mr. Alvin, you go ahead then, and I'll take Jana and the kids by your house to change." He gave Grant a thoughtful look. "Thanks for the invite, Gonzo. We'll see you shortly."

Grant could almost hear the Terminator echoing, "I'll be back."

Grant's grandmother, Roxanne Gonzales, lived on five acres of land across the highway from Grandpa in a tiny farm cottage that fairly bulged at the seams when the whole family gathered. With five extra guests, the company overflowed into the yard.

Jana had never eaten so much or laughed so hard in her life. Roxanne, an elderly red-haired sprite in bright lipstick and a yellow dress, turned out to be an endless font of rich food and useless information. Jana was utterly charmed.

After the meal, while the children rode the four-wheel ATV with Grant, she sat in the white-painted lawn glider across from Heath. Carrie had fallen asleep on Tommy's shoulder while watching a golf tournament on TV, and Grant's parents were watching Grandpa wage a cutthroat game of Ping-Pong with Roxanne.

Heath had sat down first, patting the seat beside him. For reasons not clear in her own mind, Jana chose the opposite bench. *I like my own space*, she told herself, moving her feet out of the way of Heath's enormous Top-Siders.

You didn't mind sitting close to Grant the other day in the barn, a voice in her head whispered back.

Mind your own business, she shot back.

Heath didn't seem to care. As the four-wheeler zoomed past—Grant laughing, Ty whooping, and LeeLee shrieking—he sprawled, arms flung wide across the back of the seat. He gave her his mischievous one-sided grin. "I'd watch out for Gonzales if I were you."

"He seems to know what he's doing." She had to work hard not to stand up and yell, *Slow down!* as the ATV whizzed by again.

"I'm sure he does." Heath gave her an amused look. "You do realize he's hitting on you, don't you?"

She couldn't help the little jump of her pulse. All the same, she gave Heath a cool look. "He's been very kind to us."

"I've known Grant for a long time." The amusement faded, Heath's eyes narrowing with evident concern. "He doesn't do anything without a reason."

Jana weighed the fact that she didn't know Heath well against her grandfather's positive remarks about him and Carrie's words of caution. "What could he possibly want from me?"

"Aside from the obvious—" Heath's gaze skated over her face and form, making her squirm—"he's going to be in some major financial trouble if he can't get your grandfather's river property. I'm sure he's hoping you'll butter his bread for him."

An old, instinctive flash of anger rushed through Jana. Men had always taken advantage of her—her father, Richie, a few male college professors. And now Grant and Heath were tussling over her like a couple of junkyard dogs with a bone. Ridiculous.

"Thanks for your concern, but I'm a big girl."

"Yes, you are." Charming smile back in place, Heath leaned toward her, propping his arms on his knees. "And by all accounts you're a top-grade veterinarian too. Every one of your professors—and your former employers—has highly recommended you. I figure if I don't get you to go into practice *with* me, you'll have me out of business inside a year. So how about it?"

Jana froze. "You've been asking my professors about me? You called Mr. Andrews?"

Heath shrugged. "I told you I was going to offer you a job."

"I guess I didn't take you seriously. Heath ... you know what my plans are for the wildlife refuge."

He made a disparaging noise. "Oh, that. Good grief, you can't make a living treating squirrels and deer."

Now he sounded like her grandpa. "I can get a federal grant."

"Grant schmant." He rolled his eyes. "How long do those things last, anyway? A few years tops. Do you have any idea how much equipment and medicine costs, not to mention all the manpower you'd need to run such a place seven days a week? You can't do it by yourself."

"You said you'd help me." She wasn't going to let him off the hook on that one.

"Of course I'd help you, to a point. But I'm not going to jeopardize a practice I've spent years developing. Besides, I've got more than I can handle already. That's why I'm trying to bring you in!" He took a deep breath and tempered his voice. "Come on, Jana, be reasonable. Let's build ourselves the premier veterinary clinic on the Gulf Coast, and we can doctor your little wild friends on the side."

Be reasonable. Jana was tired of being reasonable. She wanted to dream, and dream big. She wanted to do something miraculous that couldn't be explained by anything other than the power of God working through her. She wanted to treat helpless and vulnerable animals who had nobody to speak for them.

Like me. Like you rescued me, Lord.

Shaking, she refused to meet Heath's eyes.

"Won't you at least pray about it?"

Apparently he knew the right words. "I'll pray about it."

"Pray about what?"

Jana looked up. Grant stood with one hand on the frame of the glider, the other holding LeeLee's hand. Ty was on the seat of the four-wheeler several yards away, pretending to drive. She jumped to her feet.

Grant grinned and dangled the keys from one finger. "He's not going anywhere."

"I knew that." She sat down and crossed her legs.

"You want to go for a ride?"

Since she still wore the turquoise skirt and blouse, she assumed he was teasing. "Not today."

"Okay, then come get some homemade strawberry ice cream. Heath?"

"Sounds good."

"Mr. Uncle Grant, I like ice cream too." LeeLee jumped up and down.

Uncle Grant?

He blinked. "Okay, Sally. I'll loan you my fork."

"You can't eat ice cream with a fork!" LeeLee grabbed Grant's hand and towed him toward the house. "Come on, Mommy. Let's show him."

Late on Wednesday afternoon, Jana sat in the play yard outside the church's educational building. She pushed her bare toes into the sand, making the swing undulate, and looked at her watch. LeeLee and Ty should be getting out of children's choir in about ten minutes. She had enjoyed Carrie's Bible study, and when it had finished early, she'd come outside to find a quiet place to reflect. A lethargic breeze rustled the leaves of a big sycamore tree arching across the fence, but it was still hot as an oven out here. She had so few opportunities for solitude that she didn't mind.

The Lord seemed to be trying to teach her something painful. Again. How many times would she have to hit a wall before she learned to discern God's will?

Heath's job offer had thrown her for a loop. Not just any old job offer either, but a job that could lead to a partnership in a busy, thriving practice where she could do everything she'd been trained to do. She could fit into the community where she'd grown up, provide for her children, and look after Grandpa without a load of debt hanging over her head.

And if she took Heath's offer and gave up on the wildlife center, all conflict with Grant would dissolve. She could get to know his family without having to hide what mattered most to her. Grant had a lovely family, the kind of family she'd always wished for. It was clear they all adored him and wanted the best for him. They would be hurt when she ruined his plans for his camp.

But taking a job with Heath seemed too easy somehow. She remembered she'd promised him she would pray about it.

Lord, what do you want me to do? Who should I trust?

She opened her Bible, mulling over the lesson she'd just studied. The apostle John, exiled on the island of Patmos near the end of his life, had had no hope of ever going home, yet he'd remained patient, trusting. He hadn't railed at God, demanding to know what he was up to. And look what had been revealed to him.

Be still, child, she seemed to hear. *You can trust me.*

Okay, Father, I'll wait.

With a sigh, she put her marker in the Bible and brushed the sand off her feet.

Through the window behind her, Jana could hear the children laughing and singing and the orchestra rehearsing in an upstairs room. From this vantage point it sounded like a calliope performing in a high wind. There was another odd noise underneath the music.

Somebody banging on a door.

Putting on her sandals, she slid out of the swing and walked around the corner of the building. Willis Dyer stood on the front porch, hammering on the big double doors of the church sanctuary.

"Willis, what are you doing?"

His square face broke into a huge grin of relief. "Hey, Miss Jana!" Removing his cap, he clomped down the steps. His hair stuck up in wiry dark tufts all over his head. "I was looking for Dr. Redmond, but you'll do."

"What's the matter?" There was a lump inside his plaid shirt with blood seeping through. "Did you hurt yourself?"

"No, ma'am." His thick brows twisted. "I just found this little squirrel in the woods. His tail's been mauled." He opened the shirt to reveal the trembling ears of a gray squirrel.

"Oh, Willis. We'll have to get it to the clinic."

Eyes clouding, Willis put his cap back on. "Wasn't anybody there. I called Miss Dora's house, and her daughter said they were all here at the church tonight—her and Dr. Redmond too."

Just then the front door of the church opened. Heath and Grant came out, followed by several other people carrying instrument cases.

Heath's bronzed face creased in his attractive smile when he saw Jana. He strode over and slung an arm around her neck. "Hey, beautiful!" He gave her a smacking kiss on the forehead. "Had supper yet? I was just headed over to Cole's."

"I don't have time for supper. We have an emergency. Willis found an injured squirrel, and we've got to get it to the clinic."

Still grinning, Heath searched Jana's face to see if she was joking. He dropped his arm from around her neck. "A squirrel."

Jana's blood pressure soared. "Heath—"

"The kids will let out of choir in a few minutes," said a deep voice from behind her shoulder. "Want me to find LeeLee and Ty and bring them out here?"

"Oh, goodness, I nearly forgot!" Jana turned to find Grant standing close, glaring at Heath. At least *somebody* seemed to appreciate the emergency. "Would you, please? I want to take a look at this little guy."

"Be right back." Grant headed for the educational wing of the church, tossing his trombone case in the back of his truck on the way by.

Since the squirrel was calm and stable, Jana probed the injured tail without moving the animal out of the big man's gentle grasp. "Willis, you are a prince among men. He'll be fine once we treat him, but he would've died if you hadn't brought him in."

Willis turned the color of Chicago brick. "That's good, Doc. I mean, that he'll be okay."

Jana flashed a look at him. It was the first time anybody had called her "Doc" seriously.

"What are you going to do with it?" Heath peered over her shoulder. "I hope you're not expecting me to board this thing. I don't have anybody to stay overnight at the clinic, and the Wildlife Commission—"

"I'll keep him." Willis looked as if he might cry.

"Let's just get him taken care of." Jana frowned at Heath. "Then we'll worry about where to keep him."

"You are so sweet." Heath put his arm around Jana again. "You can treat him at my office."

She shrugged him off, grateful when Grant strode up with LeeLee on his shoulders and Ty trotting in his wake. LeeLee clutched a short length of PVC pipe with one hand and Grant's forehead with the other.

"Mommy! Teacher said I could bring my telephone home and practice singing to you! See, this is how it works." LeeLee let go of Grant's head long enough to twist the pipe to form an S. She put one end to her mouth and the other to Grant's ear. "Hello, down there! Anybody home?"

"Hey, that tickles." Grant shifted but managed not to lose his passenger. "Let's show her that later, okay?"

"Okay." LeeLee shoved the phone down the front of her overalls.

Grant squinted at the squirrel. "Good night, it looks like a rat. What's the prognosis?"

"Doc says he'll be fine." Willis patted Jana's shoulder as if she were Joan of Arc. "*This* doc."

Grant smiled at Jana. "To the rescue again, huh?"

"He needs a hotel for the night. I don't guess you could—"

"No, I could not! You already stuck me with a deer. I have to draw the line somewhere." He glowered at Heath. "But I'd be happy to assist in surgery."

She sighed. "Okay, Willis, go with Grant and meet me at Heath's clinic. Come here, LeeLee. Heath, can I borrow your key?"

Heath eyed Grant. "I'll unlock it myself and stay to make sure you've got everything you need."

"I'd appreciate it. Come on, Ty." Holding LeeLee by the hand, she walked toward her car, planning what she'd need to treat the squirrel. She had more important things to worry about than two men who couldn't stand to be one-upped.

chapter 8

"Just what I need, another mouth to feed." Alvin glared at the squirrel lying asleep in a cage on loan from Heath's clinic. The cage sat on the coffee table where Alvin normally kept a jar full of butterscotch candy. He stumped toward the kitchen, giving Grant a sour look on the way by. "Speaking of which, I can hear your stomach growling all the way over here, boy. Come on, let's rustle us up some sandwiches."

Grant glanced at Heath, who shrugged and accompanied him into the kitchen.

They'd both watched the operation on the squirrel's tail, then followed Jana home. This, in Grant's opinion, was asinine, but he couldn't bring himself to leave Heath alone with Jana. It was now after ten o'clock, and she had gone to put the children to bed.

"No telling what you'll get saddled with, now that Jana's here." Grant turned a chair around backward to straddle it. "She can't turn down a stray."

Alvin snorted from behind the refrigerator door. "Which could explain why you two are here."

Either missing or ignoring the inference, Heath sank into another chair with a groan. "Somebody should explain to her that she can't save every rodent in Mississippi."

"Believe me, I've tried." Alvin pulled a loaf of white bread off the top of the refrigerator and tossed it onto the table with a package of pressed ham, some sliced cheese, and a jar of mayonnaise. "Help yourselves, boys."

"I just hope she's not going to give me grief over my hunting camp. Which reminds me—" Maybe he shouldn't talk about his private business in front of Heath, but Alvin seemed to be in a rare mellow mood. "You said you'd give me an answer about your property by the first of July. That was yesterday. Alvin, I've got to start building the lodge if I'm going to have it operating before deer season opens."

Alvin dropped into a chair, old bones creaking, and gave Grant a buzzardlike glare. "Boy, you just never let up, do you?"

He shook his head. "I just don't understand the holdup."

Glancing at Heath, who was piling meat and cheese onto his bread, Alvin leaned closer to Grant. "I'll tell you one thing that makes me hesitate, but you gotta promise not to tell Jana."

Grant didn't like the sound of that. "Why not?"

"Just promise."

"All right."

"I don't want her to get her hopes up, but I may give that property to her and the kids. She's got her heart set on this California bean-sprout wildlife refuge." The old man's pale gray eyes turned watery. "She hasn't asked me for it, which is the *only* reason I'd consider letting it go for such a useless thing."

"You may not have to, Mr. Alvin." Heath took a huge bite of his sandwich. "Hey, you got any Fritos?"

Why couldn't the guy mind his own business? "What are you talking about, Redmond?"

"Fritos. Those little corn-chip things—"

"Not that, idiot. Why wouldn't Alvin have to give Jana—"

"Oh, that. She's coming to work at my clinic."

"She hasn't said anything about it to me." Grant put down his sandwich, his appetite gone.

Heath gave him a bland look. "Why would she?"

"Well now," Alvin said, tapping his chin, "that puts a new spin on things. I'll have to think about it some more." He thunked Grant's wrist with the knob of his cane. "So you just hold your horses 'til after the holiday."

Heath grinned like a pirate.

Grant stared at him, feeling inexplicably depressed for a man who was one step closer to gaining the one thing he'd always wanted. If Jana went to work for Heath, he could be losing something of much greater value.

"All right, Alvin, I'll talk to you about it later." He rose and threw away the remains of his sandwich. "I'll say good-bye to Jana and let myself out."

He walked through Alvin's tiny living room, peeking in on the unconscious squirrel. *Rodent.* "Jana!" he called softly. "Where are you?"

"In here. Come on back."

Following the sound of her voice, he found her sitting against the headboard reading to Ty. Grant checked the cover of the book. *Prince Caspian.* "Hey, I liked that book." He leaned against the doorjamb and looked around. Alvin's bedroom was small and spartan, furnished with little more than a pine chest of drawers and an iron bedstead, with Ty's single bed crowded into one corner.

"It's way cool." Ty had on a pair of blue pajamas with a red cape. "We've only got one chapter to go, but Mom won't finish!" He yawned.

Grant winked at Jana. "It'll be just as good tomorrow. You've had a busy day, sport."

Jana yawned too. "We all have. LeeLee was asleep almost before I got her out of the bathtub." She kissed Ty, then closed the book and laid it on a TV tray beside the bed. Flicking on a night-light, she turned off the overhead light and looked up at Grant. "Thank you for sticking with me tonight."

"It was kind of interesting. Squirrel's gonna be surprised to wake up and find half his tail missing."

"It would be a lot easier if I had a place to deal with emergency situations like this."

"The rescue center, you mean?" In the soft light of the hall, she looked tired. He wanted to touch the shadows under her eyes.

She nodded. "Heath and Grandpa both think it's impractical. What do you think?"

Startled to have his opinion sought, he straightened a little. "I'm a practical kind of guy myself."

"Nice way to sidestep the question. But you left a secure job to follow your dream, didn't you?"

"Baby, nothing's secure in this world," he muttered, ignoring the little jerk she gave at the endearment. "And you'd better keep that in mind if you decide to go into partnership with Heath Redmond."

"He told you about that?"

"Yeah, and it could be a good thing for you—if you get everything in writing. Redmond is the ultimate opportunist."

Jana stiffened. "Funny, he said something similar about you."

"I'll just bet he did." Grant had to smile. "Listen, what I came back here for was to remind you about bringing the kids swimming. Why don't you bring them Friday, since it's the Fourth? There's a pretty spectacular fireworks display at the river after sundown."

"That sounds like fun. The kids will like that." She looked away.

No doubt about it, she was uncomfortable. He stood there for another minute anyway, absorbing the quiet of the room. Ty had fallen asleep, flat on his back, arms flung wide. The kid was determined to be a superhero, ever protective of his mother.

God, he needs somebody to protect him too.

Heath would make a terrible father. He ought to tell Jana that, but maybe he'd already said enough.

He sighed. "Y'all come on over around one or two, and we'll have a good time." He allowed himself to touch Jana's cheek with the pad of his thumb. "Good night."

"Good night," she whispered.

I can't believe how much he's grown in just a few weeks." Jana watched from a distance as the fawn scampered to hide behind a clump of tall grass inside the new, taller enclosure Grant had built. Forrest was now big enough to jump, well, like a deer, and the flexible cast on his leg seemed not to bother him much. "You've done a great job with him." She looked at Grant, who stood beside her with his arms folded over his chest, dressed in black swim trunks and a white T-shirt.

LeeLee and Ty crouched at their feet, peering through the fence at the fawn. Jana wanted Forrest to maintain a healthy fear of humans, so it was important to limit contact with him.

"He's pretty low-maintenance." Grant watched the fawn nuzzle the bottle stuck through the mesh of the fence. "Cut enough natural oak browse to dump inside the enclosure every day and don't make eye contact, right?"

"That's right." He wasn't going to take credit for being nice, so she gave up and looked around. He and the Dyer brothers had been working hard to clear more of the road down to the landing, where the houseboat was docked. On the way over they'd passed Crowbar, running a Bush Hog in spite of the holiday. Clearly Grant hadn't given up on opening the camp.

She glanced at him, searching in vain for the tenderness that had been in his expression two days ago as he'd stood looking at her in the hallway. Here, on his turf, he was the practical man-in-charge.

The four of them watched the fawn for a while, then Grant suggested they walk down to the creek. It was a beautiful day, the afternoon sun sparkling on the water like diamonds. The creek ran smoothly between dense woods that painted pockets of deep shade along the banks, and the water lapped musically against the boat's pontoons. Jana had dressed LeeLee in her bright red one-piece and told Ty he could swim in a pair of cutoffs. Her own old swimsuit still fit, so she'd covered it up with an oversized T-shirt.

"Your backyard is amazing." Jana leaned down to pet the dogs, who were sleeping in the cool mud next to the wharf.

"I think so." Grant caught her elbow to steady her as she went across onto the boat. "Careful there, Sally." He picked LeeLee up and swung her onto the deck, watching to make sure Ty crossed safely.

"If I didn't know this was the Ketchums' boat, I never would have recognized it." Jana admired the fresh white paint and dark green trim that made the boxlike cabin gleam. A new American flag hung from a pole bracketed beside the front door.

"Take a look around while I cast off. Life jackets are hanging by the anchor." He unplugged the thick cord connecting the boat to its power pole.

Jana found the life jackets, pleased to note that a couple of them were child-sized. She buckled LeeLee into one, then helped Ty with his. "Wait a minute, honey." LeeLee was leaning over the rail. "We're not going in right here. Grant's going to take us farther out into the water first."

"This house *moves*, Mommy!" LeeLee whirled, head thrown back to let the breeze ruffle her hair.

Jana smiled, feeling like shouting with joy herself.

Grant came back onto the boat, pulling in the mooring rope and hanging it next to the anchor. "Y'all come inside while I take us out into the creek."

Jana followed him and the children through the glass door, then stopped cold.

Hanging on the wall facing her was the head of a magnificent six-point buck. The beautiful lifelike dark eyes seemed to question her as she stared. *What are you doing here, lady?*

She hardly noticed the children chattering to Grant as he sat down in the captain's chair behind the wheel. Dropping onto the sofa behind her, trying to catch her breath, she looked around. A stuffed bobcat prowled across the television, and a fox snarled at her from the floor. *Why am I shocked? This is what he does.*

Of course she'd seen mounted animals before, but this was *Grant's* home. Her gaze flew to the children. They hadn't even noticed the deer, they were so excited about all the switches and gauges, the sound of the engine, and the movement of the houseboat. Grant had set LeeLee in his lap so she could pretend to drive while he controlled the wheel. Standing on tiptoe to see over his shoulder, Ty asked one eager question after another.

Grant looked around at Jana. "What's the matter? Need some Dramamine?"

"No, I'm fine." He wouldn't deliberately offend her; he simply didn't see things the same way she did. She shuddered. How could she be so attracted to a man on the other side of this huge philosophical chasm? "I'm just wondering why you didn't go ahead and arrange a picnic in the morgue. Would have been just as cheerful."

"What?" Following her gaze to the deer head, Grant chuckled. "Oh, sorry about that. Forgot to warn you." He turned back to the wheel.

His laughter wasn't comforting. He didn't get it. She got up to stand behind his shoulder. "That's some hobby you've got. Shooting defenseless animals and hanging them on the wall for decorations."

He turned around, his expression now irritated. "They're not defenseless. They've got legs and they can run, which they most often do. Do you know how long you have to wait for a good shot, how hard it is to hit a moving target?"

"Do you know how many maimed animals I treated in vet school because of that?"

His jaw shifted. "I'm proud of the fact that I've never left a wounded animal."

"You'll have to pardon me if that doesn't make me feel any better." She pointed out the window. "You'd better pay attention to where you're going, Skipper, or we're going to get stuck on that sandbar. Guess you didn't name this thing the *Minnow* for nothing."

Releasing an exasperated breath, Grant steadied the wheel, slowing the boat to drift close to a beautiful white sand beach cupped by palmettos. He killed the motor, then set LeeLee down and put his hand on Ty's shoulder. "Come on, bud, let's drop anchor, then we'll go swimming." He gave Jana a thoughtful look. "Maybe you'd better stay out of the cabin if my decor bothers you."

Jana made sure the children were coated down with sunscreen, then sat down at the stern to dangle her feet off the side of the boat. Other than an occasional Jet Ski roaring past, creating a wake that gently rocked the houseboat, they were alone. The quiet was soothing, and Jana began to recover her emotional equilibrium. She shouldn't have confronted Grant so bluntly earlier. He'd shown remarkable restraint in his response.

The flag on the front of the boat snapped in the breeze, reminding her of the holiday. Freedom. In spite of her lingering melancholy, she felt blessed. She could hold her beliefs, Grant could hold his, and they could discuss them like adults. Surely they would do that later. Maybe she could even change his mind.

It had been a long time since she'd gone swimming in this creek. The sun on her arms, the scents of fish and fresh air and the lotion on her skin, all brought back memories of Mr. and Mrs. Ketchum's hospitality toward an otherwise lonely little girl and boy. She and Quinn had swum here most afternoons of every summer until she'd run away with Richie.

Grant, kneeling beside her, looked up from his task of inflating a pair of orange floaties for LeeLee. "Are you okay?" He'd been watching her since their conversation in the cabin.

"I'm fine." Making up her mind to enjoy the rest of the day for the children's sake, she flicked a glance at LeeLee, who was leaning over the rail again, prattling to Ty about swimming with the fish. "Watch her. She's not afraid of anything."

"I will." He slipped the floaties onto LeeLee's arms, plugging the rubber valves, then made her sit down next to Jana. Cautioning Ty to dive shallow, Grant knifed into the water himself.

Holding LeeLee's warm little body close, Jana watched Ty execute a clean, natural boy-dive that made her smile.

LeeLee bounced. "Mommy, come on, let's go swimming!"

"Let me get in first, then you can jump to me." Jana had been swimming practically since she could walk, and she'd taught both children to swim in the Andrewses' pool. LeeLee held on to the rail while Jana slipped over the side and descended the ladder. She reached up. "Okay, sugar, jump and I'll catch you."

"Wheee!" LeeLee jumped just as something grabbed Jana's ankle.

She screamed but managed to catch LeeLee before going under. Coughing and spitting, she surfaced, relieved to find that LeeLee's floaties and life preserver had kept her from more than bobbing down to her shoulders. Grant's wet brown head came up several yards away, the twinkle in his eyes visible even at that distance. Ty bobbed up as well, grinning and blowing water like a dolphin.

She shoved her hair out of her eyes. "All right, which of you two smart alecs grabbed me?"

"Not me!" sang Ty.

Grant gave her a sanctimonious look. "Not I."

"Some example of water safety you are."

"I'll have you know I'm an Eagle Scout. I'm teaching your children the consequences of failure to be observant."

"Oh, sure, blame it on me!" She splashed him, and an all-out water war started, boys against girls.

The sun had moved several notches toward the west before the children tired, and the four of them climbed back onto the boat to eat. Then they played a rather wild game of Uno, which LeeLee somehow managed to win in spite of—or perhaps because of—several cards blowing overboard.

Later, they went back down to the lower front deck to watch the sun go down. With her mouth still smeared with jelly, LeeLee fell asleep snuggled beside Jana in a deck chair.

Ty spotted a rack of cane poles on the side of the cabin. "Mr. Grant, can I fish off the side of the boat?"

"Sure." Grant, sprawled in a chair next to Jana, didn't even open his eyes. "There's a bucket of bait right there."

"Ty—"

"Come on, Mom, I'll throw 'em right back in. I just want to see if I can catch anything."

Grant grinned. "Show your mom the bait."

"Hey!" Ty exclaimed. "What *is* this?" He held a white pellet under Jana's nose.

"It smells like ... Ivory soap?"

"Yup." Grant opened his eyes and gave her a sleepy look. "Totally safe for the environment. Gentleness guaranteed." He winked.

Her breath hitched at the masculinity in that gaze. "Okay, Ty. Just be—be careful." She wasn't sure if she was talking to her son or herself.

As the sun dipped closer to the trees, a humming sound rose from the woods on each bank, sounding as if the water itself had come alive with music. Jana forgot her self-consciousness in bone-lazy contentment.

"Do you think the Singing River legend is true?" she asked Grant drowsily.

He rolled his head. "Dunno. Hey, Ty, has your mom told you that story?"

"No, sir."

"It seemed pretty morbid for children, but I guess it's part of their heritage."

"I'll tell it, then." Grant sat up, propping his elbows on his knees. "This creek is a thread off the Pascagoula River—it's always been known as the Singing River. The story goes that the warrior Biloxi Indians were jealous of the peaceful Pascagoula Indians and the richness of their land. But they agreed not to attack as long as there was no intermarriage between the tribes. Then one day the Biloxi princess fell in love with a young Pascagoula chief."

"Yuck." Ty grimaced. "Shoulda known it would be a love story."

Grant chuckled. "Yeah, well, when the princess left her tribe to marry her lover, the Biloxi came after her. Rather than send her back or submit to slavery and bloodshed, the Pascagoula waded hand in hand into the river to drown themselves, singing as they went."

"No way!" Ty looked over his shoulder in disbelief. "What a sissy thing to do."

"I have to agree." Grant shrugged. "Anyway, the legend says that the humming sound you hear in the evening during this time of year is the Indians singing from their grave in the river."

Jana watched Ty go still as he listened to the very real humming sound. "There's another version of the story that says the Pascagoula walked into the river because they were being persecuted. They'd accepted Christian beliefs and didn't want to fight back against the Biloxi. The music is God's way of reminding us of his presence in the midst of tragedy."

"I hadn't heard that one." Grant looked at her. "Well, in spite of the goofy story—" he lay back in his chair and closed his eyes—"I like the song. It makes me feel close to God."

Jana had always felt the same thing. Even in the days when nothing in her world was safe, she could come to the river or the woods and imagine someone bigger than herself, who had created every wonderful and beautiful element of the earth, and who loved her beyond reason.

Even if she couldn't quite figure out how to reach him at the time.

Just then the quiet humming sound was overlaid by the crackle of fireworks. A shower of blue, red, and gold burst against the sky. LeeLee woke up and stretched, openmouthed at the display. Grant rose to turn the running lights off, plunging the boat into darkness relieved only by the light show exploding overhead. Thrilled, Jana oohed and aahed right along with the children. As her eyes adjusted to the darkness, she turned to look at Grant and found his gaze on her.

I can't, Lord. I cannot fall in love again. Especially not with this man—this hunter. Oh, God, please do something.

Grant had reached a turning point of some sort. He felt … well, itchy, as he carried a drowsy LeeLee up the pier. Jana led the way with the swim gear, while Ty followed carrying the fishing pole Grant had given him. The itch had nothing to do with the mosquitoes beginning to swarm through the woods; it was an internal discomfort that was turning into a strong desire to kiss Jana Cutrere senseless.

How could a woman who questioned his beliefs and practices and goals be so alluring and sweet? And fun. Once she'd gotten her hair wet, she'd played with the kids in the water for hours. Her feet, encased in a pair of sparkly blue flip-flops, were as wrinkled as prunes. He shook his head. *I'm falling for a woman in flip-flops.*

In the past, Southern belle–type sorority women had always been more his style. Polished, pure as driven snow, dressed to the teeth, and no messy attachments—like children and cats and deer and crazy grandpas, et cetera ad infinitum.

LeeLee snuffled against his neck, and his heart executed a weird clench.

You are not daddy material, Gonzales. Forget this and just keep your fat mouth shut. And keep your lips to yourself.

They reached Jana's car, parked in the clearing out from the deer's pen. Grant deposited LeeLee in her booster seat and stood back while Jana loaded the car. He wished he could make sure she had a more reliable vehicle. The Subaru functioned, but the air-conditioning was temperamental. He bit his tongue to keep from offering to have it checked out.

Jana stood inside the open door and smiled at him. "Thank you so much for inviting the kids over today. They'll never forget it."

"You're welcome." He leaned down toward Ty, who sat in the passenger seat with his cane pole stuck out the open window. "You hang on to that, you hear? Don't want to spear somebody going down the road."

Ty laughed. "Yes, sir."

Grant stood and found himself only a few inches from Jana again. She was like a magnet—shiny hair dried in all directions after its dousing in the creek, the sunburned cheeks and bright eyes made luminous by the color of her blue shirt. He could just kiss her forehead. That would be friendly, right? After all, he might not see her for several days.

He leaned farther down, watching her eyes widen and her lips part. His heart began to thud in his ears.

No, wait. Not his heart. Footsteps were pounding down the road. Somebody was shouting his name. He'd forgotten all about Crowbar and Willis, who had been helping to clear timber and brush away from the entrance to the property all day.

He jerked upright. "That doesn't sound good."

"Crowbar!" Jana pushed past him. "Here we are! What's the matter?"

Crowbar crashed into the clearing. "Grant! Jana!" He panted, trying to catch his breath. "Y'all come quick. The Bush Hog broke down a couple of hours ago, so I left it sitting by the road while I went to get a part. Just now I come back to move it and accidentally knocked Mr. Alvin over. He's hurt bad!"

chapter 9

The ER of the Singing River Hospital was not a happy place to be on the Fourth of July.

Jana had signed her grandfather in an hour ago, and they were still stuck in a busy hallway, passed right and left by hospital personnel—not to mention various and sundry drunks, drug addicts, and kids with beans up their noses. Jana stood at the head of Grandpa's gurney, holding his hand and praying for a room to open up.

At the foot of the bed, Grant leaned against the wall, looking ferocious. He had apparently given up stopping people to ask how much longer they were going to be.

Jana looked at the clock hanging above her head. Eleven o'clock, but it seemed much later. She hadn't cried yet, but her throat felt tight and hard. Grandpa occasionally moaned with the pain in his leg.

Grant peered down the hallway. "What's the holdup, anyway?"

Jana couldn't answer, but she was grateful for his company and appreciated his frustration. He'd been a rock of support from the moment Crowbar had crashed their party. Because Jana was so shaken, Grant had driven her car out to the end of the road where the accident occurred, then used his cell phone to call 911. He'd waited with Grandpa for the ambulance while Jana took the kids home. She'd put them to bed and called Roxanne over to stay with them. Finally, Grant collected Jana in his truck and drove her to the hospital.

Two hours to see a doctor? Animals in a vet clinic got faster treatment than this.

"Why don't you go sit down?" said Grant. "I'll stay with him."

"I'm not tired." She yawned. Grant grinned, and she gave him a weak smile. "Well, not very."

Another white lab coat went by, and the doctor did a double take. "Grant, what are you doing here?"

"Dad!" Grant's face lit. "I tried to page you, but they said you were in surgery—this place is a zoo tonight. Mr. Alvin here's got a broken leg."

"Hi, Jana." Grant's tall, thin-faced father laid a hand on her shoulder. "I'm so sorry about this. Let's get Alvin settled in an exam room, then you can fill me in on what happened."

To Jana's relief, a noisy and belligerent crackhead was moved out into the hall, and an orderly wheeled Grandpa into the curtained room. A couple of nurses appeared, to take vital signs and start an IV drip. Fortunately, Grandpa was alert enough to answer questions that Jana wasn't able to.

"You're lucky it's not his hip," one of the nurses said to Jana while probing for a vein in Grandpa's skinny, liver-spotted arm. "How'd he fall?"

"One of our neighbors was moving a broken-down Bush Hog off the road after dark. Grandpa saw him about to hit a culvert and got out of the car to yell. The guy didn't see him in time to stop. He—" Jana swallowed tears—"knocked Grandpa down into the ditch."

"Bless your heart, I'm so sorry." The nurse touched Jana's arm in sympathy and went back to work.

Jana hovered as close to the action as possible without getting in the way. The glare of the fluorescent lights and her grandfather's obvious pain unraveled her nerves until she could hardly stand still.

While his father got the situation under control, Grant had found a chair in a corner and sat with his arms folded, watching every move the nurses made. Catching Jana's glance, his expression lightened.

"He'll be fine now," he said, rising. "Come on, they don't need us in here. Let's get something to drink."

Dr. Gonzales looked up from cutting off the leg of Grandpa's pants. "That's a good idea. It'll take awhile to get Alvin stabilized and X-ray the injury. Jana, I might as well tell you, he'll be here at least overnight."

"Oh, goodness." Jana looked at her grandfather's ashen face, gone slack as a result of the painkillers he'd been given. She didn't want to leave him.

"Grant, bring her back in about thirty minutes," said the doctor, staring over the top of his glasses. "I should know by then if he'll have to have surgery."

"Surgery?" Jana echoed as Grant led her into the hall. What was she going to do? Grandpa didn't have anybody but her and Uncle Elvin. Uncle Elvin had the Quick-Stop to run, and she had the responsibility of the kids. She had been through worse things before, but this seemed like such a pointless accident. "Poor Grandpa!" She leaned back against the wall and pressed shaking hands to her face.

"Hey." Grant pulled her against him, wrapping strong arms around her. "We'll help take care of him. Everybody in Vancleave loves your grandpa. My dad's his doctor, after all, and Granny's right across the street from you."

Too tired and worried to protest, she leaned into him and accepted his strength. He smelled like river water, and beard stubble scraped her temple, but it was still nice to be held. She grabbed fistfuls of his T-shirt. "I know, but what about the store? He wouldn't ever hire a manager, and Miss Trini's on vacation, so now there's nobody—"

"Okay, I know it looks tough right now, but don't borrow trouble. Come on, let's go find the Coke machine, and we'll sit down and talk about it."

He released her, and she stepped away.

Lord, I don't mean to be such a baby, but thank you that Grant's here.

They sat down with a couple of root beers in a waiting area just off the emergency room entrance. She began to see why it had taken so long for the staff to get to her grandpa. A parade of paramedics wheeled in victims of car wrecks, gunshots, and fireworks accidents. She closed her eyes and breathed a prayer for all the hurting souls in the room. She'd once been like them.

"Do you have a headache? I can probably scare up an aspirin."

She glanced up at Grant, and the concern in his eyes made her heart flip. Looking away, she watched a nurse question a punk with studs all over his face and tattoos on every visible square inch of skin. "I'm fine. I was just thinking of the night LeeLee was born."

"When Richie left."

It wasn't a question, and she wasn't sure Grant really wanted her to elaborate. She'd never told anyone the details of that night, not even her grandfather.

Jana jumped when she felt calloused fingers brush the back of her hand, then close, gentle and warm, around her wrist. "Where were you?"

"UT Knoxville. I walked into the emergency room all by myself, in labor. But they take ambulance patients first, so I had to wait and wait. I thought I was going to have the baby in the waiting room."

"Oh, man." Grant squeezed her wrist. "Did your grandfather know?"

"I didn't call him. Richie had already abandoned me once, but I'd let him come back." Her face burned with the shame of that stupidity. "His music career had stalled, and he needed a place to stay, so he'd hunted me up. We were living in a trailer on the Andrewses' farm."

"Where you worked, right?"

She nodded. "Andy and Lurlene didn't want me to let Richie stay, but I thought Ty needed his father. By the time I got pregnant again, I could tell Richie wasn't interested in being anybody's daddy. The night LeeLee was born, his band was playing in some honky-tonk. I drove myself to the hospital and never saw him again."

"That *jerk*—" Grant stopped, his hand so hard on her wrist it almost hurt. His lips were clamped together in a grim line.

She gave him a rueful smile. Prom night came back in vivid detail. "You tried to tell me, didn't you? I've had to find out a lot of things the hard way."

"Nobody deserves what you went through!" He released her and folded his arms across his chest.

"I'm not saying I *deserved* it. But I made some bad choices early on. I ran away from home, and Richie and I didn't get married until after Ty was born." She looked at Grant, dreading his disapproval. "And I did those things in spite of all my grandmother's warnings—I resented her harshness, and I wanted to go my own way." She sighed. "Pride. The ultimate sin."

He stared at her, that fierce expression unchanged. "I know why you ran away. I've always regretted not coming in with you that night after the prom." He looked away. "Everybody knows your dad ..."

Jana stopped him with a look. She had hated Aaron Baldwin with a rage too deep for words. "He's in prison where he belongs. But nobody forced me to give up my purity to Richie Cutrere, and nobody made me turn my back on everything I learned in Sunday school as a child."

"Do you blame *yourself* for your father beating you and Richie leaving you?" Grant looked incredulous.

That question stopped her. "I don't think so." She'd have to consider that later. "Blame is a complicated thing, isn't it?"

Grant's eyelids drooped, veiling his expression. "Yeah, I guess it is," he muttered.

A few moments of silence passed as they sipped their drinks, occupied with their own thoughts. The sights and smells of the ER returned to Jana's consciousness, and she was very aware of the quiet man next to her. She couldn't tell if he was angry with her or if he'd simply become bored with the conversation.

She found her flip-flops, which had somehow wandered under her chair, and stood up. "I need to go back and check on Grandpa."

Grant pitched both of their cans into a trash bin. "What are you going to do about Crowbar?"

"What do you mean?"

"A lot of people would sue him."

Jana shook her head. "Grant, it was a horrible accident. Nobody's going to sue anybody." She sighed. "Come on. Let's go see how Grandpa's doing."

After a long, restless weekend spent in her grandfather's hospital room, on Sunday afternoon Jana looked up from her crossword puzzle at a quiet knock on the door.

Carrie Lucas stuck her head inside. "Anybody home?"

"Carrie, come in!" Jana pushed a blanket off the extra chair. She checked to make sure Grandpa was still asleep. They had been inundated by visitors from church, and Carrie had called every day, but this was the first time Jana had seen her new friend. "I'm so glad to see you." She got up to give Carrie a hug.

She felt like bursting into tears. Her emotions seemed to be right on the surface these days. Grant had followed through on his promise to rally his family to her aid. Ty and LeeLee had moved in with Roxanne and seemed to be having the time of their lives.

Carrie returned the embrace, then leaned out into the hall. "Come on in, Tommy. The coast is clear."

Tommy appeared, staggering under an enormous flower arrangement. He set it on the floor beside an already impressive floral array. "My aunt Janelle thinks large equals love."

"Thank you." It was going to take her a week to find room for all these plants, but she wasn't going to complain.

"No problem." After peering at Grandpa, Tommy sat down and propped his feet on the air conditioner vent. He located the TV remote under a pile of newspapers, and ESPN popped up on the screen. "Bye, y'all."

"Consider yourself kidnapped." Carrie gave Jana an impish grin. "We're going for a cup of coffee."

A few minutes later Jana was sitting in the hospital cafeteria, listening to Carrie describe her morning's adventures in second grade Sunday school. Ty had been in her class and had shared a rather inventive explanation for the falling of the walls of Jericho.

Jana laughed aloud for the first time since the accident Friday night. Grandpa was doing better, but surgery on a compound fracture had sapped his strength. His recovery was slower than the orthopedist liked. Jana hoped he'd be moved to a rehab unit tomorrow.

"I'm afraid Ty's read too many comic books," she said with a sigh. "Mr. Andrews, my old boss, has collected them since he was a kid, and Ty used to spend hours in his attic reading."

"He's a great kid, Jana." Carrie's brown eyes were warm. "I'm sorry your grandpa got hurt, but Granny and I are having a ball keeping Ty and LeeLee. In fact, you may have to arm-wrestle Granny to get them back when this is all over!"

"Thanks." The compliment washed over Jana like balm. "That's one prayer the Lord answered in spades. I dreaded the thought of Ty growing up without a male role model, and Mr. Andrews was such a godly example. In fact, he and his wife are the reason I came to Christ."

Carrie leaned forward. "I'd like to hear about them."

Jana hesitated. "How much has Grant told you?"

"Nothing at all." Carrie tilted her head. "How much did you tell him?"

"Probably more than I should have. We were in the ER together for a long time." Jana hid her face behind her cup.

"After being on the houseboat all day. How did that go? Did you get a chance to ask him what's bugging him?"

Jana shook her head. How could she explain the strong connection and total polarization that coexisted between her and Grant? "We sort of had an argument—well, a discussion, I guess you'd call it—about his hunting trophies."

Carrie winced. "Uh-oh."

"Carrie, how do you deal with that? Doesn't it bother you at all?"

"I try not to think about it. Tommy hunts too, though he doesn't go as often now that we're married. He knows I don't like it, so he keeps his deer head in his office at the garage."

Jana shuddered.

"Can you not get past that?" Carrie's smooth brow wrinkled. "I know Grant's my brother, but he's a good guy, Jana. Some girl in Atlanta hurt him, and he's steered clear of dating for a while, but ..." She stopped because Jana had closed her eyes. "What did I say?"

Jana put her hand over her eyes. "It's not just the hunting, Carrie. It's what I started to tell you about my past. I messed up in just about every way you could mess up before I met the Lord. You know what a disaster my family is. When I met Andy and Lurlene Andrews, I was living in a roach motel with Ty. I used to take him to the Salvation Army to get a meal once in a while, and their church was helping out there one day." She took a shaky breath, because she didn't like to remember those days.

"Oh, Jana ..." Carrie set her cup down and laid her hand on Jana's.

"Can you believe they took me home with them?" Jana looked up and smiled at the tears welling in Carrie's eyes. "They let me work on their farm, and when they found out I wanted to go to college, they helped me apply for grants and loans. Lurlene kept Ty while I was in class. They didn't have any kids, and she said she'd always wanted a grandson." She took a breath. "It took a long time, but eventually I went to church with them and accepted Christ as my Savior. I tell you, if you ever want to see a picture of grace, just look at me."

"That's a beautiful testimony, Jana. It's nothing to be ashamed of." Carrie wiped tears from her cheeks.

Jana looked away. "Your brother doesn't think so."

"What do you mean? Grant would never judge you—"

"He didn't, not in so many words. Except for calling Richie a jerk, he was pretty quiet when I told him some of this. But he knows what I was like in high school. In fact, he was there the night—" Jana jerked to a halt. How much sludge could you dump on one person all at once?

"What? What happened?"

"Our senior prom. Your sister, Miranda, had a friend who needed a date, so she'd talked Grant into coming, even though he was already in college."

"Oh yeah. I sorta remember hearing about that. In fact, Tommy's mentioned it too."

"It was an event, all right." Jana pressed her lips together. "Grant asked me to dance. Richie, being Richie, got jealous and started a fight. Well, Grant punches his lights out, but Richie's the one who gets hauled off to jail because he's high."

"Oh, Jana."

"So there I am in my prom dress and heels without a ride home. I take off down the highway in the dark, but before I get very far, Grant drives up beside me and makes me get in."

"That sounds like him."

"Well, he wasn't very nice about it." Jana hunched her shoulders. "He lectured me all the way home about the kind of guy I was dating and the dress I was wearing, and how I shouldn't walk around alone after dark—like it wasn't *his* fault I was by myself in the first place!"

Wide-eyed, Carrie clenched her fists against her face. "He never told me all this."

"I'm not sure he even remembers it. He took one look at where I lived, let me out, and hit reverse."

Carrie winced. "That had to have hurt."

"I was humiliated. My self-esteem was at an all-time low already, and that scene was the nudge it took to send me off the deep end. I took off with Richie a month later."

"How old was Grant at the time? About twenty?"

Jana lifted her shoulders. "I guess. And you know, I don't blame him. I was one big mess at the time, and I knew your family was well-off and prominent in the church. Grant was away at college and had no reason to care what happened to me. Listen, Carrie, I don't mean to make your brother sound like a villain. He's been nothing but a prince to me since I came home, and I've grown up enough to know that people change. It's just complicated ... and you can see why I'd have a hard time believing he'd ever want a serious relationship with me." Jana gave Carrie a straight look. "And I'm not settling for anything else."

A welcome blast of air-conditioning chilled Grant's damp clothes as he walked into the Farm and Feed on Friday. He removed his cap and wiped his face with the bottom of his T-shirt. The temperature outside was up around the hundred-degree mark, and he'd been disking food plots all morning under intermittent rain showers. He'd only stopped because he needed a part for the cultivator.

That, and he was hoping Jana would stop and have lunch with him.

She sat behind the counter, chin propped on the heel of her hand as she stared at the computer screen. At her elbow were a legal pad, a calculator, and a checkbook.

What on earth had brought on that gloomy expression? Maybe old Alvin had had a relapse. He looked around and didn't see the children, but he could hear LeeLee's voice from the storeroom, singing the countries of Eastern Europe song. She had informed him the day of the houseboat swim that she could sing the countries of South and Central America as well. Which was more than he could do.

Jana didn't look up until Grant dropped his folded arms onto the counter right in front of her. "What's up, lady? Creditors at your door?"

She gave him a vague smile. "Oh, hey, Grant."

He peered at her. There were smudges of mascara around her eyes. "Is your grandpa giving you a hard time? Granny says since he's been in rehab he's been like a caged bear."

"Grandpa's a bit surly, but he's getting up and around." She flicked off the computer screen and picked up her coffee mug. "I just called to make sure he ate his lunch, and he was complaining about the watery banana pudding. I'm taking that as a good sign."

Okay, if she wasn't going to tell him what was bothering her, blunt tactics were in order. "Well, something's the matter. Are you not sleeping?"

"I'm fine." She squirmed on her grandfather's stool, watched the pencil tap against the legal pad, then looked up at him with eyes as cloudy as the sky outside. "Grant, if I tell you something, will you keep it to yourself?"

He crossed his heart and formed a Boy Scout salute. "Behold me — mum as an ice chest full of oysters. May I die a slow, hideous death at the hands of the Women's Missionary Union if so much as a syllable crosses my lips. Your secret is safe — "

"All right, all right." Jana's expression relaxed in laughter. "The thing is, all Grandpa's therapy is expensive, and his insurance isn't that great." She glanced at the computer. "From what I can tell, it's not doing as well as he likes to pretend. I think that's why he's considering selling you that property."

"Well, you know, that could be a good thing for all parties."

Jana sighed. "He's so proud of this computer, but it looks to me like he doesn't understand how it works, because his books are a mess. Grandpa used to be a wonderful businessman, but he's stuck in the twentieth century. I can't even tell who he owes money to."

"Have you asked him about it?"

"Of course I have. But he tells me not to worry, he'll straighten it out when he gets back on his feet."

Grant studied her troubled face. "But you're worried about what will happen when you start your practice and can't keep an eye on him."

"Yeah." Rubbing her eyes, she leaned back against the file cabinet. More mascara smeared. "I don't know what to do."

Grant found himself repeating a proverb he'd learned as a teen. "Granny always says for waging war you need guidance, and for victory many advisers."

Jana looked alarmed. "I'm not going to blab Grandpa's business all over the place. Remember, you promised—"

"Don't worry, I'm not risking the wrath of the WMU. But maybe I could get CJ and Tommy—and my sisters and parents and Granny—to pray for an unspoken request. Would that be okay? And you and I could pray about it together too."

She blinked. "You mean right now?"

"Well, sure, why not?" He looked around the store, miraculously empty for a Friday afternoon, and turned his palms up on the counter. "Come here."

Jana leaned forward to place both of her hands in his, and he got the full effect of the texture of her fingers for the first time. Warm, small, dainty, they curled into his palms, and he felt something just as unfamiliar curling into his heart.

He cleared his throat, closing his eyes with the desperate hope that he was capable of making sense. "Lord, we come to you with

Jana's problem. We pray you'll heal Alvin quickly, convince him to get some help with his finances, and give Jana wisdom to deal with him. Please remind her that when she seeks your will, you'll lead her a step at a time." He looked up. "Amen."

"Amen." Jana smiled and opened her eyes. "It's gonna be okay, I think."

He sure hoped so. He didn't want responsibility for Jana's faith on his shoulders.

chapter 10

"'m not settling for some half-baked camp with no lodge, no road in, and no cook," Doug Briscoe said early on Saturday morning, his tone so vehement that Grant had to hold the cell phone away from his ear. "You're making me nervous, man."

Grant stared at the deer head on the wall, wishing he could throw the phone, and Doug with it, overboard. His dream was turning into a nightmare of strong-willed personalities. He'd tried to explain that Alvin Goff, now in rehab, wasn't in any shape to be signing contracts.

Now Doug was threatening to influence the other two investors to look elsewhere.

"Look, Doug." Grant tried to sound reasonable, even while his stomach churned. "We can hunt on my land without a lodge. Y'all can camp in tents or stay on my houseboat. There's never been any problem crossing Alvin's land. And I have the best cook in the county lined up."

"Oh yeah?" Doug sounded skeptical. "And who would that be?"

"My sister Carrie." Grant didn't know why he hadn't thought of it sooner. Carrie would be glad for the business. He'd go see her today, right now. "Listen, I've got to go. As soon as old man Goff gets up and around, we'll get this thing inked. Hang in there with me, okay?"

"I'm telling you, man, if you don't give us what you promised, the deal's off." Doug let out an indecipherable growl and hung up.

Grant clipped the phone onto his belt and stood up to look out the window. In typical dog-days fashion, it had been raining for over a week. A streak of lightning slashed across the sky, thunder rocking the boat. It had better quit soon if he was going to finish disking the food plots for planting.

Instead of wasting time worrying about the camp and wondering what Jana was doing, he might as well slog on over to Carrie's and put his proposition to her. That way he could accomplish *something* positive.

A few minutes later he parked in the Lucases' driveway behind Carrie's catering van. Not bothering with an umbrella, he ducked across to the back door and knocked.

A faint burst of feminine laughter came from inside. Oh brother, that sounded like Granny's robust belly laugh and his mother's chuckle. He'd been avoiding the inevitable inquisition ever since the Fourth of July.

Too late. Carrie opened the door, surprise and welcome in her dark brown eyes. "Grant! What are you doing here so early?"

"I didn't know you had company."

"It's okay." Carrie opened the door wide. "It's just Mom and Granny. We're putting up corn."

Grant hesitated. "I don't know. I'd better go."

Carrie's smile faded as she searched his face. "Grant, what's the matter?" She pulled him out of the rain into the small vestibule.

He ruffled his damp hair. "Nothing. I was just hungry."

Carrie's eyes twinkled. "Now that I believe. Did you need to talk to me about something? You know I won't tell anybody." She sent a quick glance toward the kitchen.

He chuckled. "I know you won't. Did, uh—" he cleared his throat—"have you talked to Jana since Mr. Alvin's accident?"

"A couple of times. Why?"

He lowered his voice. "Listen, Carrie, you're a girl, right?"

She laughed. "Last time I checked."

"Okay. Well, I need Jana to help me talk her grandfather into selling me that property of his—you know what I mean?"

Carrie just squinted at him. "Grant—"

"So I just wondered if you thought I had any chance of, you know, going through her to Mr. Alvin, because I'm running out of time—"

"Grant!" Carrie frowned. Not a good sign. "As much I love you, I'm not going to let you use Jana!"

"What are you talking about?" His sister was obviously not in the mood to listen to his other proposition about cooking for the camp. "Never mind, the rain's letting up, and I've got to finish disking—"

"Oh no, you don't." She grabbed his sleeve. "Jana is very fragile right now, and her feelings for you are ..." She huffed. "I can't believe you'd manipulate a woman's feelings just for some piece of property."

"I'm not manipulating anybody!" Apparently he had miscalculated Carrie's sympathy for him. "Besides, that's not just any property; it's the entrance to my camp. In case you haven't noticed, there's only two and a half months to go before hunting season opens."

"Maybe you should have thought of that before you bought the rest."

He stared at her. She looked like she did the time she'd had mono and had to drop out of college for a semester. "What's the matter with you? Did you and Tommy have a fight?"

The pallor vanished as her cheeks flamed. "It's impossible to fight with Tommy, and you know it." She bit her lip and tugged on his sleeve again. "I'm sorry, Grant, I shouldn't bark at you, even when you're being an idiot. Come on in; I have to tell you something."

An idiot? He followed her into the kitchen, where a strong vegetable odor attacked his nose. His mother stood at a butcher-block island, shucking corn and throwing the husks into a big black garbage can. She looked up and smiled at him, the corn silk on her dark blue shirt looking like angel hair.

"Look what the cat drug up!" His grandmother, wearing a ruffled pink gingham apron, came over to hug him. "But you're out of luck, boyo—we don't have anything to eat except two bushels of raw corn."

"It's okay, I'm not hungry anymore." Grant looked at his sister. "So what's your big news?"

To his relief, focus shifted to Carrie. Mom put down her knife, and Granny, who had been squinting at the corn through the microwave door, looked over her shoulder. Carrie dropped a box of gallon Ziploc bags onto the counter. Its sound echoed over the hum of the microwave in the suddenly quiet kitchen.

"I was waiting until I could tell you all at once." To Grant's utter astonishment, Carrie began to cry. "Tommy and I are going to have a baby!"

Deafened by screaming, Grant backed into a corner. All three women gathered in a sobbing knot, hugging one another as if somebody had died.

After three minutes or so, Granny pulled away to fish a Kleenex out of her apron pocket and caught his eye. She flung herself at him, dragging his shoulders down for a hug.

Bewildered, he hugged her back. "Is this not a good thing?"

"Of course it's a good thing!" Granny blew her nose.

"Then why is everybody crying?"

She gave a hiccupping chuckle. "You are such a man. Give your sister a hug."

Grant eyed Carrie as if she might go into labor at any moment. Her face was red as a tomato, and her nose was running. Reminded him of the time he'd thrown her Barbie on top of the roof and Dad wouldn't let him go after it. When their sister, Miranda, got pregnant with Ethan, everybody had acted exactly like this. Insane.

He rotated his neck, then walked over to Carrie and put an arm around her. "I'm happy for you, sis."

She wrapped her arms around his waist and squeezed. "Thanks. I just found out yesterday. I shouldn't have said anything this soon, but I need you to pray for me. I feel icky, and I'm so scared I'm going to—" she gulped. "What if I miscarry? That would be worse than not getting pregnant at all."

"Don't say that." He tightened his hold on her. "I'll pray for you. I *thought* you looked kind of ill."

She shoved away from him and whacked him on the chest. "Thanks a lot!"

Wiping her eyes, his mother laughed. "How did you tell Tommy, honey? What did he say?"

"He went berserk. I'd fixed him a steak dinner ... the whole romantic nine yards. Now he keeps looking at my stomach and talking to it."

"I just saw him yesterday when we had our Bible study. He didn't say a word." Grant shook his head. "Had no idea he was capable of keeping a secret."

"I threatened him on pain of no divinity for a month."

"You are a hard, cold woman. So ... when is this little yard monkey due?"

Carrie sighed. "I have a long way to go. Not until next spring. April, best I can figure."

Grant did some mental calculations. "Then you'd be able to cook for me this winter."

"Cook for you? Grant, I have a business to run."

"I didn't mean for me personally. For my hunters."

She frowned. "You said you were having trouble getting the rest of the land from Mr. Alvin."

He waved his hand. "Oh, that'll work out. So what do you think about taking me on as a client? I can pay well. Hunters like to eat."

Granny, who was at the sink washing her hands, looked over her shoulder. "You're that close to opening the camp? Good for you!"

Carrie put her hands on her slim hips. "He's been pestering poor old Mr. Alvin, even while he was in the hospital."

"I have not!" Harassed, Grant backed toward the doorway. "Jeesh, pregnant women are cranky. Never mind, I'll ask you again when I get closer to an official opening. You better hope I don't take my business elsewhere." He kissed his mom on the cheek and squeezed Granny's shoulders. "See y'all at church in the morning."

Monday morning Jana pushed open the front door of the Vancleave Quick-Stop and looked around for her great-uncle Elvin. Grandpa's twin could usually be found perched on a stool behind the counter, reading the newspaper or checking inventory.

"Uncle Elvin?" She banged the bell beside the cash register a couple of times.

After dropping Ty and LeeLee off at Roxanne's, she'd stopped on her way to the Farm and Feed to fill up her gas tank and buy a cup of coffee. Uncle Elvin ran the store much like the battleship he'd commanded during the Vietnam War. Immaculate and orderly, it was stocked with essentials like toilet paper, diapers, and soft drinks—and to LeeLee's delight, the candy aisle would have put Willy Wonka to shame.

Jana hit the bell again. "Uncle Elvin, where are you?"

"Be right there—hold your horses!" A Xerox copy of Grandpa appeared in the doorway leading to the cooler. The only physical difference between the brothers was the style of their eyeglasses—Grandpa preferred round frames, and Uncle Elvin leaned toward horn rim.

"Hi, Uncle Elvin. Just wondered if you had a pot of coffee going this morning."

He grinned. "Well, if it ain't the lady pet doc. You're out mighty early."

"Yes, sir. Grandpa's still in the rehab hospital. Somebody has to open up the store until Trini gets back."

He took off his glasses and stuck one of the earpieces in his mouth. "Just brewed a pot of coffee. You want leaded or unleaded?"

"Hit me with the real thing." Smiling, she walked over to the coffee station in the middle of the store. "Got a long day ahead of me."

Uncle Elvin started wiping down a spotless countertop near the Icee machine. "How's my big brother doing?" Grandpa was all of fifteen minutes older than Uncle Elvin.

"Well enough to complain about the food service."

"Alvin's always got a bee up his butt about something." Uncle Elvin stooped to fish in a cabinet under the coffeemaker. "Got some Irish cream stuff around here somewheres if you want it."

"No, thanks. I take it black. Remnant of vet school all-nighters."

Uncle Elvin peered up at her. "Didn't never tell you how proud I am you finished and come home. You ain't been in here much. Figured you was pretty busy."

"Yes, sir." Plus she was still fighting some lingering resentment that her great-uncle had overlooked her and Quinn's need when they were small. Grandpa had been overruled by a domineering wife, but bachelor Uncle Elvin had no such excuse. Maybe ostriches ran in the family. She shook it off. Forgiveness had to run in a lot of directions. "Running the store and taking care of Grandpa and the kids are about all I can handle now."

"I'll have to go by and see the old buzzard this afternoon. Who checks on him while you're minding the store?"

"Miss Roxanne. She ignores Grandpa's grouching, and she's an angel with LeeLee and Ty."

Uncle Elvin's pale gray eyes twinkled behind his glasses. "Roxanne's raised enough children and grandchildren and foster kids, she could solve the problems in the Middle East if the state department would turn her loose." Shoving to his feet with a groan, he crammed a handful of creamer packets into the plastic bucket on the counter. "The coffee's on me. Just don't tell nobody, or I'll have freeloaders in here by the truckload." He winked.

"Thanks, Uncle Elvin." Jana stood on tiptoe to kiss his cheek. "You should go see Grandpa later. He's been asking about you."

Blushing, he scratched his nose. "Us old war eagles ain't much on spilling our guts, you know."

She grinned at the scrambled metaphor. "I'm sure he doesn't expect you to bleed all over him. Just go play a round of checkers and let him win." She sealed the lid of her Styrofoam cup. "Thanks for the coffee. I'll see you later."

"Sure thing, baby. Stop in every mornin' if you want to."

Feeling much lighter of spirit, Jana got in her car and headed for the Farm and Feed. Maybe it was just going to take time to straighten out all the kinked-up relationships she'd left behind when she and Richie traipsed off into idiocy. That didn't mean she had to give up.

Later that morning she was restocking the seed bin when the cowbell on the door jangled and Heath sauntered in.

"Hey, beautiful! How's the fertilizer business these days?"

She stood up. "We're full of it, if you'll pardon the expression."

He grinned. "Maybe you're ready to come to work at a real job now."

"A real job?" She eyed his blue scrub pants and parrot-patterned yellow shirt. A John Deere cap covered his shoulder-length dark blond hair. "You mean with dignified, highly qualified professionals who keep regular office hours?"

"I'm highly qualified. One out of three ain't bad." He leaned on the counter. "I was out at Rollie Jefferson's place—his llama came down with thrush this weekend—and I thought I'd stop by and ask how Mr. Alvin's doing."

"Well as can be expected." She frowned. "What's Rollie doing with a llama?"

"It guards his cows."

"A guard llama." She laughed. "I've never seen one. Can I come with you next time and take a look?"

"We'll go back out there right now if you want to."

"Heath, I know you find this hard to accept, but I'm working. I can't just leave the store unattended."

"Why not?" He looked puzzled.

"Because ... because I said so." She smiled to keep from sounding like Mrs. Dipiscopo, their freshman English teacher. "I looked for you at church yesterday. Where were you?"

"Overslept." He didn't elaborate, and she wondered if he'd been up late partying the night before. By all accounts, he led an active social life. "Which reminds me. How's our tailless squirrel making out? Last time I saw him he was out like a light."

"Rocky's eating and getting around just fine. But pretty soon he's going to need a bigger cage so he can exercise and get strong enough to run from predators. I need an aviary."

"Have you done any work on your grant?"

She hesitated. "I got an email from the Wildlife Commission yesterday. They're sending a rep this fall to inspect my property and review my plans for the center."

Heath's eyebrows rose. "Your property?"

"Oh, I guess technically it's not mine yet. Grandpa thinks I'm crazy. And don't you chime in with him," she added when he opened his mouth. "There are plenty of people at the Commission who think this is a worthwhile project."

"I'm sure it is. You know ..." He tugged one side of his mustache. "If you demonstrated good faith to your grandpa, say started working in my clinic, he might be a little more open to listening to you about the rehab center."

Jana folded her arms. "Heath Redmond, what is your stake in this? Why are you so dead-set on getting me to come in with you?"

He leaned closer so that his handsome Roman nose almost touched hers. "Because I said so." He grinned. "I like you, Jana. You're smart—if anybody knows what kind of brains it takes to get through vet school, I do. You've got experience that makes you an interesting lady to talk to, and you're doggone easy on the eyes." His lids closed a bit, reminding Jana of the way Grant had been looking at her the night Grandpa got hurt. It was the look of a man who wanted to kiss somebody.

She jerked backward. "Well! Thank you for the endorsement, but I've got to get back to work." She walked behind the counter and jabbed a finger at the computer keyboard to open the screen. "Next time you poke around on the llama, let me know ahead of time, and I'll make arrangements to go with you."

Heath straightened his lanky frame and gave her a hooded look. "Okay. If you need a hand around here, give me a holler."

Jana wiggled her fingers, pretending to be engrossed in the computer. To her relief Heath disappeared with a clank of the cowbell like some countrified genie. He'd presented her with three wishes, but it looked like they came with some serious strings attached.

Grant took his trombone out of its case and oiled the slide. Giving it an experimental gliss, he looked around the small room where the orchestra spent a couple of hours rehearsing every Wednesday night. On Sunday mornings it functioned as an adult Sunday school room, but tonight it was crammed with music stands, instrument cases, a drum set, and an electronic piano.

As usual he was the first one here. He liked to be early. That way he could pick out the best seat near the window and snag the only stand that didn't list like a mast in a high wind. Put his music in alphabetical order.

Actually, it never got out of alphabetical order. But he always checked anyway.

By the time he'd been through it all twice and moved "Great Is the Lord" behind "Grace Greater Than All Our Sin"—somebody had been messing around with his folder—Heath Redmond was barging in with his saxophone case bumping against his leg.

"Gonzo!" Redmond dumped the case into an empty chair in the woodwind section. "I was hoping you'd be here early."

"Why?" When Redmond missed last week's rehearsal as well as the Sunday service, Grant had breathed a sigh of relief. Dealing with his old nemesis on a twice-weekly basis would be a strain on his Christianity.

"Because I wanted to ask you something." Redmond snapped open the case and took out his instrument. It looked as if it had been dunked in battery acid.

"What have you done to that horn?" Grant kept his own instrument in perfect condition. Anytime it got a ding, he took it to the shop in Mobile for repair.

Redmond shrugged. "It was in my mother's attic for ten years. Guess there was a little humidity up there. Anyway—" he jammed the neck joint and mouthpiece on— "I offered Jana a job again, and she turned me down. Why do you think she's so all-fired set on this stupid wildlife rehab center idea?"

"You didn't tell her Alvin's thinking about giving her that property she wants, did you?"

"I'm not an idiot, Gonzales. She'll find out soon enough if he goes through with it." He pulled out a box of reeds and inspected them with a frown. "Ugh. Need a trip to the music store before Sunday. I'm gonna squawk."

"Joy Chapman always has extra reeds."

The pastor's wife, a former high school band director who functioned as the orchestra director, entered the room and stopped when she heard her name. "Oh, hello, Heath! Glad you decided to come back." She smiled at Redmond. Another female snowed by dimples and long hair. "Let me set these charts down and I'll find you a reed."

While Joy got herself organized, Grant set his trombone on its stand and crossed the room to sit down beside Redmond. He folded his arms. "Let me tell you something," he said quietly, "and I want you to hear me good. It would be to my advantage if Jana went into practice with you so she'd forget about that property. And I think it would be the best thing for her, careerwise. But Jana isn't some bar-hopping little groupie anymore. She's a godly lady with huge responsibilities. If you take advantage of her in any way—" he glowered—"in *any* way, I'll take you apart piece by piece and forget how you were put together."

Redmond stared at him for a moment. "Well, aren't you the flaming Sir Lancelot? Gonzales, I do believe that's the longest speech I've ever heard you make, including your salutatorian address." He shook his head and hooked his neck strap to his saxophone. "I have a lot of respect for Jana. This is a business arrangement, no matter what you think, so just get your butt off your high horse. She respects your opinion, and I thought you might have some influence."

Flummoxed, Grant sat there for a minute while Redmond warmed up his instrument. "I haven't even seen her since Mr. Alvin went into the hospital. What makes you think—"

"Come on, Gonzo. She's not giving me the time of day." Heath returned Grant's look thoughtfully. "Although you might as well know I'm not giving up unless you put a ring on her finger. And even then—" he grinned—"well, let's just say you better protect your interests."

chapter 11

Jana yawned as Carrie wound up the ladies' Bible study with prayer. She'd been up since five that morning, and she'd had a busy day at the store. After putting herself through college and vet school, she ought to be used to long hours. But being responsible for Grandpa's business was taking its toll. She'd asked the other women to pray for her—the only thing giving her strength to go back to the store tomorrow.

That and the fact that the end was in sight. This morning the orthopedist had said Grandpa's prognosis looked good, and he was set to come home on Friday, the same day Trini was due back from Cozumel.

After she collected Ty and LeeLee from choir, she had to go home and wash a mountain of dirty clothes, then write a few dozen emails asking for donations for the wildlife center.

She jumped and opened her eyes when Carrie cleared her throat. How long had the prayer been over? She'd almost fallen asleep!

Thank goodness the attention of the other five women in the room was focused on Carrie. "Don't forget to pray for me and the baby this week," Carrie said, blushing like a rose. "The mornings are pretty yucky right now, especially having to work with food all the time."

The meeting broke up with expressions of sympathy and promises of prayer for the new mama.

Jana gave Carrie a joyful hug. "You know I'll be praying. I'm so excited for you and Tommy."

"Can I talk to you for just a second? I'll go with you to pick up the children."

Jana blinked. "Sure. Come on." They walked down the hall toward the children's area. The old-fashioned prints Jana remembered from her childhood had been replaced by cartoonlike wall murals of Noah's ark, Jonah and the whale, and other Bible stories. The effect was bright, energetic, and fun. She glanced at Carrie. "Is something the matter? Besides the baby, I mean? Have my kids destroyed something at Miss Roxanne's house?"

"Of course not. Besides, they play outside almost all day. Granny keeps 'em busy out in the washhouse and the pecan orchard and the garden. No, it's ..." Carrie bit her lip. "Do you remember when we talked about Grant when we were at the hospital?"

"I remember." Jana looked around. The sounds of the orchestra rehearsal upstairs had ceased. They'd be coming down the stairs any moment.

Carrie seemed to realize that. She spoke in a low, hurried tone. "Well, at the risk of being a junior high–level busybody—and you can tell me to back off, mind my own business, and I will ..." She paused, knotting her fingers. "Oh, this is ridiculous! Never mind. You two are adults. I'm staying out of this."

Jana clutched her Bible to her chest. "What are you talking about, Carrie? You can't leave me hanging now!"

"It must be hereditary." Carrie shook her head. "Granny poked her nose into Miranda's love life and mine. I'm amazed she's staying out of Grant's. But here I go, stomping in where angels fear to tread." She took a deep breath. "Grant asked me to be his cook. You know, for the hunting camp. And he wants me to use my influence to get you to talk to your grandpa about the property."

"Is that right?" Anger and hurt slamming into her, Jana leaned back against the wall. The door to the children's choir room opened, and noisy laughter poured into the hallway. She didn't have the time or the energy to deal with Grant Gonzales's machinations.

"I'm sure that's not the only reason he's interested in you. I just wanted you to understand how much this thing means to him, and to be careful about letting him talk you into something you don't want to do. He can be very persistent."

"Mommy! We're gonna sing in big church!" LeeLee dodged through a gang of bigger kids and threw herself against Jana's legs, jerking her out of contemplating an autopsy on one single-minded bow hunter.

"That's great, sweetie. We'll have to get you a new dress."

"No! We're wearing costumes, and I get to be a cow. Ty's gonna be God!"

Ty slouched up, shoulders hunched and freckled face downcast. "I wanted to be a cow too."

Carrie ruffled his hair. "Sometimes you have to take an undesirable role to advance your career."

Distracted, Jana took LeeLee's hand. "I'll ... I'll think about what you said, Carrie. Pray for me."

"You know I will."

Carrie waved at the children as Jana turned and hurried them toward the parking lot. At least she'd avoided an immediate confrontation with both Grant and Heath tonight. She didn't think she could have taken one more thing.

Lord, why does this hurt so much? I told you I didn't want to resurrect any feelings for that jerk.

She made sure the children were buckled in, then, swiping a tear off her cheek, started the car—and jumped a foot when somebody tapped on the window.

When she saw who it was, she considered rolling over his big feet. She put the window down. "Grant, what are you doing?"

He leaned down, hands on his knees. "I looked for you after orchestra let out, but I missed you somehow. Are you going home?"

"Where else would I be going at this time of night?" She was in no mood to be chatty.

He frowned. "Are you in a hurry?"

"I need to get the kids in bed, and I have a pile of laundry to do."

"Okay, how about if I come over and give you a hand? Lightning fried my TV antenna, so I'm kind of at loose ends."

"Mr. Uncle Grant!" LeeLee bounced in her booster seat. "You gotta come see Rocky!"

Jana stared at Grant. At eight o'clock there was still enough milky summertime light to see hope and something like affection in the warm brown eyes. It was undoubtedly a big fat act. She pursed her lips. "No. I have too much to do tonight, and I have to get up at the crack of dawn."

She rolled the window back up before she could change her mind and backed out of the parking lot. Turning a deaf ear to LeeLee's unexpected whining, she drove past Grant's big truck and wondered how long it would take her to get over this sickening sense of betrayal.

Grant knocked on Alvin's screen door, then waited, shifting from one foot to the other, hands in pockets. There was no good reason for Jana's refusal to let him come over. He didn't buy the "too busy" excuse. Oh, he didn't doubt she had plenty to do before bedtime—but there had been something weird about the way she'd said it.

The sheer curtain over the window in the door twitched aside, and Jana's nose pressed against the glass. Her eyes widened as she jerked backward. For a minute he thought she was going to leave him standing there in the dark. Then the door opened. Reluctantly.

"What are you doing here?" She frowned. "Do you know what time it is?"

He shrugged. "Around ten, I think. I wanted to give you time to put the kids in bed." He looked over her shoulder into the living room, where the TV flickered in the otherwise dark room. "Can I come in?"

She bit her lip, closed her eyes. He thought she was going to kick him off the porch, but after a moment she sighed and the screen door screeched open. "You can't come in—Grandpa's not here—but I'll come out."

He supposed this made sense, given the nature of small-town busybodies who loved to stir up scandal where none existed. Alvin and Jana's closest neighbor was Granny, who lived across the road. She wouldn't say a word to anybody about his being here, even if she noticed. But she *would* give Grant her standard gold-star lecture about "appearances of evil." And its follow-up about a man's responsibility to protect a lady's reputation.

Besides, anybody driving by could see his truck sitting in the driveway after dark, with Alvin still in the rehab joint and nobody to chaperone except two sleeping children, an old shepherd dog, a kitten, and a gimpy squirrel. Not that he had plans to do anything about this wild attraction to Jana Cutrere that was doggone near driving him crazy. At least nothing physical.

Cool your jets, Gonzales, he told himself as she dropped into the rocker beside him without saying a word. She smelled like bubble gum toothpaste and something else he couldn't define. Something so feminine he wanted to press his face into her neck and just breathe.

He propped his foot on the porch rail and looked at her. She'd left the light off to keep the mosquitoes from eating them alive, but his eyes had adjusted to the darkness. She had on the same white calf-length pants and flowered shirt she'd worn earlier, but she'd clipped her hair away from her face with some kind of jeweled barrette. She looked about fifteen years old.

"Everybody settled in for the night?"

"Yep." Her tone was weary. "They're both asleep, worn slap out. Your granny keeps them busy. I don't know what I'd have done without her."

"I could come by tomorrow. Take 'em swimming again."

She hesitated. "Can you watch them both by yourself?"

"Sure. If it'll make you feel better, I'll take 'em to Cedar Creek where there's no current."

"Okay. They'll be thrilled. If you're not too busy. What have you been doing lately?"

"Disking. Clearing out brush. You?"

"Running the store."

Silence fell, full of crickets chirring and the occasional car passing on the road. The animals out in the barn were still, having retired for the night. He could see the dark forms of a couple of the goats lying on top of their little goat motel.

Folding her arms, Jana laid her head back against the rocker. She evidently had nothing else to say.

He wasn't much of a talker in the best of circumstances; her mood bewildered him. Heath had led him to believe ...

He knew better than to trust anything Heath wanted him to believe.

"What's the matter, Jana?"

"Nothing."

Translation—who the heck knew *what* the translation was? Grant claimed no special understanding of the female psyche.

"Come on," he said. "You're acting kind of weird. Does it have something to do with Heath renewing his job offer?"

"How'd you know about that?"

"He told me. How come you turned it down?"

"I didn't say no. I'm just not ready to give him an answer."

"You'd be smart to take it." The words scalded his throat, but what else was he supposed to say?

"You told me not to trust him." Her voice sounded odd.

"Hey, look at me." He put his feet down and took her hand, lying on the arm of the rocker. Her dainty fingers were stiff. "What's going on?"

She tried to pull away. "Why would you encourage me to work for somebody you don't trust? Believe me, I see Heath for exactly who he is. And you too."

"What are you talking about?" He reached for her other hand. "Jana, please look at me."

"No." She sniffed. "Let go of me."

Shoot, was she crying? "Not 'til you tell me what I've done to upset you."

"You asked Carrie to be your cook. And you want me to talk Grandpa into selling you his property for that hideous hunting camp."

Carrie—that little snitch. "You knew I wanted it all along."

"Of course I did. But I didn't know you were using me to get it."

Even he, blockhead that he was, heard the hurt in her voice. The partial truth of her assumption sent guilt ripping through his chest and hardened his tone more than he intended. "Did Redmond tell you that? And you believed him?"

"No, he didn't tell me that. But he didn't have to. I'm not stupid. Why else are you being so nice to the little wacko widow and her two kids?"

"How about because I'm a nice person? How about because you have two awesome kids who make me want to be a better man? How about because I can't sleep for thinking about you?"

She gasped. For half a second her fingers gripped his. Then she jerked away and jumped to her feet, putting her hands behind her back. "I've got to go inside. LeeLee gets scared if she wakes up and I'm not there."

"Jana." He rose and shifted from foot to foot. "I didn't mean—"

"I know you didn't mean it. Don't think a thing about it. I'm sorry I got snarky; I'm just tired. Really tired." She edged toward the door. "I've got to go in."

"Hey." He put his hands on her shoulders. Swallowed, because that elusive scent made his eyes close in longing, and the way she jumped when he touched her made him want to punch Heath Redmond. "Settle down, I only want to …" He wished she'd look at him. *Oh, God, help me out here.* He was drowning in the desire to forget useless words and kiss her until she understood him. As if that would help things. "I meant what I said. I like your kids, and it's no chore to spend time with them. I just don't want you to think it has anything to do with your grandpa's property." For right now he was going to pretend he hadn't just laid his heart out on a platter for her to toss out with the other leftovers.

She sighed and rubbed her forehead. "Okay, Grant. I don't know what to believe, but my head hurts too much to argue about it anymore. You can come get the kids tomorrow and take them swimming. I trust you with them."

That was something, at least. He squeezed her shoulders gently and let her go. "Good. When you drop them off at Granny's in the morning, tell her I'll be by around ten. And ask her to pack a lunch for us, if you would. She's got fresh tomatoes and—" Good gracious, he was babbling like a hormone-riddled fourteen-year-old. "Never mind. I'll call her."

She gave a rusty little laugh and stepped out from under his hands. "Good night, Grant. I'll talk to you tomorrow."

He watched her disappear inside the house, the screen door slapping softly shut.

Well. Wasn't that a fine howdy-do.

Jana leaned against the door, listening for the sound of Grant's truck driving away. She closed her eyes.

"I can't sleep for thinking about you."

Her heart thumped hard as the words played over and over in her brain like a CD with a scratch.

"I can't sleep. I can't sleep."

She wouldn't be able to sleep either.

What did he mean? Lust was a concept she was all too familiar with. She wanted no part of a physical relationship without the emotional commitment of marriage. And marriage was something else she wouldn't risk. True, she'd seen Andy and Lurlene make a go of it. Okay, she knew lots of happily married couples—look at Tommy and Carrie.

But was she herself capable of slogging through all the emotional minefields she would encounter while blending a new husband with two needy kids and the jagged scars on her own soul? Odds weren't good. Nope, in fact, they stunk.

And why was she thinking about Grant in the same brain space with husbands, anyway? What was she, crazy?

No. Just worn out. Time to go to bed.

Pushing away from the door, she picked her way through the dark living room. The little white bubbled glass lamp Grandpa liked to leave on all night cast a slash of light across the photo of Grandma on top of the TV. She stopped in front of it, crossing her arms across her stomach, and returned Grandma's stern look.

"You know, I could be petty and blame all this on you. If you'd been a nicer person, my mama wouldn't have felt the need to escape. And I wouldn't have been so dead-set on proving you wrong about Richie. And Grandpa would've come to get me sooner."

But there ya go. Blame doesn't get you anywhere.

Sighing, she wandered down the hall and stopped to look in on Ty one more time. He slept, as usual, out from under the covers with limbs flung to the four corners. Jana smiled. He'd be in third grade this year. Goodness, how did he get so big? He'd grown so much this summer that his pajama legs stopped well above his ankles. Trip to Wal-Mart for new ones due soon.

She kissed his forehead and moved to the guest room, where she slept with LeeLee. The rickety double bed was piled high with three mattresses and a feather buffer, and she always felt like the Princess on the Pea when she climbed up in it. LeeLee loved the height, though. She slept in a tidy little bundle with Glitter at her feet and a fuzzy orange Alf toy cuddled under her chin. Jana remembered scoping out yard sales one Saturday morning back in Knoxville, when she got her first paycheck from the Andrewses. Alf cost only a quarter, but LeeLee had been thrilled with her treasure.

Jana slipped into her nightgown—a treat she'd bought for herself when Victoria's Secret had an after-Christmas clearance sale. Nothing too sexy, just a green silk sleep shirt that put a scrap of luxury in her otherwise bargain-basement lifestyle. She sat on the side of the bed rubbing lotion on her feet and listened to LeeLee breathe. Resting her chin on her knee, she stilled, eyes stinging.

Lord, I have so much to be grateful for. Sorry for whining. No reason to be lonely with two beautiful, healthy kids and Grandpa getting better all the time. Please help him heal quickly. Thank you for Roxanne and Carrie and everybody who's made this ordeal easier. And Grant...

His name stuck in her prayer, in her heart, in her mind, like a song that once heard wouldn't fade. *Don't let me love him, Lord. I couldn't stand to be disappointed again.* The tears broke loose until she shook the bed, sobbing silently into her knees, trying not to groan out loud and wake up LeeLee. *Oh, Lord, don't let me...*

W atch out for that post, girl; your grandma knocked it out from under the roof more times than I can remember."

Jana pulled the El Camino under the carport and gave Grandpa a sidelong glance. His left hand was braced against the dash, with the right one bracing the injured leg. His pupils dilated with pain meds and a scrappy gray beard painting his jaw, he looked as if he'd been on a three-day drunk. She sighed. It was going to be a long day.

Mentally girding her loins, she got out of the car and went around to help him. Roxanne had come over to stay with the children and get Grandpa's room ready for the sultan's occupation. Thank goodness Trini was back, so at least she didn't have to rush back to the Farm and Feed.

Count your blessings, girl.

"Told you to drive straight to the store so I could make sure you didn't let the place go to rack and ruin," he grumbled as she offered her hand. He ignored it, grasped the roof of the car, and heaved himself to his feet. Rocking unsteadily, eyebrows beetled, he glared at her. "If you'll hand me my crutches, I'll get my diddy bag."

"I'll get it." Jana kept an eye on him as she got the metal crutches out of the backseat. If he toppled flat on his face and broke his leg again, she was just going to shoot herself and get it over with. "Grandpa, we've got to talk about the store. You can't run it one-legged with nobody but Trini to help."

"Don't have to. You're gonna help me."

"I can't for much longer. The Wildlife Commission is coming this fall to talk about the refuge. You know I have to get ready for that."

Grandpa leaned heavily on the crutches. "Wildlife Commission. Is that some federal agency?"

"Yes, sir. It's under the Department of Natural Resources." Why did his expression give her an uneasy feeling? "If they approve my grant, I'll also receive money from IFAW and the Summerlee Foundation—"

"I ain't letting the federal government get their hands on my property. And that's that."

"But, Grandpa—"

Grandpa stumped over to the kitchen door, stopped and panted for a moment, then yanked it open. "Roxanne! Will you tell this girl to take me to the store before I have to whup her?"

Roxanne appeared to offer her elbow, elfin face alight with equal parts concern and amusement. "Alvin, it's been so long since you whipped anybody I doubt you'd remember how. Come in and have a cup of coffee and some banana pudding. I hear they don't make it right at the rehab."

"That's for dang sure."

Carrying the brown paper grocery sack that served as Grandpa's luggage, Jana followed him inside the house. Clearly this was not the best time to argue with him about the property. LeeLee and Ty each attacked her with information about how the other had usurped God-given rights to various and sundry games; mewing, Glitter nearly tripped Jana winding around her legs; and Grandpa continued to grouse about the insensitivity and disrespect of his grandchildren.

Since her brother Quinn was in Mobile getting ready to be married in a few months, Jana assumed he meant *her*. She rolled her eyes at Roxanne, who shooed her toward the kitchen as she helped Grandpa into his recliner in the living room. After pouring herself a cup of coffee, she collapsed at the kitchen table. She picked up the kitten and stroked her as she randomly answered the children's questions and sorted out their arguments. A few minutes later she could hear Grandpa's stentorian snores ricocheting off the paneled living room walls.

Roxanne stuck her bright red head through the doorway and crooked a finger at the children. "C'mere, dearies. Let's give your mama a little peace and quiet. We'll have lunch in a bit, but while we're pulling it together, why don't you go play with the goat babies?"

"Can I have a hot dog with ketchup and no bun?" LeeLee turned to Jana with shining blue eyes. "Miss Roxanne makes *great* hot dogs!"

"One hot dog comin' up." Roxanne laid a hand on Ty's head. "How 'bout you, bud?"

"Yes, ma'am, but I'd like a bun, please." He tucked his Nerf football under his arm and dashed for the door. "I get to hold the boy goat."

"Nuh-*uh*!" LeeLee tore after him.

Jana looked at Roxanne. "How is it that you still have all your hair intact after a week with those two?" She shook her head as LeeLee shrieked and slammed the door. "Not to mention your hearing?"

Roxanne laughed. "I've enjoyed them. Don't get to see my great-grands near enough to suit me." She pulled a mug down from the cabinet and poured herself some coffee. "Can't wait to get my hands on Carrie and Tommy's little one."

"Oh, I imagine." Jana smiled. "How many do you have now?"

Roxanne totted up on her stubby fingers. "Fifteen grands and five greats. Carrie's will be number six."

"Wow. Quite a legacy."

"Yep. Hugh woulda been proud to see them all." Roxanne sat down across from Jana. "'Course, my daughter Cindy's gone, but her three boys are making music for the Lord and doing well in college. Miranda and her little family are in New Orleans growing like weeds. A whole brood of 'em are building computers out in California ... and then there's poor ol' Grant turning into the crotchety bachelor uncle."

Jana gave a startled laugh. The description hardly fit her mental image of the last time she'd seen Grant. She shied away from the memory of hot brown eyes caressing her face and those big, rough hands wrapped around hers.

She hid behind her coffee mug.

"I just don't know what's wrong with the girls around here," Roxanne said before Jana could figure out how to change the subject.

Everybody in Vancleave knew about Roxanne's involvement in Carrie and Tommy's courtship. *"Be afraid, Jana,"* Carrie had cautioned one night after Bible study. *"Be very afraid."* She'd been kidding, but in light of the gleam in the older woman's bright green eyes, Jana was inclined to head for the hills.

Except that she was here in her own home. She had nowhere to go.

"You should've seen him with those two children yesterday." Roxanne leaned forward. "He loaded up that big old Ford with floaties and rubber rafts and Styrofoam noodles and suchlike until he looked like a Toys 'R' Us delivery truck." She laughed, slapping the table. "Your LeeLee's got the boy wrapped right around her little pinkie."

"LeeLee's pretty fond of him too." A fact that heaped coals of fire on an already tense situation. "Mr. Uncle Grant" was the hot topic of conversation, song, and story in her little daughter's world. She set down her mug with a clunk. "Okay, Miss Roxanne, I've got to be honest with you. I appreciate Grant taking my kiddos swimming yesterday, but I'm not comfortable with him making such a big, uh, splash in their lives. It's ... complicated, you know what I mean?"

Roxanne's thin, arched red brows rose. "Complicated? What's complicated about a single Christian man getting to know a nice single Christian lady and her children? You young people these days make too big a deal out of what the Lord intended to be something simple."

Time for truth. The big guns. AK-47s to be precise. "We both want my grandpa's property, Roxanne. Grant wants it for his hunting camp; I want it for my wildlife refuge. Grandpa promised it to Grant before I moved back, but I think he's going to change his mind. I hope he will."

Roxanne frowned. "I might have known Alvin would throw a monkey wrench into the works."

"It's not his fault. It's just one of those impossible situations." Jana flattened her hands on the table. "You know, in a lot of ways I admire Grant. He really is a good guy. But we have enough philosophical differences that anything more than friendship between us would never work. And I'm scared to let the kids get too attached to him, because eventually he *will* find a woman who can put up with the hunting and the pigheadedness, and he'll get married." She swallowed against the pain that stuck her under the ribs. "I just can't see that being healthy for my babies, getting shut out by somebody they care about so much."

The bright old eyes softened. "Oh, baby girl. I'm so sorry."

Jana breathed deeply. Control. She wasn't going to start boo-hooing again. "Look, I've dealt with worse. And I've got a lot of work to do to get ready for the Wildlife Commission's visit." Her voice strengthened. "I don't have time to think about your crotchety old bachelor grandson."

Roxanne smiled. "I suppose you don't. Well, it'll be good for him to have to work for something he wants. He's always come by things way too easily."

Jana blinked. Those were almost verbatim the words that had gone through her brain some time ago, when she'd first moved home. Scary.

Still, she set her jaw. "He can work 'til the cows come home, Roxanne, but it's not going to change the way I feel about that hunting camp. You can take that to the bank."

chapter 12

Early Saturday morning Grant tromped through the woods, lugging a five-foot-tall urethane foam bear under one arm and a strutting turkey under the other. Shifting the bear to keep it from sliding out of his grasp, he looked over his shoulder. "Come on, boys, we've got to get these targets in place. I didn't want to put 'em out too early, but we need to be ready by the time the registration team gets here at eight."

Willis Dyer grunted and picked up the pace. He lumbered along with a buck, a boar, and a groundhog clutched to his massive chest. It was a good thing they weren't hunting live game; they were making enough noise to send every living creature within five miles into hiding.

"I'll sure be glad when Miss Carrie comes out to cook for us." Bringing up the rear with a doe, a coyote, and another turkey, Crowbar trotted to keep up with his long-legged younger brother. "I'm gettin' mighty tired of meetin' the Pillsbury Doughboy for breakfast."

Despite all the complications of hosting an archery tournament while preparing his land for the opening of deer season, Grant was having the time of his life. Response to the ads on his website and in a couple of regional hunting journals had been nothing short of phenomenal. He'd wound up recruiting both his mother and Granny to stuff, label, and stamp the entry information envelopes. Hunters would be coming from all over the Southeast. By cosponsoring the event with the church, which would receive all the entry fees, his new business would get invaluable exposure.

He was shelling out a lot of money. The 3-D synthetic targets for the trail and the sack targets for the practice range alone had run over three thousand dollars. Then he'd had to build signs to mark the placement of the targets, as well as registration and concession booths. The chronograph—an instrument that measured arrow speed—had been a major expense.

This tournament was going to be the talk of the ASA Pro/Am circuit. The winners in each division would qualify to compete in the World Championship Classic, held in August in Wetumpka, Alabama. Grant himself had already qualified as a pro in an earlier competition and would not participate in his own tournament. If word of mouth spread like he hoped, he'd have hunters beating down his door to hunt his camp this fall.

He came to the first clearing and stopped. "Willis, you see that marker for station one? Set the boar up a few yards away from it."

"Okay, boss."

Working quickly, the three of them placed the rest of the targets, following the path they'd cut and marked last week. They were careful to set the yardages according to American Shooters Association specifications. The setup had to be perfect.

Satisfied that the last target was turned at the correct angle from its corresponding stake, Grant led the Dyer brothers back to the truck for another armload. Within another hour all the targets were in place.

"That's it for now, boys." Grant reached inside the cab for his bow. "I want to check the placement of the practice range targets, but y'all can take a short break if you want to. I'll need you back here by nine, though."

"Can we stay and watch?" Crowbar glugged down a bottle of water from the cooler in the back of the truck, then wiped his mustache. "I always wanted to learn how to shoot one of them fancy bows."

"Sure, why not?" Grant tugged on his release glove. "I'll give you a lesson one day next week."

The Dyers high-fived and plopped onto the tailgate.

Nocking an arrow, Grant pulled the string back to his cheek. He aimed through the sight and let fly. To his satisfaction it hit the center, a twelve-point shot.

"Twelve-ring!" Willis jumped up and waved his cap.

Grinning, Grant shot a second arrow, embedding it in the notch of the first one—a shot known as a "Robin Hood."

Crowbar whistled. "Hey, you're pretty good, boss. You know, if Miss Jana could see you do that, she might not think you was such a parry-ah."

"Parry-ah?" Grant lowered the bow and frowned at his smirking employee.

"You know. Social outcast. I read me a Regency romance and learned that word."

"You mean *pariah*?"

"Yeah, whatever."

"Jana called me a pariah?" Grant's pleasure in the day vanished. "That doesn't sound like something she'd say. And when did you see her, anyway?" He'd thought they were on at least cordial terms ever since he'd taken her kids swimming.

"Willis and me took her a nest of button quail we found when we was cleaning out the woods day before yesterday. I think she's pretty mad at you for messing up the woods and upsetting all them animals and birds."

"I didn't hear her call him no purr-eye-er." The tailgate dipped with a squeak as Willis sat down again. "She just said she wished she had a place to put all the animals we been bringin' her. The birds and squirrels is the main problem. They don't got enough room to fly and run around."

Grant went to retrieve his arrows and reloaded them in his quiver. Jana and her menagerie.

"Boss, I had me an idea that might get you out of the dog-house." Willis jumped when his brother elbowed him.

"Whose idea was it?"

"Okay, it was yours." Willis sighed. "Anyways, you know that old satellite dish that turned up on the houseboat?"

"Yeah, and I told you to throw it away." Grant looked at his watch. It was nearly eight o'clock. Tommy and CJ ought to be here any minute to help him set up the registration desk.

"Well, I thought I might need it for something, so I stuck it in the Winnebago." Willis aimed a thumb over his shoulder in the general direction of the motor home.

"You've been keeping a satellite dish in the camper?"

The big man shrugged. "Makes it a little hard to get to the john, but we manage. Anyways, you can have it back."

Grant shook his head. "How is a satellite dish gonna help Jana?"

"You build her an aviary." Willis blinked as if a third grader could have figured that out.

"One major problem. I don't know *how* to build an aviary. And even if I did, I don't have time—"

"Willis and me were master welders at the shipyard." Crowbar opened the cooler and took out another bottle of water. "We can show you."

Grant put his bow back in the truck. "Okay, we'll talk about it later. Right now we've got to get the registration booth set up." CJ's truck pulled into the clearing. "Come on, we've got a big day ahead of us."

Come on, sweetie, just one more bite." Jana tweezered a bit of mashed-up worm and insect into the wide-open mouth of baby quail number one. Its siblings gaped in a circle of noisy, insistent cheeping like a preschool class at snack time.

She seemed to spend twenty-four hours a day feeding hungry mouths, beginning with LeeLee and Ty. She'd had to get up at 4:00 a.m. for the first round of feeding, just to break away long enough to go to church and take Ty to the tournament.

She shouldn't have let Ty go. But what was she supposed to do, when Roxanne was the one who invited him? She didn't need a child psychologist to tell her he needed boy-type things to do; she couldn't keep him tied to her apron strings all day long.

So she'd left Ty with Roxanne and brought LeeLee home to play with Winnie and Pooh, the baby goats.

She finished feeding the birds and moved to the squirrel cage, set up in a corner underneath a rough work table. "Grandpa, you need a bigger barn," she muttered, kneeling in front of a litter of newborn squirrels, or pinkies. Their stringy gray-brown pelts looked more like feathers than fur. "And I need about four extra hands."

She looked up when a car door slammed and LeeLee shrieked a greeting.

"Mom! Mom!" Ty burst into the barn, scattering hay and dirt as he skidded toward Jana. "Guess what? I won a door prize!" He brandished a small compound bow above his head.

"Oh, honey, no ..." She set down the syringe of squirrel formula and rose, dusting off her knees.

Ty's face fell. "I won't kill anything with it. I just want to practice on targets. Mr. Grant said he'd teach me—" he looked over his shoulder at the doorway of the barn—"won't you?"

Backlit by the late afternoon sun, Grant had a baby goat in the crook of one arm and LeeLee wrapped around his leg. The goat gave a look-what-I-found bleat.

"Don't tell me you're going to be a pain about the bow." Grant sighed. "But I'll take it back if you insist."

"Mom, no! *Please* let me keep it!"

Jana laid her hand on Ty's head. "Let me think about it." Grant had obviously never heard the admonition "Don't argue in front of the children." Well, why should he have? He'd never been anybody's husband or father.

Clearly he thought he was going to get his way. He smiled at her. "Why didn't you come to the tournament?"

"Too much to do this afternoon." She reached for the bow—a fascinating contraption with pulley wheels, taut fiberglass string, and camouflage body—and peered through the sight. She started to pull the string back.

"No, Mom!" Ty grabbed the bow. "You can't pull the string without an arrow in it. That's called dry fire—you'll ruin it!"

"Sorry, baby." Apparently Ty had learned a lot this afternoon.

Vaguely, Jana was aware of LeeLee chasing the other little goat outside and Ty kneeling to look at the pinkies, the bow clutched under his arm. She would have a time getting it away from him now.

She took a step back, avoiding Grant's intent gaze. "How did the tournament go?"

"Had a good time. Carrie won the ladies' division." Grant gave her a cautious smile. "She insists it had nothing to do with the fact that her only competition was herself."

"Good for her."

"Yeah, there'll be no living with her now." Grant bent to peer over Ty's shoulder. "Willis told me you had some new tenants. What're you gonna do when they start running around all over the barn getting into stuff? Squirrels are real pests."

Refusing to be drawn, she gave him an even look. "At the wildlife center we had nice big cages almost like an aviary—a 'squirrel-ary,' I guess you'd call it." She leaned over to pick up one of the squirrel babies, holding it in her cupped palms, close to Grant's face. The little creature twitched its nose, wiggling its ears and stump of a tail.

His expression settled into reluctant awe. "Amazing they can live without their mama when they're that small."

"Milk with a medicine dropper."

"How come you go to so much trouble and expense for these guys? People run over them on the highway and don't think a thing about it."

"You know what St. Francis of Assisi said, don't you?"

His eyes twinkled. "You mean the guy in the robe with a bird on his shoulder?"

"Yes. He wrote somewhere, 'If you have men who will exclude any of God's creatures from the shelter of compassion and pity, you will have men who will deal likewise with their fellow men.'" She glanced at Ty. "That's what I teach my children."

Grant drew his upper lip between his teeth, drawing her attention to the clean line of his mouth and the faint shadow of beard on angular chin. Jana looked down at the tiny squirrel. If only she weren't so attracted to Grant, she could keep an appropriate distance. The children were already dangerously attached to him.

"Jana." His voice was quiet.

She glanced up at him. "What?"

"Will you do something for me?"

"Depends." Her heart quaked at the soft expression she found in that hard face.

"I want you to look for every reference you can find in the Bible that has to do with animals, and see what God says about how we're to treat them. I'm sure old Francis was a good guy, but he's not the final authority."

The idea that God would approve of murdering his creation was absurd. "I know what the Bible says—I read it every day."

He sighed. "I know I told you one time I didn't want to argue about this subject. But that was before I knew we were going to be friends. Friends can talk about hard things, right?"

Were they friends, or were they enemies at an uneasy détente? She felt herself sliding off a waterfall of uncharted emotions in a leaky boat. "I'll research what the Bible says—if you'll do the same thing."

"It's a deal." Grant looked down at the sleeping goat in his arms. "Hey, do y'all want to come check on Forrest?"

Jana turned to put the squirrel back in the box. "Just let me round up LeeLee and make sure she's got her shoes on."

Grant nudged Ty with his toe. "Hang your bow on that rack over there, big guy. You don't want anybody stepping on it."

When Ty hopped to his feet without argument, Jana squelched mild resentment. It couldn't be a bad thing if her son learned to obey.

Grant backed up as Ty lined up his shot, squinting through his sight at the sack target.

Ty pulled the release trigger, and the arrow flew straight and true, hitting the twelve-ring. He grinned over his shoulder. "How's that?"

It was three days after the tournament, and Ty had been practicing every afternoon. "You're a natural." Grant grabbed the boy's shoulder. "Go get your arrows and we'll do another round."

"I want to see you shoot first. Do one of those Robin Hood things. Willis said he saw you do it the other day."

"You know how expensive it is to repair my arrows?" But Ty's admiration was gratifying. He picked up his bow, which he'd laid on the tailgate of the truck, and nocked an arrow. He released it, and it bounced off Ty's last arrow, still stuck in the bull's-eye.

Whooping, Ty did a war dance. "You're gonna win the world championship—I just know it!"

Grant couldn't help grinning. "All right, the show's over. It's your turn. Pull the arrows." Sitting on the tailgate, he reached for the jug of ice water behind him as Ty braced and aimed. "That's it. Steady. Keep the string against your cheek. Now let fly."

Teaching was almost as much fun as shooting. Maybe that explained why CJ had spent so much time with his Boy Scout troop. One summer there was a gun safety class, and many times CJ would take them all out—Grant, Tony, Heath, Tommy, and a few other boys—for a weekend of boating and fishing. Grant had learned to love and appreciate the outdoors under the old man's knowing and wise tutelage. He'd be a different man today without that influence.

Ty shot the last arrow in his quiver and bolted over to pull all six of them from the target. "Look! Fifty points!"

"Way to shoot!" Grant handed him a grape soda from the cooler. "Here ya go, bud, wet your whistle."

Hopping onto the tailgate beside Grant, Ty gulped the soda in one long pull. He belched and grinned, a purple mustache arcing up from the sides of his mouth. "Mom hates when I do that."

"I bet she does." Grant's lips twitched. "Girls."

"Yeah, girls." Ty made a face. "But if ya gotta have a mom, I guess she's a pretty good one." He cut a sidelong look, dark blue eyes cagey, a miniature Alvin. "I'm glad we moved here. I didn't get to fish or swim or nothing when we lived in Tennessee."

Grant had to admit to a strong dose of curiosity about the Cutrere family's past life. Jana had hit the high points that night in the hospital, but there were a lot of blanks to be filled in. "Why not?"

Ty slurped the last drop of soda and smashed the can between his hands. "We got to swim in the Andrewses' pool, but that's not near as much fun as diving off the houseboat." He shrugged. "You know Mom and her wildlife stuff. Mr. Andy — you know, the vet we worked for — wanted to take me huntin' one time, but she went berserko and he changed his mind. He didn't ever talk back to her like you do."

Grant's mouthful of water went down the wrong way. After he quit coughing, he said, "So your mom's pretty much used to getting her way, huh?"

"Pretty much."

"Didn't she have — uh, a boyfriend?" There was probably something reprehensible about pumping an eight-year-old for information, but it was too good an opportunity to pass up. "Somebody more her size to keep her in line?"

"A boyfriend?" Ty's freckled face screwed up. "Naw. What would she need a boyfriend for?"

Now that was the sixty-four-thousand-dollar question. Jana Cutrere was one of the most independent women Grant had come across in a lifetime of social fencing with Southern females. "I see your point. Well, you can come over here to fish and swim whenever you want. Just always make sure I'm here first. Or call me and I'll come get you."

The boy's face lit up. "That would be awesome! 'Course—" he rubbed his nose—"I can't leave LeeLee and her stupid cat all by theirselves."

This was a good kid, thinking of a pesky little sister at a time like this. "You can bring her with you. We'll figure out what to do with her."

"Cool." Ty snapped his fingers at Grant's hound Rahab, who had propped her head on his knees. "But it ain't gonna be easy to teach Glitter how to swim."

chapter 13

Late Tuesday afternoon Jana parked the Subaru in Roxanne's
gravel drive and sat for a minute rubbing her eyes. She'd been
ready to close the store when a last-minute delivery of feed stuck
her in the warehouse until nearly eight o'clock. She'd hired a
couple of part-time employees, or she might have been at it until
dark.

She didn't know how Grandpa had managed all these years.
But he was chomping at the bit to get back to work, and this
morning she'd had to all but restrain him from getting dressed
and following her out to the car. His leg seemed to be healing, but
the itching under the cast was driving him crazy. She understood
his frustration, but it added to her sense of guilt. If she hadn't been
goofing off on the boat with Grant that day—if she'd been paying
attention to Grandpa—his injury wouldn't have happened. She
would have her wildlife center plans on track and her life wouldn't
be such a confused mess.

She opened the door and got out. Regret would eat her alive
if she let it.

She wasn't going to allow it.

"Mommy!" LeeLee came pelting around the side of the house, arms stretched wide. She had on a black trench coat with a fur collar and red silk pajama bottoms dragging on the ground. A newspaper hat was cocked over one eye. "I missed you! We teached Glitter to swim today, but she don't like it."

"I missed you too." Jana grabbed her sweaty little daughter into a hug. "Mercy, you smell! What have you been doing?"

"Playing in Miss Roxanne's washhouse. She's got a box full of costumes, so we did a musical like *Hello, Dolly*. And Ty autopsied a snake."

"Autopsied a—" Jana laughed. "Did you help?"

"No, ma'am. Mr. Uncle Grant helped him. I just watched." LeeLee wiggled to be set down, then grabbed Jana's hand. "Come on, Miss Roxanne said to bring you in for supper."

"But we need to get home and check on Grandpa." Jana's stomach growled as she followed LeeLee toward the front porch. She hadn't had time to stop for lunch.

"He's over here, takin' a nap in the cowboy recliner. We already ate, but we saved you some chicken and dumplings. I helped smash out the dough."

"I hope that was *before* you autopsied the snake."

"Yes, ma'am. Ooh, and I got a surprise for you!"

"That sounds like fun." As long as the surprise didn't involve a dead snake.

Jana tiptoed through the crowded living room, smiling at the sight of Grandpa snoring with his feet kicked up. He'd be awake all night, but she didn't have the heart to wake him up. The kitchen smelled of broth and biscuits. Roxanne greeted her with a hug and made Jana sit down at the red Formica table, where a place was already set for her. Trying not to think about the poor fowl who gave his life for her dinner, she pushed aside the pieces of tender chicken and forked a soft, doughy dumpling dripping in rich cream sauce.

She smiled at LeeLee, bouncing on her knees in a chair at her elbow. "Where's your brother?"

"He's riding the four-wheeler with Mr. Uncle—"

"LeeLee, honey, Grant's not your uncle."

Roxanne looked up from her task of pasting photographs into a massive plaid scrapbook. "He's practicing the job for when Carrie's twins get here."

"*Twins?*" Jana dropped her fork. "When did she find that out?"

Roxanne's pixie grin flashed. "This morning. Ain't that a hoot?"

"That's—that's amazing!"

"Tommy's about to bust his buttons. Called Miranda and Tony to give 'em a hard time about only being able to produce one at a time."

"Winnie and Pooh is twins." LeeLee slurped grape Kool-Aid from a boot-shaped plastic cup. "I don't see what's the big deal."

"I'll explain later." Hiding a smile, Jana ate another dumpling. "These are wonderful, Roxanne. Thanks for letting LeeLee help."

"Couldn't have done it without her. She's a whiz with the rolling pin." Roxanne winked at her apprentice chef.

"I'll have to get your recipe. Grandpa loves dumplings." Jana hesitated. "Roxanne, I've got to think about hiring somebody to manage the store. I can't keep doing this, and Grandpa's still not in shape to take over."

Roxanne peeled a sticky tab off a coil on the table. "You should ask Grant. He knows everybody in the county, and he's got a good head for business."

"Ask Grant what?"

Jana jumped. She hadn't heard the door open. Ty ducked under Grant's arm, charging straight for the refrigerator. Grant shut the door behind him and yanked open a cabinet to take down a couple of plastic stadium cups. He looked over his shoulder, eyebrows raised.

She looked away. "I'll—talk to you about it later." Maybe. He would ask her about the Bible study thing, and she wasn't ready to argue about it yet. Discuss. Whatever they were going to do. Meanwhile, safety in numbers. She was grateful for the presence of Roxanne and the children.

Grant sat down at the table next to LeeLee. "Nice coat there, Sally. Wind-chill factor in here must be at least seventy-five."

"Huh?"

"Say 'sir,' LeeLee." Jana met Roxanne's twinkling eyes. "Did you have to give her one with a fur collar?"

"Don't worry, it's genu-ine fake." Roxanne turned the scrapbook around so Jana could see. "Here's Grant wearing it when he was about seven."

Jana got a glimpse of a gap-toothed moppet wearing the coat, a cowboy hat, and boots before Grant yanked it away from her.

"Granny!" He took one look and slammed the book shut. "I can't believe you kept that picture, let alone put it on public display. I have a reputation to uphold."

"But you were so cute!" Jana pulled the scrapbook away from him and flipped through the pages. Grant and his two sisters— along with a multitude of rowdy cousins—appeared in costume, dressed in Sunday best, goofing off in shorts and T-shirts. At the river, on the beach, in Roxanne's yard. Over birthday cake, under the Christmas tree, in a fort in the woods. The Gonzales family clearly enjoyed one another.

She couldn't help a little surge of envy. Had Mama ever even owned a camera? She didn't think so. If there were any snapshots

from her childhood, she didn't know where to find them. Memories
of holidays were blurry—which was probably a good thing. Who
wanted to remember arguments and disappointment?

She came to the cowboy picture again and studied it. Grant
had been very blond as a little boy, the deep dimple giving him a
cherubic look belied by a mischievous sparkle in the brown eyes.
She smiled up at him.

Ears glowing like stoplights, he tugged at the bill of his cap.
"My sisters liked to play *Little House on the Prairie.* I always had
to be Pa."

"Mommy, are you through eating?" LeeLee slid down off her
chair. "I wanna show you something."

"Sure, honey. What is it?"

"C'mere. I told you, it's a surprise." LeeLee took Jana's hand
and tugged her toward the back door. "Come on, Mr. Uncle Grant,
you too."

Skipping across the yard behind her daughter, Jana looked
over her shoulder. Grant shrugged, apparently as mystified as
she.

Roxanne's washhouse, situated some twenty yards behind the
house, was a tin-roofed cinderblock building with jalousie windows cranked open. LeeLee jumped to reach the string hanging
beside the door to turn on the fluorescent lights.

Jana had never had occasion to enter the little building. The
washer and dryer squatted along one wall, flanked by a couple of
folding tables. But her attention zeroed in on a variety of musical
instruments at the other end of the room: an electronic keyboard,
a couple of guitar cases, a drum set, and a table holding a tambou-
rine, a cabasa, and a set of claves. Before she had time to ask Grant
who it all belonged to, LeeLee ran to the keyboard and pressed a
power button. The amplifier buzzed to life.

Tossing her hair with elaborate ceremony, LeeLee pushed back her coat sleeves and placed her small hands on the keys. Tongue between her teeth, she began to play.

Jana's mouth dropped open. Music poured out of the keyboard. Not just a single-line melody, but fully harmonized, two-handed, ten-fingered music. The little smart alec had even figured out the damper pedal. *I can't help falling in love with you . . .*

An Elvis tune Jana sang to put the children to sleep when they were babies. She laid her hand over her mouth and leaned back, not surprised to find Grant's solid chest behind her.

He squeezed her shoulders. "Holy cow. Can you believe that?"

LeeLee rippled off a final arpeggio. "See, Mommy? Aren't you surprised?"

"I'm . . ." Jana cleared her throat. "I sure am. Who taught you to do that, sweetie?"

"I teached myself. Alls they got at choir is this little xylophone stair thingie and a stick to hit it with. I like to play all the notes at once." LeeLee looked grieved. "Teacher won't let us bang on the piano."

"Does Miss Roxanne know you've been out here playing?" Jana was so stunned she hardly knew what to say.

"Oh, sure. She lets me come whenever I want to."

"Who does all this stuff belong to?"

LeeLee grinned. "The boys." The *SpongeBob SquarePants* theme bounced from the keyboard.

"What boys?"

Grant chuckled. "My cousins, the Galloways. They're on the road most of the time now, based out of Nashville. They used to practice out here when they lived with Granny."

"Oh yeah." Jana put her hand to her head. "I knew that, of course. I guess I forgot. But LeeLee . . ." How could LeeLee have this amazing talent pouring out of her little self with no training whatsoever? It came from Richie, she supposed.

Grant's hands were gentle on her collarbones. "Let it be for now," he whispered into the top of her head. "It'll be okay."

She swallowed. If her life hadn't been complicated enough already, here was one more awkward twist. LeeLee loved music, sang constantly, and moved in time to some inner rhythm nobody else heard—a sort of personal life dance. How could Jana have been unaware of the depth of her daughter's talent?

She couldn't ignore it now.

"LeeLee, honey."

LeeLee stopped playing and looked up. "Ma'am?"

"We've got to get Grandpa home, and you and Ty need a bath before bedtime. I've got some work to do on the computer too. Let's shut down the piano, okay?"

LeeLee sighed. "Okay. But can I come back tomorrow?"

Grant sat on Granny's porch swing in the dark, slapping at mosquitoes and wishing he could've helped Jana get cranky old Alvin and the two kids to bed. He wished he could erase the purple shadows from beneath her eyes and pull her head down to his shoulder and hold her for a little while, just to let her know another human cared what happened to her.

He was getting to be a sorry mess, and there was about as much likelihood of her letting him close as there was the sun coming up in the West in the morning.

When Granny dropped into the swing beside him, he let out a sigh. No use pretending with her. She was like the oracle of whatever that mythological place was he'd had to study about in high school English. Granny sees all, knows all.

He came out on the offensive. "What was all that about when I came in the kitchen with Ty? I heard you take my name in vain."

Granny chuckled. "I was telling Jana she should ask you for suggestions about somebody to help manage the store. Everybody knows you're the best business head in town."

"Huh. Didn't do such a great job with mine."

She patted his leg. "You did a fine job. Not your fault you hooked up with a crook."

"Yes, it was. Something looks too good to be true, it usually is."

"Nathan Winters fooled a lot of people. Apparently even the IRS. Doesn't make you stupid; it just makes you a good man. A kind man."

Grant hunched his shoulders. "Granny, I appreciate the 'shore up Grant's tender little feelings' session, but I don't think I should go messing around with Jana Cutrere's personal problems."

"Why not?"

"Things are just a little ... complicated between us."

"Is that a good complicated, or a bad complicated?"

"It's just ..." He reached for his cap and remembered he'd left it in the truck. "Just complicated, that's all." Talking about his deepest feelings, even to his grandmother, who knew him better than anybody but God, made him feel like a worm on a hook. "There's something between us, but she's got too many issues." He changed the subject. "Did you know LeeLee's a doggone little Mozart?"

"Isn't she something?" There was a smile in Granny's voice. "Jana's done a good job raising those two kids."

"Of course she has, but—"

"A fellow would be lucky to get to help parent such sweet younguns."

"Granny—hold up right there." Grant's shoulders felt like a bowstring pulled to launch an arrow. "Maybe Miranda and Carrie let you railroad them into getting married, but you're gonna have to leave *my* love life to me." He pulled in a calming breath. "Are we straight on that?"

"Oh, sure. Whatever." Granny didn't sound offended. In fact, he suspected she planned to ignore him.

"Anyway," he said after a short silence, "back to LeeLee. You can understand why Jana would be sorta unnerved by a musical talent like that." Granny didn't answer. Confused, he continued, "What with Richie's screwups and all."

"I have an idea."

Grant's neck tightened even more. "Granny, I don't think—"

"You know who used to be the best piano teacher in Jackson County?"

Yes, he did. But he wasn't going to let her say it. Because if he knew about it, then he'd have to try to stop it, and motto number three was *Never interfere when a woman thinks she's doing something for someone's own good, or you'll be picking your scalp up off the side of the road.* He lurched out of the swing. "I've got to go home and feed the dogs. See you later."

"Shelby Cutrere."

Grant paused, halfway off the porch on the middle step. Dang. He sighed and turned. "Granny, if you suggest to Jana that she send LeeLee to take piano lessons from Richie's mother, I'm gonna have you carted away to Whitfield in a jacket that buckles in the back."

"And they call Miranda the drama queen." Granny laughed. "It's the perfect solution. I've been trying to get Shelby back in church since she finished the program at the Home of Grace. She needs a purpose and she needs her grandchildren. LeeLee needs a teacher."

Looking up at the starry velvet summer sky, Grant resigned himself to hunting for his hair somewhere down the road. "Okay, but what about Jana? What about her feelings?"

"If you talk to her about it, she'll see the wisdom of—"

"*Me?* Granny, you may be willing to ride down Niagara Falls in a barrel, but I have no intention of losing what little good opinion Jana has of me."

Granny sniffed. "I had no idea you were this self-centered."

"Now that's not fair. When did this get to be *my* issue?"

"When you decided to show up here every time those children come over to play, with or without their pretty mother. They need a daddy, and you'd make a good one, but what's not *fair* is pretending you want the job and then letting go of the oars when the water gets a little choppy. Like your Grandpa Hugh used to say, boyo, it's time to fish or cut bait."

Grant stared at the red nimbus of his grandmother's hair and tried to regain the breath she'd just knocked out of him. In the end he just grunted, wheeled, and sauntered to his truck.

That was the thing about women. They were just plain dangerous.

Jana put off approaching Heath for nearly two weeks. Promoting Trini to store manager, training her, and hiring an assistant took time. Besides, she wanted to make sure Grandpa was truly on the mend before she pulled the trigger.

The second Saturday of August she entered the back door of the vet clinic and called Heath's name. She'd vetoed his suggestion that she come to his apartment to discuss the partnership. Business. That was all she needed or wanted from him.

Heath's voice came from the bowels of the clinic. "Come on back, Jana. I'm in my office."

The clinic was quiet this afternoon. Heath tried to keep the weekends free, taking only emergency cases—a policy she appreciated. Maybe this deal was going to work out.

She found him reading the newspaper, feet propped on his desk. He looked up and grinned around the cigar in his mouth. "Things just got a lot more pleasant around here. Welcome to my world, pretty lady." He got up and shoveled a pile of journals off the extra chair. "Sit down. Want some coffee? A beer?"

"No thanks. Roxanne's got the kids, and I don't want to leave them any longer than I have to. Can we get down to business?" She sat down, coughing at the reeking cigar smoke.

"Sorry, I'll put this out." Heath stubbed the cigar in a Skoal can and flung himself back into his chair. "So what made you change your mind? I'm glad, mind you, but you were pretty adamant about working on your own."

"I decided you're right. This is my best option for getting Grandpa to take me seriously. He's starting to get around some, and he'll be back at the store soon. I've got to start making a living. But before we sign anything, I'm going to set some ground rules."

He whistled. "Boy, that sounds serious. What'd I do to put that schoolteacher look on your face?"

"To start with, you've got to quit calling me stuff like 'pretty lady.' It makes me feel like a barmaid."

Heath grinned. "Nobody ever accused me of being politically correct."

"Well, I'm not either, particularly, but at least you can call me 'Dr. Cutrere' when we're working. Okay?"

The grin faded. "Okay. What else?"

"Do not, on pain of death, insinuate to anyone that there's anything between us except a business partnership."

Heath scowled. "I never—"

"Yes, you did. People have noticed you sitting beside us in church, and they're asking pointed questions. I want it to stop."

"I can't believe you're telling me not to come to church."

"That's not what I said, and you know it. It's the way you look at me—Yes, *that* look."

Heath scratched his nose. "Lady, you drive a hard bargain." He sighed. "Okay. No more looks, no more insinuations. But if you'd wear a bag over your head, it'd make it a lot easier."

Jana rolled her eyes.

Bye, Glitter! You be a good girl for Mommy!" Wearing a tiny denim backpack and carrying her VeggieTales lunch box, LeeLee slammed the car door and skipped up the sidewalk of Vancleave Lower Elementary School for her second day of kindergarten. In the school uniform of khaki shorts and red shirt, with a red barrette in her dark hair, she looked like a happy little robin.

Jana hadn't expected to feel this strange, dropping her baby off and leaving. Yesterday she'd been inside the building with LeeLee for registration but hadn't had time to look around. Now she scanned the neat grassy grounds, flat roof, modern adobe siding, and tall flagpole. Much nicer than the old brick building on the highway she'd attended as a child.

She jumped when the minivan behind her in the drop-off circle let out a blaring honk. Muttering, she pulled into the street and headed for the store. She had nothing to be anxious about. LeeLee knew kids from Sunday school and children's choir. Besides, she didn't have a shy bone in her body and would be five next month. She could already read circles around most second graders.

Jana gripped the blistering hot steering wheel hard. It was August 11, and the air conditioner was still broken. Even with the windows down, the temperature neared a hundred—probably frying her brain as well as her spirit. Just because she'd been a misfit herself was no reason to worry about—

Do you trust me, child? she heard a quiet voice in her heart say.

Lord, you know I do. But this is my little LeeLee.

You can trust me with her and Ty too.

Jana sighed. Was it wrong to try to control her children's environment so they wouldn't wander into the same mistakes she'd made? So they didn't have a father. At least they would never have to deal with the violence she and Quinn had grown up with. And they had the influence of their grandfather, who was a good man.

A good man to whom she owed a lot. Which meant she was going to keep an eye on his store, even while she started a new job, until he was back on his feet.

The sight of a big dark green Ford pickup in the parking lot almost made her circle back home.

Oh no. I cannot deal with this right now.

Grant had been scarce lately—since the night she'd found out LeeLee was a musical prodigy—and she assumed he'd decided she was more trouble than she was worth. Which was a relief, except for the fact that LeeLee had been driving her insane, wanting to call Grant to ask if they could go swimming. And Ty couldn't understand the sudden distance.

Gritting her teeth, she pulled up beside Grant's truck and climbed out with the kitten in her arms. "Come on, Glitter. Let's see what your hero wants and get him out of here."

She wasn't prepared for the flood of awareness that pumped through her as he leaned out the open window and smiled at her.

"Mornin'." He touched the bill of his cap like some old-fashioned courtier. "Thought you might have slept in this morning."

"No, I had to take the kids to school before I could open up."
She hugged the kitten to her chest as if Glitter could stop the
bounce of her heart.

"Oh yeah. I wondered what the sudden traffic in town was all
about."

"Haven't seen you around for a while." As soon as the words
came out of her mouth, she could have cut her tongue out.
Sounded as though she'd *missed* him.

"Had a little project going."

A project, huh. If he wasn't going to tell her about it, she wasn't
going to ask. "Did you need something special this morning, or
did you just stop to say 'hey' on your way by?"

She could tell by the droop of his eyes he was choosing his
words. "I was hoping you'd have time to come look at my project.
Tell me what you think."

"I have to open the store. You know that." She took a step
toward the door.

"Jana. Come here." He crooked a finger, and doggone if she
didn't find herself edging toward the truck.

She put on the brakes. Shook her head.

He sighed. "There won't be a soul here before ten o'clock, and
Trini can open. You've got two solid hours. Come on, it's a nice day
and the kids are in school. Give yourself a little break. I've made
coffee on the houseboat ..."

Responsibility. A business to run. *What are you thinking,
Jana?*

"You're gonna like this. Besides, Willis and Crowbar will be
disappointed if you don't show up."

"Willis and Crowbar?"

"This is like a joint undertaking. They want it to be a surprise.
So act surprised, okay?"

Jana snuggled the kitten up to her chin. "What do you think, Glitter? Can we trust him?" Glitter mewed. "Looks pretty shady to me too." She laughed at Grant's injured look. "Oh, all right. Want me to take my car, or will you bring me back?"

"I'll bring you back. Hop in." He leaned over and opened the passenger door.

Jana tucked Glitter under her arm and pocketed her keys. "I hope I'm not going to be sorry."

chapter 14

There was something personal about having Jana as a guest on his boat. Especially without the children. Knowing the stuffed bobcat and fox and the deer head offended her, Grant had taken them down a few days ago and moved them to one of the cabins in the woods. Now the wall beside the TV looked blank, but it was a small price to pay for having her here.

Instead of entering the cabin, though, she found a deck chair and dragged it into the shade while he went inside for coffee. Smiling her thanks, she took the mug from him and sipped. "Good stuff." She scanned the pier. "Where are your sidekicks?"

"In the woods. Getting the—uh—thing ready."

"Grant, you're starting to scare me." Her nose wrinkled in that sassy way that had attracted him way back in the days when he had no business being attracted.

As if the attraction was any safer now.

He swallowed irrational fear. Granny's lecture two weeks ago, laden as it was with her typical scrambled metaphors, had given him a lot to think about. Fish or cut bait.

Maybe—just maybe—he was ready to throw out a line.

He leaned back against the deck rail instead of taking the other chair. A little distance seemed prudent. "Finish your coffee. They'll whistle when they're ready for us." Taking a hasty swig from his Hunters for the Hungry mug, he burned the roof of his mouth. "Shoot—I mean, how are the kiddos liking their new school?"

His watering eyes seemed to amuse Jana. "So far, so good. It's only their second day, but LeeLee already has the class organized into rotating play groups. And Ty's found a couple of potential best buds."

"That's good. School can be a jungle for new kids—at least so I hear. Me, I was stuck in Vancleave from the ground up." He paused. Jana had been too. Maybe this wasn't such a great conversational topic. But doggone it, sooner or later they had to shovel out the past.

She gave him a thoughtful look. "It's not always being new that's the problem. You never had anything to prove, did you?"

"Guess not." Dad being a doctor, and the parental units having maintained something of a Ward and June Cleaver marriage, there'd always been plenty of money and moral support to go around. Family and church formed a bedrock of moral foundation that gave him a launching pad for a fairly stable adulthood. "Is that what sent you off on the skids, Jana? Why would you care what juvenile idiots like me thought?"

"I don't know. I just did." She sat looking down, elbows braced on the knees of her jeans, the bright blue of her cotton shirt setting up a stark contrast to her olive-toned skin. The breeze ruffled her wavy hair, lifting it away from her face to reveal pinkened cheeks. "I had such a crush on you . . ."

He stared at her. "No way."

Dark jewel eyes cut his way. "How could you not know? Don't you remember church youth camp, the summer before your senior year?"

He struggled to dredge up a time that by now was little more than a blur. "Maybe. What did I do?" He gave her a nervous glance.

"Nothing. But your sister Miranda had made an effort to try to bring me into church, so she invited me to come with her. I think your dad even paid my way—they called it a scholarship. So I went, even though I was scared to death of you rich kids."

"Rich?" Grant snorted. His parents gave away so much money that the family had never been rolling in dough. But, okay, they were comfortable. "Whatever." He squinted at Jana, unable to remember her presence at camp, though she'd sure been a knockout in that pink prom dress a few years later. "Are you sure it was *that* summer and not the next one? I don't remember ..."

"You wouldn't. I was keeping a low profile at the time, and you older guys didn't have much to do with us pre-freshmen dorks." She smiled. "But Miranda was nice to me all week, and I started to think I might fit in after all. I had a wonderful time."

He shook his head. "Then what happened? Why didn't you come back to church after school started?"

She sighed. "Like the White Mouse said, it's a long, sad tale."

"I'm not in any hurry. Tell me."

"School started that fall." Jana sat back and cradled the coffee mug to her cheek. "The first day, I went outside at lunchtime to see if I could find Miranda. I knew she was a JV cheerleader, but I thought she might let me sit with her and her friends. You know, since she'd hauled me all the way to camp the month before."

A hollow sensation gripped the pit of Grant's stomach. His little sister had grown into a godly, compassionate woman, but as a young teenager Miranda was flighty, self-centered, and very much aware of her own beauty. "She didn't mean whatever she said to you," he said helplessly.

A faint smile curled Jana's lips. "She didn't say anything to me. I was sort of hiding behind one of those brick columns on the patio, eating my bologna sandwich and trying to work up the nerve to approach them, when you walked up and asked her for a quarter."

Grant winced. "I was a colossal mooch, and Miranda always hung on to her money."

Jana laughed. "She wouldn't give it to you. Her girlfriends ragged on her for being mean."

"I'm not remembering this."

"No reason you would. Just a day in the life." She shrugged. "Then Miranda asked if you'd seen Jana Baldwin, and you said 'Who?' like she'd asked for directions to the bathroom."

"Oh, gosh, Jana—"

"And when you realized who she was talking about, you said, 'You mean the little frizzy-haired wild child with the animals in her pockets?'"

Grant looked down at his feet. Shame inched from the soles of his boots all the way to his hairline. He felt sick.

"So I thought—I'll show 'em wild."

He made himself look at her. "I cannot tell you how sorry I am."

Her eyes were soft. "The funny thing is, I wasn't mad at you. Or Miranda. I just knew I wasn't in your league—so I invented my own. Tommy and I were friends. And I met Richie pretty soon after that. They liked me just the way I was."

Yeah, and look how well *that* turned out. Though he kept the thought to himself, it made Granny's crazy idea about LeeLee taking piano from Richie's mother pop into his head.

"How well did you get along with Richie's parents?"

She blinked at the sudden jerk in the track of the conversation. "I was never around them much. Richie and I spent most of our time driving up and down the highway to Mobile, playing his gigs. Why?"

Shoot, he never should have opened his mouth. That *was* a very weird question. "I just . . ." He shrugged. "Granny mentioned Miss Shelby the other day. Said she's out of rehab at the Home of Grace and back in Vancleave."

Jana's glowing complexion went a dead white. "I didn't know that." She jerked to her feet, sloshing coffee. "I mean I didn't—" She looked down at the coffee stains on the deck. "I'm sorry."

"It's okay. *I'm* sorry." In two steps he was beside her, taking her mug and setting it with his on the deck. The boat had dipped with his sudden movement, and he took her hands to keep her from overbalancing. "I shouldn't have thrown that at you. I thought you knew."

"No." She slipped her hands free and pushed her hair back from her face. "I knew she'd been in jail, but I lost track of . . . Oh dear."

"Hey." Grant cupped her elbows. "Let's sit down. I'll get you a glass of water or something."

"No." Her color flooded back. "I'm just being silly. I knew I'd have to see her sooner or later. I'm glad you warned me before I ran into her in the grocery store or somewhere."

"Is it gonna be that bad?"

She sighed and looked away. "Maybe I thought I'd never have to explain to the kids about my parents and Richie's family. I hoped they'd get a little older before they knew what a mess . . . That's one big reason I waited so long to come home. If it weren't for Grandpa—"

"Jana." He closed his eyes against the sudden urge to hold her. "Let me say two things, and you can take it for what it's worth.

First of all, you have a couple of *awesome* kids, and they're not as fragile as you think they are—which has a lot to do with who you are now. The other thing is, people move on and change. After all, *you* did, right? Don't you think it's possible Shelby Cutrere might have gotten her life together by now?"

Jana scrubbed her hands down her face. "I don't know. Maybe. She's been in the Home of Grace?"

"That's what Granny said."

"Well. That's good, isn't it?" She looked up at him, and the confusion in her eyes struck him to the heart. "Do you think I should go see her?"

He marveled that she'd asked his opinion. *Thanks, Lord.* "Yeah, I do. I think that would be the right thing to do."

"Okay. Then I will. But she'll want to see the kids, and I'm not sure that's a good idea."

Uh-oh. He'd have to sit on Granny to keep her from interfering. "You can decide that after you've met her, right?"

"I suppose." A whistle shrilled from the direction of the woods at the top of the bank. Jana blinked like a sleepwalker waking up. "Grant, we've been talking for almost an hour, and I've got to get back to the store. What did you bring me over here for?"

Remembering, he smiled. "Come on. Sounds like they've got everything ready. Watch your step on the gangplank."

J ana stared at the aviary with tears in her eyes. Putting her fingers to her lips, she walked all the way around it. Cast-iron poles supported a six-foot-radius round roof and mesh walls, the whole thing coated with shiny black enamel paint. She'd never seen anything like it. "The roof looks just like a satellite dish."

"That's 'cause it is a satellite dish." Willis's broad forehead was corrugated with anxiety. "Is it okay?"

She flung her arms around his massive shoulders. "Of course it's okay! It's exactly what I needed, only I never expected ..." She gulped. "What a wonderful idea. It's just so *big*! How am I going to get it back to Grandpa's house?"

"I dunno." Willis glanced at Grant, who was standing back watching the show, a peculiar expression somewhere between pride and embarrassment crinkling his eyes. "We kinda thought you might leave it here. You know, so I could help you take care of whatever you put in it."

"Leave it here?"

Grant took off his cap and shoved his fingers through his hair. "Yeah, I don't mind. Forrest needs some company."

"Forrest will be going home soon. And these little guys who'll be staying here ... They require a lot of care. I'm not sure y'all want to—"

"Won't you be stopping by to check on them?" Grant spread his hands. "I mean, you're the vet and all. We wouldn't do anything you didn't tell us to, but we could handle the day-to-day stuff, feeding and cleaning. Isn't this what you wanted? To have a place to put your injured animals?"

Of course it was. But she wanted to be in control of it. She wanted the hospital on her own property—and this place belonged to Grant. Every time she came here, she'd be in his territory.

Gratitude, Jana. Say thank you.

"Thank you," she managed, giving Willis and Crowbar each a wobbly smile. "This is beyond the call of friendship. I'll bring the little quail over this afternoon after I close the store."

"Good deal." Crowbar hooked his thumbs in the belt loops of his jeans. "I told the boss you'd like it."

Her gaze flashed to Grant.

Color flooded his brown face. "There's one more thing we wanted to show you."

Something was going on here beneath the surface. She ran her hand across the slick black mesh of the aviary and backed toward Grant's truck. "This is already too much."

He smiled. "Just come see."

Willis, practically jumping up and down, led the way down the path toward the Winnebago. A few yards along, he stepped aside to let Jana pass, opening his arms like a magician. "Wah-*lah*!"

She caught her breath. The St. Francis quote she loved so much had been artistically burned with a Dremel tool on a series of wooden plaques, stapled low to the ground on wooden stakes lining the path from the camper to the sanctuary. The idea was simple, exquisite, and utterly out of character for Grant Gonzales—she would have thought.

"That's ... beautiful, guys. I don't know what to say." And that was the honest truth.

On the way back to the store with Grant, she wetted her lips. "Okay, let's have it out."

"What? What's the matter?" His eyes cut her way.

"If you think getting Willis and Crowbar to build me an aviary, and using them to soft-soap me with those plaques, is going to get you that property, you're barking up the wrong pine tree."

"I don't know where you'd get an idea like that." He sounded hurt.

"You just admitted not thirty minutes ago that you've been conning people out of what you want since childhood."

He flinched. "That's a low thing to say, Jana. I'm not an eighteen-year-old moron anymore."

"I'm sorry, but experience tells me to be careful about accepting gifts that come with hidden price tags." *Why* had she let down her guard and opened her mouth like this?

He clamped his lips together, then said in a strangled voice, "Jana, you can't put me in the same sack with your dad or Richie or any other dirtbag who mistreated you. You can't even put me in the same sentence with who I was twelve years ago."

"I know." She dropped her chin. "But I don't know how to trust the way you want me to. I don't know if I'll ever ..." She couldn't finish the sentence.

He sighed. "I told Willis this wasn't a good idea, but he wanted to do it so bad. I got the materials, and he showed me how to put it together. He was so excited. So can't you just ... overlook the whole thing with me and you and the property and let him help you and the animals?"

Overlook it? Overlook what was at the heart of everything important to her?

She'd learned to look for the Lord's hand in everything, but this situation was just beyond her comprehension. Which scared her to death because she still didn't trust her own judgment.

"I have to get back to the store. Grandpa's coming back to work next Monday, and I've decided to take the partnership with Heath. I have a lot to do in the next few days."

His brows knit. "You're going in with Heath? When did you decide that?"

"A couple of weeks ago." She shrugged. "It's the smartest thing to do. The Wildlife Commission will be here soon, and they'll be looking to see how I operate as a vet. And I need the income."

"I guess so. But—"

"Look, I know you and Heath have this competition thing going on, but he's a great vet, and we get along fine." She looked away. "Besides, it's really none of your business."

There was a strained silence. "True." He gave her a tight-lipped smile. "And that's that."

Grant opened the spit valve on his trombone slide and blew moisture onto the floor. Joy had just wrapped up rehearsal with prayer, but he could hardly remember what they'd practiced. The time had dragged by with his mind on other things.

Things like Willis's hangdog expression this past week as he farmed the food plot and cleaned the cabins and mourned over the empty aviary. The contraption just sat there in the woods like the oversized birdcage it was, collecting leaves and pine straw and bugs that slipped through its mesh sides. The least Jana could have done was bring over a few critters to give Willis something to do besides stay up all hours of the night playing his harmonica like some lugubrious Arlo Guthrie haint. It was enough to give even a well-adjusted former engineer the willies.

But he had seen neither curl nor freckle of her since a week ago Monday morning when she'd made it clear she didn't trust him. Okay, so she had good reason to be leery of the male species. How was it she could put her professional career in the hands of Heath Redmond—who was over there charming the socks off the preacher's wife—yet *he* wasn't good enough to help out with her little hobbyhorse?

Rubbing a felt cloth along the bell of his horn before putting it in the case, Grant contemplated life's unfairness. "Competition thing," Jana had called it. There was no competition. There was Iago. There was the Sheriff of Nottingham. There was Wile E. Coyote.

Well, beep beep, I'm outta here.

He latched his case and eased out of the rehearsal room. Tommy had to be around somewhere. He always played basketball with the high school boys after their Wednesday night Bible study in the church gym. Tommy could be counted on for common sense and humor when Grant needed it most.

Sure enough, he found his brother-in-law shooting hoops with a bunch of lanky teenagers whose britches hung four inches below colorful boxers, threatening to trip the unwary. The game was loud, fast, and obnoxious, the squeak of sneakers on wood counterpoint to trash talk and laughter. Comforted, Grant sat down to watch on a section of bleachers that had been pulled out from the wall.

At the first break, Tommy caught his eye and sailed the ball at him. "Heads up!"

Grant caught it and jumped up to hook a long shot straight through the net, no rim. Whistles and jeers from the kids coaxed him into the game, and thirty minutes later he was leaning over hugging the ball, sweat dripping off his chin onto the floor.

Tommy ran past, jostling him, and stole the ball. "Come on, old man, you're not giving up, are you?"

"In your dreams." Grant took off after him.

The game broke up not long after that, the rec director having a wife and three little kids to get home to. After sending the teenagers off to deal with parents and homework and Internet flirting, Grant and Tommy lingered in the dark, leaning against Grant's truck.

He jerked a thumb at Tommy's motorcycle. "You keeping this thing after the babies come?"

"Sure, why not?"

Grant snorted. "You got no idea what those two additions are going to do to your life, do you?"

"I know it's gonna be different." Tommy scratched his head. "But what's that got to do with my motorcycle?"

"You should see Tony, when he and Miranda and the kids come home for Christmas. Ethan's like a little leech, won't let his daddy out of his sight. And RoseNell's got him wrapped around her little baby pinkie."

"Okay, so I get a double infant seat on the bike for the twins. They can't weigh much."

Grant snickered. "I want to be around when you suggest that to Carrie."

"All right," Tommy said with a sheepish smile. "So I have no idea how to be a daddy. I'll learn—which reminds me. How's your campaign to win the fair Jana going?"

Grant shrugged. "I told you there's no campaign. At least there wasn't. I had no idea how much I cared about her—until she threw a perfectly good satellite dish in my face, that is."

"You know, if you'd speak English, we'd have a conversation here. Are you telling me Jana Cutrere heaved a two-hundred-pound metal disk at you? With what, a forklift?"

"Good night, Tommy, I didn't mean literally." Grant had to laugh. "Willis and Crowbar and I made her an aviary out of an old dish, and she decided she didn't want it."

"I find that hard to believe."

"Well, you can believe it. For some reason she's downright suspicious of my motives."

Tommy was quiet for a moment. Then, "You have no concept of what she survived as a kid."

Grant hunched his shoulders. He wasn't sure he wanted to know, but maybe it was time to quit being an emotional coward. "I took her home one night twelve years ago and saw her place. I can use my imagination."

"You saw the outside." Tommy's voice was grim. "Take what you *think* it was like and quadruple that. Her old man was a mess."

Cold chills crept across Grant's shoulders. "No wonder she—"

Tommy waited. "No wonder what?" he prompted.

"The other day she accused me of soft-soaping her to get Alvin's property." Grant ran his hand around the back of his neck.

"Tommy, this situation is impossible. How can I be falling in love with a woman who's as skittish as a doe with a couple of fawns to take care of?" Now that he'd said it out loud, he wondered if he ought to check himself into a psych ward. Or call for an exorcist or something. *In love?*

"All things are possible with God."

Grant sighed. "I knew you were gonna say that. It's not that I don't have faith, in the normal course of things. But I'm just doubting my own sanity. And you know what? I have enough respect for her to wonder if it wouldn't be better for *her* if I backed off. I feel like a guy stumbling around in the dark and stubbing my toe over and over."

"If it's any consolation, I felt like that after the first time I kissed Carrie."

"At least you got a kiss," Grant muttered.

Tommy laughed. "Yeah, and it was a scorcher, but she was so messed up she pushed me away and said she was sorry and it wouldn't happen again."

"So what did you do?" There was something a little twisted in hearing about his sister's love life, but he was desperate. He'd been living in Atlanta when Tommy and Carrie got together. He'd never cared much about the particulars.

Tommy chuckled. "I let her go."

"Huh?"

"I took my hands off and told the Lord if he wanted me and Carrie together, he was going to have to do it. Kind of like the way we prayed about the getting pregnant thing."

Grant didn't want to go there. "Er, I see what you mean."

"So God had Skywalker do cupid duty."

"Skywalker?"

"Yeah. And about twenty pounds of green wedding mints." Tommy waved a hand. "Never mind, it's a long story. Suffice it to say, it all worked out."

"So you think I should back off and see what happens?"

"Well ... I think you shouldn't push her. But stay close so if she needs a hand, you're there." He paused. "Okay, I have an idea. What if we each take a kid on the church's father-son camping trip?"

"Tommy. There's a major problem. Neither one of us is a father. And what would that have to do with Jana anyway?"

"I'm thinking lots of little guys with no dad will need a stand-in. I'll find somebody to sponsor, and you could take Ty."

"That sounds to me like a recipe for trouble. A bunch of kids with poles they could beat each other with? And a nice big lake to drown in? No thanks."

"You have no sense of adventure."

chapter 15

Jana thought if she heard "I Believe in a Hill Called Mount Calvary" one more time, she was going to cart Dora's CD collection down to the Salvation Army. Not that she objected to the content or to Heath's receptionist's sincerity. It was a blessing to have at least one other person in the clinic who was passionate about her faith.

But really, enough was enough.

"Dora, could you turn that down a little?" she yelled over the yips, meows, and squawks of sundry animals waiting for treatment. "The parrot's going crazy."

Gloria Gaither's stentorian alto dropped to a soft croon.

"What?"

"I said you're scaring Amos." Jana poked her head into the office, where Dora, singing along at the top of her lungs, had been entering prescription drugs into the pharmacy log. "He's not used to so much … um, excitement."

"Oh dear, I'm sorry." Dora tittered. "Dr. Heath is gone so much during the middle part of the day, I forget there's anybody here but me and Bitsy."

Anybody less like a "Bitsy" than Heath's six-foot-tall Chewbacca-voiced clinic supervisor Jana had yet to meet.

She frowned. "Where is Bitsy, by the way? I need her to help me move Mrs. Yates's boxer into the recovery room."

"She's outside, hosing down the dog run." Dora pushed the print button on the pharmaceutical report. "Which reminds me, Heath said if you don't find adoptive families for the animal show crew by the end of this week, he's going to have to ..." She made a face. "He said he can't afford to keep feeding Maddy, and the parrot's driving him nuts."

Jana walked over to the big cage in the hallway where Amos "The Real" macaw hung upside down from one massive claw. He made eye contact, flipped right side up, and let out an ear-splitting whistle. "Shut up!" he screamed.

"I don't know where he learned that," Jana sighed. She opened the door of the cage and held out her arm for Amos to step onto. "He was such a polite old man when he got here last week."

Heath walked in the back door. "Can't you get that confounded bird to *shut up*?" Amos lunged at him and Heath swore. "One more nip like that and you're cat bait, you lousy featherbrain."

Dora's shoe-button brown eyes twinkled as she met Jana's gaze. "You may have to take a bar of soap to everybody's mouth before the day's over with."

Jana put the bird back in the cage and closed the door. "He knows you don't like him, Heath; that's the only reason he attacks you." She reproached her new partner with a look. His habit of swearing was one of many unpleasant surprises she'd had to cope with since coming to work at the clinic.

"Uninvited and *unpaying* guests don't have any room to complain about the service." Heath combed his fingers through his hair. "I'm all for rescuing starving animals, and I sure don't like to see them go to the pound, but, Jana—we can't keep taking in every stray that waddles or flies in off the street."

Jana gave him a pleading look. "You didn't see that animal show trailer these guys were in. They didn't have a drop of water, and it hadn't been cleaned out in two days. Poor little Cody was half dead before we got him back to—"

Closing his eyes, Heath held up a large hand. "I know, I know. I told you, I was glad to save them. But this is a vet clinic, not a Hollywood retirement spa. You've got to find a place to put them."

"I've got notices out on the Internet. There's some interest in the chicken, believe it or not, but nobody seems to want a macaw or a potbellied pig or a miniature horse. I promise if they're not out of here by Friday, I'll take them home with me." She tipped her head and smiled up at Heath.

He rolled his eyes. "Oh, all right. But Friday's it."

"Thanks, Heath." Jana slid open the door to exam room two. "Would you help me get this boxer into a recovery crate?"

For the next few hours as they worked together, Heath introduced Jana to pet owners, loudly extolling her superior veterinary skills and education. Bitsy buzzed in and out, her job mainly consisting of giving vaccinations and testing fecal samples in the lab. By closing time at five thirty, Jana was so tired she could barely put one foot in front of the other and had no idea what she was going to feed the crew at home. Ty and LeeLee had been at the store keeping Grandpa company since school ended at three.

Yawning, she leaned against her car as Heath locked the back door. "You've got the beeper, right?" They shared the emergency load. Next week was her turn.

He glanced at the device clipped onto his belt. "Yup. Bitsy's staying upstairs on night duty, but she'll call me if there's a problem."

"She's a good worker. You're lucky." Jana heaved herself upright. "I'll see you tomorrow."

"Just a sec, Jana. I wanted to run something by you, but didn't want to mention it in front of the other girls." Heath slouched toward her, jingling his keys.

She had to give him credit: he hadn't put any offensive moves on her since they'd been working together. Still, her guard went up. "What is it?"

"I heard the guys talking at church Wednesday night about the big father-son camping and fishing trip this weekend."

"Oh yeah?" She hadn't paid much attention, because from her perspective, fishing ran a close second to hunting in regard to the ick factor. Besides, obviously Ty didn't have a father.

"It occurred to me I might take Ty."

The hair on the back of her neck stood up. "Heath—"

"Wait, don't dismiss it out of hand." He leaned against her car, arms folded, and regarded her with a teasing smile in his eyes. "Don't you think he needs outdoor guy-type stuff to do?"

She shrugged. Grant had quit coming by to take Ty out to the woods for target practice. That was a relief on a lot of levels, but she couldn't help worrying about her son's disappointment and restlessness. And his recent tendency to shut himself up in his room with his comic books. "I suppose."

"Then let me help. I like to fish, and I can teach him some things."

"I don't know." She looked away. "I'll think about it."

Heath sighed. "Jana, what's the problem? Ty and I get along fine."

"I know you do." Ty loved to hang out in the clinic on weekends and play with the dogs. He was good at sweeping up, and Heath often slid him a little cash for his work. "It's just the whole 'father-son' thing. I don't want Ty to get the wrong idea."

"You mean the idea that you and I are more than partners?" Heath's expression took on a bland innocence that she had learned to mistrust back in the days when she first started wearing a bra.

She lifted her chin. "Yeah. That idea."

Leaning down a bit, he murmured, "Would that be such a bad thing?"

"That would be a very bad thing." She met his eyes, refusing to back away. He was so attractive in that rakish, crooked-nosed, daffy way of his. But he was also full of himself and had the spiritual depth of a dandelion patch.

He smiled—a slow, knowing grin that made her want to smack him. "I think you like me, but you're scared of me." He nudged her shoulder. "But I promise I won't give Ty any undue ideas about his mama's intentions toward Uncle Heath, if you'll let him go on the trip. Come on, you know it'll be good for him."

It would be. Plus, a lot of good Christian men would be participating in that trip. Tommy Lucas for one, Mr. CJ for another. Wouldn't Heath benefit from their influence? Which, in turn, would positively affect her job.

Hadn't she been praying for Heath?

"Okay," she sighed. "All right. You win. I'll sign Ty up to go."

Heath placed his palms on each side of her head and kissed her forehead loudly. "Good girl. I'll pick him up tomorrow afternoon after school."

Jana got into her car and watched Heath drive off. She laid her forehead on the steering wheel. "Boy, I hope I don't regret this."

All things are possible with God, Grant reminded himself Thursday night as he pulled up Jana's cell number on his phone menu. Her photo popped up on the screen, a snapshot he'd taken here at the houseboat on the Fourth. A rather distant shot, because she was camera shy, but he'd Photoshopped it, enlarging and cropping until he had just those sapphire eyes and the mischievous curling smile.

He'd been sitting on the deck in the dark for at least an hour, sipping a root beer and summoning the sense of adventure—as Tommy so aptly put it—to ask her to let him take Ty on the fishing trip.

Come on, Gonzales, it's not like you're asking her on a date. Although a date had its appealing aspects, he thought, touching his finger to the picture of her straight little nose. To have Jana to himself for a few hours, away from everything that reminded them of past hurts and present complications. Dinner and a movie and a good-night kiss. Simple.

He'd done it plenty of times in college, then when he was living alone in Atlanta. And he'd come frighteningly close to getting engaged. Looking back on it, he thanked God that it hadn't worked out. He hadn't done anything to deserve that narrow escape, but he was grateful to be here now, facing the challenge of winning Jana Cutrere.

Gonzales life maxim number four—*Nothing worth having is easy to get*—was never truer than in this case.

He pushed the call button and put the phone to his ear. After a couple of rings, a chirping little voice answered. "Cutrere residence! LeeLee speaking!"

Caught off guard, Grant stammered, "S–Sally! Hey, squirt, where's your mom?"

"Hi, Mr. Uncle Grant!" LeeLee sounded thrilled to hear from him. "Mommy didn't hear the phone, 'cause she's blowing off her hair."

"She is, huh? Well, do you think you could have her call me when she gets done? I need to ask her something."

"Yessir, but first she'll have to get—"

"LeeLee!" He heard Jana's breathless voice in the background. "Give me the phone, honey."

"It's Mr. Uncle—"

"I know, baby, but you were supposed to be in bed. Now, good *night*." Grant heard a door closing before Jana's voice returned to the phone. "I'm sorry, Grant, I was—"

"I know," he said, releasing pent-up laughter. "You were blowing off your hair."

"Blowing off my—" Jana gulped, then laughed. "What is she going to say next?"

There was a pause, during which he pictured her settling somewhere. When his imagination got a little too creative, he stood up and walked to the rail to look out across the creek. "How's the new job going?"

"Busy. I don't know how Heath managed by himself."

"The area is growing. More animals to care for, I guess."

"Yeah." Another pause. Finally, Jana said, "Did you need something, or did you just call to hear me breathe?"

Since that was painfully close to the truth, Grant blurted, "I thought you might still be mad at me. You never brought the squirrels over to the refuge."

Jana sighed. "I'm not mad at you, Grant, I just haven't had time to get over there. I told you I've been—"

"Then how about if I come get Ty and take him on the church fishing trip?"

There was a startled silence. "Oh, Grant—"

"I promise I'll take good care of him, and we'll throw back any fish we catch."

"It's not that. I already told him he could go with Heath."

Grant nearly dropped the phone overboard. "You did *what*? How could you do that?"

Jana's voice dripped icicles. "I did that because Heath asked this afternoon, and I thought it was a good idea. I *am* Ty's mother, remember?"

"Of course you are, but—" He should have called last night, even though it had been late when he got home from church. Or this morning before Jana left for the clinic. Now he wouldn't be there to watch out for the boy, and he would spend the whole weekend worrying about Redmond letting Ty fall in the river. "Okay. Well, I'm glad he'll get to go. That's good. I just didn't want Ty to get left out." An idea popped into his head. "Listen, Jana, I have to make another phone call. Tell Ty I'll see him tomorrow at the lake, okay?"

"Okay." Jana sounded confused. "Good night, Grant."

"'Night." He canceled the call and started another hunt through the menu. Never let it be said that a Gonzales quit before the final round.

With Tommy's bass boat on a trailer hitched to the back of the F-250, Grant maneuvered into the campground at Parker Lake. Bouncing around in the backseat were Jason and Roy Porter, a couple of half-grown boys from the children's home down in Kreole. The houseparents at the home, Grant's friends from way back, had been thrilled at the kids' opportunity to get away for the weekend. Grant supposed he should have thought of it a long time ago, but better late than never.

Tommy jumped out of the passenger seat and opened the back door. "Come on, guys—are y'all ready to par-*tee*?"

"Yes, sir!" Whooping with joy, the boys tumbled out of the truck.

Grant scanned the campground, looking for Redmond and Ty. They didn't seem to have arrived. He hoped Ty had the right equipment and supplies; you never could depend on Redmond to come prepared.

"Hey, man, you having a meditation session right here in the parking lot?"

"Huh?" Grant looked over his shoulder to find Tommy, grinning broadly, hoisting a couple of tents out of the truck. "Oh, sorry. Let me give y'all a hand."

The four of them hauled the equipment down to the camping area by the lake, where CJ, as point man, was already directing traffic in his soft-spoken and laconic way. After scoping out an open area away from the water and not too far from the restrooms, Grant and Tommy pitched the tent. They let the boys take turns hammering the metal pegs into the ground, and Grant supposed he should be grateful he survived the process with nothing more than a blackened thumbnail.

Shaking the aching digit, he stood up and tossed the hammer into his tool chest. "Good job, guys. Now we need firewood. Look for limbs that are short enough to carry, not too green but not rotten either."

Half an hour later they were returning from the woods with armloads of firewood, when Jason, a gawky, towheaded eleven-year-old, stopped in his tracks. "Whoa! Would you look at the size of that boat!"

Grant peered toward the parking lot. Might have known Redmond would show up at a boys' campout with a fishing boat the size of the QE2.

"It belongs to Heath's dad," Tommy said wistfully. "Mr. Dwight took me out on it back in March, right after he bought it. It's a seventeen-foot Deep-Vee Polar 1700 with a hydro-lift transom. One day when I get to heaven, I'm gonna be fishing off one of those."

Grant snorted. "Sitting in an expensive boat doesn't make you a good fisherman."

"Well, it sure couldn't hurt." Tommy gently cuffed the back of Jason's head. "Come on, guys, let's show 'em how a real man builds a fire. I'm ready for a hot dog myself."

Thirty minutes later, Grant was crouched beside Jason, teaching him how to trim a slender, straight limb for a roasting stick without cutting off his thumb, when he heard a loud crash. He looked up just in time to see Tommy take off after Roy. The ten-year-old, a freckled blond carbon copy of his older brother, had dashed around somebody's pop-up camper, howling like a Comanche, a three-pronged metal frog gig brandished in one fist.

"Good night!" Grant jumped to his feet. "Tommy, grab that kid before he falls and gigs himself!" Just then Ty Cutrere raced by, teeth bared, a ferocious scowl twisting his face. "Ty!" Grant shouted. "What's the matter?"

Ty glanced over his shoulder but kept running flat out. "I'm gonna kill him!"

Grant had no idea where Heath was, but he took off after Ty and caught him just as Tommy snatched the gig out of Roy's hand and jammed it into the ground. Grabbing Roy around the waist, Tommy hauled the boy into a headlock.

Ty struggled like a wild man, forcing Grant to subdue him with both arms and simultaneously dodge flailing heels. "Ty, stop it! Settle down, dude. What's the matter with you?"

Ty was sobbing with rage. "Let me go! I'm gonna smash his ugly face in!"

Grant exchanged bewildered looks with Tommy, who held a red-faced and kicking Roy Porter.

An ear-splitting whistle shocked both boys into limp silence, and CJ ambled up to survey the scene of contention. "What's goin' on over here?" He stuck his pipe in his mouth.

"Ty!" Heath shouldered through the ring of spectators. "I thought I sent you to gather up firewood."

"That's what I was doing." Ty swiped the tears off his cheeks and glared at Roy. "But I saw this jerk trying to jab that spear thing into a squirrel, and I told him not to; but he wouldn't listen, so I told him I'd gig *him* if he didn't quit, and he dared me to catch him, so I—"

"Whoa. Holy Toledo, kid, take a breath." Heath frowned at the sullen Roy. "This is supposed to be a *fishing* trip, you little twerp. Where'd you get that thing?"

"I found it." Roy cast a guilty look at Tommy.

"I had one under the backseat of my truck." Grant clamped down on Ty's stiff neck. "Settle down, man," he muttered, "we'll take care of it." He frowned at Roy. "Which means you took it without permission. What've you got to say?"

Roy performed a penitent shuffle. "I'm sorry. I won't do nothin' like that again."

Tommy sighed and pulled the boy into a rough hug. "Come on back to our camp spot and we'll talk about it." The two of them walked off, Tommy's arm looped across Roy's skinny shoulders.

Heath glowered at Grant but spoke to Ty. "Come on, let's go finish up supper."

Ty looked up at Grant. "Can't I stay with you?" His dark blue eyes were so much like Jana's that Grant had to blink.

Glancing at Redmond, he lifted his shoulders. "Not this time. You and Dr. Dolittle see what you can do for the squirrel. I'll go lock the gig back in the truck." He ruffled Ty's hair and walked off before he said something he'd regret.

Something like *I wish you were my kid.*

LeeLee's kindergarten teacher, Miss Mahon—having apparently attended a curriculum workshop—had assigned a book report project designed to frustrate a NASA engineer, let alone a brain-fried working mother. Which explained why, at seven o'clock Friday evening, Jana stood in the checkout line at Martin Grocery, wondering how she was going to turn a cantaloupe into a bunny rabbit.

She looked down at her happy little daughter, crouched in front of the candy display with the pink tip of her tongue sticking out between her front teeth. "LeeLee, are you sure you want to do *Max's Chocolate Chicken?*"

LeeLee looked up and grinned. "Yes, ma'am. That's my favorite."

"But it's an Easter book."

"I know." Clearly seasonal considerations had little impact on LeeLee's literary taste. "Can we put a bow tie on Max so he'll look like he's going to church?"

"I guess we can try." Jana rolled the cantaloupe toward Irene, a checkout clerk who had been working here at Martin's since Jana was a child. The woman's platinum-blonde perm and wrinkled mahogany skin testified to regular patronage of Cheryl's Cut 'n Curl and Tanning Bed down the highway. Some things never changed.

Irene leaned across the conveyor belt to wag a finger at LeeLee. "Stick to your artistic vision, honeybunch." She weighed the melon and rang up the other items Jana slid toward her. As Jana dug in her purse for her checkbook, Irene said, "Your mother-in-law was in here less than an hour ago."

Jana's heart jolted. Another thing that never changed was the fact that one's personal business rarely remained personal. "I'm sorry I missed her," she said evenly. "Can I write my check five dollars over the total, for cash?"

"Sure, love." Irene folded her arms across her comfortable stomach and leaned back to watch Jana write her check. "Mr. Martin let Shelby put an advertisement for piano lessons on the community bulletin board over there. I hope she gets some students. Poor woman looks kinda pitiful these days."

Jana glanced at LeeLee, who appeared to be absorbed by the prizes in the gumball machines at the end of the checkout counter. It was silly to worry. LeeLee wouldn't know who Shelby was anyway. "It's good to see you, Irene. Thanks for your help." She put her wallet back in her purse and held out a hand to LeeLee. "Come on, sweetie, we have to get home and work on your project."

"Mommy, can I take piano lessons?"

Jana stopped in her tracks. "Piano lessons?" There was no reason to be surprised. She'd been thinking about the idea ever since that night she'd heard LeeLee play on the keyboard in Roxanne's washhouse.

"Mm-hmm. That lady said somebody is teaching to play the piano. You said I could learn."

"Ooh, look at this ring, LeeLee! It looks like a sapphire, just the color of your eyes."

LeeLee blinked up at Jana. "I don't need a ring. What about the piano?"

"Sweetheart, we don't have a piano for you to practice on."

"Miss Roxanne said I could use hers whenever I want to."

Jana clutched the little hand in hers. Staring at the corkboard at the store's entrance, she could almost hear Richie laughing at her. *He* had put her in this position. She let LeeLee pull her toward the bulletin board, where a mélange of colored papers and business cards and brochures had been fastened with plastic pushpins. Her eye went with the unerring efficiency of a metal detector to a small yellow notice bordered by hand-drawn music notes: "Mrs. Shelby Thomas Cutrere, piano lessons for beginning, intermediate, or advanced students. Twenty years' experience." A phone number followed.

She could find LeeLee a piano teacher without having to call Shelby Cutrere—Richie's mother.

LeeLee's grandmother.

Lord, are you sure? It can't be a good idea to expose the kids to that kind of person. I mean, she was a drug addict!

Her thoughts wheeled like seagulls circling a fishing boat until LeeLee yanked on her hand. "Mommy, I gotta go to the bathroom."

"Just a minute, darlin'." Jana pulled a pen and a small spiral notebook from her purse. Bowing to the inevitable, she jotted down the phone number, though she knew it by heart already. It was Richie's old number when they were running around in high school.

She felt the Lord's nudge. She just hoped she was headed in the right direction.

chapter 16

"Somebody starts singing 'Kum Ba Yah' and I'm outta here," Heath muttered to Grant as he dropped down beside him on an oak log near the campfire.

Grant sympathized. Past midnight, and they'd just settled the boys down so the adults could have a short devotion before turning in themselves. After a rowdy two-hour game of capture the flag, only a threat to cancel the fishing expedition in the morning could convince a bunch of testosterone-laden preteens to knock it off and go to sleep. Muffled giggles and rude noises still emanated from the tents and pop-up campers around the campsite, but all trips to the outhouses had been accomplished and flashlights confiscated. It wouldn't take long for the kids to crash from sheer exhaustion.

Grant yawned. "Don't worry, CJ's style is short, sweet, and to the point. We'll be done in ten minutes." He glanced at Heath. "You having a good time?"

What he wanted to know was if *Ty* was having a good time. But he couldn't ask without sounding like a doofus.

Heath took a minute to sandwich a roasted marshmallow and a chocolate square between a couple of graham crackers before answering. "Yeah," he said slowly. "I guess I was expecting all these religious guys to be boring."

Amused, Grant watched orange-and-red firelight flicker on Redmond's sharply planed face with demonic playfulness. "You think *I'm* boring?"

"No, but I've never thought of you as particularly religious, either."

Whoa. Now that was a low blow.

Heath stuffed his s'more into his mouth, yelping when he burned his tongue. "I mean—I know you've got strong beliefs. With your family history, who wouldn't? But I don't see you as the Bible-thumping turn-or-burn type. You're just sort of—I dunno, more casual about it."

Casual? Did that mean watered down? Lord knew he *wasn't* a loudmouth about his faith, not nearly as good a witness as Tommy, who was always dragging somebody down the aisles on Sunday. Grant had a horror of doing something wrong in front of other people and being thought a hypocrite.

He took a deep breath for courage. "I promise you I take my relationship with Christ seriously. I'm sorry if I led you to think otherwise."

"But ..." Heath stroked his mustache. "Why? I don't see why you have to get all bent out of shape over it. I go to church once in a while, and I understand the basic story. I believe in God too."

"Well ... well, that's good." Grant fumbled around in a morass of insecurity. What if he said the wrong thing? What if Redmond laughed at him? He looked around. Where the heck was Tommy when he needed him?

Conferring with CJ on the other side of the fire. The slacker. Hands on thighs, Grant started to get up. Time to hand Redmond off to the experts.

"But you know," said Heath, forestalling Grant's bolt for safety, "lately I get the crazy feeling I'm missing something. Some information everybody else knows but me." There was genuine confusion in that cocky, craggy face.

Huh. Who would've thought the king of the world ever had doubts? "What do you mean?"

"I always thought it was Dora that was the freak, but even Jana seems to speak a different language. She doesn't always get my jokes, and sometimes she looks at me with this—" Heath spread his hands and grimaced—"this *patient* expression that makes me wonder what I've done ... or haven't done." He gave a short bark of laughter and picked up a wire coat hanger to straighten it. "I'm sounding like a fool. Just ignore me."

Boy, did he ever want to. How could you want to slug somebody you were supposed to be talking to about Christ? "Let me get this straight. You want to be religious to impress Jana?"

"At first I did." Heath jabbed at the embers of the fire. "I would've tried just about anything to separate Jana Cutrere from her clothes."

"I always knew you were a real hero, Redmond." Grant dug his hands into his thigh muscles.

"Oh, shut up, it's not like you weren't thinking the same thing."

"No," Grant retorted. "I wasn't."

Heath shrugged. "But like I said, for whatever reason, now that I'm here and watching what's going on, it looks to me like there might be something to this church thing that I've missed out on. So I want you to explain it to me."

This was so wrong. Grant had come on this campout to keep an eye on Ty and—let's face it—maybe make a good impression on Jana while he was at it. Oh, sure, somewhere in there was a desire to have a Christian influence on a lonely, mistreated little kid named Jason Porter.

But were his motives any purer than Redmond's?

Not much.

As if he were entering figures in a calculator, he sorted out the facts. Jana was no dummy, and she was careful of the influences on her kids — she wouldn't take on a relationship with Heath unless he became a solid believer. Grant could scotch that possibility with a few well-chosen words. The power of that knowledge made him light-headed. On the other hand, if Heath became a serious contender for Jana, the two of them would gang up on Alvin and sweet-talk the old man into handing over the land. Grant could kiss his hunting camp good-bye.

Talk about the horns of a dilemma. *Thanks, God. Thanks a lot.*

"Okay, sure. It's pretty simple." He took the wire away from Redmond and stuck a couple of marshmallows on the end of it. When he got it too close to the flames, the candy puffed, burst, and disintegrated into a charred black blob.

This is you. This is your life after Jana.

Swiping his hand over his face, Grant sent up a quick SOS. "You know, I used to design GPS transmitters. I have a patent on one the FAA used up until a year ago."

Redmond snorted. "Gonzo, your thought processes make me wonder how you ever stayed in business as long as you did. What's that got to do with anything?"

"Just listen." Grant's stomach churned. *Please, Lord, don't let me screw this up.* "The thing about GPS is, you don't have to know where you are for it to work — you just have to know where you *want* to go, and you have to be connected to the system. In fact, the key is knowing you're lost and letting the satellites find you."

He glanced at Redmond, who stared at him with the concentration of a psychiatrist tuned in to the ravings of a mental patient.

"So?"

"Well, spiritually we all start out lost. Problem is, most people won't admit it. God gave us a GPS transmitter—the Bible—and what you have to do to start finding your way is read it. Get connected to the, uh, satellites, which would be … I guess, God. The analogy breaks down a little because there are four satellites involved in GPS, but I guess you could relate it to the Trinity, which is the Father, the Son, and the Holy Spirit—although—"

"Gonzales." Heath was grinning. "Can you just cut to the chase? Okay, I'm lost. Tell me how to get found."

Grant was sweating, but hyperventilation was not an option. What would Tommy say? "All I know to tell you is what happened to me a long time ago. I realized God loved me and didn't want to be separated from me. But the wrong things I was thinking and doing, and the things I was supposed to do that I *didn't* do, kept me from him. So the only option was to acknowledge I was headed off in the wrong direction and ask for help."

"You mean pray."

Grant kept forgetting that Heath might be a clown, but he wasn't stupid. "Yeah, pray. As in tell God you're sorry you've gone off your own way, and you want to go his way." He gave Heath a firm look. "No matter how easy that seems—and it is pretty simple; after all, I was just a little kid when I did it—it's a serious commitment."

Letting out a soft whistle between his teeth, Heath ran his hand around the back of his neck. "So … no more partying or chasing skirts, no good movies or music, right?"

Grant hesitated. If he made Christianity sound unattractive enough, Heath would forget about it and leave him the heck alone.

What kind of person am I, to be this self-centered about somebody else's salvation? God, I don't know how you put up with me.

"I'll tell you something, Redmond. You're not gonna miss what you think you'll miss, because you'll get something a lot more valuable."

"You mean Jana?"

Redmond *was* an idiot. Why was he wasting his time? "No guarantees on that one, man." Grant scraped the blob of marshmallow off the end of his wire, tossed it into the fire, and started over.

Heath sighed. "I've been watching you handle this fracas over Alvin's land. I'd have sued him a long time ago."

"I'm not suing Alvin." The more Grant thought about it, the dumber that idea sounded. "We'll work it out."

"I don't know how you can know that. Alvin's a squirrelly old codger. In fact, I wouldn't put it past him to sue *you*."

"For what? I haven't done anything to him." Grant was getting impatient with this pointless conversation. Heath wasn't interested in finding Christ or anything else except the short route to his own desires. Besides, CJ looked as if he was ready to begin the devotional time. "Listen, Redmond, I'll be glad to answer your questions anytime. But I'm not gonna talk to you about Jana. You're on your own in that arena."

Jason and Roy Porter, it turned out, had never been in a boat—much less climbed in one while juggling tackle boxes, cane poles, and mesh creels full of crickets. That they managed to do so without landing in the lake Grant considered a direct answer to prayer. The four of them—with Tommy operating the small outboard motor—pushed off from the dock at about 6:00 a.m., the first team on the water.

When both boys seemed inclined to stay seated and in their life jackets, Grant relaxed, lifting his face against the stiff, water-laden breeze. The blackness of the night had faded with the first pink rays of the sun, though a milky moon still floated above the trees along the west bank. It was his favorite time of day, and he got a kick out of the excited jabbering of the boys. They'd have to shut up eventually, though, or they'd never catch anything.

On the other hand, maybe a big fish wasn't the most important concern. Grant watched the boys trail their hands in the spray off the sides of the boat, expressions of utter rapture on their sun-burned faces. He could hardly imagine the road that had taken them through physical abuse, broken homes, and endless chaos. What did he have to offer them?

He couldn't help thinking about that stupid conversation with Heath last night. Man, had that been a royal disaster. At least CJ had followed it up with the fishing passage in Luke 5. Maybe not the most original topic for a campout devotional. But apropos, he figured, for men who needed to be the spiritual leaders of their homes. Who should they "fish" for, if not their own kids?

Tommy cut the motor, interrupting his musings.

"Okay, boys," Grant said, picking up an oar from the bottom of the boat, "time to chill." He and Tommy paddled into a deep shadow under a copse of trees leaning over the water. Dropping anchor, he pointed to the limbs overhead. "Watch out for water moccasins."

Both boys looked up wide-eyed and bobbed their heads in unison.

Neither of the brothers had ever baited a hook, but they seemed to delight in the process of capturing a cricket bare-handed. Grant held the boat steady while Tommy demonstrated circling the pole and flicking the line across the water with a quick snap of the wrist. Though it took Jason several tries to get the hang of it, Roy was a natural. Before long he'd caught a one-and-a-half-pound bream, big enough to keep.

Around midmorning, three father-and-son teams fishing off of CJ's big pontoon boat came within hailing distance. They leaned over the rails waving as the boat floated downstream.

Grant looked up from helping Jason take the hook out of the mouth of a huge catfish. "You boys're looking a little sunbaked. I don't think we're gonna get one much bigger than this. Ready to head for camp?"

"Can we cook what we caught for lunch?" Roy rubbed his stomach. "I'm hungry."

"Sure. We'll have a lesson on cleaning and—" Grant looked around when a shout went up from the direction of the dock across the lake. "What was that?" He dropped the catfish into the ice chest, squinting against the glare of the sun on the water.

"Let's go see." Tommy moved back toward the motor and gunned it to life. "Boys, y'all hold on."

The bass boat went leaping across the lake, jouncing across choppy water, smoothing out and slowing as they neared the boat launch area.

"That's Heath's boat floundering around!" Tommy shouted. "What you reckon's the matter?" As they reached shallow water, he cut the engine, tipping the outboard motor up into the boat. The shouts got louder.

As he and Tommy rowed closer, Grant saw that the Polar 1700 sat a bit low in the water. He put his hands to his mouth. "Redmond! What's the matter?"

A string of colorful language painted the sweet midmorning breeze as Heath looked over his shoulder. "Somebody stole the plug out of the boat last night, and I didn't notice it until we were in the lake. We're taking on water faster than we can bail!" Ty and Redmond were both bailing hard and fast with bait buckets, but

Heath paused long enough to glare at Grant. "You got any suggestions? If this boat winds up in the bottom of the lake, my dad's gonna disinherit me."

Since Ty was wet from head to toe but safe, Grant had a hard time not laughing. "Drive the boat around, numskull, or you *will* sink. You'll take in less water if you're moving. Tommy and I'll go get your trailer and back it in so you can haul the boat out and drain it."

Heath tossed aside the bucket and reached for the motor's ignition. "Thanks, good idea. The truck keys are under the seat."

As the Polar 1700 roared away, Tommy paddled the bass boat close to the dock. "I'll help the boys with their gear. Don't worry about them. Just rescue that boat."

Grinning, Grant climbed out onto the dock. "Okay, but you better believe Mr. Valedictorian's never living this one down."

It took him less than ten minutes to locate Redmond's maroon truck in the parking lot, fish the keys out from under the seat, and back the trailer into the water. Meanwhile, Heath had looped the Polar 1700 around in a large circle. By the time he got back to the dock, it had sunk nearly to the gunwales. It was going to be a close shave getting the vessel onto the trailer before it went to the bottom of the lake.

Grant thought it might do Redmond's ego good to suffer the consequences of losing the boat. But he'd always liked and respected Heath's dad. Mr. Dwight, who'd managed the sawmill down at Cumbest Bluff for thirty years, didn't deserve forfeiting his retirement money just because he'd raised a moron.

So he locked the brakes on the truck, slung his arm across the back of the seat, and watched Redmond struggle to get the boat — now holding almost two feet of water — up onto the trailer. Grant's main concern was Ty, who sat in the front of the boat, both hands clutching his head in apparent humiliation. At last the job was accomplished, and Redmond killed the motor. When he signaled to indicate the boat was locked in place, Grant released the brake and pulled the trailer out of the water.

Before Grant could get out of the truck, Ty had clambered out onto dry ground. The boy yanked open the passenger door. "Take me home, Mr. Grant. I've had enough of this stupid camping trip."

Grant sighed. "Come on, man. You haven't caught anything yet. All Heath has to do is drain the boat, put the plug back in, and y'all are good to go. Give it another shot."

"Uh-uh." Ty shook his damp blond head. "I don't even like fish that much. I'd rather go swimming at your place."

Grant stared at him for a moment. How should he handle this? Glancing at the rearview mirror, he could see Heath stand up in the boat. After an experience like that, the animal doc had probably lost his penchant for fishing too.

"Okay. But first let me see if Heath needs some help. Are you all right?"

Ty sniffed and swiped his hand under his nose. "Yes, sir. I'm just hungry. We didn't have nothing for breakfast but a Pop-Tart."

Figured. Grant got out and walked to the back of the trailer. Heath and Tommy were on the ground inspecting the boat—which seemed not a bit the worse for wear—while the Porter boys engaged one another in a cane pole sword fight.

"Stop that, you two, before somebody gets hurt," Grant said on the way by. He leaned on the boat. "Don't feel bad, Redmond. I did the same thing when I was about fifteen, out skiing one time with Tony and the girls."

Redmond looked up from under thickly knit brows, as if he didn't know whether to spit or say thanks. "Guess that's how you knew what to do."

"Yup." Grant couldn't help a smirk. "You can thank me after you've dried out and calmed down. Ty asked me to take him home. I think he's had enough for today."

Redmond's scowl deepened. "And *I* think you planned this fiasco, Gonzales."

"What?" Grant jerked erect. "You gotta be kidding!"

Tommy shook his head. "Heath, you know better than—"

"I'm dead serious. I checked to make sure the plug was in that boat yesterday when I stowed the life jackets in the bow compartment. That's why I didn't notice it this morning before we took off."

Grant had had just about enough of Redmond's paranoid malarkey. "And what makes you think I had anything to do with it?"

"You're jealous."

The mustard-seed element of truth in the accusation tripped Grant into acting before his brain could get in gear. He reached over, flipped the lock that fastened the boat to the trailer, and let it slide down the ramp into the lake.

Redmond watched it for a stunned moment before he swung at Grant, accidentally hitting Tommy, who was in the way. "Gonzales, I'm gonna destroy you. Move, Tommy."

"Wait a minute!" Grant prepared to defend himself.

Tommy flung out his arms, dancing like a guard on a basketball team. "For Pete's sake, Heath, you got kids watching this whole thing. Chill."

Reminded about the boys, Heath blinked and stiffened. He lowered his hands.

Grant shook his head. "Redmond, this is crazy." He met Tommy's eyes, saw relief there as Heath came to his senses.

"Dang straight." Tommy wiggled his jaw, which had already started to swell. "You both need to have your heads examined."

Grant looked at the three wide-eyed boys peering over the back of the truck for all the world like one of those "Kilroy was here" cartoons in his grandmother's World War II scrapbook. He cleared his throat. "I vote we all calm down and have a little chat."

Roy Porter stepped out from behind the boat. "Mr. Grant, I have to tell you something." He took a deep breath. "I pulled the plug out of the boat. It's my fault it sank."

A Saturday morning to herself. Jana shook her head. When was the last time she'd had that? But today wasn't going to be any picnic in the park.

Slowing to turn off Old River Road onto a one-lane gravel track that was so familiar it put a knot in her stomach, Jana passed a tumbledown building that, according to Grandpa, had started out as a honky-tonk known as the Bloody Bucket. In the eighties it became a beer joint called Bud's, where her father would take his paper mill paycheck every weekend and get soused. These days it flourished as Serendipity, a trendy flea market where upwardly mobile Gen Xers could purchase things like antique farm implements and European carousel horses and handmade dulcimers.

Thank goodness times changed.

And praise the Lord for good neighbors like Roxanne Gonzales, who had "borrowed" LeeLee for the day. If Jana timed this right, they would have turned that cantaloupe into Max the Easter bunny before she got back.

However, she almost—almost—would rather be decorating melons than paying a visit to her former mother-in-law. Wait, was Shelby *still* her mother-in-law? She had no idea of the etiquette of doomed marriages and failed relationships. Not that it mattered. This was something she had to do.

Get it out of the way and pray it doesn't lead to something worse. Is it okay to pray that way, Lord?

By the time she got to the bottom of the lane, which ended in a cloud of dust at Shelby's gray-blue trailer, the knot in Jana's stomach had turned into a boiling ache. It took her a few minutes to unwrap her fingers from around the steering wheel. The problem was, all she had to do was look across the soybean field twenty degrees west and she could see the humped roof of the rusted white double-wide she'd grown up in.

Or fallen apart in—whichever way you wanted to look at it.

This is not about you, Jana. Get over yourself.

She checked her hair in the mirror—if that wasn't a stupid thing to do—then opened the car door and got out. A marmalade cat glided out from under the old black sedan parked by the trailer, and she was reminded how much Mrs. Shelby loved cats. The one thing they had in common. She realized with a sting of the heart that it was something she and LeeLee shared too.

When the cat wound around her ankles, she bent to pick it up, snuggling it under her chin. Poor thing probably had fleas, but Jana needed its comfort right then. She carried it with her to knock on the door. While she waited, she noted that the Plymouth was dusty but neat inside. A set of keys dangled from the ignition.

"Who's there?" came a soft, deeply musical woman's voice, and Jana closed her eyes, unable to answer for a moment. The cadence was Richie's.

"It's—it's Jana, Miss Shelby. Richie's Jana."

"Jana?" The door opened. "Jana? What are you—? Oh my!" Shelby Cutrere, barefoot and dressed in old Wranglers and a pink cotton shirt, stood with her hands to her pale cheeks, staring at Jana as if the dead had come to life.

Which in a lot of ways was exactly what had happened.

"You might not want to see me ..." Jana searched the faded gray eyes, looking for some clue as to how she should proceed. "I just felt like I needed to come. I didn't know you were here until a few days ago."

"Oh, my dear, of course I'm glad to see you." Shelby let out her breath as if she had been holding it and reached for Jana. Then laughed when the cat meowed and jumped down. "Sadie knows I don't let her inside. Come in, come in."

Feeling empty-handed, Jana stepped inside the trailer and found herself in a living room that was familiar yet somehow felt like an alternate universe. The brown velour sofa was threadbare but clean, the carpet freshly vacuumed. A pressboard lamp table and bookcase, smelling of lemon wax, contained stacks of paperback books and several versions of the Bible. She recognized the Formica breakfast table, but instead of piles of dirty dishes, it held a brilliant coral daylily stalk in a white bud vase.

Reminding herself to close her mouth, Jana smiled at Richie's mother.

"Won't you sit down?" Twisting her shirttail, Shelby gestured toward the sofa, then pulled one of the kitchen chairs into the living room for herself. "If I'd known you were coming, I would have made tea."

"No, that's okay. I came sort of on a whim. You know, to see how you are. I heard—" She cut herself off. Stupid to bring up Shelby's troubles.

Shelby looked away, straightening the tail of her shirt. "I'm doing good now. I had a bad spell after I heard about Richie. But I was able to get help." She brushed a hand over her neat gray ponytail, then linked her fingers in her lap again. Her eyes brightened with something firm and—Jana could only describe it as *happy*. "The Lord's my help. Every day."

"I wondered. Roxanne Gonzales said you—not that she was talking about you behind your back—but she was the one who told me you came back to Vancleave. And then I saw your piano ad in the grocery store last night." Jana couldn't seem to straighten out her thoughts. Richie's home had always been as chaotic as her own, and this scene of peace and simplicity sent her tongue running faster than her brain.

"Oh, the ad." Shelby's cheeks flushed. "I didn't expect anybody to hire me to work with their little darlings. I haven't taught in such a long time. Not since I left the high school."

"You mean nobody's called you?"

Shelby shrugged. "Everybody knows how far down I went." She smiled and exhaled a little breath as if to blow away the sadness. "So tell me how the children are. Do you have pictures?"

"Yes, but ..." Jana swallowed. "I wondered if you'd like to come to LeeLee's birthday party? She's turning five in three weeks."

"Five? Oh my. Then Ty must be—"

"Eight. His birthday is in January."

Shelby's eyes filled. "It seems so odd that I've never seen my grandchildren."

Jana leaned over to grab Shelby's rough hands. "I'm sorry." Her throat thickened until she couldn't get anything else out.

"Baby, there's nothing to be sorry for. That's just the way it is. Can't undo the past."

Jana sniffed and blinked. "Yeah, but don't you wish you could?"

chapter 17

Grant pulled up in Jana's driveway—when had he started thinking of it as *her* house and not Alvin's?—at 2:15 that afternoon.

Ty flung open the door and pelted up the front porch steps. "Mom! Mom, guess what? Me and Dr. Heath were in his boat when it sank! And he tried to punch Mr. Grant!"

Oh yeah. This was going to be a fun afternoon.

With a deep sigh Grant got out to unload Ty's fishing gear.

Tommy had taken Roy and Jason back to Kreole; Redmond, the coward, had accepted Grant's apology, agreed to let him take Ty home, and beat a hasty retreat back to the safety of his bachelor apartment.

Now Grant was going to have to explain why he'd responded like a seventh grader to that absurd accusation of sabotage. He wasn't sure he could justify it even to himself. Jealousy, maybe. Of what? Jana's time and attention? Ty's regard? Before today Grant would have described himself as a man with a higher-than-average boiling point. Once that point was reached, however, he had a previously unsuspected tendency to explode all over anybody within a five-mile radius.

Yeesh. A fistfight, for crying out loud, with his best friend as collateral damage.

As he stowed Ty's pole and bait creel in the barn, Jana's soft voice quoting St. Francis floated through his mind. *Men who will exclude God's creatures from compassion will deal likewise with their fellow men.*

Come on, Lord. He closed his eyes but couldn't shut out images of Tommy's bruised jaw and the knowing glint in Heath's eyes. *I'm not uncompassionate.*

He wasn't. He was a scrupulously humane hunter and fisherman.

But you also reek of selfishness. Let somebody get in the way of what you want, and you run over 'em like a Bigfoot at a monster truck rally.

What did he really want? Now that he thought about it, most of his priorities had shifted since he'd moved home last year. He used to want land—acres and acres of it, to tramp around in, to hunt, to brag about. But lately he'd gotten more focused on the little plot he already owned. The sweetness of the woods, the soil, the water.

He'd always wanted to win every competition. To be the best archer, hook the biggest bass, bag the six-point buck that nobody else could capture. Date the most beautiful woman around. Once he laid eyes on Jana Cutrere, though ... Those desires might still be there, but they faded in comparison to the thrill of making her smile. Lately his dreams had been filled with the possibility of waking up to that smile every day.

Most notably, the challenge of besting somebody else's record had been supplanted by a growing inspiration to please his Creator in everything he did. Would God be pleased with his performance over the last twenty-four hours? Hardly. He and Heath had shaken hands, but it would take more than that to erase the negative impression they had made on three impressionable young boys.

Lord, help me. Show me how I can redeem myself.

He was halfway across the yard when Ty burst through the front door.

"Grant! Mr. Grant!" Ty waved, bouncing on his toes. "Come here quick!"

"What's the matter?" Grant rubbed his forehead. If he had to deal with one more crisis today, he was just going to shoot himself and be done with it.

"It's that dumb cat. She's got herself stuck in a tree again, and Mom can't get her to come down. LeeLee's crying, says she's been up there for two hours now." Judging by the white around his blue eyes, Ty was relishing the drama.

Grant sighed. "Where are they?"

"Mom's on the phone with the fire department, but I don't think they're coming, 'cause they're busy with a fire." Ty led the way into the house, slinging the screen door back against the wall in his excitement.

"I told her the cat would figure out how to come down when it gets hungry enough," Grant muttered, cautiously optimistic that his own sins might be overlooked in the uproar over Glitter's acromania. He didn't see Alvin anywhere as he passed through the living room. "Where's your grandpa?"

"At the store. He's feeling a lot better since—"

"How're *you* doin', sweetie?" said a loud, sultry voice from the vicinity of one of the bedrooms.

Grant stopped and looked down at Ty. "What was that?"

"Oh, that's Amos."

"It sounded like a woman."

Ty grinned up at him. "Amos is a macaw. He can sound like just about anybody or anything he wants to. You should hear him do a doorbell."

"Where'd he come from?"

"The animal show that came through a couple of weeks ago. The guy that ran it took off and left 'em. Dr. Heath kicked Amos out of the clinic because he was too loud and too messy and eats too much."

"Hmph. Sounds like the pot calling the kettle black."

Ty snickered. "Cody, the miniature horse, is really cool. He can bow and count to ten."

"Which is probably more than Redmond can do." Grant paused in the kitchen doorway.

Jana was leaning against the refrigerator with her back to him and the phone receiver to her ear. She looked over her shoulder, eyebrows raised.

"What I mean is—" *Shut up, Gonzales, before you get in more trouble.* "Never mind." He gave Jana what he hoped was a re-assuring smile. "I've come to talk the patient down off the ledge."

She slapped the phone into its cradle on the wall. "What are you doing here?"

"Gosh, you're welcome. Happy to help." He tried to look both harmless and useful.

She stared at him for a moment, her expression unreadable. "Thank you for bringing Ty home. Where's Heath?"

"Took off for parts unknown. I promise you he's all in one piece, and we got the boat back out. The only one with bruises is Tommy, and that was an accident. He's already forgiven me, so can we just move on?"

"I suppose." She bit her lip. "Glitter's in the tree again. Duke must've chased her up there."

"Doubt it. That dog's so senile he's forgotten how to bark. Seems to me the cat's just got a tree fetish." He sighed when she didn't smile. "All right, so I'm persona non grata right now. Just show me which tree and I'll figure something out."

A few minutes later he and Jana and the kids stood in the middle of a cluster of trees in the woods behind Alvin's house, staring straight up into a longleaf pine. He could hear Glitter mewing like a lost baby, but all he saw was the white tip of her tail twitching under a limb about sixty feet up.

He scratched his head. "You may have to call the fire department after all, Jana. I don't have a rope that long."

LeeLee flung her arms around his leg and sniffled. "Oh no ... She's gonna be a car cuss."

"Not on my watch." Grant put a hand on Ty's shoulder. "Go get my rod and reel out of the truck, and throw a couple of your smallest brim in the bait bucket. We're gonna go cat fishin'."

Waiting for the junior rescue squad to return, Grant ruffled LeeLee's messy dark hair. But his focus was on Jana, whose pinched mouth and glassy eyes warned him he'd better tread carefully. He began to get the least bit aggravated. Who, after all, was the one who kept riding in on a white horse when her animals needed food, transportation, housing, and medical attention? And who knew what other outlandish rescue stunts he might have to stage, should the Lord decide to torture him by abandoning him permanently in this desert of unrequited love?

Love? *Love?* He mentally slapped himself. This was not love. This was a mental handicap.

"Jana, what's the matter?" he blurted, unable to handcuff his feelings and therefore his tongue. "I promise I didn't mean to set a bad example for Ty. I told him even grown-ups do things they're sorry for, and there's a price to pay when they do. He understands a lot more than you think he—"

"Shut up, Grant. I'm not mad at you." Jana glanced at LeeLee, who blinked up at Grant with drenched blue eyes. "I've just got a lot on my mind."

"Oh." He knew he shouldn't pursue this right now. But relief had him babbling like an FBI witness on Sodium Pentothal. "Okay, but if you need somebody to talk to, I don't have anything to do tonight. Maybe I could take you and the kids out for pizza or—or veggie burgers or whatever they like."

"Thanks, but we had pizza last night. Here comes Ty with the fishing equipment. Let's see if we can help poor little Glitter get down."

Ty ran toward them, the bucket clanking against his leg and the rod and reel waving over his head. "Mr. Grant! Here ya go—I got it. Can I try first?"

"I reckon." Grant took the rod and checked the weight tied to the end of the line before handing it back to Ty. "Only problem is, all these trees are gonna make your cast kinda tricky. Remember how I showed you to snap your wrist that day you were out at the houseboat?" He demonstrated. "Make sure the line goes straight up. That's it. Now aim for the branch just like you were out on the water ... easy ... easy. Okay, now cast!"

Craning his neck, Ty tipped the rod back, then whipped it forward, releasing the line into the air. The fly sailed in a perfect arc, just missing several branches on the way up. It flipped neatly across the limb on which Glitter crouched.

"Way to go, man!" Grant whacked Ty's shoulder.

"Yay, Ty!" LeeLee jumped up and down clapping her hands.

The boy grinned. "Now what do I do?"

"Reel out the line until the fly comes down far enough we can tie the bucket to it. Good. Jana, hand me the fish."

In short order, the bucket was on its way up. The kitten, smelling food, peered over the limb.

"Glitter, don't look down!" shrieked LeeLee. "You'll fall!"

Apparently suicide wasn't on the cat's agenda. Without a moment's hesitation she hopped into the bucket and rode down like Queen Nefertiti in her royal litter. Arriving at lobby level, she exited, smelling of bream but sublimely unconcerned about the trauma she had provoked in her human slaves.

Grant picked the kitten up by the nape of the neck and glared at her. "Look, you. We're getting tired of rescuing your fluffy little buns. Next time somebody bullies you, send 'em to me. Got that?" He winked at LeeLee as he handed her the kitten. "Might as well let her have those fish. Doubt anybody'll want to eat 'em now."

"Come on, Glitter. Let's go play dress-up." LeeLee waggled one of the kitten's paws. "Tell Mr. Uncle Grant thank you." Glitter mewed on cue, and the two of them skipped toward the house.

Ty looked up from his task of untying the line from the handle of the bucket. "Hey, I was the one that got her down this time."

Grant laughed. "Most good deeds go unappreciated. Be careful reeling the line back in—don't let it snag. Think you can put the rod back where you found it?"

"Yes, sir. Did you ask her yet?" Ty jerked his head toward his mother. "You know, about the—?"

Grant's gaze flashed to Jana. "Uh, nope, I haven't had a chance."

She put her hands on her hips. "Ask me what?"

Oblivious to undercurrents, Ty jumped to his feet and hugged his mother's arm. "About the ASA Classic in Wetumpka next weekend."

Grant had planned to wait until he had her alone to bring that up. Now he had to think on his feet. "Ty and I were talking about it on the way home this afternoon." He stuffed his hands into the pockets of his shorts. "It's an overnight trip, but he can stay with me, and I'll pay his way into the tournament and everything. It won't cost you anything." He knew Jana didn't have a lot of extra money to throw around.

"Come on, Mom, please, can I go? Mr. Grant's competing, and if he wins, he'll get his third national trophy in a row. Please, Mom!"

To give her credit, she didn't immediately say no. But she looked away with a sigh. "Oh, Ty ..."

Grant regretted putting her on the spot, and Tommy's "hands-off" advice came to mind. He swallowed his natural impulse to press for victory. "Hold on, dude." He put a gentle hand on top of Ty's head. "This is your mom's decision, and you need to give her time to think about it."

Jana stared at him, as if he'd said something out of character. Maybe he had.

"He can't miss school." She folded her arms.

Was she thinking about letting Ty go? "No problem. We can get up early Saturday morning and get to Wetumpka in time for registration."

"Wetumpka? Where's that?"

"Alabama—just outside Montgomery." Something in Jana's expression made him throw good money after bad. "You could come too, if you wanted to. I doubt if LeeLee would get into it, but maybe she could hang out here with Granny or Carrie—" Shoot. Babbling again. He sent Ty a look that said *Keep your mouth shut.*

Taut, humid silence fell. Some small animal rustled in the underbrush; a bird called overhead. A pinecone fell with a soft thud.

Jana looked Grant in the eye. "You won't be hunting live animals, will you?"

"No!" He raised a hand in a Boy Scout salute. "Genuine 3-D fake ones. Nothing but polystyrene and paint."

"Okay, well, no promises, but I'll think about it and let you know tomorrow at church. Will that be soon enough?"

Grant resisted the impulse to do a war whoop. "That'll be fine. Are you sure you don't want to go out for—" he stopped when she shook her head. "Right. Then I'll just be moseying back to my place. Gotta practice my, uh, trombone." Like he ever took the thing out of its case except on Wednesday nights and Sunday mornings. "I'll see you in the morning."

"Wait, Grant." Jana was smiling as if he'd said something funny. "It's time to release Forrest back into the wild. Maybe we could come over tomorrow afternoon after lunch and you could go with us?"

"Yeah, I'd like that." Warmth surged through his chest. He felt a peculiar sense of absolution in the way she looked at him. "I'll give Forrest a pep talk tonight, make sure he's ready for the big bad world."

Jana gave him an inscrutable look. "I guess you'd be the one to do that."

All the way home he wondered what she meant by that.

Jana held a finger over her lips to remind the children to be quiet as Forrest sidled closer to the open door of his pen. Behind her Grant stood with both hands tucked into his back pockets, his favorite stance. Ty and LeeLee, wide-eyed and mouths open in excitement, crouched side by side with hands on knees.

Jana's heart pounded in anticipation of the deer taking his first walk in freedom in nearly two months. If everything went as she hoped, he wouldn't come back. "Wilding" an animal who had lived even briefly among humans could be a tricky process. Sometimes they got so attached to their human caretakers that they'd forget they belonged in the wild. Returning again and again, they'd often meet with a predator or poisoned food, or get run over by a vehicle.

Housing and treating Forrest in the woods had increased the chances of his successful return to the wild. After the first couple of weeks of hand-feeding him, Jana had shown Grant how to set the baby bottle into the grid of the fence so Forrest could feed himself. The broken leg had strengthened until the splint could come off—a brief trip to the clinic took care of that—and lately he'd come close to jumping over the fence.

Now most of the young deer's white spots had faded away, leaving his coat a beautiful sienna brown dappled with umber. Only the underside of his tail was pure white. His ears were large, sensitive, rabbitlike, his eyes bright and liquid with health. He was ready for freedom.

Jana blinked back tears of emotion. She'd done everything she could to rescue this little guy. Now he'd be on his own. She leaned back against Grant's chest as Forrest found the open gate, and LeeLee reached for Ty's hand—the four of them united in an experience that was more than a project, more than a hobby, more than simple kindness to a dumb animal. If she'd had to describe it, Jana would have called it a smile of the Holy Spirit.

Oh, Lord, this is what I want to do with my life.

It was just so hard to know whether she was pushing for her own desires or following the Lord's plan. She would have given anything for some formula to analyze the data she'd been given, like the lab experiments she used to do in vet school. Unfortunately, the process of interacting with other people—and even diagnosing her own emotions, for that matter—made that kind of analysis way too complicated.

Freedom. Was there really any such thing? Even as a child roaming these woods, nobody caring where she went, she'd been hostage to fear. Maybe God's simple creatures could truly be free.

But the human ability to make choices, the ability to *feel*—with those gifts came responsibility.

She felt Grant's chest expand with a sharp breath as Forrest took a long look over his shoulder, as if assessing the safety of the fence, then disappeared into the woods.

Gone. A chapter closed, and with it came the realization that she had been holding off making decisions, fearful of doing the wrong thing. Drifting into the job with Heath. Avoiding the threat of Grant's affection. She closed her eyes as the stillness of her children, the warmth and solidity of the man behind her, the scent and live sounds of the woods filled her spirit.

A fragment of Scripture came from somewhere: *"Now faith is being sure of what we hope for and certain of what we do not see."*

Lord, I don't know how I functioned before I knew you. Hold on to me and make me grow.

Grant released a sigh. "Wow. I feel like I'm watching my kid get on the bus for his first day of school."

"He'll be fine. You did a great job taking care of him." Jana turned and extended a hand to each of the children. "Come on, guys, time to go home."

Ty backed away. "I wanted to stay here and go fishing off the boat."

Gracious, he was getting independent lately. Jana took LeeLee's chubby little hand and turned toward the highway. "Grant's got other stuff to do this afternoon. Besides, you'll see him next weekend when we go to the archery tournament." The decision seemed right.

"Mom! You're gonna let me go?" Ty threw a fist into the air. "Yahoo!"

Jana smiled into Grant's astonished brown eyes. "Yes, but I'm going too."

"Double cool!" Ty danced around a tree. "Can I bring my bow?"

"Absolutely." Grant's lazy, lopsided grin spread all over his face. "We'll show your mama what a real bow hunter's made of."

Realizing what she had just committed to, Jana looked away. This particular bow hunter was entirely too real already.

Jana was flipping pancakes early Saturday morning when Grandpa leaned around the side of his recliner to holler, "Can't you teach this bird a hymn or somethin'?"

It was barely six, and Amos had been shrieking his "Easy on the Ice" mantra for over an hour.

"He just wants some attention." She turned another pancake. "Try singing to him."

She'd been looking forward to the excursion yet dreading two days spent on Grant's turf. This was probably the worst decision she'd made in a long time, but it was too late to back out now. She'd left Trini in charge of the store, along with one of the college students who sometimes temped during the summers, pacifying Grandpa with a promise to call in and check on them during the day. Ty was outside cleaning his bow and arrows, which he'd carefully packed in a canvas case Grant had given him. Jana had never seen her little boy so excited about going somewhere.

At least LeeLee and Grandpa would be well cared for while she was gone. "Sure," Roxanne had chirped when Jana called to ask her to come over. "I'll bring my Penney's catalog, and we'll make paper dolls."

Grandpa was gonna love that. Grinning to herself, she put the last pancake on a plate and turned off the stove. She still had to hunt up bug spray and sunscreen before Roxanne and Grant arrived.

On her way through the den, she plunked Grandpa's breakfast on a TV tray. "I want to know why you got so upset about the deer eating your peaches, when you feed them to Amos by the bushel."

"He looked hungry." Grandpa put away his pocket knife, then fed the last bit of a peach to Amos, who sat on his shoulder. The bird snatched the fruit and flew to hang upside down from the perch in his open cage.

"Howdy, gorgeous!" He let out an ear-splitting whistle.

Jana shook her head. "I'll put the cover on, if you want."

"No, I want to see what he'll do with Roxanne's hair." Grandpa cackled.

Jana rolled her eyes and went to wake LeeLee up for breakfast.

Half an hour later she sat in the cab of Grant's truck, headed for Alabama, with Ty already asleep in the backseat.

"Thanks for the pancakes," Grant said. "You didn't have to feed me too." He glanced at her with a grin. "But I'm glad you did."

"I like to cook, and it's no trouble to fix for one more."

"That's what Carrie says. She'd just as soon feed an army as one person."

"She's going to have a hard time doing that once her babies come. I don't think she realizes how much attention they'll demand."

Grant was quiet for a moment. "I still don't know how you did that all by yourself."

She didn't know what to say. *I covet your family* wasn't an option.

"So what did you do—I mean, after you got out of the hospital with LeeLee? Did you go right back to school?"

"Pretty much. Before she was born, I'd managed to finish my bachelor's degree. When I was in vet school, Lurlene Andrews played grandma and kept the kids for me."

"That's amazing."

Jana blushed. "If you want something badly enough, you do whatever it takes." She grinned. "But I didn't sleep much, that's for sure."

"Your grades must have been phenomenal. I know how hard Heath worked to get into vet school."

"I had Dr. Andrews's recommendation. He's an MSU alum himself." She paused, then took a chance on getting laughed at. "I feel like I'm *called*—you know, by God—to be a wildlife veterinarian. Do you know there are very few textbooks on the subject? Wildlife volunteers across the country share information in newsletters and on the Internet, but a lot of vets work pretty much in the dark."

"Really?"

She glanced at him. He wasn't scoffing. "Yes. I want to write a book about wildlife rescue and treatment in the southeast region of the U.S."

"That's a great ambition." Grant chewed the inside of his lip. "You've thought about this a lot, haven't you?"

"All the time," she said quietly. "Next to my relationship to God and my kids, it's the most important thing in the world to me."

Grant adjusted the radio to find a Christian station in Mobile. "That's how important my camp is to me."

She took a deep breath. "I did what you asked me to do. I did a topical study on animals in the Bible. How God speaks of them, how he cares for them, how we're directed to treat them."

"There's not much there, huh?"

"On the contrary. The Bible's chock-full of references to the Lord's creation. How it praises him in its pure existence.

"Jana, the animals, all creation in fact, were given for our use. *Human* use."

"Yes, but in the beginning, God didn't intend us to murder them for food."

"You're not going to get into that 'Jesus was a vegetarian' thing, are you?"

She just looked at him. "You can turn this truck around and take me home right now if you're going to taunt me."

"I'm sorry. That's not what I meant. But can't you see why this seems so outlandish to me? The Jews—God's chosen people—have practiced the sacrificial system for centuries. At his direction, I might add. How can you claim he doesn't approve?"

"What about the new covenant making the old one obsolete? Because Jesus came to *be* our sacrifice, once and for all. The new covenant makes the old one obsolete."

He looked thoughtful. "I'm no theologian, but that doesn't apply in this context. You just can't equate some off-the-wall view of the animal kingdom with Jesus' sacrifice for the crown of his creation, which is mankind. Jana, I love your tender heart, but think about it. Psalm 8 says we're created just a little lower than the angels. We're created in God's image. Do you know what that means?"

"I understand your point, but I still can't reconcile myself to indiscriminate taking of animal life." Jana clenched her hands, hating to be upset with Grant. "Maybe it's one of those 'disputable matters' we can agree to disagree on. Like it or not, your beliefs affect me and my kids. Somehow I have to make you see how serious I am about this."

chapter 18

Grant regretted provoking this conversation to begin with. It just wasn't fair that the first woman he cared for outside his family would be on the other side of a philosophical chasm even the Golden Gate Bridge couldn't span. He sighed. "I've told you before, I respect your position. I just want you to stay open-minded toward folks who don't quite line up with it."

"I'll try." She leaned her head back against the seat and closed her eyes. Beyond her pensive profile the green and brown hay fields of Jackson County, interspersed with farm buildings and dinky little houses and trailers, flashed past. He knew what had drawn him home a year ago. The solid sense of belonging in the place of his birth, where you could depend on people to behave with common decency and right thinking. How could Jana come back here and expect something different?

He couldn't remember being this confused about a woman since Mary Katherine Blackmon had dumped him for a dentist two years ago. Well, truthfully, *that* hadn't been all that confusing. MK wanted to get married, Grant wasn't ready, and that was that. Bye-bye, redneck surveying engineer—hello, Dr. Toothy Smile. Grant had been relieved to leave Mary Katherine and Atlanta behind.

Jana wasn't at all the sort of woman he'd thought would get under his skin. And it wasn't just the two little people who came permanently attached to her—though that was disconcerting enough. She'd come right out and admitted that she'd lived in sin with Richie before getting married, and that she'd done some drugs. And she had some serious emotional issues, dating from her childhood.

How did a person leave all that behind and become the sane, godly woman she seemed to be? Chances were, she had buried emotions that were apt to explode all over the poor, unsuspecting guy who fell in love with her.

She sighed, breaking into his thoughts.

"This wouldn't be so painful, Grant, if I didn't like you so much."

Great. The *L* word, only it wasn't *love*. *I like you*—the ultimate kiss of death.

He found a smile somewhere in the recesses of his home training. "I know what you mean. But for the sake of the little guy in the backseat, let's suspend hostilities for a couple days and pretend we're having a good time, okay?"

After coating herself and Ty in an aromatic layer of Deep Woods OFF, Jana followed Grant from the parking lot to the registration tables located in a wide-open field near a stretch of woods. As Grant stood in line to register, she looked around with interest. Instead of rampant camouflage, as she'd expected, she found that collared shirts and tailored shorts or slacks were required tournament attire. This was no redneck yee-haw, but a well-organized, friendly affair run by men and women with an obvious love for the sport of archery.

She watched Grant tuck his scorecard into the back pocket of his khaki shorts. In his royal blue golf shirt and distressed-leather belt and hiking boots, he looked handsome and relaxed—as if he'd forgotten their tense conversation.

Looking over the crowd, he suddenly smiled and raised a hand. He beckoned over a silver-haired, barrel-chested man with a neat goatee. "Jana, this is Bo Eubanks. He owns the pro shop in Saraland where I get most of my supplies. Bo, meet my good friends Ty and Jana Cutrere."

Bo winked. "I won't hold it against you." He slid an assessing look from Jana back to Grant. "Something you're not telling me, boy?"

"Yeah, you're gonna get beat today."

Jana raised her brows. Masterful deflection of a tricky question.

"I don't think so. I've got serious motivation to win." Bo's expression sobered. "The cash prize plus the publicity could make the difference in my staying in business for another year."

"Come on, man." Grant elbowed him. "We've been praying about that. You're gonna be fine."

"Hope so. I'm hanging on." Bo's voice lightened. "But look out, boy, because I *am* gonna win." He leaned in again. "Hey, I saw Doug Briscoe's name on the registration list. Did you know he was gonna be here?"

"Figured he would be." Grant shrugged.

Bo pulled out his wallet to replace his ID. "Better watch your back, big guy. Lawyer with a deadly weapon."

At that, Grant grinned. "As ambulance chasers go, he's harmless enough." He glanced at Jana. "Come on, you two, I need a few practice rounds before my one o'clock shotgun start."

"Yeah, me too," said Bo. "Nice to meet you, Jana."

"Same here." Jana nodded, then slung an arm around Ty's shoulders as they followed Grant toward the practice range. *Focused* was a word she associated with Grant, but his attention seemed to be disseminated into the crowd of spectators and shooters milling around. She'd given up the right to question him about anything personal. But as he set down his bow case and gym bag at the target range, she touched his arm. "Who's Doug Briscoe?"

"Potential business partner." He unzipped the bag and pulled out a fingerless leather glove.

"With the hunting camp, you mean?"

"That's right." Grant pulled on the glove and fastened its Velcro opening.

The lack of elaboration told Jana volumes. She retreated a step. "Oh. Okay. Where should Ty and I stand?"

Grant crouched to open the bow case. "You're fine right here for now. There'll be marked locations for the gallery to watch from during the tournament." He glanced at Ty before looking up at her. "We'll have time to talk later, okay?"

Talk about something he didn't want to discuss in front of Ty? Carrie had asked her to find out what was bothering Grant. She'd almost forgotten it. But did she *want* to know about some cut-throat lawyer who was into the hunting industry?

Actually—yes, she did. Might as well admit it. She wanted to know everything that made Grant Gonzales tick. She touched Ty's shoulder, and the two of them backed up to give Grant room to shoot.

She was so far in over her head it was going to take a backhoe to dig her out.

During the first round of the tournament, Grant had a hard time focusing his attention where it was supposed to be.

For one thing, he couldn't help wondering whether Bo was in as much trouble as he claimed. Competing at the pro level, the two of them wound up in a group with three other shooters representing the states of Tennessee, Georgia, and West Virginia. Grant watched his friend shoot with cool, determined, and deadly accuracy. He understood all too well the stakes involved in competition at the national level. The hunting industry could be unpredictable—particularly in a region where recent hurricane activity had wiped out game, put miles of hunting land under water, and discouraged potential hunters. Bo's pro shop had done well in years past, but a depressed local economy had forced him to consider folding the store and shifting careers. Sickening prospect for a man with a family to support.

Adding to Grant's distraction was his awareness of Jana and Ty in the gallery. Every time he lined up to shoot, he felt his focus waver just a bit. He wanted to impress the woman, and he wanted to set a good example for the boy. At the same time, he almost physically felt their prayers and encouragement.

And at the end of the round, Grant held the high score, just one point ahead of Bo.

"I'll get you back tomorrow." Bo grinned as he shook hands, then left for the old town square, where a barbecue supper was being catered for the tournament contestants.

Knowing Jana wouldn't find much to eat there besides coleslaw and hush puppies, Grant asked where she and Ty wanted to go for supper. "And don't say the Golden Arches," he warned Ty with a wink.

"Mom doesn't do McDonald's. I've never even had a Happy Meal."

"You're so deprived." Grant skinned a hand across the kid's head. "How about this Chinese buffet I know of over in

Montgomery? There ought to be bushels of veggies for your mom, and good stuff for me and you too."

"Cool!" Ty's cloudy expression cleared. "Can I eat with chopsticks?"

Jana rolled her eyes. "Only if you promise not to make a weapon out of them."

It was a short fifteen-minute drive to the state capital. The restaurant turned out to be busy, but they managed to get a table in the small courtyard out back. Soft lights colored a fountain burbling in the corner, and exotic plants complemented traditional black and red tablecloths. The place was nothing fancy, but Jana seemed to enjoy its restful atmosphere. While she scoped out the buffet and came back to the table with her plate loaded with colorful and bizarre vegetables, Grant ordered sweet-and-sour chicken off the menu. It was the only Chinese food he liked.

After the waitress brought their iced tea, Jana bit into a crispy egg roll. "You came here just for me, didn't you?"

He shot a paper wad through a straw across the table at Ty. "I came for the entertainment." He grinned at Jana.

She shook her head as Ty returned fire. "LeeLee's got better manners than you two. Who's that man over there staring at you?"

Grant looked over his shoulder and nearly sucked a paper wad down his throat. Doug Briscoe, dressed in a tailored sport coat and crisp oxford shirt, sat at a table across the courtyard. His companion was a beautiful, polished blonde — not his wife. Before Grant could think what to say or do, Doug excused himself to the woman and crossed the courtyard.

"Gonzales! I thought that was you." Smiling, Doug held out a well-manicured hand. "Never would've thought you'd pick noodles and rice for dinner. For some reason I never caught up to you at the tournament today."

Staying seated, Grant shook hands. "Hey, man. What're you up to?" *Please don't let him mention the camp in front of Jana.*

Doug gave him an odd look. "I'm competing, of course. Not on your level, but still ... I've been practicing." His gaze drifted to Jana. "Looks like you're doing well since last time we talked."

Grant had no desire to introduce Doug to Jana, but not to do so — well, that would be even more awkward. "This is Jana Cutrere and her son, Ty. Jana, this is Doug Briscoe."

Her eyes widened. "How are you?"

"Better than I deserve." Doug's stock response, and Grant had begun to wonder if it might not be true. "How're things going with old man Goff?"

Grant's stomach started to hurt, and it wasn't from the deep-fried chicken. "Not now, Doug." He met Jana's dark, suddenly opaque eyes. *Please, Lord, don't let him sit down.*

Doug leaned down on the empty chair between Grant and Ty. "I'm trying to figure out a way we can sue, if you'll just say the word. You can't let the old goat get away with stealing your property." Jana caught her breath, drawing Doug's attention. "What? What did I say?"

"Doug, Jana is Mr. Goff's granddaughter." Grant felt like crawling under the table.

"Ah." Doug's thick black brows rose as his eyes skimmed Jana again. "I guess you've got the situation under control." A smirk curled his mouth. "Then I'll leave you folks to your meal. I'm sure we'll run into each other at the tournament. Pleasure to meet you, Jana." With a nod at Jana, he turned on his heel and returned to his table.

Watching Ty twirl noodles around his chopsticks, Grant avoided Jana's eyes. "You'll have to excuse him. He doesn't know what he's—"

"Yes, he does, Grant. He *does* know what he's talking about. And so do I." Jana glanced at Ty, who seemed oblivious to the undercurrents of tension that swirled around their little corner of real estate. Her voice remained soft and intent. "This is what I was afraid of. You conniving against Grandpa behind his back. With a—a *lawyer.*"

She said it as though Doug were some species of adder.

"I'm not conniving, and I'm not going to sue Alvin. I don't need to. We're going to work this out like two Southern gentlemen."

She pressed her lips together. He could tell it was killing her not to argue in front of Ty.

What killed *him* was the fact that every bit of goodwill he'd built up over the day had dissipated like dew under a hot Mississippi sun. Back to square one. Again.

The rest of the meal was accomplished in silence except for Ty's chattering about the tournament. Grant found himself responding rather at random, watching Jana's blank face and wishing he could think of a way to bridge the gap between them.

Nope. Not gonna happen now.

So he paid the bill and drove the three of them back to the Sleep Inn in Wetumpka. The little old town had long since rolled up the sidewalks, so even if Jana had been in a mood for entertainment, there was nothing to do but check in to the hotel.

She marched up to the registration desk, plunked her purse on the counter, and whipped out her wallet. "Single room for me and my son. Jana and Ty Cutrere." She slid out a credit card. "This is how you spell it."

Grant picked up the card and stuffed it into her purse. "I'm paying. I'm the one who invited you."

She gave him a fulminating look. "No. That wouldn't look right." Her gaze went to the young male desk clerk. "And make sure our room is on the opposite side of the hotel from him."

"Yes, ma'am." Stonefaced, the clerk looked at Grant. "I'll be right with you, sir."

"Jana—"

"Somebody might ask," she whispered over her shoulder, "and appearances matter."

"Yeah," he said, "let's make sure we've got all the outside surfaces covered."

She didn't respond, so he backed off and waited his turn, watching Ty trundle his suitcase around the lobby like a lawn mower with full sound effects. Sometimes he wished he could go back to being eight years old, when the thorniest issue in his life was Mom refusing to let him use his roller skates in the house.

Later that night Grant lay on the hard motel bed, listening to the roar of the air conditioner, thinking and praying. He missed the sound of the water lapping against the houseboat pontoons and the hum rising from the surrounding woods. He missed the gentle rise and fall of the boat on the water.

He also missed Jana's companionship.

Grant bunched the squishy hotel pillow under his head and flopped onto his stomach. What was God trying to teach him? Granny always said when things didn't go your way, you needed to *change* your way and get in line with the Holy Spirit.

Problem was, he didn't know how to do that in this situation. He'd been convinced God was telling him to leave the engineering business, to disentangle himself from partnership with Nathan Winters, to come home and strike out on his own. *"To a land that I will show you,"* like he'd once told Abraham. Did God still ask people to give up precious things, like he'd asked Abraham to sacrifice his promised son, Isaac?

No way. He couldn't be asking me to give up the hunting camp. That would be just plain ridiculous, after all the time and effort and money he'd put into it. Why did God give a man good common sense, except to use it?

I want to go your way, Lord. Just not too far. Okay?

Feeling righteous, he fell asleep.

Jana endured a tense continental breakfast at the hotel, then, with Ty at her heels, watched the morning round of day two progress uneventfully. Grant's friend Bo edged him out over the last three targets to win the round. After lunch—this time, an unappetizing crawfish boil—the five-man group reassembled, along with its gallery, for the final best-two-out-of-three round.

Afternoon shadows were drawing long; the crowd shuffled and whispered, tired from walking and standing such long hours, yet excited to see the conclusion of the tournament. Several kept score along with the shooters, who carried official scorecards in their pockets.

Jana had long since lost track of every man except Grant and his friend Bo. They were the two to watch, anyway. The last target was a deer, gazing into the forest with such lifelike eyes that it made Jana sad. How could she root for Grant to win when his object was to shoot an arrow into the grooved circles around the heart of that beautiful replica? How could she root for him when he'd betrayed her? In cahoots with a lawyer, for heaven's sake, who wanted to sue her grandfather.

Even now, remembering the man's smirk as he looked her up and down made her skin ice up and her hands shake. Like she was some cheap piece of jewelry Grant had picked up at Wal-Mart. She couldn't wait to get back home where she belonged. At least this was the end of the tournament. One more shot for each man, and it would be over. She just had to get through the awards ceremony.

Watching to make sure she didn't lose Ty, she pressed between a couple of guys in camo caps, where she'd have a better view. Bo stood at the stake ready to shoot. He lined up quickly, too quickly Jana thought, and his arrow pierced the second ring from the center, the ten-ring. He flinched with disappointment, then moved to the side, bumping his bow against his leg.

If Grant hit the center ring, he would win. He'd only missed once during this whole round.

Jana pressed Ty's shoulder and shifted her gaze to Grant's face as he retracted the string to line up his shot. He hesitated, all his muscles bunched, feet planted. One eye closed, he laid his nose against the string, trigger finger alongside his cheek, bow steady. There was absolute silence from the crowd.

Then it happened, so quickly that Jana would have missed it if she hadn't been watching Grant's every move for the past two days. His gaze flickered to Bo, then back to the target. There was a minute adjustment to the angle of the arrow, and he squeezed the trigger.

The arrow flew to the outside edge of the eight-ring.

Half the crowd groaned, Jana and Ty among them, and half cheered for Bo—who looked both astonished and delighted.

Grant shook hands, congratulated Bo, and accepted backslaps of commiseration from the three other shooters. "Guess the pressure got to me," he said over and over, his expression chagrined.

Jana stood there gripping Ty's shoulder, letting the crowd mill past her. How was she supposed to keep from falling in love with a man who would give up a prize of this magnitude for friendship? And give it up so subtly that the friend would never know?

She held her peace through the awards ceremony, during which Grant seemed almost giddy—not the reaction she would have expected from a man with a mile-wide competitive streak who'd just lost the tournament he'd been preparing to win for nearly a year.

In fact, she said nothing until that night on the way home, as they crossed the magnificent arched bridge over the Alabama River at Stockton. Glancing at Ty conked out in the backseat, hugging the big second-place trophy to his chest, she cleared her throat.

"I noticed something when we were at your houseboat that day."

"That it needs another coat of paint?" He smiled and turned down the radio.

"No. I noticed you have three ASA Shooter of the Year trophies holding up the bathroom sink."

He frowned. "So?"

"So you could have won this tournament in your sleep with one arm tied behind your back."

He laughed. "Now that'd be a sight."

"You know what I mean. You let Bo win today."

"I did not." The denial was immediate and loud.

In the dark cab, she couldn't tell whether or not he was blushing. "I *saw* you move the sight just before you shot. Why did you do that?"

"I told you, I got nervous."

"Grant, you were not nervous. You aimed, you looked at Bo, you moved the sight."

He was silent for half a minute, then sounded almost sullen. "You must've been watching from a funny angle. I don't play to lose."

"I know you don't. That's why this confuses me so."

Jana saw Grant's jaw shift as an interstate light flashed across his face.

"Okay, look, it's not that big a deal." Still looking flustered, he glanced at Jana. "I could take home another trophy to stick under the bathroom sink, get a bit of publicity, maybe brag a little at the feed store next week. But in the grand scheme of things, my website's doing more for my purposes than a shooting title."

She linked her fingers together and waited.

He sighed. "Bo, on the other hand, has a wife and two kids in college, and he's got everything invested in his shop. That title will bring him endorsements that'll boost his sales through the roof." He chuckled. "And if you want to know the honest truth, I *was* sorta nervous with Ty over there jumping up and down like a kangaroo on a trampoline."

Jana shook her head. "You're not blaming any of this on Ty."

"Of course I'm not. I'm just trying to explain ..." He glanced at her. "Any of what?"

"This thing, this ... whatever it is, between us." She spread her hands, looking at the ringless fingers, feeling the responsibility she held in them. "If you're trying to impress me with what a good and harmless guy you are, I'm not buying it. Some time ago, your sister said something happened to you while you lived in Atlanta—something that made you come home with this hunting camp embedded in your brain. I think she's right. You're so focused on whatever it is you're trying to prove, you're not seeing anybody else's needs but your own."

"How can you say that, when Heath Redmond is the ultimate opportunist? I've done everything in my power to make you and your kids feel welcome and secure—"

"The difference between you and Heath is he's right out in the open. You're like one of those camouflaged hunters moving around in the woods. Sneaking up on people and—zing—you've shot somebody through the heart."

"Is that what it looks like to you?"

"Yes. You don't know how that feels, and there's no way to describe how much it hurts."

"I beg to differ."

"Huh?"

"I know how it feels."

"Oh, sure. You with your intact family and generations of churchgoing ancestors in your pedigree."

He remained silent for a moment, posture relaxed, one wrist draped over the steering wheel. Finally, he sighed. "Okay, listen. The FBI told me not to talk about this. But I think you understand the concept of holding a secret better than anybody."

"Talk about—the FBI?"

"Can you keep this to yourself?"

"Of course, but—"

"All right then. Doug was my lawyer before he decided he wanted in on the hunting camp. My last partner was a crook. A real one. Embezzled over a million dollars through a tax shelter before I wised up. I got out before I ratted on him, and he's still under investigation. Unfortunately, he's a Slick Willy who may never get what he deserves." He sucked in a sharp breath and exhaled it slowly. "This guy was like a brother to me at one time. I got my trust factor reduced to zero. In a hurry."

Jana sat there a moment, absorbing not only his words but the pain behind them. "Well … maybe you do get it a little."

"You better believe I do. Jana, I'm sorry if you feel like I'm running over you sometimes. I get … focused, as my family always puts it. But I'm not a liar. The only time I'd hide anything from you is if I'm afraid it'll hurt you."

"It hurts worse to be kept in the dark." She reached up and turned on the cab overhead lamp, slanting yellow blobs of light across his cheekbones. The revelation of his hard, strong features, the gentle set of his mouth, was reassuring. "And I'm not as fragile as you think. So here's the light. If there's anything you're keeping from me in order not to hurt me, Grant—say it now."

He swallowed, then glanced at her. "Okay. Here's one you're not going to like at all. I promised Ty I'd take him hunting on the first day of bow season."

Never tell a woman the unvarnished truth unless you're pre-
pared for a nuclear meltdown.

Grant's collection of maxims was growing daily, right along
with his personal list of dumb mistakes. After driving thirty miles
in frozen silence, he pulled into Jana's driveway and snapped off
the ignition. "Wait, Jana. Don't wake up Ty. I'll carry him in."

"I can get him."

Oh yeah. Those teeth were clenched so tightly it would take a
jackhammer to blast them apart. So much for a good-night kiss.

"He's heavy. Don't be silly."

He heard her breath hiss in. Too late to salvage anything of
this miserable trip. Not only had he made a fool of himself by letting Bo win the tournament, he'd destroyed any chance he ever
had of winning Jana's respect—let alone her love.

Resigned, he got out of the truck, opened the passenger door,
and scooped Ty, a sleeping deadweight, into his arms. Jana went
ahead of him to unlock the front door. By the front porch light he
could see how screwed together her face was. She looked as if she
might shatter if he touched her.

Which he was not about to do. No, sir. He knew when it was time to cut bait.

He carried Ty to the bedroom he shared with Alvin, who slept flat on his back like a mummy all wrapped up in sheets, and waited for Jana to turn Ty's single bed down. LeeLee was spending the night across the road with Granny; at least Jana wouldn't have to worry about the little widget tonight. Stepping back, he watched her slip Ty's sneakers off, shuck him out of his jeans, and pull the sheet over him. The kid was out like a light.

"Thank you," Jana whispered stone dead. "Good night." She stood beside the bed as if willing him to leave.

Which cemented his determination to stay. Since when did a Gonzales give up like a total wimp? Back to the caballeros of old Mexico, they went after what they wanted with swashbuckling valor. *This bold renegade carves a Z with his blade . . .*

"Come here," he whispered.

"No." Her voice was still soft but strained.

"You have to let me explain why I promised—"

"No," she repeated. "It doesn't take a rocket scientist to figure that out."

King Tut muttered and turned over in his sleep.

Grant looked at Jana's beautiful, mulish face and folded his arms. He made no effort to lower his voice. "Okay, then we'll discuss it right here."

"Shh!" She glanced at her grandpa in alarm and put her hands against Grant's chest, pushing him out of the room. "Are you crazy?"

"I reckon so. Otherwise, I don't know why I brought home a deer with a broken leg." He kept backing until he was in the living room, dimly lit by a lamp on the TV. "I don't know why I built an aviary out of a satellite dish. I don't know why I took a vegetarian to an archery contest. And I sure don't know why I'm fixin' to do this."

He put his hands on each side of her face, tipped it up, and kissed her. He started gently enough because she wasn't expecting it—well, shoot, neither was he—but when her mouth dropped open, there was no way he wasn't going to take advantage of it, and before he knew it, they were in a full-blown lip-lock with her arms around his waist, straining together as if to erase their differences by sheer proximity.

It lasted who knew how long before one of them realized what was going on—he was pretty sure it wasn't him—and shoved away. In any case, by the time he got his wits back again, Jana was standing behind the recliner with her hand over her mouth and her eyes as wide as dinner plates.

His hands felt empty. He looked down at them, startled to find them shaking. "Well, that was interesting," he said, sounding exactly like that drunk pirate in the Disney movie.

"That was not interesting." Her voice was a hysterical hiss. "That was cataclysmic. And you better get out of here before I call the police."

He had to laugh. "The police? I'm pretty sure I wasn't the only one participating in—"

"You started it."

"No. *You* started it, twelve years ago."

"*Me?* You were the one who belted my boyfriend and then dumped your prom date to take me home."

"I was protecting you."

"Yeah, big bad protector. Leave me at the doorstep and hightail it without once looking back."

She was crying. *Oh, God, this isn't going like I wanted it to.*

He took a step toward her. "Jana, we were both different people then. We're adults now."

"We are. But too much has happened. We're too different from each other. You attract me, Grant—you know you always have—but you scare me too." Her hands moved, fluttered like butterflies, as if she didn't know what to do with them. She grasped the top of the chair. "You've got to leave Ty alone. You've got to leave me alone. I can't live like this."

He shook his head. "This is an awfully small town, Jana. We're going to see each other."

"Yes, but it can't be ... personal. It can't be ..." She touched her lips again.

"I love you, Jana."

She made a small noise as if he'd hit her. *God, what's wrong with this woman? What's wrong with me?*

He stuck his hands in his pockets and felt the sharp jab of his truck keys. *Okay, Zorro, get your butt out of here while your dignity's still mostly intact.* "All right. I'm leaving. But do me a favor. Don't tell Ty the hunting trip's off. At least let me do that. I need to explain what happened."

She turned her head away. He wasn't sure she'd even heard him.

He let himself out the front door.

Jana lay on her back in the high antique bed, wishing she had LeeLee to cuddle. She was going to fly into a million pieces without something to hold on to. She grabbed LeeLee's pillow, rolled over, and pressed her face into it. It smelled like coconut sunscreen and Barbie shampoo.

Lord, I can't stand it.

It had been all too easy, holding on to Grant, big and solid and warm with his own internal fire. Clutching handfuls of the back of his shirt, as if she could climb inside him ... Oh, how she missed being held and kissed. She hadn't realized how needy she was. This was frightening.

It was the right thing to do, pushing him away. Making him stay away. All she had to do to renew her anger was remember he was suing her grandfather. And he'd gone behind her back to promise her son a hunting trip.

The villain.

Who kissed like a hero in a romance movie.

She flopped onto her quivering stomach, shoving the pillow against her mouth.

Lord, please give me strength to stay away from him.

The Gulf Coast rainy season started early that year, plunging Grant into a gloomy premonition that his hunting camp was doomed no matter what happened with Alvin's property. By the end of August, the National Weather Service was predicting record numbers and intensities of tropical storms, warning residents of southern Louisiana, Mississippi, Alabama, and Florida to be prepared to evacuate at a moment's notice.

But every day he crammed his feet into rubber wading boots and slogged through mud up to his knees, clearing brush and working the food plots. Now all he had to do was get Alvin's signature. Bow season would start the first of October, and he was determined to be ready.

The first Saturday of September came with a brief respite from the waterlogged weather, beaming in on a shaft of warm sunshine. Feeling like Noah poking his head out of the ark after the flood, he dressed in his best jeans and a polo and called Tommy.

"Hey, man, what're you up to today?" He took the cell phone out onto the deck and stretched. "Want to ride up to the bow shop with me?"

He heard a clatter from Tommy's end that sounded like dishes rattling, and then water running. "Not today, thanks. Me and Carrie are going to Mobile to pick out cribs for the twins and get a birthday present for LeeLee. You want to come?"

He could just see himself in the baby store, tagging along with the prospective parents like a third wheel on a motorcycle. "I'll pass. When's LeeLee's birthday?" He missed the little squirt more than he wanted to admit to anybody. He'd seen her arriving at church last Sunday from a distance, dressed in a girly little dress with black patent shoes. She'd waved at him before Jana whisked her off.

"It's today. Didn't you get an invita—? Ow! Carrie! That wet towel stings."

Grant could hear scuffling noises over the phone and almost hung up in disgust. Carrie came on the line. "Sorry about that, Grant. He can go with you next week. I want to start decorating the nursery, and I need to know what the furniture's going to look like."

"Did he say LeeLee's birthday is today? And you're going to the party?" He felt like a little kid who'd been the only one left off the invitation list. Which he probably was.

Carrie sighed. "Yes, it's this afternoon at two. I didn't want Tommy to rub it in, knowing Jana didn't want … well, you know."

Yeah, he knew. He'd gone down in flames.

"I feel like I'm in the middle of two divorced people," Carrie said. "I've been trying to get her to listen to me, but she's awful pigheaded."

"You can say that again." He walked over to the rail and breathed in the river-scented breeze. "Don't worry about it, Care Bear. I'm a big boy."

"I know, but this is ridiculous. Just because she doesn't want to go out with you is no reason to punish the kids. They love you so much."

Grant felt his throat tighten. Good grief. He was turning into a sappy wuss. He cleared his throat. "Yeah, well, tell Sally Mr. Uncle Grant said 'happy birthday' and to eat an extra piece of cake for me."

"Okay. Bye, little brother."

Grant closed the phone, stuffed it into his pocket, and leaned out over the water. He could take the houseboat downriver and go fishing all by himself. Of course, it would be more fun with Tommy or even Ty, but *that* was out of the question too.

Muttering under his breath, he locked the cabin and stomped across the gangplank. He'd be hanged if he'd let Jana keep him from giving LeeLee a birthday present.

Jana woke up when LeeLee pounced on her bed at—yawning, she looked at the clock—nine o'clock? Goodness, she should have been out of bed hours ago.

"Mommy, I waited and waited, but you was still asleeping, so I made myself a waffle." LeeLee knelt at Jana's hip, still in her babydoll pajamas, with Glitter under one arm. Alf, who was only for nighttime security, was primly tucked under the covers beside Jana.

Jana blinked up into her daughter's cherub face. "You're a big girl, but I wish you'd gotten me up. What's Grandpa doing?"

"He went to the store to put up a sign that says 'Closed for Birthday Party.' I made it. I cooked him a waffle too!"

Jana laughed and leaned forward to kiss LeeLee's blooming cheek. "Happy birthday, punkin. I'm sorry you had to cook your own breakfast. Okay, I'm 'awaking' now." She sat up and scrubbed her hands over her face. She'd had dreams all night, probably why she'd slept so late. Dreams of being fiercely kissed and—

Whoa. Not going there.

"Did Ty go with your grandpa?"

"No, ma'am. He's outside feedin' the goats."

"Oh, what a good boy he is." Jana pulled LeeLee into a hug. "Let me get up and get dressed. Would you go tell Ty I'll be out to help in just a few minutes? I need to talk to you both about something."

LeeLee skipped out of the room, singing, "Happy birthday to me!"

Jana made the bed, then donned a pair of khaki shorts and a red cotton blouse in honor of the birthday party. She'd never considered herself much of a hostess, but LeeLee deserved a little extra attention today. The fact that Jana had been gone a lot lately was weighing on her conscience. Maybe she'd always been a working mom, but with LeeLee in school now, the time seemed to whiz by faster than ever.

She skipped breakfast in anticipation of nine thousand or so calories due for consumption at the party and hurried out to the barn, where she found Ty and LeeLee cleaning stalls. When she pitched in to help, the job was quickly dispatched.

"Come here, kiddos, we need a little family conference before Grandpa gets back." Jana sat on a hay bale and drew the children close. They both would need baths before company arrived, but the odor of straw and manure and animals had never been off-putting to Jana. She nuzzled her nose against the top of LeeLee's head and laughed when Ty sneezed. "Thank you for letting me sleep in this morning. I'm proud of the way you're taking responsibility around here."

Ty shrugged and swiped the back of his hand under his nose. "Mr. Grant said I should help you out whenever I could. Besides, I like the animals."

Jana was dying to know when Grant had had such a conversation with Ty.

"You're a sweetie," she said, earning a roll of Ty's blue eyes. She grinned. "Sorry—but you are. Anyway, I wanted to tell you about somebody special who's going to come to the party today." She'd rehearsed this over and over as she dropped off to sleep last night. There had to be a proper way to introduce the children to a grandmother they never knew they had.

LeeLee gasped. "Is it Santa Claus?"

Ty snorted. "Wrong song, ding-dong. It's not even Christmas."

"Ty." Jana chided him with a look, letting him know he'd just lost a bunch of brownie points. "No, darlin'—" she kissed LeeLee's cheek—"it's somebody better than Santa. You have a Grandma Shelby, your daddy's mama. I went to see her the other day, and she's looking forward to meeting you both."

LeeLee's forehead wrinkled. "Daddy had a mommy? That's funny!"

"Everybody has a mother and a father," Ty said. "Just like the baby goats."

"That's right." Jana's stomach tightened. With homicide and addiction in her and Richie's family trees, this conversation could get very weird very fast. She'd asked Roxanne and Carrie to pray for her about it.

"Where'd Dad's dad go? Is he gonna show up today too?" Ty's expression was curious, but not particularly anxious.

"No, he doesn't live in Vancleave anymore. Just Grandma Shelby."

"Oh. Okay." Ty pushed off the hay bale. "Can I go see if Jesse Paul Allen can come to the party? There seems to be an awful lot of *girls* coming."

Relieved to have dodged most of the potentially embarrassing questions—at least for now—Jana smiled. "Of course you can. I should have thought of that sooner. But, Ty—"

He paused in the barn door, looking over his shoulder. "Ma'am?"

"You'll have to have a bath before lunch."

"Mo-o-m!"

He disappeared, and Jana rubbed noses with LeeLee. "Boys are gross, huh?"

Grandpa's house was way too small to hold LeeLee's entire guest list—seven doting adults, three little girls from Miss Mahon's kindergarten, plus Ty and Jesse Paul—so Jana decided to move the party out into the yard. By ten after two, everyone except Shelby had arrived, and Jana stood on the porch surveying a scene of utter mayhem.

LeeLee's taste in decor included balloons left over from Roxanne's Sunday school party, silver tinsel strung in clumps on the cedar tree beside the front porch, and orange and black crepe paper streamers flying from the martin houses. Eclectic, to say the least, but somehow appropriate for a birthday girl wearing an angel costume from last year's Christmas pageant.

Jana smiled at the glittering flutter of wings and bob of halo, then beckoned Heath, who had shown up a few minutes earlier dressed in a red pearl-snap Western shirt and cowboy hat. "Come here, Wild Bill, I've got a job for you. You can saddle Cody and start the pony rides."

Technically, Cody was a miniature horse and should have been insulted at the misnomer, but Heath gave Jana a thumbs-up, whistled the giggling children into order, and marched them toward the barn. Fat little Cody took his assignment in stride with a resigned professionalism that had Jana resolved to ply him with apples and carrots for dinner.

Meanwhile, Grandpa managed to harness Molly to the home-made two-wheeled carriage without letting Jack take a plug out of him, and Tommy and Carrie set up the lawn darts. There would be plenty of entertainment for the afternoon.

Half an hour later, Jana, who had joined in the darts game, squinted as a cloud of dust kicked up at the end of the driveway. A black sedan emerged from around the mimosa tree; it looked as though Shelby had decided to come after all. Reuniting Shelby with her grandchildren in the confusion of a birthday party might not have been the best idea—but it was too late to undo the invitation. *Please, Lord*, she breathed, *let this be a sweet time for us all.*

Jana met Shelby as she got out of the car and gave her a brief hug. "I'm so glad you came."

Shelby thrust a lumpy, gaily wrapped package into Jana's hands. "Almost didn't. But Roxanne called this morning and said I should." She smoothed her hand over her gray-streaked blonde hair and tugged the white blouse down over her hips. Today she wore neat khaki slacks in place of the Wranglers. She glanced at the package, eyes worried. "I don't have much money to spare, but that's a little something for the birthday girl."

"Trust me. She'll be thrilled." Jana took her mother-in-law's hand. "You remember Tommy Lucas, right? Have you met his wife?"

With several colorful lawn dart hoops looped around his neck like leis and his usual friendly grin in place, Tommy went straight for a hug. He chuckled at Shelby's stiff response. "Hey, I promise I'm not gonna run over your flowers with my motorcycle anymore!"

Shelby relaxed, smiling. "And I promise not to squirt you with the garden hose."

Carrie approached with her hand extended. "I'm Carrie. Welcome."

Shelby's eyes lit. "Aren't you one of the Gonzales girls?"

"Yes, ma'am." Carrie gestured over her shoulder. "Matter of fact, Granny's here too."

Roxanne chugged over with a huge plastic jar full of bubble gum under her arm, her turquoise muumuu flapping around her bare calves. "Shelby! I'm so glad you decided to brave the ravening hordes! Listen, I need somebody to count all this gum for a game—are you up for it?"

Shelby blinked. "I suppose …"

Jana winced as Ty and Jesse Paul skidded to a halt behind Tommy, faces smeared with purple and crimson streaks. Heaven knew what they'd gotten into. And here came LeeLee pelting across the yard, wings flapping. "Ravening hordes" was about right.

Jana tugged Ty forward. "Shelby, somewhere under all this war paint is your grandson. Ty, say hello to Grandma Shelby."

Ty grinned. "Hey, Grandma. Wanna see me shoot my bow?"

Before Shelby had time to do more than raise her eyebrows, LeeLee flung her arms around her grandmother's waist, tipped her head back, and beamed up at her. "I know you! You're the piano lady! Can you teach me to play 'Ding Dong! The Witch Is Dead'?"

Shelby chuckled and hugged LeeLee tight. "We'll see."

With that social hurdle successfully leaped, Jana relaxed and met Carrie's amused brown eyes. "Will you and Tommy help me bring the refreshments out to the picnic table?"

"Sure."

The three of them lugged from the kitchen gallon jugs of blue Kool-Aid, soft drinks, and an ice chest containing the obligatory ice cream. Satisfied that everything was ready, Jana looked around with her hands on her hips. Getting everybody together would be like herding fleas.

"Huh. Leave it to me." Tommy issued an ear-splitting two-fingered whistle that brought the entire guest list running—including the dogs and cats.

Everyone clapped and cheered when Ty, singing a loud and off-key rendition of the birthday song, staggered down the porch steps. In his arms was a monstrous three-layer chocolate cake covered in chocolate buttercream frosting topped by confectionery roses the size of small cabbages. He'd made it yesterday afternoon after school in Carrie's shop while Jana was at work. He plunked it on the picnic table. "Happy birthday, sissy."

LeeLee strangled her brother in a hug. "*Thank* you! Choc'lit's my *favorite*!"

"Hey, get your feathers out of my mouth." Ty spit, pretending annoyance, but his cheeks reddened at her obvious excitement.

Jana reached over to straighten the cake's tipsy pink number five candle. "Thanks, Mrs. Lucas. I owe you one."

Smiling, Carrie laid a hand on her already blooming tummy. "My pleasure. Ty may give Emeril a run for his money one of these days."

"When are we gonna cut it?" demanded the chef. "I'm hungry."

"Presents first." Jana smiled at Ty's resigned sigh and handed LeeLee the gift from Shelby, which was on top of the stash. "This is from Grandma Shelby."

"Ooh, that's pretty!" LeeLee tore into the wrapping to reveal three coloring books and a large box of crayons. She hugged them, eyes shining. "Thank you, Grandma! That's my favorite!"

Every item LeeLee opened turned out to be her favorite, and Jana couldn't help wondering if gratitude was in direct proportion to the lack one had experienced.

I'm grateful, Lord. Don't think I'm not.

Inexorably her thoughts turned to the one missing guest. She shook her head, still feeling guilty. *Lord, I just couldn't face Grant being here today.*

Carrie had made one more stab at getting her to call him at the last minute. But every time she thought about that blistering kiss in Grandpa's living room—which happened fewer than ten times a day now—panic flooded every cell of her body. She wasn't grateful for that yet.

Finally, LeeLee opened her last gift, a pair of sparkly purple plastic high-heeled slippers from Heath, and tried them on.

Ty eyed them with barely disguised impatience. *"Now* can we have the cake?"

"Just a minute." Roxanne pinched his cheek, laughing. "One more thing from me and—" she waved her hand—"somebody else. Tommy, there's a box in the trunk of my car. Would you go get it?" She tossed over her keys.

Exchanging a look with Carrie, Tommy shrugged and obeyed. He came back with a large rectangular box wrapped in newspaper and set it on the ground beside LeeLee. "Here ya go, princess. Check that one out."

The sound of ripping paper was followed by stunned silence.

"Oh boy!" LeeLee clapped her hands and jumped up and down. "A keyboard just like Miss Roxanne's!"

Jana managed to get her breath back. "Roxanne, you can't give her a piano. It's too—"

"Don't worry, I had a little help." Roxanne's bright green eyes sparkled under those arched red eyebrows.

A nasty slug of suspicion slithered into Jana's stomach. "Please tell me he didn't."

But she knew he did; it was his MO, and everybody was looking at her. If she pitched a fit, she was going to look like a Grinch. So she ground out a smile. "After we have our cake and ice cream, maybe Grandma Shelby will help you set it up in the living room and give you a lesson."

"Okay." LeeLee squatted to examine the picture on the outside of the box. "But first I gotta call Mr. Uncle Grant and tell him thank you."

Jana frowned. There was no card with the piano. How did she know it came from Grant?

LeeLee looked up at Jana. "How come he didn't come to my party?"

chapter 20

On Sunday Tropical Storm Umberto hit the Yucatan Peninsula and surfed his way up through the Gulf of Mexico to souse Louisiana. Coastal Mississippi also got several days of steady downpour that flooded the creeks meandering in and out of the Pascagoula River. Grant decided the better part of valor would be temporarily moving in with his grandmother until hurricane season ended.

This decision had nothing to do with the fact that from Granny's front porch he had a clear view of Alvin Goff's little house across the highway.

The Saturday morning after LeeLee's birthday, Grant was sitting in the swing by himself, eating oatmeal out of a Teenage Mutant Ninja Turtles bowl and watching the rain come down in gusty spatters, when his cell phone rang. He unclipped it from his belt and stared at the display, where Jana's eyes sparkled at him. Oatmeal congealed in his stomach.

Did she know he'd been watching her house like some sicko stalker?

He flipped open the phone. "Hello?"

"Hello, Mr. Uncle Grant! This is LeeLee! Mommy said I could call and talk to you on the phone if I didn't take too long 'cause she's got stuff to do in Mobile today and—ma'am? Okay." She gave a little huff. "I'm supposed to say thank you for the piano and get right off the phone."

Grant couldn't speak for a moment. He could picture Jana standing over LeeLee, wanting to do the right thing, wanting to teach her daughter manners, but wishing she could ignore an unwanted gift. He'd known it might cause trouble, but doggone it, that little girl deserved a piano, and he'd wanted to give her something extravagant. He just wished he could've been there to see her open it.

He pressed the spoon against the side of the bowl like a lever and watched oatmeal blob into the bowl. A fine mess. "You're welcome. Have you had a lesson yet?" Granny'd told him Shelby Cutrere was going to teach LeeLee.

"No, sir, not yet. Grandma's going to come over this afternoon and start me. She says I have to learn the black keys first. Don't you think that's weird? I like the white keys too."

Grant felt a rusty chuckle erupt from his chest. He hadn't laughed in nearly two weeks. "Yeah, but you do what your grandma says. She's the expert."

"Okay." LeeLee sighed. "Can you come over and listen to me play, soon as I learn something?"

"Of course I will." He could just see Jana hyperventilating on the other end of the line, but he didn't care. Well, the problem was, he *did* care. For her and the kids. He felt like a man in an emotional straitjacket. "Tell you what, Sally, just give me a call and I'll be right over, okay?"

"Yessir. Mommy says I gotta go. But I really, really, really like my piano."

"I know," he managed to get out, inexplicably choked. Probably the oatmeal. "I'll see you around, Sally."

Jana took the phone from LeeLee and walked straight to the front window. The sheers were already closed as usual, but she yanked the drapes shut as well. She didn't want to see Grant sitting on his grandmother's porch. It had been hard enough when he was living over at the river on the houseboat—but to know he was right over there at Roxanne's, keeping tabs on when she and the children left the house ...

She clenched her teeth. She should call him back and tell him to go inside.

Then she realized how ridiculous that would sound. He'd know she was standing at the window looking at him, like some giggly junior high twit twirling her hair. Why should she pay attention to where he ate his breakfast?

Snatching the drapes wide again, she marched into the kitchen, where LeeLee was peeling an orange and feeding it to the cat. She unplugged the coffeepot and started to rinse the carafe. "Run and tell Ty to hurry brushing his teeth so we can go. We're meeting Uncle Quinn for breakfast."

Lee Lee's eyes lit. "At Krispy Kreme?"

Jana nodded. "It's his favorite place."

LeeLee hopped off her chair but paused in the doorway. "Will we be back in time for my piano lesson?"

Jana sighed, leaned her arms on the sink, and watched rivulets of rain descend against the window. "Yes, baby." She turned her head and smiled to reassure her daughter. "I promise."

There were some things you just didn't go back on, no matter how much you might like to.

The next Wednesday night Grant arrived at church in time for supper, parked in his usual spot next to the sanctuary doors, and dashed through the monsoon with his trombone in a black plastic trash bag. He propped his maroon-and-white golf umbrella in a corner of the foyer, then started up the stairs to the rehearsal room where he usually left his instrument while he ate in the fellowship hall. The sound of piano music caught his ear, however, and he paused with his foot on the second tread.

That sounded an awful lot like one of the songs from *The Wizard of Oz*. What was it? Not "Munchkinland." Not "Yellow Brick Road," either. He thumped his head trying to remember. He must have watched that movie a hundred times as a kid at Granny's house.

But come to think of it, why would Faye King, the church accompanist, be practicing Broadway tunes on the church piano?

He retraced his steps through the foyer and cracked open the doors into the sanctuary. And nearly fell out on the Nile green carpet. There was LeeLee, perched on the bench behind the grand piano, hands on the keys, head tilted like a little bird. Tweety Pie — that was who she reminded him of.

And then he recognized the song. "Ding Dong! The Witch Is Dead."

Stifling his laughter, he tiptoed into the sanctuary and sat down on a back pew. After all, he'd promised he'd listen to her play sometime. Jana wasn't anywhere around — if he wasn't mistaken, that was Shelby Cutrere sitting in a folding chair beside LeeLee with her back to Grant.

Evidently LeeLee had won the war over black versus white keys. She was playing all over the instrument.

Ten minutes into the lesson, Shelby sighed and closed the lid over the keys. "LeeLee, I want you to look at your music!"

Frustration filled the big blue eyes. "But I already know it by heart!" Then LeeLee looked across Shelby's head and saw Grant. "Oh! Oh! Mr. Uncle Grant!" She hopped off the bench and came tearing down the aisle to fling herself at him. "I didn't know you was here!"

He hugged her, something painful snagging in his chest at the feel of silky dark curls tickling his chin. "I didn't know you would be either. I thought you were having your lessons at your house."

"Grandma said we needed neutral territory."

He glanced at Shelby, who had stood up, pencil and notepad clutched in both hands. She smiled, sheepishly, he thought.

Releasing LeeLee, he took her small face in his hands. "I think that was a great idea. What did I tell you about Grandma being the expert?"

LeeLee's eyes fell. "Oh yeah. I forgot."

"You listen to what she says. Delayed obedience is no obedience. Got that?"

"Yes, sir." She looked at him, eyes shimmering. "I'm sorry."

"Tell your grandma."

"Okay." She heaved a sigh. "Now, I guess."

"That's right."

In one of her lightning mood shifts, LeeLee grinned, threw her arms around his neck, and kissed his cheek. "I love you, Mr. Uncle Grant." She was flying back toward the platform, shouting,

"I'm sorry I delayed, Grandma. I'll look at the music and play the black keys for the next two hundred years!"

Grant slid down against the pew, feeling like a blob of Play-Doh. *God, just squish me right now and tell me what to do. I can't take this anymore.*

enjoyed the Bible study so much." Shelby walked beside Jana to the children's wing to pick up Ty and LeeLee after choir. "Thank you for inviting me."

"I should have thought of it sooner." Jana smiled. Shelby had agreed to pick the kids up after school and bring them to the church for LeeLee's lesson. "LeeLee has been so excited about playing on the big piano." A thought tightened her stomach. "How'd she do today? Did she cooperate?"

Shelby's soft mouth turned up. "We had a bit of a head-butting until Grant came in to listen."

"Until—what?" Halfway down the hall, Jana stopped, letting other moms filter past.

Shelby laughed. "I don't know what he said to her, but she was good as gold afterward."

Jana's mouth opened and closed. She was not going to stand there and rant like a fishwife in front of Shelby. She wasn't going to rant period. "I'll talk to him and ask him not to interrupt her lessons anymore," she said carefully.

"No, no, don't do that. He didn't stay long, and like I said, LeeLee minded her p's and q's while he was there." Shelby adjusted the neckline of her blouse and looked away. "Don't mean to be nosy, Jana, but folks say you got pretty close to Grant this summer. I just wanted you to know that I think that would be a good thing for the children. To have a daddy like him, I mean. The

Gonzales family is a fine one ..." Her voice trailed off, gray eyes misting.

Jana sighed. "Thanks, Shelby. I know you mean well. But we're doing great by ourselves. Grant and I aren't ... It's not like that, you know?" Boy, was that the understatement of the year.

"Oh." Shelby gave Jana a puzzled look. "Sorry if I assumed the wrong thing. It's just that from what LeeLee said, I thought—"

"What did she say?" Jana leaned against the wall as her knees buckled.

"She said Mr. Uncle Grant-Daddy wanted her to learn to play 'Here Comes the Bride.'"

Jana felt as though her skin were going up in flames. Her eyeballs even seemed to be on fire. Whether he knew it or not, Grant was tearing her children apart. In many ways this situation was worse than losing their father. At least Richie had mercifully died and gone away, never to inflict his sorry self on them again. What was she going to do about this good and gentle man whom she couldn't give herself to and yet couldn't seem to do without?

She had no doubt the "Here Comes the Bride" comment was the sole fruit of LeeLee's fertile imagination, and Grant would be horrified to know he'd had anything to do with planting it. Still, Jana knew she'd somehow have to yank such baby yearnings out by the roots. Otherwise, they were going to grow into one fine dysfunctional mess. Ugh.

She pushed away from the wall and gave Shelby a wan smile. "Well. Wasn't that creative? I'll have to talk to her about it. Looks like they're letting out. How many minutes do you want her to practice this week?"

On a soggy mid-September afternoon, the rain paused long enough that Grant made up his mind to go home and stomp around in the woods for a while. If he didn't get some exercise, he was going to climb the walls. There were only so many episodes of HGTV—Granny's favorite channel—a guy could watch and still retain any semblance of manhood.

Driving past Alvin's house, he forced himself to keep his eyes on the road. Early this morning he'd watched Jana put the kids on the school bus and then putt off to the clinic in that scuzzy little Subaru of hers. He hadn't approached her or even called her since the night he'd kissed her. Easier just to pretend it hadn't happened.

Parking the truck by the side of the road, he got out and walked into the woods, nothing in his hands, not even his bow. He stepped over wet pine straw and sloshed through standing puddles, letting the familiar odors of vegetation and earth soothe the restless jitters that had turned him into a bear lately. Granny was a saint to put up with him.

He stopped in a clearing where weak sunlight dripped onto his face when he looked up. The foliage was turning, brown and yellow dappling the leaves. Fall was on the way; he could smell it in the lichens on the trunks, sense it in a certain edge to the wind rushing through the tops of the trees. The animals were moving too. Soon his plans for the hunters would chase away this terrible pointless, centerless feeling in his gut.

He wished CJ would come along and tell him some story from years gone by when things were simple—when you had to hunt just to stay alive. When your family didn't eat if you didn't take your gun out every day and come home with meat for the pot. Man, he wished he could've lived back then, in the days before "work" meant putting on a dress shirt and driving for hours to an office where you sat in front of a computer for even more hours, figuring out formulas to make some techno-gizmo that would make life faster and easier for other people.

Who would then have to find ways to spend the extra time on their hands.

He shook his head at his own circling thoughts. *To be or not to be*: *that is the question.*

Whatever. Why was it when he waxed philosophical he tended to resort to movie quotes or lines of Shakespeare he'd learned in high school English? Wasn't the Bible where you were supposed to turn? At the moment he couldn't come up with a single verse that applied.

Well, maybe 1 John 1:7, which had shown up in his devotions a couple of days ago. "If we walk in the light, as he is in the light, we have fellowship with one another, and the blood of Jesus, his Son, purifies us from all sin." Ha. Things were just about as dark as they could get, including the weather, and he certainly didn't have fellowship with the one person in the world who mattered the most to him.

He'd heard people say you were supposed to be content with just the Lord's company. A nice idea in theory, but since he hadn't been called to live in a monastery, somebody was going to have to give him some instructions on how to deal with this ache of longing for Jana.

You hear that, Lord? I'm getting desperate.

He walked on and found himself following the little road that led to Willis and Crowbar's camper. He hadn't seen much of the Dyer brothers in the last few weeks. Maybe they'd gotten rehired at the shipyard. Maybe one or the other had been sick. He should go check.

"Yo, Willis! Crowbar!" he called when the Winnebago came into view. He didn't want Crowbar letting loose with the .44 he kept just inside the front door. "Anybody home?"

"Down here, Mr. Grant!"

Sounded like Willis's voice—surprisingly light for a man his size—coming from the woods behind the camper, where Forrest's empty pen was. Curious, Grant headed that way.

Grant stopped, staring. "Willis, what have you done?"

During the two weeks Grant had been living at Granny's house, Willis had transformed a three-thousand-square-foot area of woods into a working animal shelter. Eight-foot-high chain-link fencing supported by wooden posts composed a series of three long, open-air runs, plus one rectangular section covered with a tin roof. The aviary, now enclosing an oak sapling, housed a family of squirrels. A couple of raccoons, a coyote, and a nest of field mice—all in varying stages of bandaging and recovery—were among the inmates of this amazing facility. There were undoubtedly more underneath the shelter.

Willis, seated on a stump with a snake in one gloved hand, looked up and grinned. "I'm taking care of the refuge until Miss Jana gets off work."

Where is she?" Grant placed his hands flat on the counter at the receptionist's window in Heath's clinic. He did his best to block out the Cathedral Quartet—who, as far as he knew, had been retired for at least a decade—belting out "Don't It Make You Want to Go Home" from the boom box in the corner.

Dora took a red Dum Dum sucker out of her mouth and looked at him with patent confusion. "Who?"

"Dr. Tree Hugger."

She put on her glasses as if that would clarify his meaning. "Are you lost, honey?"

"Where is Jana?" he enunciated clearly.

"Oh!" She gave his hand an aren't-you-cute swat. "She and Dr. Heath went out to Rollie Jefferson's to geld his llama."

He couldn't help wincing in sympathy. For the llama. "When will they be back?"

The glasses bounced onto Dora's matronly bosom and the sucker returned to her mouth. "These things take time," she said around it. "Got to watch and make sure there aren't any complications." She paused. "You can wait, if you like."

The CD switched to "I've Read the Back of the Book."

"No, thanks. I think I'll drive out there."

He walked outside and wandered down to the goldfish pond. His thoughts darted and swam with just about as much purpose as the fish. The trouble was, he knew he shouldn't be upset with Jana—she'd been very clear from the beginning that she wanted her grandfather's property.

Talking to Jana wouldn't do a bit of good, now that he thought about it. *Alvin* was the conniving liar who'd backed out on a gentleman's agreement.

If only he'd gotten something in writing. *Stupid, Gonzales. You of all people know not to trust anybody's word.*

Okay, so he'd just have to figure out a way to make the old man settle out of court for his road access without letting it drag on indefinitely. Doug Briscoe would probably have some ideas.

J ana loved the house call part of her job, and it wasn't just Paco the llama's whimsical way of pursing his lips just before blowing spit all over the front of her scrub shirt. If she'd had to stay inside that clinic with Dora's gospel quartet music one more minute, she would've committed hari-kari.

She patted her sleeping patient's wooly brown neck. "Paco will be fine, Rollie. Just keep an eye on him until he wakes up and give me or Dr. Redmond a call if anything looks unusual."

Rollie hitched up his sagging pants. "Yes, ma'am, I will. Reckon he'll quit chasing Dandy around the pasture?"

Jana laughed. "I can't promise. But he should be a lot less aggressive."

"My wife said Paco scared the mess out of her last week when he first started that screaming business. She thought one of 'em was dying."

"Boys will be boys. It's just their way of trying to establish control." Jana walked out of the barn with Rollie and spotted Heath out in the paddock, checking the feet of one of the Jeffersons' prize quarter horses. She sighed. Goodness knew she'd had plenty of experience handling the alpha male ego lately.

Rollie leaned on the top rail of the paddock and called out to Heath, "Hey, Doc, you hired yourself a winner here. Better watch it or she'll be taking over your practice."

Heath released the chestnut's hoof and winked at Jana. "There's plenty to go around. Besides, two heads are better than one, right?" He walked over to Jana and dropped a casual arm around her shoulder.

She rolled her eyes. Flirting was like breathing to Heath. "This head needs lunch before we go back to the clinic. I've got appointments scheduled for the rest of the afternoon." She slid out from under Heath's arm and headed for the truck.

"Rollie, we'll send you a bill. Let us know if you need anything." Heath caught up to Jana and opened the passenger door for her. "You okay, Jannie?"

"Don't call me that." She frowned. "That's what Richie called me, and I can't stand it."

He looked at her for a moment. "Sorry. I didn't know."

She made herself smile. "That's why I just told you. Come on, let's go get a sandwich."

Heath shrugged and went around to the driver's seat. "Cole's okay?"

"Sure." She'd been avoiding restaurants since LeeLee's birthday, but that was ridiculous. So what if she ran into Grant? They were both grown-ups, right?

They got their food—Heath insisted it was his treat—and found an empty table on the porch. Jana ate her grilled cheese, then picked at her fries, staring off into space. She jumped when Heath cleared his throat.

"Are you gonna tell me what's going on with you and Gonzales?" Heath's deep, sexy gray eyes held their usual twinkle. He'd long finished eating and sat relaxed, chewing on his straw.

"Nothing's going on. Nothing has ever been going on." She looked away. "Why?"

"I'm getting to know you pretty well, Jana. You're looking over your shoulder."

She jerked her head around straight. "I am not."

He chuckled. "I knew he'd eventually screw things up. Was it the keyboard?"

"I don't want to talk about Grant or that keyboard."

"Good. Then let's talk about us."

She stared at him. "What do you mean, *us*?"

"You know. Moving this partnership forward a little. I'd like to take you somewhere nice this weekend. Maybe Atlanta."

Her mouth opened and closed. "No." She couldn't come up with anything less bald. "Um, no."

"Come on, we could stay downtown and do the sights there, then go to a ball game the next day. The Braves are in the playoffs."

"You mean overnight? Are you crazy?"

He shrugged. "Why not? You went to that overnight thing with Gonzales last month."

"That was ..." Her face felt as if it were on fire. "Ty was with us the whole time. There was nothing—Oh, I knew I shouldn't have done that. I'm a Christian woman, Heath. I do not—" she lowered her voice and whispered—"sleep around!"

"At all?" He looked incredulous.

"No!"

He thought about that for a minute. "Oh. Well then, we'll just drive over to Mobile and go to a movie or something."

Jana dropped her chin into her palms and studied Heath. "You know what I think?"

His confident expression faltered under her regard. "I'm afraid to ask."

"I think the only reason you want to take me out is to step over Grant."

"No way!"

"That's also the reason you've been helping me with fundraising for the wildlife center. You two are like a couple of juvenile llamas chasing and butting one another back and forth across the pasture."

"You don't have to insult me." But he took his straw out of his cup and concentrated on tying it into a series of knots.

She sighed. "It's just so ridiculous. You two are both intelligent guys with enormous talent and good friends and great families. Why can't you just leave one another alone and be happy?"

A minivan drove into the parking lot of the body shop next door. Heath squinted at it. "Hey, that's the pastor's wife. Wonder what she's up to?"

Jana just watched him until he looked at her.

"There's something missing," he mumbled.

"Missing from what?" She'd never seen Heath confused. Ever. But he was chewing on the end of his mustache.

"Me. I asked Gonzales about it, and he gave me this rigma-role about GPS systems and praying and finding your way back to God."

A bubble of laughter floated up and almost escaped. *Oh, Grant.* "Heath, don't you ever pay attention in church? Pastor David talks about this all the time."

"When I'm in church I'm usually thinking about you."

Dismay killed the laughter. "Well, just stop it right now! I don't want you thinking about me."

"I don't mean anything ... lewd. I'm just trying to figure out what makes you so different from most of the single women I know. You've got your head on straight, Jana. And as long as we're being honest, so does Gonzales. That's why I can't understand why you keep pushing him away."

This conversation had more twists than a pretzel. "On the campout you threw a punch at him."

Heath tugged his mustache. "I was provoked."

Jana struggled to stay on point. "If you say so. Back to the original topic. Grant tried to explain to you how to know the Lord?"

"Yeah, but what he said to do seems too hard. I don't want to get fanatical or anything. I just want to be religious enough to be a good person and feel, you know, peaceful."

Looking at her handsome, happy-go-lucky partner, Jana was filled with deep sadness. *There I was twelve years ago.* "Heath," she said gently, "that's like asking somebody how to play chess and then deciding you're gonna replace all the game pieces with marbles. Jesus said, 'I'm the way, the truth, and the life, and no one comes to the Father except through me.'"

His eyes narrowed. "So ... basically I've got to decide how bad I want you, huh?"

"No!" *Oh, Lord, have mercy!* "This has nothing to do with me. It's between you and God. Please don't put me in this position." She reached across the table and grabbed one of his big, gentle hands. He was a healer, and he had so many good qualities, but he was one of the most pigheaded men she'd ever known. Outside of her grandfather and Grant Gonzales. "Heath, I'm praying for you to listen when God speaks to you. But whether you say yes or no to him, I won't—I will *not* be anything more than your friend and your partner." She squeezed his fingers. "Do you hear me?"

His mouth twisted. "I hear you," he muttered. "Are you gonna eat the rest of your fries?"

c h a p t e r   2 1

been lookin' for you, boy," drawled CJ Stokes.

Head down, Grant was getting the back of his neck shaved by Tommy's cousin, volatile proprietress of Cheryl's Cut 'n Curl. Looking up carefully so as not to get sliced and diced by her razor, he met the game warden's amused gaze in the beauty shop mirror. "Well, you've sure got a captive audience." Grant flapped the cape strapped around his neck. Cheryl was the best barber in town, so he was willing to put up with a flamingo pink garment once a month. "What's up, CJ?"

"Gotta talk to you about somethin' serious." CJ slid his hands into the pockets of his coveralls. "When you get done here, why don't you meet me out to the house?"

"Sure." Understandable that CJ didn't want to talk here. The fastest way to get news spread across the entire tri-state area was to mention it in front of Cheryl Lamont.

Twenty minutes later, barbered and itching like a kid with chicken pox, he presented himself at CJ's carport door. CJ let him in and offered freshly brewed coffee. Mugs in hand, they sat across from each other at Pearl's cloth-covered breakfast table. The Stokes' home was small, simple, and filled with old, homemade furniture and hand-made curtains and upholstery. Tones of orange, olive green, and brown reminded Grant of the woods. He relaxed.

CJ slurped his coffee, then set it down and took off his John Deere cap. He looked at it, turning it in his hands. "I found our poacher."

"Poacher?" Grant tipped his head. CJ was always nosing out poachers. Why would he call Grant over to tell him about this one, unless—? "You mean the one who shot that doe in Alvin's woods back in June?"

"Yep. Caught him headlightin' last night. Shell casings from the June incident matched his ammo."

Grant licked his lips. "Who was it?" He had a feeling he didn't really want to know.

"Crowbar Dyer."

"No way." Grant thought he might throw up. The coffee all but sloshed out of his cup, his hand shook so hard. He managed to get it on the table. "Why would he do that?"

"Said he had to eat. He's been out of work for several weeks now."

Grant hadn't had any work to give either of the Dyer brothers during the rainstorms, but he thought Willis had been working for Jana. He'd assumed … Well, he'd assumed she'd been paying him something. Remorse hit hard. "I feel like this is my fault, CJ. I should have checked to make sure they had food."

If nothing else, the church had a benevolence fund. It could have provided for the brothers.

CJ shook his head, replacing his cap. "We got laws for a reason. To protect everybody. You can't go around shootin' a gun out of season. You know that."

"Yeah, but—"

CJ's thin lips tightened. "Don't be feelin' sorry for that weasel. It'd burn you up to see the little deer he hit last night. Not much more'n a fawn."

Grant winced. What if it had been Forrest? That would be too much of a coincidence, but he couldn't get the idea out of his head. "Is Crowbar in jail?"

CJ nodded. "Didn't have any way to pay the fine. The reason I wanted you to know was so you can tell his brother, make sure he's fed and don't get in trouble himself. I know the two of 'em's been living out there on your property."

"I'll pay Crowbar's fine." Grant gripped the edge of the table. "I want to help him and Willis both, if it's not too late."

A glimmer of a smile lit CJ's deep-set eyes. "You're a good boy, and I knew I could count on you. But Crowbar's prob'ly better off right where he is. He can't get in no trouble, and at least he's fed and out of the rain."

"I guess you're right." Grant took a deep breath. "Okay, I'll go look for Willis and make sure he's taken care of." He held out a hand to CJ, who took it in a hard grasp. "Thanks for letting me know."

Being responsible for somebody besides himself gave Grant the odd sensation of walking in his father's shoes. Maybe because he was here in the hospital, his dad's turf.

He'd found Willis curled on the floor of the camper, white as a sheet, holding a bleeding hand to his chest. One of those nasty little gray squirrels had bitten the tender pad between thumb and forefinger as Willis tried to change its splint. Grant couldn't even imagine the pain. So he'd half-carried two hundred thirty pounds of hulking giant nearly a quarter mile out to his truck and driven like a maniac to the emergency room.

"My dad'll be here soon," he said for the fourth time, resisting the urge to pester the nurse again. She'd been nothing but nice already, but there wasn't anything she could do until a doctor became free. The ER staff was all busy with the victims of a car wreck.

Willis nodded and gulped, tears of pain leaking out of his little black eyes. He put his head down on his knees.

Grant couldn't help thinking of the night Crowbar ran over Alvin. The night he'd first gotten to know Jana. Amazing how his life had gotten all twisted up with the Dyers and the Cutreres. He was a different person now, and he didn't think he wanted to go back to the freedom of that pre-Jana time. There were a lot of things he'd do differently, of course—but since he couldn't change the past, at least he could walk straight in the present.

His phone buzzed against his hip, and he snatched it out of his pocket. "Dad! Where are you?"

"I'm on my way, son. Sit tight, I've got some other bad news. Alvin Goff fell again and apparently busted up that same hip. He and Jana will be there any minute."

"You're kidding." What else was going to go wrong today? "How did that happen?"

"He was up on a ladder at the store—where he didn't have any business in the first place, in the shape he's in—and lost his balance. He crawled over to the phone and called Jana. She called the ambulance. I've paged Buddy to come in off the golf course, so he'll get there as soon as he can."

"That's good." Dad's partner in the Vancleave family practice clinic was a good man, always ready to help. "Hurry, Dad. Willis is scaring me."

"You know I will."

Ten minutes later, the ER doors burst open, and the EMT team wheeled in a gurney from the ambulance parked outside. Alvin. And Jana ran in right behind the stretcher. Grant stood up, shaken by a strong sense of déjà vu.

Jana was so intent on her grandfather she barely glanced at Grant as she followed the gurney to the registration window. But she did a double take when she passed Willis.

"Willis! What's the matter?"

Willis looked up, pasty-faced, but put his head right back down again. "Hey, Miss Jana," he mumbled into his knees. "How ya doin'?"

"One of your doggone squirrels bit him." Grant patted Willis's massive shoulder. "I'm just hoping it wasn't rabid."

"How long ago?" Jana glanced at her grandfather, who was being signed in by one of the emergency techs. Tension vibrated from her tall, slender body.

"An hour maybe? I found him lying on the floor writhing in pain and rushed him right over here, but we've been waiting awhile. My dad and his partner are both on the way."

"Are you sure it was a squirrel?"

"That's what Willis said."

"Then he's going to be fine. Squirrels rarely get rabies."

"Oh, I didn't know that." Grant looked at her, chagrined.

She knelt beside Willis and laid a hand on his head. "I've been bitten a time or two myself. It really hurts."

"Ms. Cutrere?" called the registration clerk. "We're moving your grandfather down the hall now. Would you like to come with him or wait here?"

"I'll come." She stood up, her expression troubled. "Willis, I'm so sorry this happened. I'll be praying for you." Her gaze dragged over to Grant as if against her will. "Would you pray for Grandpa? I'm so scared."

"Of course I will." Grant got to his feet, torn between the need to stay with Willis and an equally strong urge to make sure Alvin was attended to. He grabbed Jana's hand as she turned. "I have to talk to you."

She pressed her lips together, her gaze darting to the orderly pushing her grandfather away. "I've got to go. After Willis is settled, come find us."

"Do you need me to pick the kids up after school?"

"No." She backed away. "I called their grandma — Shelby," she added when he looked confused. "She was happy to help out."

He didn't know whether to be relieved or disappointed.

Just then the ER doors slid open again, and this time it was his dad. Grant flung his arms around his startled sire. "Boy, am I glad to see you."

Jana was staring out the window of Grandpa's hospital room when she heard a knock on the door, followed by Grant's voice softly calling her name.

Heart bumping up a notch, she turned. "Come in, Grant."

"Hey, lady ..." He stepped inside, closing the door behind him. "How is he?"

"He's asleep right now — they've got him sedated because of the pain." She stayed where she was. Maybe she could deal with him as long as he was on the opposite side of the room. "How's Willis?"

Grant stuffed his hands into his jeans pockets. "You were right. He'll be good as new in a day or two. They gave him a shot of penicillin, bandaged him, and I took him home. He's conked out too." He scratched his nose. "I, uh, checked on your critters while I was there. Everybody seems to be fine."

"Good. Thanks." She moistened her lips. "Your dad told me about Crowbar. Did you know he was in jail?"

"Yeah. Mr. CJ told me this morning. That's how I happened to discover Willis. I went to check on him."

"I'm so glad you did. Rabies or not, an animal bite can get infected easily."

He shrugged. "I just feel bad that I didn't know they were in such dire straits. I should've looked in on them a long time ago."

"I know. I've been all wrapped up in getting my feet on the ground at the clinic. I left Willis in charge of the refuge, assumed you were paying him, like you had been, and—" She lost the thread of her words abruptly. There was no excuse for such callous inattention. Focusing on Grandpa's shallow breaths, she clutched her hands together to hide their trembling.

"I haven't had any work for him all week because of the rain. I guess ... It looks like your grandpa decided to give you the property after all."

The stiffness of his tone got her attention. She looked up. "What do you mean?"

His expression was wooden. "I saw all the pens set up in the clearing where we put the aviary."

"Grandpa's still holding out. But people keep bringing me injured wild animals. Heath didn't want them at the clinic, so he found funds for a couple of new pens. Are you telling me you didn't know they were there?"

"That was weeks ago. I've been living at Granny's house for a while now. I walked over to check things out and all of a sudden, there's this ... this full-blown animal hospital, practically on my doorstep." He frowned. "So Alvin didn't give you permission to build that stuff on his property?"

"Alvin most abso-dang-lutely did not give her permission to build no varmint hospital on my land. Especially if it's gonna be regulated by the federal government."

Jana's head whipped around to find Grandpa wide awake and hopping mad, if the crimson mottling of his complexion was any indication. "Grandpa! You're supposed to be asleep!"

"How's a body supposed to sleep with people carryin' on an argument loud enough to wake the dead?" Grandpa glared at Jana. "And I want to know who's minding my store?"

"Trini's visiting her daughter in New Orleans, so I closed it for the day, Grandpa. Everybody understands when there's an emergency."

Grandpa's face got, if possible, redder than ever. "You can't close my store! How'm I supposed to keep food on the table with no income? That's what a man's supposed to do, take care of his family. And if you're a real woman of God, you'll back off and let this boy run his camp like he wants to and quit throwin' a dad-blame monkey wrench in his business."

"Grandpa—"

"Be quiet, missy!" There was nothing feeble about Grandpa's voice. He was practically roaring. "I tried to keep my nose out of y'all's love life and let you two settle it on your own. I figured if you wound up gettin' married, it'd keep the property in the family and I wouldn't have to worry about you and your babies no more." He glanced at Grant and snorted. "But since you ain't got the sense to cooperate, I'll be snookered if I'm gonna lay around and watch you turn land that's been in our family since before Jeff Davis bought Beauvoir into some California bean-sprout animal resort!"

Jana sat down, too shocked to utter a word. She locked eyes with Grant, who looked as if somebody had dumped a bucket of ice water on his head.

Grandpa laid his head back down on the pillow, panting. He crooked a bony finger at Grant. "You still carryin' that deed around in your truck, boy?"

"Y–yes, sir."

"Go get it. I'll sign it right now."

That's what I said. Right now." Grant paced down the hall toward the elevator, hoping a nurse wouldn't catch him with the cell phone and make him turn it off. He was fortunate to have caught Doug between appointments on a Tuesday afternoon. "He'll sign the deed right now, but we've got to have a notary. And I need a certified check."

And a lobotomy to remove the image of Jana's betrayed expression from his memory bank. Maybe it was a good thing he was right here in the hospital.

But this was obviously God's will. He was meant to have this property, this camp, this business. Jana wouldn't have anything to do with him anyway. He might as well have *something* to fill his time.

"Don't worry about that," Doug said. "I'll have the money wired to your account before two o'clock. And I'll send my paralegal over with her notary seal. I was beginning to think it might not happen. Bow season opens in a week. Guess it's a good thing the old coot fell and knocked some sense into his head."

Grant had a sudden qualm. "You think this might not be legal if Alvin's under the influence of painkillers?"

"From what you told me, he sounds lucid. We gotta get this thing inked before he goes into surgery."

"Which is first thing tomorrow morning." The elevator dinged and opened. "Listen, I gotta get to the bank. Let me know the second that money's wired."

"You got it, man. Congratulations."

"Thanks." Closing his phone, Grant got on the elevator and went down. For some reason he didn't particularly feel like celebrating. He hoped that wasn't an omen.

Jana heard a rumble of thunder overhead and figured that was just par for the course. Trini was back from New Orleans, so she'd taken the opportunity to get outdoors. The woods was the only place she could think to go when she felt like this. Cradled in God's womb—safe from people, who hurt and rejected one another without a second thought. Now it looked as though even this safe place was going to get dangerous.

A streak of lightning could hit and set her on fire.

For three days she'd lived with the knowledge that, once again, family had let her down. Grandpa had tried to defend himself with the it's-for-your-good shtick. But she didn't believe that. He needed the money, pure and simple. Between ICU visiting hours, she'd gotten a closer look at his accounts. Money had been disappearing from the store faster than it had come in. The Farm and Feed was teetering on wobbly underpinnings, and one more good puff of financial strain would send it crashing into the bayou.

She'd stayed up late last night, staring at the plans for the wildlife rescue center on her computer screen. She and Willis had made a good start with those three pens and the covered shelter, but what was she going to tell the Wildlife Commission rep when he showed up in a few weeks? She had a real estate agent helping her look for an alternate piece of property, but she had no funds to pay for land. Heath had given her a list of animal protection enthusiasts in the area who might be able to help, but nothing had turned up yet. Time was short.

The rain started as she sat down on a fallen tree trunk. Dripping through the trees, it refreshed and cooled her skin but couldn't wash away her confusion. How could she have so grievously misunderstood God's will? She wished she could talk to her mentors, the Andrewses. Lurlene would give her a hug and pray with her; Dr. Andy would counsel her to wait in faith.

She remembered the day she and Grant and the children had released Forrest back into the wild. Everything seemed possible then, even a relationship with Grant. But that was before he'd proven he had no regard for anything except himself. Even his gifts were full of self-interest.

He'd ruined everything. Now she had no close friends to go to in her grief, because they were all related to him. Naturally they would take his side in the controversy.

Oh, what did it matter anyway? The deed had been signed and notarized. Grant owned the land. She had no choice but to look for God's will somewhere else.

The rain began to pelt her head and shoulders. She got up and walked on until she came to the pens Willis had built for her. Strong, sturdy materials, wonderful craftsmanship. The animals had taken shelter under the brush and trees. They'd be fine here, unless the creek happened to rise this far.

It occurred to her that she hadn't seen a weather report for several days. Better go home and check it out. She wheeled and strode toward her car, which she'd left parked by the side of the road. By the time she reached it, she was sopping wet and shivering. Starting the car, she headed for home. Maybe there was time to take a hot bath. The kids would be getting off the school bus in an hour, and she'd promised to take them to the hospital to visit Grandpa, now that he'd been moved to a regular room.

The windshield wipers swashed back and forth against the onslaught of what looked to become a crashing storm, and Jana slowed. She didn't want to take out any more of Mr. CJ's cows.

Heath was being very sweet about letting her have time away from the clinic to take care of Grandpa. *But, Lord, I'm exhausted. I don't know how much more of this I can take.*

Come to me, she seemed to hear him say. *If you're weary and burdened, I'll give you rest.*

That sounded good. But how was she going to take hold of it when she hardly had a moment to herself? And it seemed as though every time she *did* get alone, she only wound up more depressed and confused.

Then it occurred to her there was at least one person who could pray with her objectively and who would understand her load of regret and insecurity.

She passed Grandpa's driveway and kept going. A hot bath could wait.

This time as she drove down Magnolia Road, the memories seemed not so suffocating. Maybe in spite of everything, she'd begun to heal. She parked in front of Shelby's trailer door, turned off the car, and listened for a minute to the soothing sound of the rain pounding on the roof.

She might have stayed longer, but Shelby opened the door and peered out. Recognizing Jana, her lined face lit, and she beckoned.

Taking a deep breath, Jana dashed through the rain and into the trailer, where Shelby welcomed her with a threadbare brown towel. Laughing, Jana toed out of her wet sneakers and toweled her dripping hair.

"Girl, what in the *world* are you doing out in this weather?" Shelby demanded with affectionate amusement. She opened a cabinet and took down a couple of coffee mugs.

"Crazy, huh?" Jana peeked out from under the towel. "I might have to swim back home."

"You know I'm always glad to see you." Curiosity lifted the end of the sentence, but Shelby held her peace. Another restful thing about her.

Which made Jana long to confide in her. "I need you to pray with me." She let the towel fall and twisted it between her hands. "I need you to ..." Her eyes filled, her mouth trembled. The ugly little brown and orange kitchenette blurred as Shelby's thin, warm embrace absorbed her dampness, her sadness, her loneliness.

"Dear Father," Shelby said quietly, "I don't know what's bothering Jana, but I pray you'll be her strength and her wisdom and her peace. I pray you'll hold on to her through whatever you've got her walking through. And protect her and the children. Oh, you know how grateful I am for those children." Shelby's voice shredded until she and Jana were shuddering in tears together. Cleansing tears.

Jana stood wrapped in her mother-in-law's arms, astonished at this twist in her road. She began to hope, just a little bit, that the Lord was going to take her beyond the trouble gripping her.

The Sunday morning before bow season opened, Grant sat in the congregation watching LeeLee and Ty—and the rest of the children's choir—sing the special music. The only thing that got him through it was the fact that LeeLee waved at him as she skipped onto the platform. Ty, standing with his hands in his pockets and moving his lips as little as possible, didn't look at anybody. Grant wished he had a video camera.

He slid a glance at Jana, who sat two pews ahead of him near the aisle, with Heath beside her. Apparently having caught on to the dress code, Redmond had neatly combed his hair away from his face, so that it just brushed the collar of a blue button-down shirt. Even had a Bible in his lap. Maybe something from CJ's camping devotional had sunk in.

Hostilities between Heath and himself had cooled somewhat with the passage of time. During orchestra rehearsals they circled one another like junkyard dogs guarding a stash of bones. Grant hoped he wasn't going to have to spend the rest of his life feeling like this.

When the kids finished singing and trooped out for children's church, he whistled and clapped along with everybody else, enthusiastically enough that Granny elbowed him. "This is a worship service, not a ball game."

Hot-faced, he folded his arms. "Psalms says to clap your hands and make a joyful noise."

She gave him that eyebrows-up look she was famous for. "All this rain's mildewed your brain."

He'd have to agree that the good Lord had seen fit to dump half the Gulf of Mexico on them over the last three or four weeks. The river had risen over his section of land until the houseboat floated twenty-two feet in from its normal mooring. And more nasty weather was predicted. Tropical Storm Wendy threatened to upgrade to hurricane status. Doug had been calling nearly every day to affirm his plans for the camp. All Grant could do was assure the lawyer that short of a flood he'd be open for hunting on October 1.

That afternoon he drove Willis down to the jail in Pascagoula to check on his brother. They found Crowbar lounging on his bunk, perfectly content reading a Western from the sheriff's library and eating brownies donated by the WMU.

I should have it so good, Grant thought, negotiating the truck through the woods as he took Willis home.

Willis leaned forward. "Hey, boss, who's that truck belong to?"

"I dunno." Grant squinted through the flapping windshield wipers at the big black Yukon Denali parked at a cockeyed angle on the edge of the clearing. Looked like Doug Briscoe's vehicle, but what would he be doing out here on a day like this? And if it was Doug, where had he gone?

Grant pulled up beside the Dyers' Winnebago and fished around behind the seat for his umbrella. Getting out in the pouring rain, he stepped in a mud hole. "Shoot." He still had on his church shoes. "Doug! Is that you? Where are you?"

Willis got out of the truck with an armload of the groceries the church ladies had loaded him up with this morning. "I'm gonna put this stuff in the trailer, boss."

"Okay. I'll take a look around." Grant watched where he was going this time as he moved into the trees, looking for signs of Doug's footprints in the mud. "Doug! What are you doing out here, man?"

"Hey, Gonzales! Come look at this!"

Doug's cultured voice sounded funny. Grant's stomach, not too steady anyway these days, started to hurt worse. "Where are you?"

"Back here." Doug's pale face and dark hair appeared in the gloaming. A big, sloppy grin came and went just before he turned and staggered back where he'd come from. "C'mere," he yelled over his shoulder, "gotta show you what some nut's been doin' on our property."

Doug was headed in the direction of Jana's animal enclosures.

"Oh no ..." Grant tossed aside the umbrella and started to run. He passed Doug, jostling the lawyer into the underbrush. A string of colorful language followed Grant as he reached the sanctuary, but he couldn't have cared less. He stood there in the rain, feeling the blood drain from his face.

The aviary lay on its side, with its central tree chopped into three sections. The fencing sagged as if it had been run over, and the posts lay on the ground like timber tossed by a tornado. Probably Doug had done this with the big Yukon—which, now that Grant thought about it, had looked oddly banged up.

But worse than the actual condition of the pens was the fact that most of the animals were gone. And the ones left had been brutally shot.

Blood, fur, feathers, carnage.

Grant put his hands over his face and felt the heavens roar above him as he tried to shut out what he had just seen. In that one rending moment he saw through Jana's eyes. He wanted to vomit.

He felt Doug grab his shoulder from behind and spin him around. This time Tommy wasn't there to deflect the blow, but Doug was too drunk to aim more than a glancing blow off his cheekbone. Hot blood gushed down Grant's face.

"Why did you do this?" He shoved Doug onto his rear in the mud. "These animals were in a hospital. They couldn't run, they couldn't hide. That's not sporting, Briscoe—it's murder!"

Doug gaped up at him. "Whassa matter wi' you? You can't run an animal hospital in a huntin' camp!"

"You're drunk," Grant said in disgust. "Don't you know it's Sunday?" Not that that had anything to do with anything, but somehow it seemed like an added obscenity in the situation.

Doug didn't seem to notice the absurdity of the question. "I already been to church this morning. I was just havin' a few beers with the guys during the ball game, thought I'd come out here an' make sure you got everything ready for the first day. Jus' three days away. Gonna be awful wet. D'you know it's rainin'?"

There was no point in arguing with this drunken idiot in the pouring rain. But if Grant left him out here, Doug would probably drown.

Which had its appealing aspects.

He swiped a hand over his face, surprised when it came away smeared with blood. His own blood. He looked around at the dead birds and animals flung about in the mud and leaves. His stomach surged. *Get Briscoe out of here, then come back and clean it up.*

Oh, God, what have I done?

chapter 22

Monday morning Jana managed to talk Dora into tuning her boom box in to the local weather station. As she wormed a litter of Boston terrier puppies for Mrs. Harris, she kept an ear out for news of the gulf storm that had overnight become Hurricane Wendy. A category two headed for Mobile, it was certain to bring more nasty weather, and if it turned even slightly to the west, things would get ugly. Evacuation might even be in order.

She looked up when the noise level changed with the opening of the back door. Heath had been out in the hospital barn, delivering a foal out of one of their boarded mares. Judging by the state of his jeans and boots, he seemed to have slogged through quite a bit of mud on the way back in.

"Hey." She grinned at his sour expression. "Are we giving out blue or pink bubble gum cigars?"

"Neither yet. This foal's decided it's too wet to come out and play right now."

"You're not letting her go another day, are you?"

"No. Bitsy's with her." He stretched, rolling his shoulders and watching Jana cuddle the smallest puppy. "I just came in to tell you there's a woman out in the barn looking for you."

"What woman?" She rubbed her nose into the soft white fur at the puppy's neck and received a lick of appreciation on the cheek. "Aren't you sweet?"

"Thanks," Heath said and ducked when she swatted at him. "I don't know. Just some dried-up old lady in a suit, asking for Dr. Cutrere. That would be you, right?" He backed toward the door. "She didn't want to get her shoes messed up, so I told her to wait in the barn and I'd send you out."

"Great," Jana muttered as Heath disappeared. "So I get to get *my* shoes messed up." Once Heath got the message that she wasn't interested in any sort of romantic liaison with him, he decided to treat her like a little sister. Which was much more comfortable on one level—but in many other ways ironically inconvenient. Heath could be a bit of a boor.

She put the puppy back in the crate with her littermates and returned them to the kennel. Singing softly to herself, she yanked her umbrella out of the stand, took a deep breath, and braved the storm. For the most part she was able to forget about her worry over the wildlife center while she was here at the clinic. She was just plain too busy. Or maybe it was faith. Or blind optimism.

She only knew in her heart of hearts that God was trustworthy. The Bible said so, and she had to believe it or go crazy.

By the time she got to the barn, she was soaked from the waist down, her hair a curly mess. The rain blew in gusts that circumvented the umbrella and left her panting with the effort of navigating the muddy yard. Heath opened the door for her, and she barreled laughing into the warm, humid center aisle. The familiar odor of animals and hay and antiseptic was a welcome she always appreciated.

But the elegant gray-haired woman standing with a clipboard under the fluorescent lights sent her good humor into a tailspin. "Professor French?" Jana collapsed the umbrella, sending a cold, miserable rivulet of water down her back. "What are you doing here?"

"Weren't you expecting me?" Dr. India French stepped over a pile of loose hay Heath had dragged out of the expectant mare's stall. "I've come about the wildlife research grant."

Last night Grant had only managed to get the belligerent, noisy, and profane Doug Briscoe loaded into his truck by threatening to call his wife. The lawyer was passed out with his head bouncing against the window within five minutes. Grant drove to Mobile, hauled his snoring partner into his ten-thousand-square-foot Springhill home, and called it good riddance.

Now he sat in his truck in his rapidly flooding hunting camp trying to figure out what to do with Doug's scratched-up luxury SUV. Willis wanted to tow it to the river. Grant had never seen the gentle giant so riled up. And he would have confessed to a certain amount of sympathy. Once upon a time he would've traded his birthright to own a vehicle like this. Now all he could think was how repellent he found Doug's attitude and lifestyle.

To say the least, this partnership was not working out. He could almost hear Tommy quoting from Second Corinthians — *"Don't be yoked together with unbelievers."* At the time they'd studied that passage, Grant had argued that the apostle Paul was talking about marriage.

What a miserable turn of events. Jana would never believe he didn't have anything to do with killing all those animals and tearing up the fences. He hadn't seen any reason to make her move them. At least not yet. He was getting around to that.

He was also getting around to telling Ty he couldn't take him hunting on Wednesday. For one thing, Jana made sure he never got within shouting distance of her kids. Besides that, Grant hated to disappoint Ty.

He handed his keys to Willis, seated beside him in the truck. "I'll drive Briscoe's SUV to Mobile, and you follow me in my truck. Then we'll get back here and clean up the mess. I promise I'll help you put everything back good as new."

Willis stared at the keys. "You're gonna let me drive your truck?"

"You've got a license, don't you?"

"Yep. Had to drive a concrete truck at the shipyard once't in a while."

"All right then." Relieved, Grant got out so Willis could slide over. "Just don't speed, and stick close to me. Everything's gonna be fine."

With Dr. French on her heels, Jana marched through the woods with umbrella aloft like some redneck version of Mary Poppins. She'd tried to explain that the best time to inspect property was not during the approach of a hurricane. The good professor insisted, however, that, as she was getting married at Christmas, she was in a personal time crunch. As the board member assigned to field visits, it was crucial that she complete her inspection now and turn in the necessary paperwork before the end of the federal fiscal year.

Jana glanced at Dr. French. What a bizarre turn of events for her toughest vet school professor to show up as her field inspector. How was she going to explain that she didn't own this property and that it wasn't even her grandfather's anymore? She could say that the setup here in the woods was a facsimile of what she wanted to do with the grant.

Either way she was going to sound like a disorganized lunatic.

They reached the clearing where the Dyer brothers' camper squatted like a big brown and white loaf of bread.

"Um, here's where my onsite caretaker lives." Jana gestured toward the Winnebago, hoping Willis wouldn't come bounding out to greet her with his usual unbridled enthusiasm. He was a big precious teddy bear, but he didn't exactly exude professionalism.

"Good idea." Dr. French made a note. Today she had donned a sensible pair of walking shoes with canvas pants and a rain slicker. The rain and mud didn't seem to bother her one iota. Her eyebrows rose as her gaze took in the series of wooden plaques along the path. "Ah. St. Francis."

"Yes. My caretaker, Willis, is quite artistic. The sanctuary itself is right past these—" Jana jerked to a halt, stifling a scream with her fist. "Oh no!" she choked. "Grant, what have you done?"

B riscoe clearly had a hangover, but Grant was in no mood to put things off. If he was going to clean up the mess at the wildlife sanctuary before the hurricane hit, he had no time to waste.

Doug's wife, Allison, hovered in the doorway of their den— which looked as if it could be featured on one of those shows Granny liked so much—until Doug snarled at her to "go find something constructive to do." She disappeared, looking hurt.

Feeling sorry for Allison, but not up to tackling marriage counseling on top of everything else, Grant glanced at Willis.

The big guy was standing at the French doors gazing out on the Briscoes' backyard patio and pool with a look of dumbfounded wonder on his honest, square face. "Boy, I wish't Crowbar could see this. Can I go stand out there and look at it?"

Grant smiled. "Sure, why not. I'll be ready to go pretty quick."

Willis opened the patio door and stepped out. He sat down in one of the cushioned rockers on the porch and seemed content to watch the rain sluice down into the color-coordinated flower beds around the patio.

"What's so all-fired important it couldn't wait until tomorrow?" Doug sank back into his recliner, raising the footrest. "I feel like—"

"I'm sorry, Doug. But I might as well tell you now that I'm gonna buy you out of your part of the camp as soon as I can get the money together. I have a lot of respect for you as an attorney, but we're not cut out to be business partners."

Doug's half-closed eyes burned with enmity. "My money not good enough for you?"

Grant sighed and ran a hand through his hair. "The problem's not your money. I've just realized we're too ... different ... to operate a business together. I don't believe in mixing alcohol and firearms, for one thing."

"Okay, so that was stupid." Doug sat up a little, holding his head. "I don't normally drink that much."

"But that's not the only thing." Grant fumbled with how he was going to say what he needed to say without sounding like a holier-than-thou stiff. He couldn't help thinking of Heath's accusation of "casual Christianity." Maybe it was time to quit being casual. "Listen, Doug, I've made a decision that's going to affect everything I do from now on. I'm letting Jesus Christ be in complete charge of my life. I don't think he's real happy with me right now, and I've got to step back and figure out what that means."

Doug frowned. He looked ill but intrigued. "I didn't know you were *that* religious."

"You know what? That's the problem." Grant gave a dry laugh. "Anyway. You kept threatening to find another hunting club to invest in. It might be best if you did that after all. I'll do some checking around and get you hooked up with a place that'll suit you a lot better than my swampy little bayou. What do you say?"

"I say I feel like puking. Go get your Paul Bunyan buddy and get out of here. I'll call you tomorrow and we'll work out how to untangle ourselves. Okay?" He closed his eyes and lay back again.

Grant hustled over to the patio door and called Willis. Sometimes a caballero's best plan of action was to get while the gettin' was good.

I don't understand what happened." Jana lifted her coffee mug to her lips with shaking hands. "Willis was right there to keep an eye on things." Some part of her brain wished she had a bottle of brandy to lace with the caffeine. *Leave me alone, you hideous snake*, she told the nasty voice that still sometimes threatened to slither back in under stress. *I don't belong in that place anymore.*

Dr. French, seated across from her at Grandpa's kitchen table, looked up from the manila file in front of her. "Looked to me like your caretaker went nuts on you. That was the biggest mess I've ever seen."

"Oh no, Willis would never do something like that. He loves animals as much as I do. But he got bitten by a squirrel recently, and he's been pretty sick. Maybe he just didn't hear the vandal, unless ..." Jana shook her head. Maybe Grant had gotten Willis busy in another part of the camp while he destroyed the enclosures.

Dr. French stopped writing and looked up. "Jana, if the foundation is going to invest this much money in your research, we've got to be sure you can hold things together. Maybe you should consider moving onto the property, where you can keep a closer eye on things."

Jana set down the mug and closed her eyes. Here it was. The truth, which was going to blast all her dreams into a puff of smoke. *Lord, please give me grace.* "I'm afraid I can't do that."

Dr. French's blunt features softened. "I realize you've got many other responsibilities — your grandfather's health, the children, and your vet practice. But maybe you could put a double-wide or something onsite, and — "

"That's not it." Jana held her breath, then let it out with a whoosh. "That property's not mine to move onto. My grandfather sold it to a hunting camp enterprise last week." The words scalded her lips, but she forced herself to continue. "In fact, I've been in the process of looking for another place to house the research center. But with the weather and so many distractions ..." She moved her hands apart in a helpless gesture. "I haven't had any luck."

Dr. French sighed. "Jana, there's a bigger problem than the search for a location. After talking to Dr. Redmond, I believe you have the resources and connections to raise funds for supplies and medications, and can probably even find a land donor." Her dark eyes shifted, and she tapped a finger to her lips. "But your stationery letterhead has contained what I recognize as distinctively Christian symbolism, and after seeing the St. Francis plaques at the site today ... I knew I had to broach it. You do realize that since this is a federal grant, you have to eliminate any references to religion from your correspondence, signage, and any articles or research data you generate." She shrugged. "If the media reports any alliance between the wildlife center and an established church ... I'm afraid the funding for your research would be cut."

"But I'm not an established church! I'm a scientist and doctor who happens to be a Christian. I can't deny the most important part of my life — in fact, the whole reason that I do what I do!"

Dr. French pressed her thin lips together and closed the folder. "That's a choice you'll have to make. You can express your faith in whatever way you choose—after all, this *is* America." She smiled faintly. "But if you do that, you'll have to forfeit federal money." Jana sat stunned as her former professor rose and put on her sopping rain slicker. "I've made all the notes I need for now. I'll write up my evaluation and email you a copy next week. The board will make a decision from there." She offered her hand to Jana. "Good luck, Jana. I wish you the best."

After the door closed behind Dr. French, Jana laid her head down on the table, shoving the mug of cooled coffee away.

Oh, God of mercy and grace, what am I going to do? I can't run a wildlife center and never mention your name.

Her favorite lines from Coleridge twisted and turned through her mind until they became part of her prayer. *Let me pray well, let me love well ... man and bird and beast ... all things great and small, dear God. You made me, you love me, you have a plan. Please ... help me know it.*

Grant spent Monday and Tuesday calling hunters to cancel trips and summoning the nerve to approach Alvin about buying back the property. He and Willis also cleaned up the wildlife refuge, straightened the fencing, and replaced the broken and toppled posts. The animals were gone, but he figured it wouldn't take Willis long to find sick and injured creatures to take their places.

He tried several times to get hold of Jana, desperate to explain what had happened, but she had apparently fallen off the face of the earth. Heath said she'd taken a leave of absence from the clinic and refused to say where she was. She certainly wasn't returning his calls.

On Tuesday afternoon, he called CJ and Tommy and asked the two of them to meet with him for prayer and counseling.

He'd been fasting since Monday—a radical concept to a man who loved food in every form—and he was feeling a bit light-headed when Tommy opened his front door to let him in. He collapsed in Tommy's La-Z-Boy and closed his eyes. "Where's your bride?"

"Catering a dinner over at the Old Gautier House." Tommy grinned and plopped onto the sofa. "I'll be eating good for the next couple of days. What's the matter with you?"

"Wait 'til CJ gets here and I'll explain."

The game warden showed up a few minutes later, and Grant filled them in. "Bottom line," he finished, "I don't know what I want to do about a hunting camp—or my life, for that matter—but I know I've got to get untangled from Doug Briscoe."

CJ sat silent and thoughtful, chewing on his pipe stem—unlit, out of deference to Carrie's pregnancy.

Tommy whistled. "I told you that guy was bad news."

"Thanks. That's real helpful." Grant lifted his hands. "Any suggestions?"

Tommy scratched his head. "You said Briscoe's willing to sell back his share of the camp? What about the other two investors?"

"I think they'll come around too. The main problem is getting hold of the money. The only thing I can figure is talking Alvin around to buying it back."

"Man, you worked so hard to get him to sell it to you in the first place. He's liable to throw you out on your keister when you bring up reversing the deal." Tommy made a face. "Glad I don't have to be there."

Grant looked at CJ. "I was hoping you'd talk to him."

"Nope."

Grant hadn't expected immediate acquiescence, but neither had he expected flat-out refusal. "Why not?"

CJ just looked at him. "We ain't prayed yet. I don't do nothin' 'til we pray."

"Oh. Yeah." Grant looked down, ashamed. "I've got a long way to go, don't I?"

CJ grinned. "You'll catch up."

Grant rapped on the door of Alvin's hospital room. CJ had offered to come with him for backup, but he decided to take Alvin on like a man. Slingshot and twelve smooth stones. When the old man growled out an irascible "Come on in," he sent up a prayer for favor and stepped inside.

"How're you feeling?" Grant walked over to the bed and shook hands. Alvin's leg was stabilized by a cast, but he looked better than the last time Grant had seen him.

"I'll live," Alvin laid aside the Sudoku puzzle he'd been working on. "What're you doing here?"

Grant sighed. "I thought I'd see if you needed anything. Where's Jana?"

"Made her go home to look in on the kids. She spends too much time in here. Wearin' her out." Alvin's eyebrows beetled. "I don't need a thing, and you look like a man with an agenda. Spit it out."

Stalling, Grant picked up the puzzle. He saw where Alvin had made an error and started to fix it. *Not a smart move, Gonzo.* He put down the paper and stuck his fingers in his back pockets. "I came to see if you'd be interested in buying back your property."

Alvin gaped at him. "Why in Sam Hill would I want to do that?"

"Come on, Alvin, I'm asking you for a favor. My business partnership turned out to be a disaster, and I'm in a jam." He hesitated. "Did Jana tell you what happened with the wildlife center?"

"She did." Alvin folded his skinny arms over his skinny chest. "Your fault for letting her build those pens on your hunting property to start with."

"I guess it was. But things just kind of took off that way. Listen, Alvin, I'm not going into partnership with a guy who can't control his drinking. Doug Briscoe lost it the other day. And I've decided I'd rather Jana get what she wants than to make a mistake like I did before. If you want her to have the land, I'll figure something else out." He lifted his shoulders, meeting Alvin's eyes. "God's in control of my life, and if he wants me to have a hunting camp, he'll provide it without me having to stomp all over everybody I love."

Alvin stared at him expressionless. "That's mighty noble, Gonzales."

Grant looked away. "Well, better late than never."

"Are you saying you love my granddaughter?"

"Yes, sir. I do." He brought his gaze back to Alvin's. It was time to quit denying it. "She's refused me more than once, and I'm not begging. If you'll buy the property back, I'll be able to pay back my investors, and you can do whatever you want to with it. What do you say?"

Alvin shook his head. "I say you've got a loose screw. But if that's what you want, I'll get you a cashier's check tomorrow. Bring the deed over and we'll work it out."

Grant shook hands and tried to smile. "Thanks, Alvin. You're a good man."

CJ came to the door in his bathrobe and slippers. Grant's eyes widened. "Uh-oh, I didn't realize it was so late. I'll come back tomorrow."

"Naw, come on in, boy." Chuckling, CJ opened the screen door. "We're watching a movie, and Pearl made popcorn. We'll be glad to share."

Grant shifted. "I don't want to mess up your evening. Just wanted to tell you Alvin agreed to buy back the property, so I'm in the clear."

"That's good." CJ grabbed Grant's sleeve and towed him inside the house. "Pearl, put on another bag of popcorn. We've got company."

The smell of the popcorn made Grant's stomach growl, reminding him he hadn't eaten since lunch. It was now nine. "Okay, if you insist." He heard Pearl rummaging in the background, the beeping of the microwave. He walked to the door of the kitchen. "Hey, Miss Pearl. I hope you don't mind—"

"Goodness, sweetheart, we're always glad to have you." Pearl, comfortably plump in a startling pink housedress, handed him a root beer. "Go sit down with CJ in the den, and I'll be right there."

Soft drink in hand, Grant took the unoccupied armchair. He laid his head back.

"So Alvin decided to cooperate for once in his ornery life?" CJ's tone was amused.

"Yes, sir. I could hardly believe it. We'll straighten out the details tomorrow."

"That's good. So what are you going to do now?"

"I don't know." Grant rubbed his forehead. "I feel like I'm in a rubber raft in the middle of the Gulf."

CJ cleared his throat. "Since you're at loose ends, I have an option for you."

Grant looked at him. CJ rarely made suggestions, preferring to let people figure things out on their own. "What's that?"

"I'm retiring at the end of this year."

"Whoa. Really?" He shouldn't be surprised. CJ had worked well beyond most people's retirement age.

"Yep." The old man folded his hands across his lean stomach. "There'll be a spot open in our unit if you're interested. I'll recommend you."

"Me? A game warden?" A rush of possibilities flooded Grant's head. "I'd never thought about it. You think I'm qualified?"

"I can't think of anybody better qualified. You'd have to go through training, of course. But you've got the basic skills. The pay's not what you were used to as an engineer, but it'd keep body and soul together, and you could stay here in Jackson County. Why don't you think about it. Let me know, and I'll get you an application."

"Wow. Okay, I guess." Grant listened to the mad noise of popcorn popping in the kitchen and felt his dreams and expectations explode likewise. "I'll think about it."

Hurricane Wendy turned out to be little more than a sneeze on the Mississippi Gulf Coast. She made a sharp eastern turn just before landfall and roared with category three force into Pensacola, Florida—which in recent years had already taken its share of poundings. Grateful for the reprieve, Jackson County residents moved into clean-up mode and went about their business, cutting and dragging limbs, repairing leaky roofs, and dealing with downed telephone and electrical wiring.

With Grandpa in the hospital, Jana had decided not to evacuate —a decision that had kept her shut up in the house with the kids, since the schools had been closed. They reopened on Wednesday morning, by which time Jana was in a nearly catatonic state of indecision. This perhaps explained why she didn't notice that Ty was missing until it was time to walk him and LeeLee out to meet the bus.

"What do you mean, he's gone hunting?" Jana stared at LeeLee, who had her lunch box under one arm and a sack of Dum Dums that Dora had donated for the class under the other.

"You said not to tattle, and he told me not to tell." LeeLee looked down at her shins. "Mommy, would you mind pulling up my socks? They're falling down."

Jana fell to her knees, absently hiking up the little striped socks. She took LeeLee's hands. "Honey, you can *always* tell me when Ty does something dangerous. Remember when he ran into the woods after the fawn?"

"Oh yeah. But he said he was going with Mr. Grant, so that's not dangerous, is it?"

"*What?* But I told him not to—oh no!" Jana jumped to her feet. "Today's the opening day of bow season, but surely he wouldn't—" Then she thought about the destroyed pens and dead animals. He would. After she found Ty, she was going to have Grant arrested for kidnapping or child endangerment or whatever other charges applied.

It just went to prove that men were all alike. You couldn't trust a single one of them, no matter how completely they suckered you in.

"When did he leave?"

LeeLee shrugged. "Before you got up. Me and Glitter was playing ballerina." She squinted. "Is Ty in trouble?"

G rant was on the roof, inspecting hurricane damage, when Granny hallooed from the back step.

"Phone's for you, Grant!"

He crab-walked toward the ladder propped on the eaves and peered down at his grandmother, standing on the lawn still clad in her flowered muumuu and house shoes. "Can you ask 'em to call back in an hour or so? I'm almost done up here."

"Okay." Granny headed for the carport. "It's Jana."

"Wait!" Grant nearly fell off the roof. "Granny, don't let her hang up. I'll be right there."

He managed to make it into the house without breaking a limb, but he was shaking so hard from lack of food that he couldn't get the phone to land on his ear. "Jana! Hey, I'm sorry it took so long, but I was up on the roof—"

"Where's Ty?"

Well, he hadn't expected her to be especially friendly. After all, he hadn't explained about Doug's rampage yet. "I don't know. Did you lose him?" It was a half-facetious question, but her silence scared him. "Jana, did you think he was supposed to be with me?"

He heard a sharp inhalation from the other end of the line. "He told LeeLee he was going hunting with you."

He folded into a kitchen chair. "Today's the first day of bow season." Of course the date was burned into his brain. But with the rain flooding the woods, there wouldn't be any hunting today.

The crash of his heart threatened to turn into a heart attack. Ty wouldn't know that.

And Grant had never gotten around to canceling their hunting date.

"He's not here," he said, his voice a suffocated rasp. "You reckon he thinks I'm still staying at the houseboat?"

"I don't know *what* he thinks, Grant!" Jana sounded hysterical. "You said you'd tell him the hunting date was off!"

"I meant to, but everything's been insane around here ... Why didn't you ever answer your phone?"

"I was so angry I didn't want to talk to you, you monumental jerk! How could you do that to my sanctuary?"

"Whoa. Whoa, whoa, whoa." He clutched his hair. "This won't help us find Ty. I'm going over to the houseboat to look for him—"

"Don't you dare leave without me!" she shouted. "I'll be right there."

She hung up on him.

Grant looked at Granny, who stood in the kitchen doorway, fists planted on her hips. "What's going on?" she demanded.

"Can I borrow your four-wheeler?" He reached for the back door latch.

"Of course you can, but—"

"Ty thought we were still going hunting this morning and apparently went over to the woods by himself. I've got to go after him."

Granny's face went white. "Grant, that whole area's flooded right now!"

"I know it. Call CJ and tell him to get together a search-and-rescue team. Jana's on her way."

As if Grant needed one more lesson in relinquishing selfish behavior, God just kept hammering in the nails. Grant raced out to the toolshed where Granny kept the four-wheeler, his pounding heart keeping time with his feet.

Please, God, if you'll help me find that kid and bring him home safe, I'll never ask you for another favor. Well, probably I will, but this one's life and death. Please, Lord. You know I love you. Please keep him safe until I can get to him.

*P*lease, Lord, don't let him leave without me. Please let us find Ty.

Jana braked the Subaru in a deep rut in Roxanne's driveway, flung open the door, and jumped out. "LeeLee, go in the house and stay with Miss Roxanne." She opened the passenger door. "I'll come back for you when I find your brother."

"Okay, Mommy. Glitter and me will pray." LeeLee skipped toward the house with the cat draped over her shoulder and banged on the door.

Jana watched to make sure she made it into the house, then looked around. Grant's truck was parked behind Roxanne's big white Buick, so he hadn't left yet. Then she heard the four-wheeler roaring around the side of the house and realized Grant was on it.

He was going to drive it right past her.

"Stop!" Waving her arms over her head like a madwoman, she ran to cross his vision. "Grant, stop!"

He had to, or run over her. "What are you doing?" he shouted over the idling of the ATV's motor. "I have to go look for Ty."

"Take me with you!"

"No, I've got to have room to bring him back. Look, CJ'll get an S and R team together—maybe they'll let you come with them. I'm not waiting."

"That's why I'm going with you." She saw that he had a blanket, a hatchet, a flashlight, and what looked like a rifle case strapped with a bungee cord in the basket at the rear of the ATV. At the front was a powerful electric winch mechanism. He was well prepared, but still ... "If you find him and he's hurt, he'll want me."

Their eyes locked for a moment, and Jana could see the anguish burning in the deep brown eyes. Whatever his failings, Grant loved her son. If anybody could bring Ty back, he would.

"Jana ..." His mouth was hard; the hollows under his cheekbones shifted. "All right. Get on and hang tight. We're gonna hit some rough spots."

No time for argument. Jana had dressed in loose, ripped-at-the-knees jeans, boots, and a long-sleeved T-shirt, with a baseball cap pulled on over her curls. She was ready for anything.

Except, it appeared, for the shock of putting her arms around Grant. Her child lost in a flooded woods, and she still ached with a piercing longing for this man's love. How could she even think about that when—

No, she wasn't going to consider that anything bad might have happened to Ty. He was good at taking care of himself, he had great common sense, and he wouldn't try to cross any flooded roads.

Unless he saw an injured animal, and then who knew what he was likely to do?

Jana closed her eyes and prayed as the four-wheeler jounced over Roxanne's lawn, across the highway, then through Grandpa's yard. *Please, Lord, please* ... Her prayers were becoming incoherent.

They passed the house, then the barn and the peach trees where the water scarecrow lounged with fine nonchalance on his metal pole. The ground was so saturated that the ATV came close to getting stuck once or twice; once they entered the woods, Grant had to twist and turn the vehicle continuously to avoid slick spots and mud holes.

When he slowed to negotiate a sharp dip in the path, Jana leaned up to shout in his ear. "Where do you think he went?"

He glanced over his shoulder. "I'm guessing he tried to meet me at the houseboat. That's what scares me. The creek was way over the banks even three days ago."

Chilled, Jana settled back, pressing her cheek between his shoulder blades. If *Grant* was scared . . .

The four-wheeler stopped with a jerk, and she sat up. "What's the matter?"

Grant turned. His expression was troubled. "I'm sorry. I didn't mean to scare you. We'll find him." He hesitated, looking away. "You know how awful I feel about this, don't you?"

"Of course I do." She couldn't imagine him endangering either of her children on purpose. "I take part of the blame. Like you said, I didn't want you talking to Ty after what you did to the animals in the refuge. And I forgot all about you telling him you'd take him—"

"Wait a minute, Jana. I didn't tear up the refuge. I was just as sick about that as you."

Impossible to gauge the sincerity of his expression. "Then who did?" If she sounded truculent, so what?

"Doug Briscoe, my ex-partner. Sunday afternoon he came out here drunk and decided there wasn't any reason to have an animal hospital in our camp."

"Then it's still your fault, isn't it?"

Grant's mouth tightened. "I reckon so."

She swallowed. "What ... what do you mean, 'ex-partner'?"

"I killed the deal after he did that. I'm not putting up with that kind of stuff."

"But—" she felt her mouth open and close. "I thought you couldn't afford to open the camp without those guys as investors."

"I can't."

"So you'll have to find some other—"

"Jana, there's not going to be a camp. Your grandpa is buying it back. He's free to do whatever he wants to with it."

Twenty-four hours ago she would have been delirious with joy. Now her awful worry for Ty overshadowed everything. "I guess that's good. But we need to get going." She glanced up at the fulminating sky, where steel-gray clouds bulged with rain. "Looks like the bottom might fall out again any minute."

"You're right. I just wanted you to know." Grant touched her hand. "Now hang on and let's go find your kid."

She grabbed him hard around the middle as the ATV jerked into gear. *Please, Lord, help us find Ty.*

The ground beneath the wheels of the ATV got soggier as they penetrated the woods, and Grant was afraid they were going to have to abandon it and walk. He and Jana both were spattered with mud up to their shoulders. Once, when he glanced over his shoulder at her, he almost smiled in spite of his anxiety at the brown-speckled princess in her dirty brown baseball cap and ratty jeans. A true Jackson County debutante.

At least she'd seemed to believe he planned to dissolve the camp. At least one of them would be happy. Maybe she'd forgive him for his part in Ty's winding up out here by himself.

No matter what she said about sharing the blame, he didn't know if he could ever forgive himself.

On that morbid thought, he steered the four-wheeler through a copse of sweet gum trees in an effort to shorten the route to the swollen creek. The terrain was rougher, less traveled here; even the forest animals apparently avoided the area. Gritting his teeth, he negotiated roots, sudden gullies, and standing tables of water. This had been one of his stupider ideas, bringing Jana with him. If she got hurt—

A sudden jolt had him bracing against the handlebars. The ATV skidded downward, sliding on a film of mud toward a surge of water rushing across the path.

"Jump, Jana!" he shouted. "We're gonna flip!"

He felt her release him, felt the loss of her warmth. No time to look and make sure she landed safely. He flung himself sideways just as the ATV rolled—in the same direction he jumped. The heavy vehicle slammed him against the wet ground. He could barely breathe. Excruciating pain radiated from his kneecap to the roots of his hair.

He must have blacked out for a few seconds; he opened his eyes to find Jana's pale, dirty face suspended above him.

"Grant!" She laid her hands on each side of his face, little mewling sounds escaping. "What are we gonna do? This thing's too heavy for me to move!"

"Okay, it's all right. I'll push it—" Vision blurring, he folded backward onto the ground. He could hear the stream rushing just a few yards away, smelled the mud beneath his shoulders. All he could see was a wavy canopy of dying leaves and stripped branches as a backdrop to Jana's face. She was crying.

And then a child's scream ripped through the woods from the other side of the stream.

Jana jumped to her feet. "Ty!"

Ty's screams grabbed Jana's nerve ends and twisted until she felt electrocuted. She couldn't see him, but her imagination unreeled like a horror film. How had he gotten on the other side of that wild rush of water?

"Jana?" Panting, Grant gasped her name again. "Jana, come here."

She collapsed beside him. Her bruised hip protested, but his drawn, ashen face and terror for Ty made her own discomfort seem minor. "I'm here."

"Where's Ty? Can you see what's happened to him?"

"No, there are too many trees, and it's starting to rain again."

"See if you can stand on the four-wheeler and get a better view across the stream."

She stared at him in horror. "It's on your leg! If I stand on it—"

He grunted. "I'm mostly numb down there. I'm sure it's broken; you can't hurt it any more."

"That's crazy. It could slip and roll right on top of you. I'm not doing that."

He sighed. "Okay. Then at least stand up and look again. Get my field glasses."

"Good idea." Jana searched among the items that had tumbled into the mud when the four-wheeler flipped, and found the binoculars under the blanket. Then on rubbery legs she stumbled around to the other side of the ATV, where the ground was higher, and climbed onto a thick fallen tree trunk whose bark gave her boots slippery purchase. Focusing the lenses, she still saw nothing—until she scooted a foot or so to the right.

Something pale, flesh-colored, was wrapped around the trunk of a partially uprooted red oak hanging over the water. Leaning at a forty-five-degree angle, splitting the stream at its base, the tree trembled against the force of the flood. A shout tore Jana's throat muscles. "Ty!"

Ty's white, muddy face appeared from the other side of the tree trunk. "Mama!" he screamed.

"Hang on! I'm coming to get you!" Jana staggered back around the four-wheeler and fell to her knees beside Grant. "He's c–caught on a tree in the water. I'm going to swim over to—"

"Jana!" Grant raised his head and lifted himself onto his elbows. "The water's too fast and too deep. It'll pull you down to the river."

"I can't leave him there! He'll fall and drown." She started to get up, slipping in the mud, but Grant grabbed her by the wrist before she could get to her feet.

"No, wait a minute. We can use the winch and the cable, but you've got to get this ATV off me first. Go get the longest, stoutest limb you can find."

She stared at him, uncomprehending.

A faint smile curved his white lips. "Basic physics, sweetheart. We need a lever. But, uh, hurry."

Jana scrambled to her feet. Before she did anything else, she was going to check on Ty. She climbed onto the fallen tree again and focused the field glasses. Ty's arms were still around the oak. *Please help him hold on*, she prayed.

She lowered the binoculars. And jerked them back up as she caught something in her peripheral vision—the unmistakable markings of a water moccasin wrapped around a limb just a few feet from Ty. She was already cold, shaken, terrified. Now she wanted to scream with fear.

"Ty! Don't move! We're coming to get you, but there's a—" Choking back the words, she dropped the glasses and stumbled to the ground. Better not to frighten Ty into losing his grip. "Just *don't move!*"

She glanced around the area. Limbs lay all around, most of them too small or rotten. Kicking aside a pile of wet leaves, she uncovered a long, thick, straight branch. "Thank you, Lord," she whispered and dragged it to where Grant lay under the ATV. "We've got to hurry." Her voice came out unnaturally shrill. "I saw a moccasin. It's in the tree close to Ty."

Grant's eyes widened. "Poised to strike?"

"I don't think so. It was wrapped around a limb several feet away."

"Okay." He tipped his head back to catch his breath. "We'll get to him before the snake does. That limb'll work fine. Push the thickest end of it into the mud right by my leg. That's it. All right, when I say 'go,' lay all your weight on it while I pull my leg free. Understand?"

"Yes." She hurried to follow his instructions.

"Okay, you ready? Go."

Jana concentrated on keeping her balance as she shoved down on the limb with her entire body. If she slipped, the four-wheeler could fall on Grant again and deepen his injury. Slowly, slowly it lifted. She could hear Grant panting as the weight came off his leg, and then she heard a faint cracking sound from the center of the limb. *Oh, Father, don't let it break!*

Several heart-stopping seconds passed.

Grant grunted. "I'm out. Let it go."

As she moved off the limb, the ATV fell against the mud with a thick, sickening glump. It slid several inches closer to the water.

Grant sat up with a deep groan. "Hoo-boy. Remind me to jump the other way next time."

Jana clenched her hands together and looked over her shoulder. *Lord, please be with my baby.* The rain was coming down again in sheets. "I ought to splint your leg," she said to Grant.

"No time. The longer we wait, the higher the water's gonna get."

"How are we going to get to him?"

"First I'm gonna stabilize the four-wheeler as a fulcrum for the winch." Grant rolled onto his good knee. He wasn't looking at her, but she could see his pain in the way he held his shoulders. He unclipped the radio from his belt and passed it to her. "I want you to call CJ. You know how to operate this, don't you?"

"Of course. Grant, what are you planning to do?"

Grant used the limb as a cane and pushed himself to his feet. His right leg hung at an odd angle. His face was the color of papier-mâché. "I'm going upstream a ways so I can jump in and get to him easier. Let the current carry me to him."

Her mouth opened in new horror. "No."

"I'm the stronger swimmer. I'll take the cable out with me, and you'll winch us back in. Simple."

"What if I can't?"

"Jana." There was a whimsical, tender glint in his eyes. "You got the four-wheeler off me. God's been with us so far. You think he's gonna abandon us after all this?"

"No." She sucked in a breath and gripped the radio. "No, of course not." As Grant fumbled with the ATV, fastening it with a nylon cable and hook to a sturdy tree, Jana turned the radio on. "Mr. CJ, come in." Her voice shook, then strengthened. "This is Jana. We found Ty, but we need help! Come on, Mr. CJ, answer the stupid radio!" She smeared rain and tears off her face. "Come on, come on!"

Nothing. Frustrated, she walked over to the creek bank where she could keep an eye on Ty. He peered around the tree, his little face white. "Mom!"

"Hold on! I'm calling CJ, and Grant's coming after you right now!" Without the binoculars she couldn't see the snake. Dread curled in her stomach.

The radio crackled. "Jana, this is CJ. Where're y'all at?"

"We're about a mile up from Twin Creek Bayou where Grant's houseboat is docked. Ty's stuck in a tree in the middle of the stream. It's moving too fast to swim across. Grant's going to try to get to him, but his leg is broken and—" She looked over her shoulder just as Grant, teetering at the edge of the water with the cable tied around his waist, dropped the limb he was using for a crutch. She threw the radio into the basket of the ATV and grabbed the winch remote control. "Grant! Wait for me!"

"I've got to go now!" He jumped in.

Jana watched helplessly as the current jerked Grant twenty yards downstream in less than five seconds. At first he drifted closer to the near bank. Then the eddy shoved him away, toward the tree where Ty hung on for dear life.

Oh no, he's going to get swept past, and then what will we do? Dear Lord, please do something ... My baby. My love. Oh, Father, I love them both so much.

Blinded by tears and rain, Jana clutched the winch remote control and prayed with dogged faith. She didn't realize she'd been holding her breath until, at the last possible second before being swept past Ty, the current swirled Grant in a sudden arc that slammed him backward against the oak.

He went under, came up coughing. He grabbed for the tree trunk close to where Ty clung. A moment later, he circled strong arms around her son. Ty turned and latched on to Grant, sobbing.

Jana could have wept with relief, but this was no time for weakness. The stream was inching higher as Grant loosened the noose around his waist and struggled to encircle Ty. She waited, dancing with impatience, until Grant looked around, grinning.

He lifted a hand. "Pull us in!"

Momentary panic set in as her finger slipped on the button, reeling the cable out instead of in. But with a deep breath and another quick prayer, she forced herself to calm down. The winch whined, the cable jerked, and Grant let go of the tree. He and Ty were in the water headed for the bank near her.

Before Jana had time to worry, they were crawling out onto the mud. She stopped the winch as Ty scrambled to his feet, then watched Grant fold onto the wet ground. She rushed over to him and knelt to lay her hand on his icy, wet cheek. He was out cold.

She grabbed Ty in a crushing hug and kissed his dirty, wet freckled face over and over. "Oh, thank God, thank you, God!"

Ty hugged her back. "Mom, I'm sorry—I didn't mean to get stuck. But it wasn't raining like this when I left this morning, and that creek was just a little bit of spit, and when I tried to get back across—"

"I know, sweetie; we'll talk about it later. Right now I need you to run get the radio—it's in the basket of the four-wheeler."

By the time she had dragged Grant, a complete deadweight, farther back from the edge of the stream, Ty had returned with the handset. "Here, Mom." He knuckled his eyes. "Mr. Grant's gonna be okay, isn't he?"

Pausing in the act of activating the radio, she looped an arm around him. "Of course he is." With a shaking hand she put the radio to her mouth. "CJ, this is Jana."

"Jana, thank the Lord you're okay! What's going on?"

"Ty's safe, CJ, but Grant's unconscious. We'll need a stretcher and a splint."

"You got it, baby doll," CJ drawled. "We're almost there, so you just hang on and pray. Help's comin'."

Clutching Ty, Jana drew Grant's head across her knees and did as CJ suggested. She hung on and prayed.

Grant came to on a stretcher in the rain. He didn't know who was behind him, but Tommy and Matthew Lamont carried the front poles, zig-zagging with care through the dripping trees. Apparently they had better sense than he'd had, driving a four-wheeler into a flood during the aftermath of a hurricane.

"He's awake!"

Grant moved his eyes to one side and found Jana skipping along beside him as if she were on a Sunday walk in the park instead of a miserable, tedious slog through a rain-soaked forest. She had her arm around Ty.

"Hey, Mr. Grant," he said. "I knew you were a good swimmer! Boy, I was glad to see you and Mom."

Grant didn't have the energy to answer. He managed a feeble grunt.

"Hush, baby," Jana said, presumably to Ty. She looked at whoever was behind Grant's head. "How much farther?"

"We're practically in your grandpa's backyard," CJ reported. "There's the paramedic truck. Run tell 'em we got him."

Grant found himself bundled onto a gurney, stuffed into the back of the truck, and rushed to the hospital. This time it was his turn to experience the almost out-of-body leaps between unconsciousness and the most excruciating pain he'd ever endured. How had poor old Alvin survived it?

After what seemed like hours but was probably no more than forty-five minutes, the paramedics wheeled him into the ER. Jana gave him a timid wave and backed away with Ty, letting his mother and father take over. He loved his parents, but he would rather have had Jana.

chapter 24

Jana sat with Ty—and Grant's parents and grandmother—in the surgical waiting room. With them, and yet oddly apart.

She had to decide what she wanted.

She could call together all the prayer warriors she knew and take a poll. Or she could list pros and cons on a ledger sheet, like she used to do when making decisions in college.

But this seismic shift in the fabric of her life seemed to require something more elemental than polls and ledger sheets. Something involving the heart rather than the head. Something requiring faith.

Lurlene used to tell her love wasn't a feeling—it was a decision. That might be true, but her feelings were more than involved. She'd never known such powerful feelings existed. Feelings so strong they'd yanked her from passion, respect, and admiration to terror and back again.

One thing was for sure. These feelings scared her out of her mind. And not least because they involved her two precious babies. Here was Ty, snuggled up against her sound asleep, wetter than a trout and just about as smelly. Ready to die for Mr. Grant. Ty had told her he'd changed his mind about going hunting—"Kill a deer, Mom? I don't think so"—but didn't want to disappoint Grant, so he'd gone to tell him in person. And there was LeeLee, practicing her piano every day without fail, mostly because it was Grant who gave it to her.

Could she trust God to iron out the difficulties between them if she let go and handed them over? Could she give up the fears ingrained by years of abuse and abandonment?

Smoothing Ty's rough blond hair, she looked at Grant's parents holding hands across the room. And his red-haired, wizened little grandmother reading a golf magazine with all apparent fascination. How on earth would Jana fit into the tight circle of their extravagant love? That was supposing Grant still wanted her.

Just then the waiting room door opened and the surgeon walked in. "Good news," he said, smiling. "The surgery went well. Grant's leg is nicely pinned together, and with a little physical therapy he should regain normal use of it."

Relief drained the last of Jana's energy, leaving her feeling like a noodle cooked past al dente. Hiding her face, she let her tears drip onto Ty's head as the doctor talked to Grant's parents. They had the right to first information.

"Miss Cutrere?" Jana looked up. The surgeon was at the door. "Grant asked to see you. You can have just a few minutes to check on him while he's in recovery, before they move him to a room."

"Me?"

"You." The doctor winked and disappeared.

Roxanne crossed the room and patted Ty's cheek. "I know Ty wanted to see Grant," she said to Jana, "but I don't think they're going to let him today. Why don't I take him home for you? Carrie's having a ball with LeeLee, and she won't mind keeping her a few more hours."

Jana looked shyly at Linda Gonzales. "Don't you want to—?"

Linda smiled. "I'll go up later, when he's back in his room. I imagine he'd rather see you right now."

"Okay then." She took a deep breath and slipped Ty's head under Roxanne's shoulder. "I'll see you at home. Thanks." Blinking back fresh tears, she hurried from the room.

The recovery room nurse told Jana where to find Grant. Eyes closed, he lay on a gurney behind a curtain, dressed in a hospital gown, with a white blanket covering him from the waist down. He still looked pale and, oddly, very thin. Maybe this wasn't such a good idea.

But his eyes blinked open before she could back out, and he smiled, just a faint curving of his lips. "Hey, you," he said, curling his fingers to beckon her. "C'mere."

"You don't look very well. I can come back later."

The smile faded. "I heard you stayed, so I thought you wanted to ..." He turned his head away. "Okay. Ne'er mind." His voice was slurred, tired.

"I *did* want to—" Want to what? She hadn't had time to decide anything. She made the final step toward him and took the curled fingers, lacing them into hers. "I'm so glad your leg's going to be okay. Thank you for risking your life for Ty."

"I love him," he said simply. "Like he's my kid. I wouldn't ever want anything to happen to him."

Was this drugs talking? Did it matter? Her heart turned into a big, goopy blob of syrup.

"And I love Sally too. If you don't want her to have the keyboard, I'll take it back, but I think you ought to reconsider, because if anybody's meant for the stage, that one is." He looked at her. "You know what I mean?"

She couldn't speak past the lump in her throat, so she nodded.

His eyes burned into hers. "And most of all I love you. I love you, Jana, more than anybody I've ever known in my life. I love you more than hunting and I love you more than fishing, and I love you more than my mother and my father. I love you so much I'll move away if it'll make you happier, because I know how hard it's been for you to be around me all the time and have to avoid me."

Jana reached up and laid her free hand across his chapped lips. "Now I *know* you're still under anesthesia. I've never heard you talk this much all in one whack." A laugh bubbled up. "I wish I had a tape recorder."

He cupped her hand and kissed her palm. "You smell like mud."

"So do you," she retorted. "We both need a shower."

He grinned. "Well, anyway, I feel better now that I've told you. Would you go get my mama?"

"Only if you promise we can finish this discussion later when you're sober."

"It's a deal, Lucille." He brought her other hand to his mouth, kissed it, and let her go.

Feeling giddy, Jana backed through the curtain.

Whoa, Nelly.

It's about time somebody showed up to tell me what's going on around here." Grandpa looked like he was about to jump out of the bed, cast and all.

Jana hurried over to him. "Can I get you a drink of water? Are you hungry?"

"I don't need anything but information. Roxanne calls and asks me to pray 'cause the boy's lost in the woods with a major tropical storm going on, and now I can't get ahold of her to find out what happened. Since you're here, I assume everything's all right."

"Yes, sir." Jana put a hand on Grandpa's shoulder to make him lie back. "Ty's perfectly fine, sound asleep at Roxanne's house. She may have turned off the phone to keep from waking him up." She pulled over a chair. "Grant and I went after him. Grant's leg is broken, but he came out of surgery fine."

"Surgery? What the Sam Hill is the matter with everybody? Did all the telephones go broke around here?" He picked up the receiver and put it to his ear. "Nope, that's a dial tone." He dropped the phone, scowling at Jana.

"I'm sorry, Grandpa. It's been a little hectic today."

He snorted. "Reckon I should be glad you decided to grace me with your presence. You need something else?"

Jana picked up Grandpa's hand. His feelings were hurt. "I just wanted to say thanks for buying back the property from Grant. And to tell you how much I love you."

His cheeks reddened. "Back atcha, baby doll." He gripped her hand. "And I don't see where I had no choice about the property. The boy was caught between a rock and a hard place." He gave her his cagey look. "Wanted to talk to you about that before I signed anything, though."

She looked at him in alarm. "Grandpa, please don't waffle on this. Grant deserves everything we can do for him."

"You're dang straight he does. Which is why I can't figure out what your problem is. Are you blind?"

"I don't know what you —"

"Way I see it, you got a choice between building your house on sand or rock. The Gonzales boy is a bedrock of courage and integrity, and there you are setting up housekeeping on a beach with that shiftless Heath Redmond."

"Grandpa!" Jana gave a startled laugh. "First of all, Heath's not exactly shiftless. He runs a perfectly respectable veterinary practice. But what gives you the idea we're … setting up housekeeping?"

"What else am I supposed to think, the way you been running away from Gonzales? Are you in love with him or are you not?"

She thought of the flame in Grant's eyes when he'd looked at her in the recovery room. It had ignited something inside her that no difference of opinion could extinguish. It burned down long held notions and clarified her spiritual vision. Maybe she *had* been blind.

"Yes, Grandpa. I do love him. More than anybody I've ever known." Her face crumpled, and she laid her head down on the bed beside Grandpa's arm. "So what am I going to do?"

Make sure that stupid cowlick's not sticking up." Grant bent to let Carrie reach the back of his head with the hair dryer.

"I'm sure Jana's seen a cowlick before." His sister shut off the dryer and yanked the cord out of the wall.

"Yeah, but last time I saw her, she told me I needed a shower." He winced. "And I'm pretty sure I told her she stunk."

"That's what you get for declaring your undying love while under the influence." Carrie put a hand against the little bump of her stomach. "You want me to put the bed back down flat? You don't look very comfortable."

Truthfully, he *wasn't* comfortable, not with his leg in traction and a bedsore the size of a basketball on his backside. But he wanted to be sitting up when Jana arrived. "No, thanks. Just bring me my toothbrush."

Teeth brushed, hair combed, deodorant on, he felt like a human being again. Ordering his long-suffering sister to report to the cafeteria for lunch, he turned on ESPN and settled down to wait. He couldn't believe how nervous he was. *Lord, what did I say yesterday? I hope I can recover from whatever idiocy came out of my mouth.*

He'd just flicked the channel to catch Dr. Phil flaying some poor soul alive for failure to commit, when a soft knock came on the door. His heart jumped into his eyebrows. "Come in!" He muted the television.

Jana came in with Alvin hobbling right behind her on a pair of crutches.

"Alvin!" He tried to sound enthusiastic. "Good to see you up and around."

The old man responded with a sour smile. "I told her you wouldn't give two cents for my ugly mug, but would she listen? Why, no. Insisted I get my exercise stumpin' all the way down two floors on these dang torture sticks."

"Sit down and rest then." He risked a look at Jana. She was looking all around the room, everywhere but at him. "There's a chair right there behind you."

"Lord knows I'm familiar with every square inch of this dadgum hospital," snarled Alvin, but he sat down anyway. "Take these crutches, would you, Jana? And push that stool over here so I can prop up my foot."

When the old man was comfortable, Jana looked for a chair. Finding none, she leaned against the wall.

"You can sit on the end of the bed." Grant slicked at the incipient cowlick with a restless hand.

She looked at the arrangement of pulleys hoisting his cast in the air and shook her head in alarm. "I'm fine."

Rats. This wasn't going well at all. "I'm sorry for whatever I said to you in the recovery room," he blurted.

Alvin looked interested, and Jana's face flamed. "I promise you I don't remember," she said.

Grant would swear whatever it was had been burned into her brain as if with a blowtorch. But how was he going to address it right in front of her grandfather?

He slid a look at Alvin. "Did you tell her about the property? You said you were going to—"

"That's what I come down here to talk to you about. Me and my girl been having a right interesting conversation here in the last day or two."

Grant braced. Alvin's interesting conversations usually resulted in his ulcer acting up.

Alvin nodded, as if Grant had asked some deep question. "Yep. We both decided there ain't no sense lettin' the federal government get mixed up in our business, when we can take care of it ourselves."

"What do you mean?" He looked at Jana.

Her expression had become soft and bemused as she regarded her wily old grandpa. As if he had done something admirable and unexpected. She smiled at Grant. "Grandpa and I are going to do the wildlife research center without the federal grant."

"How? I thought—I thought you had to have the money."

Alvin cackled. "She got the idea somewhere that the Farm and Feed was goin' under." He waved a hand. "I just been taking all my profits and puttin' 'em in technology stocks. I got more money than I know what to do with."

Grant looked at Jana. "I thought you found a bunch of outstanding invoices."

She shrugged. "Grandpa had been receiving the money into one of those accounts I didn't know anything about."

Alvin gave his granddaughter a fond scowl. "I told her not to go messing around in my business when she didn't understand it."

"But Alvin, why didn't you give Jana the land to start with?" Grant's head was hurting.

"For one thing, I'd promised to sell it to you. And like I said, I thought that wildlife stuff was foolishness. Once you decided you didn't want the property, I started lookin' into all that medical research stuff, and dang if she ain't a pretty smart little chickie. I'd kinda like to see my name on the dedication page of a book."

So much for Don Gonzo, the Great Caballero, winning the hand of the heroine with daring exploits and golden tongue. Grant put his head back against the pillow. He was happy for Jana. She'd gotten what she wanted, and she deserved it.

Her eyes clouded. "You must be tired. Grandpa and I will go. I just wanted to tell you about—"

"No!" Grant's voice came out much louder than he intended. "I mean, no, I just have something else to tell you."

Jana's color came and went as her gaze cut to her grandfather.

"Oh, it's nothing private," Grant said, aiming for nonchalance and hitting coldness. "It's just that CJ's retiring at the end of the year, and he's talked to me about being the new game warden." He flicked a finger at his cast. "Of course I have to get out of traction and therapy first."

"I'm assuming you mean *psycho* therapy," said Alvin. "Boy, if you ain't the most cockleheaded, brain-dead varmint in Mississippi. Are you gonna lay there like roadkill and let her think you got no feelings for her?"

Grant bristled. "Roadkill? Alvin, if you don't get out of here, I'm gonna clobber you with one of those crutches." He looked at Jana, whose eyes were dancing. "If I take the game warden job I could be outdoors all the time, work with kids who want to learn fishing and gun safety, be available to help you with the sanctuary some. Maybe work on a new patent as a hobby in my spare time." He paused. "What do you think?"

"I think ..." She took a breath. "That's fine if it's what you really want to do. But Grandpa and I had a suggestion. We were hoping you might want to do the camp after all. If Grandpa came in as your backer, you could—"

"Wait. Just hold on." Grant shook his head. "You're taking the property for the wildlife center."

"Yes, but there's plenty of room for both. Just like we had it before Briscoe ruined it. We can rebuild."

Confused, he looked at her earnest face. "You know what you're saying, don't you? Are you telling me you've changed your whole philosophy about hunting?"

"I've done a lot of thinking, praying, and studying Scripture. I've been wrong about some things. I don't know that I'm ever going to be comfortable with the whole hunting thing, but as long as I don't have to live right on top of it, I can accept that not everybody believes like I do. I've seen your passion, and your gifts have a place in God's work, just like mine." She paused for a breath. "I respect your integrity, Grant. I think we can do this together. If you want to."

"If I want to?" A wild spurt of elation flooded him, from the crown of his head to the bare toes sticking out of his cast. "Oh, Jana. Come here." He stared into her eyes, watching hope and joy and something even stronger color her expression.

Instead of moving closer, however, she picked up her grandfather's crutches. "Grandpa, the nurse said we could only stay a minute. Come on. I'll help you back to your room."

Alvin sighed. "Just when things were getting interesting." He heaved himself to his feet and took the crutches.

Grant watched the door open and close as his two visitors left the room. Delirous with impatience, he closed his eyes.

Ten minutes later he was almost asleep when he felt something soft press against his forehead. Opening his eyes, he found Jana leaning over him, hands propped on the bed rails.

His heart began to thud in his ears. "Hey. You came back."

She didn't move away, but she didn't come closer either. Exquisite torture.

"Yep. I wanted to see if you remember what you said last night in the recovery room."

Distracted, he looked at her sweet mouth, which had quirked up on one side. "W—what I said? What did I say?"

"You said I smelled like mud."

"Well, if it's any consolation, you smell really good right now. In fact—"

"Grant."

"What?"

She leaned closer so that her lips brushed his ear. "That's not all you said."

He must have insulted her beyond forgiveness. "Maybe you should call the nurse. I'm feeling kind of faint."

"That's probably because of all the blood rushing to your head. I've never seen anybody blush like this." Unless he was delirious—which was a distinct possibility—she had kissed his cheek. Twice. She drew back just far enough to stare into his eyes. "Grant ... last night you said you loved me."

"Oh." He stared back at her, falling into those sapphire eyes.

"Were you out of your head with painkillers when you said that, Grant Gonzales? Or did you mean it?"

A beat of silence passed, and he passed his tongue across dry lips. Here was the moment of truth, his shot at gaining the world. He had to make sure he did it right.

He took so long that Jana pulled away, and he slid his hand around the back of her neck. "Look at me, Jana. I don't know exactly what I said yesterday, but this I do know. You're so deep in my life now that I can't imagine living it without you and Ty and LeeLee. I know I want to be your husband and I know I want to be their daddy. And if you love me the same way, I know I'll do everything in my power to keep y'all safe and happy the rest of our lives. Hunting camp or no hunting camp."

She blinked and nodded, and two brilliant tears dropped onto his nose. She sniffed.

"I think I'll take that as a yes." He brought her lips to his and kissed her, slow and deep. Then he pulled back. "Was that interesting enough, or should we go for cataclysmic?"

"Hey," she said, "why not shoot for the moon?"

off the record

elizabeth white

A secret past with journalist
Cole McGaughan could end
Laurel Kincade's judicial career...

Or will the truth set
them free to love again?

Read an excerpt from Elizabeth White's
Off the Record, Coming in 2007

chapter 1

Laurel Kincade, surrounded by reporters in the rotunda of the Alabama Judicial Building, suddenly understood her great-great grandmother's propensity to shoot Yankee invaders on sight and ask questions later.

How was she supposed to remember the most important speech of her life with *him* hulking in their midst like a Great Dane infiltrating a pack of Jack Russell terriers?

Okay, so Coleman Davis McGaughan IV—having burst upon this mortal coil some thirty-three years earlier in a Tupelo, Mississippi, delivery room—couldn't *technically* be called a Yankee. And if the threadbare khakis were anything to go by, Cole had somehow mislaid his family carpetbag full of filthy lucre. One might also note that under the tweed sport coat hugging those defensive-end shoulders, there was no place to hide a gun.

Still. He'd spent the last eight years in New York City (never mind how Laurel knew that) and marched onto her turf toting notepad and Bic pen. This, in her experience, could be infinitely more dangerous than a gun.

Yankee invader. As a southern woman, hyperbole was her birthright.

Outwardly as cool as the Italian marble beneath her feet, she looked up at the white dome soaring overhead. *God, please give me strength.* The weight of the occasion, its historic significance, mashed her insides to pudding. She wasn't the first woman to declare candidacy for Alabama Supreme Court chief justice, but she could be the first one to win.

Unless Cole was here to make trouble.

Behind the crowd of supporters gathered for Laurel's campaign launch, a few reporters from Alabama's backbone papers — the *Montgomery Advertiser,* the *Birmingham News,* the *Mobile Register,* the *Huntsville Times* — as well as the wire services, stood in a circumspect clump, shuffling cameras, PDAs, recorders; Cole was the only one standing there like Fred Flintstone with a notebook and pen.

Laurel checked her watch. It was almost time for her speech. She adjusted the tail of her navy pinstripe suit jacket, though it already hung with military precision. People expected a judge to look sober, so she bought designer suits in the boutique at SteinMart, where she could get a good fit for ... okay, face it, her *statuesque* figure.

Which was one reason the six-foot-four Neanderthal had managed to pull her under.

Ignore him, sister, Renata would say. *Not worth a wasted brain cell.* Her best friend and campaign manager, standing over by the entrance to the law library with Laurel's family, caught her glancing at the dark-haired giant at the back of the press pack. Laurel and Renata went all the way back to a dorm room at Springhill College, though after graduation they'd gone their separate ways. And Laurel had always kept to herself what happened with Cole. So when Renata's brown eyes widened, Laurel knew it wasn't in recognition, but because Cole still had that inexplicable something.

Charisma. Never pretty-boy handsome, Cole had a way of tucking his chin, brows knit over eyes like raw magnesium. A ragged white scar, new since the last time she'd seen him, cut into his top lip and veered upward across his left cheekbone. What wasn't new was the gladiator stance that dared men to take him on and women to tame him.

Renata raised her eyebrows at Laurel and fanned her face. Then with a little smirk she tapped her watch.

As Laurel moved to the podium, debate-team training took over. Gathering herself, she drew a breath and released it. "I'd like to thank everyone for coming out to support me today. My decision to run for chief justice wasn't made lightly, though many will be surprised to learn that it's been in my plans since I was young."

The irony wasn't lost on her. Some would claim that, as the youngest woman ever to run for Supreme Court, she didn't have enough judicial experience to handle the job. But she'd worked and planned and kept her nose firmly to the grindstone to get here. Smart voters would recognize that youth and femininity didn't equate stupidity.

She glanced at Cole, fumbled for her notes, and remembered she'd left them in the hotel room. Her photographic memory had blanked as if erased by acid.

Don't look at him again. Cold sweat ran between her breasts. She looked down at her hands gripping the edges of the lectern.

A camera flashed. She looked up and found a cameraman standing next to Cole lowering a big zoom lens. He elbowed Cole and stepped back.

Blinking against red and yellow spots, she lifted her chin.

In return, Cole raised his pen: a silent toast—or more likely a challenge. *Go ahead, baby, let's see what you're made of.*

She jerked her gaze off him and looked at her grandfather, who smiled his pride and encouragement. The next line of her speech clicked back into place. "I'm honored to come from a family with a rich tradition of public service. Beginning with my grandparents and continuing with my parents, they have supported me, encouraged me, taught me, and presented me with incomparable examples of hard work, faith, and personal integrity.

"These values undergirded the laws of our country and state from their inception, and once elected, they will guide me as I fulfill that law. These values will guide me as I seek this critical judicial post."

Once she got rolling, the words flowed. She'd practiced. She'd prayed. Didn't matter what Cole was up to. God was in charge of this whole thing.

She hoped.

J udge Kincade looks nervous." Matt Hogan spoke with unnecessary relish.

"Nervous? I don't think she looks particularly nervous." Cole stepped in front of Hogan's camera. Laurel might be famous for nerves of steel, but she was definitely distracted. He'd known it might not be a good idea to show up like this without warning.

"You said you could get an interview with her." Hogan lowered the camera, more interested in excavating Laurel's checkered past than taking her picture. "Have you arranged it yet?"

"I just flew in this morning. Give me time."

"We don't have any to waste." Hogan's whisper took on an aggrieved tone. "I've been here a week and haven't found out diddly about this dirty little skeleton in her closet—at least nothing we can document."

"Have you considered the possibility that she might be as clean as she claims to be?" The question had to be asked.

Hogan gave him a *yeah, right* look. "We're talking southern politics here."

Cole sighed. "Point taken. Now shut up so I can take notes." He leaned away from the column behind him to stare at Laurel. Half the copper-laced mahogany hair was twisted in a complicated knot on top of her head, with the rest swirling in fiery waves past her shoulders. She'd always worn it that way, and he wondered if she knew how telling it was.

He forced his pen across the paper.

Neutral umpire on any dispute to come before her court.

He couldn't help remembering the last time they were in the same room. She'd told him not to color her world until Jesus came back—at which time he'd undoubtedly be bound for that place of weeping, wailing, and gnashing of teeth anyway.

Editor of Law Review, *clerk for Eleventh Circuit Court of Appeals, youngest partner in firm history, state Attorney General's staff, well-rounded lawyer with extensive experience in the state court system.*

She'd gained a little weight, filled out into womanly curves that catapulted images across his brain like Rockettes in a Christmas Eve show. *Oh, Lord, help me out here.*

Would interpret the law, not legislate it; loved the judicial process and promised to bring experience, leadership, and integrity to Alabama's highest court.

Hogan and his buddy Field would crucify her if they found out the truth.

He felt a sharp jab in his ribcage and looked down.

Hogan was peering at Cole's notepad. "You writing an article or drawing her portrait?"

Cole flipped to a clean page. "Go over there and listen in on her family. The old man with the cane—that's her grandfather, Judge Gillian. The middle-aged couple are her parents."

Hogan perked up, a hound on a scent. "I'll meet you back here after the speech."

Cole was left alone to take notes like a good boy.

Laurel would make a fine justice. She'd been the only one of her law school friends with a lick of common sense—as if he'd cared about her brain back then. The evening he met her at a university picnic, she'd been sitting at the edge of the group, a fine queenly decorum in the turned-up corners of that lush mouth. He couldn't quit staring at it—beautiful and unglossed in the natural deep rose that came from her high Scots coloring. Then she'd spiked his guns with the humor, and he'd felt like a kid slammed in the gut with a volleyball. The fact that he could still remember it was a measure of its impact, considering his brain had been half pickled with a six-pack of Budweiser.

"I thank you all for coming out today." Laurel beamed her warm smile, and the cameras took advantage of it. Flashes went off everywhere. "I look forward to the upcoming campaign with great anticipation."

A cheer erupted. Cole stuck his hand in the air. "Excuse me, Ms. Kincade! Judge Kincade, I'm sorry. I have a couple of questions."

The applause halted. Laurel froze in the act of removing the mike attached to her lapel. Her beautiful, elegant head turned his way. "I'm sorry, I wasn't planning to—"

"I won't keep you long." He let his voice slide into the familiar southern cadence he'd worked hard to eradicate. Charm, his stock in trade. "I'm from the *Daily Journal* in New York."

One fine line creased Laurel's milky brow. "You may call my campaign manager and request an appointment." Her smile gave him a private warning.

"I promise, just a couple of questions."

She hesitated, then grabbed the lectern and swallowed. "All right."

They stared at one another for a long moment. Somebody in the crowd coughed.

He cleared his throat. "All right, then. Your grandfather, Judge Gillian, was involved in the Ten Commandments issue back in 2004 — when the Alabama Chief Justice was impeached for refusing to remove the monument from this very building. Tell us how that will affect your interpretation of the Constitution regarding religion."

Laurel's grip on the lectern relaxed. "My grandfather, as much as I love and respect him, will not be seated behind this bench. My decisions have always been my own and are solely based on Alabama law." She smiled faintly. "They always will be."

"Um, that's good." He jerked his gaze away from Laurel and cased her family.

Judge Gillian didn't seem to recognize him. Silver head poised like a hawk, the old man watched his granddaughter handle this unexpected inquisition. Laurel's parents, Dodge and Frances Kincade, were lined up in front of the library, in solidarity with several other people Cole had never seen.

There was so much he hadn't had time to learn about Laurel.

He glanced at Hogan, who was making circular "keep going" motions. But Cole didn't want to antagonize Laurel.

"You said two questions. Do you have another?" Laurel was back in control, smiling and confident, ready to walk off with her family and supporters.

"Yes. Yes, I do." His voice jackknifed off the marble of the rotunda. "Actually I have several more questions, Judge Kincade. Would you like to have dinner with me tonight?"

O   ne has to admire that young man's nerve." Fafa handed Laurel a tray and waited for her to collect her silverware. "Quite the bold tactician."

The Commerce Café, located in the Center for Commerce a few blocks down from the Judicial Building, was nothing fancy but was quite the weekday place to see and be seen. Laurel often had lunch here when in Montgomery on business trips.

She snatched a container of coleslaw at random from the salad array. Her hand still shook so hard the bowl rattled against the tray. "I can't believe he asked me out in front of all those people."

Actually she *could* believe it. It was just like Cole to embarrass her. What was completely out of character was the fact that he'd let it go with just the one question—well, technically two, if you counted the dinner invitation. When she'd stared at him, openmouthed and speechless, he'd backed off, lips curved, leaving her to face a barrage of laughter.

Pretending to find the humor in the situation, she'd smiled and removed the microphone. "I think I'm going to rescue myself," she'd said dryly.

But Fafa's patent curiosity wasn't any laughing matter. Avoiding his gaze, she moved to the entrée kiosk. "Catfish, please," she told the server. Most of the world's ills would be cured if all its bottom-feeding scavengers were fried to a crisp and served with hushpuppies.

If she weren't such a big chicken she'd have taken Cole on right there in the rotunda; tried to find out what he was doing down here. Instead she'd ducked out, letting Renata and Fafa carry her off for a celebratory lunch with the family.

They clustered around a table by the window looking out on downtown Montgomery. Daddy had already taken off his suit coat and loosened his tie—"left-wing Communist inventions," he always called them with a wink, ignoring the fact that Communists had gone out of style with stirrup pants and shoulder pads.

Her father got up and pulled out Laurel's chair as she approached the table. "Here's our woman of the hour. Appetite come back yet?"

"More or less." She never could get food down before a big speech. And this had been one of the biggest of her life. She sat down and opened her napkin. "Where's Mom?"

"I think she went to powder her nose." Daddy gave her a searching look. "What's the matter? You knocked their socks off, little girl. You're a shoo-in."

"Daddy. The media thinks I'm a spoiled, ultraconservative rich girl with too many political antecedents and not enough experience. Didn't you hear that last question from—" she stopped. She shouldn't have brought up Cole.

Sure enough, Renata, seated across from her, joined the fray. "You mean the dinner invitation? I don't know what's the matter with you, Laurel. You should've jumped on it. Jumped on him." She laughed. "Whichever came first."

Laurel frowned. "Renata—"

"You are so prissy." Renata sighed. "But he sure was cute, in a Russell Crowe kind of way."

Fafa bent an indulgent smile on Renata. "You've got the right idea, sugar. Best way to handle the press is to give them the old soft soap. Let 'em think you're rattled, and they'll hound you to kingdom come." He picked up his tea glass and jiggled the ice. "Which is why I sent your mama back over to the judicial building."

The gargoyle of impending doom, crouched on Laurel's shoulder since meeting Cole's hot green eyes, suddenly swooped down and took a chunk out of her stomach. "Fafa, what have you done?"

"Honey, a New York paper wants an interview, and we need all the name recognition we can get. Your mama lived in New York City for three years. She'll know how to talk to him." Fafa sipped his tea, then dabbed his white mustache with a napkin. "She can give him your statistics and background and sell you like a Prada handbag."

At one time Laurel might have objected to the auction block terminology. At the moment she was more worried about what Cole might say to her mother. She pleated her napkin. By the world's standards she hadn't done anything so terrible; besides, it had happened a long time ago. The problem was, she'd set herself very publicly above the world's standards—back in law school days and certainly in her recent career as a public servant.

Laurel Josephine Kincade, family values candidate.

She pushed away from the table. "I've got to go talk to him."

Renata's smile leaped out. "I knew it."

"Stay and finish your lunch." Daddy patted her hand. "I'm sure he'll call your office later—"

"I'm not hungry." She picked up the plate of cooling catfish. Too bad to waste it. Too bad about a lot of things.

Leaving the uneaten food on the conveyor belt, she pushed through the café door and stopped in the deserted lobby. Tracking down her mother would be easy enough. She fumbled for her cell phone, then hesitated.

Seeing Cole like this—out of the blue after all these years—was shocking. She'd thought to never lay eyes on him again, had managed to put all that behind her and move on. Okay, maybe she hadn't committed to another relationship since then, but at least she'd tried. Several times. One day there was going to be somebody who would measure up to that staggering infatuation she'd encountered and lost with Cole.

One thing was clear from the jellified state of her knees. She wasn't ready to confront him. She needed time to get her head together first. Talk to the Lord. There might not be an immediate solution to her problem, but He would bring her through somehow. Look how far she'd come. Look what she was on the verge of accomplishing.

"Laurel! Sweetie, what are you doing out here by yourself?"

Laurel jerked around. "Mom!" Her mother was coming up the stairs with Cole in tow like a trained bear on a chain. "I was just about to call you." The impulse to dive under the nearest sofa translated into smoothing her skirt.

"Look who I brought to lunch!" Hooking an arm through Cole's, Laurel's mom charged across the lobby, Linda Pritcher sandals clicking against the tile.

Laurel thought of her junior year of high school when her parents had arranged for the pastor's son to invite her to the prom. They'd paid for the tickets and rented his tux, and she wouldn't be surprised to discover they'd bought her corsage too. Some things never changed.

Looking at Cole, though, she forgot her mother and everything else. What did you say to the man who'd taken your virginity as if it were a free toaster at the bank?

"How are you?" There. She managed that just fine. She smiled at her mother. "Daddy and the others are waiting for us inside the cafeteria."

"In a minute, darlin'." Her mother's southern-belle charm lay in almost visible droplets on her still-dewy skin. "I want you to meet Cole McGaughan. It turns out he's not really from New York after all. He grew up over in Tupelo, just like Elvis—" her mom actually giggled—"and graduated from Ole Miss not too long after you were there in law school. Isn't that a coincidence?"

"Yes, ma'am, it's downright amazing." Laurel met Cole's eyes again. Dense piercing green, they burned her straight through.

Then his voice rumbled, deeper than she'd remembered, shaking her. "You've been mighty kind, Mrs. Frances, but I wonder if I could have a little time alone with Judge Kincade." An infinitesimal wink appeared to delight Laurel's mother.

Mom pretended to think. "I don't see a problem with that."

"No! I mean—" Judging by her mother's demeanor, so far Cole hadn't brought up past indiscretions. Likely he was waiting to get Laurel alone and dump the whole load. How to get him away from her? "Wouldn't you like to meet my grandfather?"

Cole's expression was impossible to interpret. "You sure you want me to?"

How could she be so stupid? What if Fafa recognized the name? She was more rattled than she'd thought. How odd that Cole had warned her. Was this honor between enemies?

The whole situation was crazy. She swallowed. Well so be it. Get it over with. Her house of cards was collapsing anyway, and she didn't even have time to pray.

Might as well stick her head in the guillotine and pull the cord herself. Before one Not-really-from-New-York reporter got the chance.

Fireworks

Elizabeth White

Susannah is out to prove that pyrotechnics genius Quinn Baldwin is responsible for a million-dollar fireworks catastrophe during a Mardi Gras ball.

With her faithful black Lab Monty, she moves to the charming backwater city of Mobile, Alabama, to uncover the truth. But this world-traveled military brat with a string of letters behind her name finds herself wholly unprepared to navigate the cultural quagmires of the Deep South.

Captivated by the warmth and joy of her new circle of friends, Susannah struggles to keep from falling for a subject who refuses to be anything but a man of integrity, compassion, and lethal southern charm. *Fireworks* offers a glimpse into heart of the South and a cynical young woman's first encounter with Christ-like love.

Softcover: 0-310-26224-0

Pick up a copy today at your favorite bookstore!

Off the Record

Elizabeth White

Judge Laurel Kincade has it all—brains, beauty, and an aristocratic Old South family to back her up. A political rising star, she's ready to announce her candidacy for chief justice of the Alabama Supreme Court.

Journalist Cole McGaughan has ambitions too. Working as a religion writer for the *New York Daily Journal*, he longs to become a political reporter. Then his old friend Matt Hogan, a private investigator, calls with a tip. The lovely young judge may be hiding a secret that could derail her campaign. Would Cole like to be the one to break the story?

Cole sees a clear road to his goal, but there's a problem. Laurel's history is entangled with his own, and he must decide if the story that could make his career is worth the price he'd have to pay. Can Cole and Laurel find forgiveness and turn their hidden past into a hopeful future—and somehow keep it all off the record?

Softcover: 0-310-27304-8

Pick up a copy today at your favorite bookstore!

Three ways to keep up on your favorite Zondervan books and authors

Sign up for our *Fiction E-Newsletter*. Every month you'll receive sample excerpts from our books, sneak peeks at upcoming books, and chances to win free books autographed by the author.

You can also sign up for our *Breakfast Club*. Every morning in your email, you'll receive a five-minute snippet from a fiction or nonfiction book. A new book will be featured each week, and by the end of the week you will have sampled two to three chapters of the book.

Zondervan *Author Tracker* is the best way to be notified whenever your favorite Zondervan authors write new books, go on tour, or want to tell you about what's happening in their lives.

Visit *www.zondervan.com* and sign up today!

ZONDERVAN®

ZONDERVAN.com/
AUTHORTRACKER
follow your favorite authors